HIGH PRAISE FOR
LULLABY AND GOOD NIGHT:

"Man—I like a sizzling novel with a great true sex scandal all poured into a terrific law story of the 1920s with mobsters, gun-flappers—the works!! Bugliosi again is great!! Read LULLABY AND GOOD NIGHT!"
—Melvin Belli, "The book paints a wonderful portrait of New York during the Roaring Twenties."
—David Freeman, co-author of *Death of an American: The Killing of John Singer*

"Bugliosi tells a gripping true-crime story of Tammany Hall corruption, judges on the take, a woman driven by a mother's love who is forced to embrace the political machine which can crush her, and one of the most celebrated murder cases defended by the legendary Sam Leibowitz."
—Milton J. Silverman, author of *Open and Shut*

"A nostalgia-steeped political and sexual thriller . . . a large and lively cast of real-life characters . . . highly satisfying feel for time and place."
—*The Daily News*

"In the manner of E.L. Doctorow's *Ragtime*."
—*Detroit News*

"SMASHING GOOD READ!"—*USA Today*

LULLABY

AND
GOOD NIGHT

a novel inspired by the true story
of Vivian Gordon

VINCENT T. BUGLIOSI
WITH WILLIAM STADIEM

A SIGNET BOOK

NEW AMERICAN LIBRARY

SIGNET TRADEMARK REG. U.S. PAT. OFF. AND FOREIGN COUNTRIES
REGISTERED TRADEMARK—MARCA REGISTRADA
HECHO EN CHICAGO, U.S.A.

SIGNET, SIGNET CLASSIC, MENTOR, ONYX, PLUME, MERIDIAN
and NAL BOOKS are published by NAL PENGUIN INC.,
1633 Broadway, New York, New York 10019

First Signet Printing, December, 1988

1 2 3 4 5 6 7 8 9

PRINTED IN THE UNITED STATES OF AMERICA

To my wife, Gail
                —V.T.B.

To my mother
                —W.S.

1

1924

"Do you think I'm being selfish?" Emily Stanton asked her friend.

"Not at all," Cassie Laverne replied with deadpan mockery. "You're being insane." She paused, then continued. "If you want to be scrounging for crumbs on Broadway when you could be eating cake on Park Avenue, that's just swell."

"Oh, Cassie," Emily pleaded for understanding. "I'm betting on myself. That's what I'm doing."

"Honey, I love you dearly, but I suggest you confine your gambling to the racetrack."

Emily had been showing Cassie around her new apartment on Forty-fifth Street and Tenth Avenue, the precarious dividing line between Hell's Kitchen and the Theater District, where both young women were aspiring actresses. The Royale, as the building was known, was a large six-story structure that had been a hospital at the turn of the century. Emily sometimes imagined a faint trace of ether in the gloomy corridors. Inside the furnished apartment, Emily had tried to enliven the tattered couches and sagging chairs with bright pillows and flowers she would pick up at the street market on her way home from auditions.

"The light's really good in the late afternoon," Emily said, doing her best to sell Cassie on her new living arrangements.

Cassie wasn't buying. She looked out of the sooty windows at the Salvation Army mission across the street. "Please excuse my brutal frankness"—she stretched her syllables in her Louisiana drawl—"but I would run out of

1

here and back to Warren faster than Red Grange at the Rose Bowl."

"Cassie! I am not going back there. All I want to do is what you do."

"And all I want to do is what you *did*," Cassie parried. "You have a rich husband on Park Avenue begging you to come home. And I'm still out there just begging."

Emily and Cassie had met in 1916, when Emily, only sixteen, had fled to New York from her Michigan convent school and had moved into a two-dollar-a-week room at the Hotel Elysium. Cassie had lived there for the two years since she had come up from New Orleans. Cassie, who had been rejected as a Ziegfeld girl for being too flat-chested, had been working in a number of second-string vaudeville shows. She helped Emily get her first Broadway part, in the chorus of *War Babies*, in which Cassie was playing.

A slinky honey blonde who never believed she had real talent or anything else going for her other than her looks, Cassie didn't really care what the shows were. She was in the theater marking time until she met a rich man. Getting the parts was a means to that end. To Emily, on the other hand, the theater was the end in itself. When Emily got married in her very first year on Broadway, Cassie was wildly envious of Emily's security. Emily, however, envied Cassie's insecurity, which she saw as freedom.

"Is it selfish to want to be an actress?" Emily asked again, though she was really talking to herself. "It was always my dream. I can't help it, but I feel so guilty about Jessica, taking her away from all that comfort."

"I'm worried more about you than about her," Cassie said, trailing a finger through the dust on the windowsill. "You said she liked it here."

"She really does, thank goodness. She's made friends. She doesn't need nannies. She's not spoiled."

"And she never will be, at this rate," Cassie said.

"Come on. I've been getting work. Look at *Something in the Air*."

"Emily, it closed opening night."

"But it was a solo. I'm making progress. I'm up for the *Scandals* next week."

"But, Emily, honey, do you really want to live on the edge, going from show to show, no to no?"

"Yeah. Because you know, Cassie, how sweet the yeses are," Emily said. "It's the life I want. I couldn't have it with Warren." For six years, Emily had given up the theater to raise Jessica and please her husband. When she had tried to please herself by getting back into the theater again, he was vehemently opposed to it, in fact, violently so. After a series of brutal beatings, Emily saw no choice but to leave him. "God knows, I tried. I really tried," she said.

"I'd try again," Cassie urged her.

"I can't. You know I can't."

"He begged you to come back. Go. You'd have a net."

"A net that could be yanked out any second," Emily said. "I can't live like that. Warren hates the theater. He was insanely jealous. He doesn't understand what I need."

"Sometimes I don't either." Cassie shrugged. "He's going to have really big money someday."

"I don't care. We were all wrong. We should never have gotten married. If it weren't for Jessica . . ." Emily reflected soberly. "I gave him over six years. But it was always the same. He felt he had done me the biggest favor, *rescuing* me from Broadway. By the end, I felt he was holding me hostage on Park Avenue. It was hopeless."

"He let you try *Bicycle Built for Three.* He was open . . ."

"He almost killed me. Please. I can't . . . talk about it."

Cassie backed off. Emily had told her a little, though not all, of the nightmare confrontations Warren had put her through. Cassie had dismissed them as bouts of temper, but there was more that Emily didn't want to tell, more that had scared her into leaving. Despite Warren's profuse apologies and flower-bedecked entreaties to return, Emily knew there was no going back.

Cassie realized she could plead her position no further. "Honey, if this is what you want," she assured Emily, "I'm always gonna be in your corner. Even if it's in the poorhouse." The two women laughed.

"Cassie, you're great," Emily said.

"Who knows?" Cassie looked Emily up and down admiringly. "With those incredible green eyes you can't go far wrong. You're beautiful. You can sing. Maybe you'll be a big star. Maybe you'll meet another man."

"No more men, thank you."

"Famous last words. Listen, it's been glorious, but I have to get back to my place and pack."

"I'll miss you," Emily said.

"My glamorous road show. This time it's Huron. Fargo. Sioux City. I used to dream of Paris. Now I'm grateful for Omaha," Cassie said.

"Cheer up. You may meet a famous fur trapper," Emily laughed, as she opened the door to the dismal hallway.

"*You* cheer up, honey, and stop feeling so damn guilty," Cassie urged Emily. "You want to sing and dance? Sing and dance. You don't have to be a saint just because you went to that convent school."

"I know. I promise you I know. Don't forget, Cassie"— Emily smiled knowingly—"I ran away from that convent."

Emily took Cassie downstairs in the creaky elevator and outside into a crisp and brilliant January morning and a jumble of Italian fruit vendors who set up their colorful market of rickety pushcarts in front of Emily's building every day except Sunday.

"*Arancie fresche! Arancie buone! Arancie della Florida!*" the Italians shouted. All were selling the same oranges and grapefruit, and all of them were thronged with immigrant customers. At the stand beside Emily's door, three Greek Orthodox prelates in flowing robes were intently squeezing and examining the citrus fruit. At the one next to it, the vendor was boxing the ears of a redheaded Irish boy who had tried to make off with a bunch of bananas without paying. "*Delinquente! Ladro!*" the Italian cursed the boy.

Cassie grimaced at the crowds and the noise. "You've gone from Park Avenue to Ellis Island," she said through the din. "I thought they had immigration quotas now."

"They do," Emily said. "But these people aren't making enough money to move on from here. So they just stay. Think of all the languages Jessica can learn."

"Emily, Emily," Cassie chuckled. "Only you could find the bright side here."

After Cassie left, Emily discovered herself in the rare

4

situation of having some free time. With no audition to go to this morning and with her six-year-old daughter Jessica in school, Emily decided to go for a walk. She liked her neighborhood. She liked all the young show people hurrying back and forth to their Broadway rounds. She liked the immigrants, some of whom were so new to the New World that they would back away whenever they came near one of the many skyscrapers going up in the area, peering up with wonder at the height, and terror at the thought that it might fall. Here in New York, fifty-, sixty-, seventy-story buildings would spring up in a matter of months, buildings that would dwarf the greatest cathedrals of Europe that had taken centuries to construct. No wonder the newcomers were in awe.

So was Emily. Giant steel skeletons were everywhere on the horizon, thrusting to the heavens, making the bold statement that no other city in the world could soar as high as this one. Looking down toward the docks from any intersection in the West Forties, Emily could see the gleaming ocean liners that were coming in from Europe and South America. She was truly in the center of the world, the greatest city on earth, the colossus on the Hudson, full of surging energy and opportunity.

Of course, Emily was more than a little scared by it all. She was taking an enormous risk, both for herself and for her daughter, in the enormously risky business of the theater. Yet, despite her fears, she was exhilarated by the challenge. This was the city of hope, of dreams, of success, and she had as good a chance as she would ever have to find her own place in it.

2

Emily's husband, Warren Matthews, was at his club on Union Square. The club, Tammany Hall, was housed in a Georgian red-brick building that, on the outside, bore a distinct resemblance to New York's exclusive gentlemen's clubs—the Union, the Knickerbocker, the Racquet and Tennis, the Links. Large black Cadillacs and Lincolns were parked outside, some with waiting chauffeurs in uniform. There was a palpable air of power and exclusivity. Nevertheless, the men who filed into Tammany Hall were different from the men who filed into the Union or the Knickerbocker. The latter's members had blood ties to the American Revolution, society ties to Mrs. Astor's "Four Hundred," school ties to Groton and Harvard. Tammany men, on the other hand, were not particularly pedigreed or educated. Although the first great leader, or "Boss," of Tammany was the patrician Aaron Burr, most members were of peasant stock, Irishmen with a potato famine rather than a *Mayflower* in their past. But Tammany men had a tie of their own, a tie that the men of the Union and the Knickerbocker well envied. This was the tie to City Hall. Tammany Hall was above all a political club, much more so than a social club, and it had immense power. Tammany Hall, for all practical purposes, ran New York City.

Tammany's main power—to control elections—had inevitably led to corruption. From the venal hegemony of "Boss" William Marcy Tweed in the 1860's to the present day, the symbol of Tammany Hall had been a fierce tiger that political cartoonists had depicted as devouring a helpless island of Manhattan. Because Tammany's power was so all-pervasive and daunting, few reformers, including the cartoonists, had made much headway against it. One who did was the Reverend Charles H. Parkhurst, minister of the Madison Avenue Presbyterian Church and president of the Society for the Prevention of Crime. As far back as the 1890's, he had mounted an all-out assault on Tammany from his pulpit. Describing New York City as "hell with the lid off," Reverend Parkhurst charged that Tammany and the New York City Police Department were "a lying, perjured, rum-soaked, and libidinous lot" who fostered prostitution and gambling. To prove his point that New York City was "rotten with a rottenness which is unspeakable and indescribable," the reverend disguised himself as a free-spending man on the town and made what became a famous tour of the city's brothels and gambling dens. Parkhurst's railings did lead in 1894 to the resignation of the notorious Tammany Boss Richard Croker, who retreated to England to race his thoroughbred horses. By 1897, however, Boss Croker was back, and successfully ran his candidate, Robert Van Wyck, for mayor. The critics came, and the critics went, but Tammany rolled inexorably on. Now, in 1924, the Tammany tiger had its powerful jaws around the fatted calf of New York politics as securely as the big cat had ever held it.

This afternoon, the men of Tammany were having an initiation ceremony. The large assembly hall was dominated by two flags. One was a Stars and Stripes. The other was a tiger. The hall was dark except for the candles held by each of fifty men in two long lines running the length of the room. Warren Matthews stood in the line on the left. With him was such politically august company as the Manhattan police commissioner, district attorney, and county clerk, several state senators and assemblymen, two magistrates, and, most important to Warren, the subway commissioner, Terence McCarey. McCarey was important because Warren Matthews was on the verge of closing a contract with the city to supply the station tiles for the new line to Queens. Over the next few years of construction, the contract would make Matthews Tile a profit of several hundred thousand dollars. Warren was proud to be here in Tammany Hall, as had been his father, and his father before him. Tammany had everything to do with loyalty and continuity.

Tammany had been founded after the Revolutionary War—as a patriotic society, taking its name from Tamanend, an Indian chief whose advice to his tribe was "Stand together and support each other and you will be a mountain." As the society grew, the Indian theme remained. Members were called braves, elders called sachems, the hall itself the wigwam. Today a new brave was being initiated. A gawky, freckled Irishman in his mid-twenties walked up the candlelit gauntlet toward a sachem named Charles Sullivan, a white-haired sage who was one of the most powerful lawyers on Wall Street. Sullivan was holding a red tomahawk.

"He's not very distinguished-looking," Warren Matthews whispered to Terence McCarey.

"Not everyone's got a mug like yours," McCarey said, smiling up at Warren, who was tall and quite distinguished-looking—"senatorial," as the thirty-six-year-old aspiring captain of industry liked to see himself.

"Can we trust him?" Warren asked.

"He's here," McCarey assured Warren.

The initiate reached Charles Sullivan, who raised his tomahawk as if to strike him. Just at the point when the ax was to begin its downward trajectory, another white-haired elder, this one known as the sagamore, stepped forward with his own tomahawk and deflected Sullivan's blow. The sagamore was Edward Flynn, political boss of the Bronx, a man capable of swinging entire elections.

"Why are we taking young cops into the Hall?" Warren sneered.

"He's more than just a cop. Vice squad," McCarey continued under his breath to Warren, describing the initiate. "Arrested five hundred whores last year. Damn good man."

"Sago. Sago. Sagamore," Sullivan addressed the deflector, Flynn.

"Sago. Sago. Oly," Flynn replied in the arcane Indian argot known only to Tammany.

"Is this stranger worthy of a seat among us?" Sullivan

continued the ceremony, as the initiate stood bolt-straight at attention.

"Etho," Flynn answered.

"Does he love freedom?"

"Etho."

"Will he bear adversity, torture, and death in defense of liberty, like a true son of Tammany?" Sullivan asked.

"Etho."

Both elders dropped their tomahawks. Charles Sullivan stepped forward and put his hand, in benediction, upon the initiate's shoulder. "Timothy Shea," he intoned, "I now confirm you as a Son of Tammany and a member of the Columbian order." The young vice officer broke into a big smile and shook hands with Sullivan and Flynn.

The braves in the gauntlet raised a cheer and began to sing, "Our hearts sincere shall greet you here. With joyful voice confirm your choice. Etho! Etho! Etho!"

Warren Matthews raised his voice, spirited and high. He wasn't embarrassed at all. He didn't find the ritual silly or foolish. In fact, he took it very seriously. After all, these were the men who controlled New York, and he was one of them. He placed his hand over his heart and sang loud and clear. He was honored to be a Tammany man, to be part of this tradition. Never interested in books, Warren had dropped out of New York University in his freshman year and gone straight into his prospering family business. He liked politics and had been a loyal Tammany brave, working hard for the Tammany slate of Democratic candidates in each election, making large annual donations. Now this loyalty was on the verge of paying off. "Any fool can make tiles," Warren liked to say, "but you've got to be smart to make contacts." Warren had made his contacts. He had paid his dues. Already well-to-do, Warren, thanks to Tammany Hall, was going to be a very rich man. "Etho!" the braves concluded.

After the ceremony, Warren Matthews and Terence McCarey went to Greenwich Village for dinner and more contract discussions. Because of McCarey's position, they took the subway. The Union Square station was a roaring cave, its cleanliness and gleaming white tile walls offensively counterpointed by the ear-splitting screeches of the

9

train brakes and the acrid stench of burning iron. Warren didn't complain. He simply thought about the new stations and how much he would make from them and did his best to make small talk that would keep Commissioner McCarey amused. They chatted about Knute Rockne and his great team at Notre Dame and about Washington and what a raw deal the late President Harding—he had died in August and been succeeded by Calvin Coolidge—and his men were getting in the Teapot Dome scandal. "It was just business," McCarey lamented. "Nothing but business."

McCarey was a jovial, rotund Irishman in his early fifties. He had a plain face that was a road map of broken capillaries, a red balloon one alcoholic breath away from bursting. McCarey was Warren Matthews' mentor and benefactor at Tammany, although sometimes Warren wasn't sure who was the donor and who the donee. In order to ensure that Matthews Tile's "bid" for the subway stations would be chosen, Warren had given McCarey a not insignificant block of stock in the company, held in the name of a shell corporation no one would ever trace to McCarey. Tammany Hall did not operate on mere public service and party loyalty. There was generally a profit motive, an unspoken *quid pro quo*. Whatever, Warren didn't mind. He only wished he could find an equivalent trade-off that would allow his personal life to keep pace with his professional one.

"Stop brooding about your wife," McCarey yelled at Warren as the subway train hurtled into the Astor Place station.

"I'm not brooding," Warren replied defensively. He wanted to maintain a facade of bonhomie at least until the subway contract was signed, but it was hard. The dissolution of his marriage was tormenting him. He felt betrayed, abandoned.

"I'd trade the thirty years I've put in with Mary for your six with Emily. No, make that one. One year with a beautiful woman can carry you through the sorrows of a lifetime."

"I know what you mean."

"You had a good run with her, Warren boy. Now let her go."

"Oh, she can go. It's not her I want. It's my daughter." Emily's taking Jessica away had imbued Warren with a renewed sense of fatherhood. He was sorry he had been so busy, that he had given so little attention to Jessica. Now he wanted her, almost to the point of desperation. His desire also contained an element of competition. First, Emily had defied him about the acting. Now she had taken away his daughter, which Warren saw as the final humiliation. In a sense, Jessica had become a trophy. Warren wanted his daughter, all right. He also wanted to win.

"You can't get a child away from its mother, Warren. That's tough. You heard what the lawyers said."

"I don't need lawyers," Warren said, "I need a drink."

They left the subway station and walked through Greenwich Village. The monolithic skyscrapers that had turned much of Manhattan into office canyons had not lumbered into the area. The small-scale feel of the nineteenth century endured. There were makeshift coffeehouses, ragtag theaters, fragrant bakeries, long-haired men and short-haired women, young NYU students hugging and kissing right in the street while their old philosophy professors calmly played chess under the pin oaks and Oriental plane trees of Washington Square Park. Warren was uncomfortable. He would have never come down here had McCarey not insisted on it.

"It's all Bolshevism and free love," Warren complained.

"I thought you liked free love," McCarey joked.

They arrived at an old brownstone on MacDougal Street that housed a pawnshop on its first floor. Under the stoop was an uninviting black steel door that a passerby never would have noticed. McCarey rang a bell concealed by ivy vines. A moment passed. Then a confessional-type peephole slid open. Two eyes peered out. "Cross the Delaware," McCarey said. With that shibboleth came a clang of locks. The steel door was unbolted and flung open by an obese sweaty man who greeted McCarey with a bear hug. The man was Tony, and Tony's was one among the hundreds upon hundreds of illegal speakeasies, or "resorts," that comprised New York's imaginative free enterprise during Prohibition.

Tony's narrow dining room, with its brown tin ceiling,

was dominated by a long redwood bar stacked with level upon level of bottled liquors. There were twenty tables with red-and-white-checkered tablecloths. Despite the Spartan, workhouse atmosphere, the tough steaks, and the waterlogged spaghetti, Tony's, as usual, was jammed, three deep at the bar, the tables all filled, except the one McCarey had reserved. Tony's was a great favorite of Tammany Hall. So many Irishmen were in the place that Warren could never understand why veal parmigiana, rather than corned beef and cabbage, was the menu staple.

Warren and McCarey could hardly sip their contraband Scotch without being interrupted by countless hellos and handshakes, all with that hail-fellow-well-met camaraderie that made Warren a very satisfied member of the club. The place was mostly all male. The women seemed very short-term companionship—young, overly rouged, overly endowed, meat-and-potatoes floozies who sat patiently and giggled while the men blustered and got drunk.

"Looks like we've got special entertainment tonight," McCarey said. At an upright piano in the corner, an imperially slim, dapper little man in a suit with a pinched waist and wide lapels, still boyish, with only the crinkles around his eyes betraying the fact that he was over forty, had sat down to play a song, "Will You Still Love Me in December as You Do in May?" He was much too elegant to be the house pianist and was getting far too much undivided attention from the drunken patrons.

The player was Jimmy Walker, the bon vivant state senator who wrote Broadway songs as a hobby. The one he was playing had been a huge hit.

"Aren't they supposed to be in session up in Albany?" Warren asked.

"You know how much Jimmy likes Albany?" McCarey guffawed and threw back his Scotch. "About as much as you like Bolsheviks."

"He's good. He could have made it on Broadway."

"There's still time, Warren boy. Give him time."

When Walker finished his song, the patrons at Tony's cheered him wildly. On his way to his table, he stopped by to say hellow to McCarey and Warren.

"'Evening, Terry. Warren. You all set on the tiles?"

"All in place, Senator," Warren said.

"There's no one like you, Jimmy," McCarey said, embracing the little man.

"Sorry about your missus, Warren," Walker said. "She was a beauty. I know you'll miss her."

"Word really gets around the Hall," Warren said, ill-at-ease at the prospect of gossip that he couldn't hold on to his wife.

"When they're that pretty, you're bound to have trouble. That's why I have Allie," Walker said, referring to his own wife, whom he rarely took out in public. "We want to help you, Warren. The Hall's behind you a hundred percent."

"I appreciate that, Senator," Warren said. "I'm sure I can work things out."

"I'm sure we can," Walker said. "I'm sure we can." He shook hands and was off to work the next table, though not without sending a complimentary round of drinks over to Warren and McCarey.

"Great man, Walker."

"What did he mean by the 'we'?"

"How he talks. He's a team man. You're a team man, Warren. You know we're all team men. So who are you seeing now?"

"Seeing?"

"I know you. You're not moping around the house all night."

"Isabelle Millbank."

"Millbank. Millbank Sugar?"

"Her uncle." Warren nodded. "Nice girl."

"Oh, Warren, you've got a way with the ladies." McCarey elbowed Warren's ribs. "Millbank. Pretty highfalutin. Now, don't go and get uppity on us, boy. Remember your old pals when you're at Mrs. Astor's."

"Don't worry, Commissioner."

"Hell, you don't even *need* the contract. You marry her and . . ."

"She's from the poorer side of the family. Besides, I couldn't marry her if I wanted," Warren said.

"Why not?"

"I'm still married, remember? I can't even get a divorce," Warren said bitterly as he sipped the liquor Walker had sent to him. The only grounds for divorce in New York State were adultery. He might try to argue that Emily had abandoned him, but that wasn't enough. His hands were tied. He wanted a wife. If Emily wouldn't come back, then Isabelle, if things progressed the way he hoped, would be even better. She had been a debutante. Despite financial setbacks, her family was still in the *Social Register*. She wouldn't leave him to join a chorus line. But right now he was paralyzed. "I can't do a damn thing."

"If you could make a wish, what would it be?"

"I'm too old for wishes."

"Go ahead, Warren, tell me. Would you want Emily back?"

"Not the way she is."

"The way she was?"

"She was always that way, wanting what *she* wanted. She wanted to be on Broadway, that's all she ever wanted. Why the hell can't she just give me Jessica back? She can't raise her!" Warren felt himself opening up. He didn't really want to talk about Knute Rockne or Cal Coolidge or tile-glazing processes. He wanted to talk about what he perceived to be the gross impropriety of Emily's conduct. The alcohol had loosened him up. The crowd didn't inhibit Warren. He was among friends. Besides, with all the noise, only McCarey could hear him, and McCarey was more than sympathetic. "She can't raise Jessica. She's going to ruin her. Damn her!" Warren felt the fury rising, the same wild fury that he sometimes couldn't control, the fury that obliterated his composure and drove him to beat Emily. He didn't *want* to. He couldn't *help* it. "She's an unfit mother."

"I know what you mean," McCarey said. "Problem is, under the law, being an actress—"

"Don't dignify it, Commissioner. She's a chorus girl."

"Whatever. Being a chorus girl doesn't make her an unfit mother. I told you what Charlie Sullivan said. He's a lawyer, he knows."

"Well, then what does?"

"Something bad. What did he call it, dereliction of motherly duties. She'd have to commit some kind of crime, Warren. Trying to succeed on Broadway's not a crime, even though she is a married woman."

"It should be," Warren said, lighting a Havana cigar to compose himself. "So should ingratitude. All I gave her. The home, the clothes, the thousands and thousands spent. Jesus!" That the material goods he had provided Emily didn't satisfy her infuriated Warren. What disturbed him more, but what he left unsaid, was the thought that *he* didn't satisfy her, emotionally or physically.

"Lord help us. They sure can fool you. She was such a pretty, sweet thing . . ." McCarey offered.

"She's not what I thought she was."

"So you really don't care about her anymore. You're sure. You don't want her under any—"

"Commissioner, what are you, some kind of marriage counselor?"

"I just wanted to be sure I understood how you felt."

"I feel like hell. What she's done, I hate her just as much as I used to love her. I hate myself for being blind. But she's got me, sir. She's got my daughter, and I can't get her back. There's no way. She's got me. There's not a damn thing . . ."

"If you love that little girl that much, if you want her bad enough, Warren boy, there's going to be a way," McCarey said in a confident fatherly tone that somehow strangely reassured Warren. "Now, let's have another round. Waiter!"

3

George Gershwin was rude, Emily Stanton thought. He should have at least taken the cigar out of his mouth when he turned her down for his show. She had just finished her audition, singing "Somebody Loves Me." What her voice lacked in vibrato, she made up for in lyrical quality. Emily had poured her own dreams into Gershwin's pretty new song. She thought she had the part and was, therefore, crushed when Gershwin seemed to mumble "Not for us" through the side of his mouth.

"Thanks, anyway," Emily said. Eyes cast downward, she was walking off the rehearsal stage when she overheard the producer, George White, say, "Dame's good," to Gershwin.

"Nice voice," Gershwin now enunciated more clearly, and when he did, Emily realized that he was repeating what he had originally said, not "Not for us." In her efforts to get back into Broadway, Emily had become so attuned to the endless nuances of rejection that sometimes yeses could sound like nos.

Catching the compliment, Emily stopped, pivoted, and smiled a belated thank-you. "It's a wonderful song," she added.

"I like the way you did it," Gershwin said, cigar still clenched between his teeth as he sat at the piano. "Good job."

George White shrugged quizzically at Emily's nervous behavior. "We'll be calling you, Miss Stanton."

Emily's hope was renewed. In her delicate balance between the reality of rejection and the fantasy of success, she had regained her equilibrium. Despite her actress's superstitions about the hubris of optimism, Emily now began to imagine herself on opening night, bowing to endless curtain calls, winning raves in the *Times*, plunging into the heady delights of a long run.

The show was *George White's Scandals*. It was the only revue in town that was any kind of competitive threat to the *Ziegfeld Follies*, and thus to Emily represented the Big Time. White's shows in fact were Ziegfeldian, packed with stunning showgirls sweeping down grand staircases in creative dishabille—as Tahitian rain-forest nymphs, as Wild West cowgirls, as mock Buckingham Palace guards. If the women were the bait, the music was the hook. That was why impresario White had hired Gershwin. Songs like "Drifting Along with the Tide" and "Stairway to Paradise" had made earlier versions of the *Scandals* among the hottest tickets on Broadway. Emily Stanton loved singing Gershwin's music. She was up for a small featured role that would pay sixty dollars a week. She wanted it, needed it, badly.

"I wanted to tell you how terrific you were," a voice cut through Emily's flights of fancy as she stepped out of the sepulchral plush of the theater into the glaring daylight flooding the marble lobby. Emily squinted. Standing near the closed ticket window was one of the handsomest men she had ever seen. In his late twenties, he had jet-black wavy hair, the noble head of a statue, and, despite the strength of the rest of him, blue eyes that could cry if you hurt him. They called the type Black Irish, from the Iberian seamen washed up on Ireland's shores during England's wars with Spain. He was tall and imposing, in a navy blazer and an azure ascot that picked up his eyes. He looked like a matinee idol, but Emily could tell he wasn't Broadway at all. Nevertheless, she warned herself, she wasn't the slightest bit interested in him. Emily hadn't thought about men, other men, since she left Warren, and Warren had made her life such a hell that she didn't want to think about men, not in that way. "That's very kind," was all she could respond.

"It's not kind. It's business," the man said. He offered Emily a cigarette from a gold case. She almost never smoked, but this time she took one. He lit the cigarette, leaning over. She could smell his cologne, the scent of lime, rugged and masculine. She was embarrassed for paying so much attention to him. "I'm thinking of becoming one of White's backers," he went on. "The better talent we get, the less likely I lose my shirt."

"I see," Emily said.

"So I'm going to put in a good word with the two Georges. That is, if you don't mind," he said. "You probably don't need it."

"No," Emily laughed lightly. "I need all the help I can get."

"I'll do whatever I can for you. You're good. Awfully good. You made me feel that song. I think we could make money together," he said. "I'm Amory Longworth."

What a beautiful name, Emily thought. Fitting. "I'm Emily Stanton. Nice to meet you."

"You must have a lot of love in you to sing like that," he said.

Emily laughed again. "Well, maybe . . . I mean, it's a great song. All credit to Mr. Gershwin."

"Don't be so modest. I'll bet there's a very lucky man in your life."

"No, there really isn't," Emily replied.

"Hard to believe."

"What can I say?"

"Emily . . . will you have a cup of coffee with me?" Amory asked in a way that melted all of Emily's reserve.

"Gosh, I would . . . but I've got an errand."

"Let me come with you. If I'm not imposing . . ."

"But the auditions . . . Don't you want to hear the other—"

"I know whom *I* want. Where are you going?"

"Just up to this toy store on Fiftieth Street. I have to get a Barney Google doll," Emily said.

"You look very girlish, but . . ." Amory teased.

"It's for my daughter."

"Daughter?" Amory raised an eyebrow. "I thought you, er, weren't . . ."

"In love," Emily finished his sentence. "I'm separated from my husband."

18

Amory seemed relieved. "Let's take a walk," he said, gesturing toward the door.

Emily and Amory left the serenity of the theater and plunged into the carnival maelstrom that was Broadway. The howling January wind whipped up tiny cyclones of ticket stubs, gum wrappers, peanut shells, and other debris. Emily and Amory weaved through the crowds, savoring the absurd tawdriness of the urban circus. Despite the more salacious attractions of the peep and strip shows, many men in the throngs couldn't help but stare at Emily. She was a sweet whiff of freshness in Broadway's rancid miasma of exhaust fumes and chop-suey grease.

Emily was five feet five inches tall. She had a willowy figure and thick, auburn hair. With her fresh, open-faced beauty and even features, one wouldn't have found it difficult to imagine her on the Coca-Cola billboards lining the nation's highways. Small town. Heartland. Uncomplicated. But close up, one saw a softness and vulnerability in her delicate, cameo face which was at odds with an unmistakable sensuality and mystery in her large, haunting, almond-shaped green eyes. Her face had a feral complexity that was an irresistible invitation to men to explore, to experiment with, an invitation that bespoke delicious ecstasy—as well as danger. Although Emily's appearance was completely without calculation, hers was a beauty that could easily get her into trouble.

Emily told Amory about her recent career. A bit in *Bicycle Built for Three*, the chorus of *Horse Latitudes*, a solo in the short-lived *Something in the Air*. Not a lustrous curriculum vitae, yet Amory seemed fascinated. "All that and raising a daughter too. I'm impressed," he said. "How can you manage both?"

"Magic," Emily answered.

Amory's attentions were all business. Here was someone genuinely interested in her career. Yet the more business he talked, the more Emily wanted him to get personal. Was he married? Involved? She couldn't stop herself from being increasingly curious about him.

"Look . . ." Emily motioned toward a boarded-up restaurant front. "Blackstone's is finished."

"They closed last month."

19

"Rector's is gone. Reisenweber's. Now Blackstone's. They're all gone, all the famous restaurants. It's sad. Broadway used to be glamorous."

"That's what happens when you can't serve liquor. Those places couldn't survive on food alone," Amory said.

Emily stopped to peer through the wooden slats and saw the crystal chandeliers and fluted columns of the deserted grand dining room. Emily remembered when she first came to New York, how hungry and alone she was, wandering up Broadway. It was then a boulevard of swells. Pressing up to the beveled windows of Blackstone's, she would watch the fancy people in their evening clothes sipping champagne and dancing to the Gypsy orchestra. The scene would have impressed anyone who wasn't rich. To a teenage runaway from a Midwestern convent school, it was overwhelming.

Now all the grand restaurants—or lobster palaces, as they were known—were gone. In their place was a new Broadway, a midway of low-budget pleasures for the masses. There was the Little Havana, a synthetic-orange-drink stand with plastic palm leaves. There was the Château Tango, whose strident shill, dressed as Napoleon, lured passersby with the promise of a choice of thirty lovely hostesses, "direct from Paris," a steal at five cents a dance. There was a grizzled old prospector in a sidewalk booth festooned with more artificial palm fronds, selling land on the Gulf Coast of Florida. There was the House of Sound, a discount phonograph store with "Ain't We Got Fun" blaring out of at least ten sets at the same time. These were some of the current attractions of the Great White Way Emily and Amory passed while talking about the more rarefied pleasures that had populated the street before the Volstead Act took New York's real nightlife underground to the speakeasies.

"Now all you can eat on Broadway is chop suey," Amory lamented.

"I love chop suey," Emily said. "It's the staff of life for struggling actresses."

"Be thin. Be rich. Be happy," a woman in a bonnet cried out. Although she looked like a suffragette, she was actually peddling reducing belts. "Be thin. Be rich.

Be . . ." The woman locked eyes with Emily for a second, saw that Emily didn't need what she was selling, and scanned the throngs for a better mark.

"You don't look like a struggling actress," Amory said. "That's a beautiful coat."

"I had a successful husband. About all I have to show for it are some clothes," Emily said with much less rancor than relief. "I'm all on my own. What about you?" she asked demurely.

"I'm from Philadelphia," Amory said.

"Are you a lawyer?"

"Why?"

"I thought every man in Philadelphia's supposed to be a lawyer." She smiled.

"Then I feel left out."

"What do you do?"

"My . . . My family makes soda and ginger ale. Polar brand. I'm trying to open up a New York market."

"That's a great business to be in now," Emily said. "People have to drink something."

"You're absolutely right. When you're used to paying for whiskey, you don't even notice the price of water. And at a lot of places they'll charge two dollars for a soda and then throw in the Scotch for free. That way, they're not *selling* liquor. Prohibition's a joke."

"And you're laughing all the way—"

"To the theater," Amory cut her off. "The business pretty much runs itself. And sales are good, so good I can back shows. I love Broadway."

"Why?" Emily asked.

"To pick up my dull life. You can only do so much with ginger ale. I'm fascinated by show people. You've got something extra, something special. You're so *alive*."

What a terrific attitude, Emily thought. If only Warren had felt that way.

"Here's your toy store," Amory said. The facade of H. B. Greene's Castle of Toys was that of a crenellated medieval fortress. It stood between a flea circus and a hat shop. "I have to go back to Philadelphia and sell some water. Miss Stanton, it's been a pleasure." Amory put out a proper hand to say good-bye. Shaking hands made

21

Emily uneasy. She didn't want Amory to notice the scar where Warren had burned her.

Luckily, Amory was looking only into her beautiful green eyes. "Listen," he said, "this has absolutely nothing to do with the *Scandals*. You've got my vote on that. I'm going to call George W. about you tonight. But I would like to see you again. You're a very interesting person."

Emily couldn't have been more elated at that moment if George White had run up waving a contract at her. "Amory, you're too nice."

"I'll be back in town next week," he said. "Would you have dinner with me a week from Friday?"

"Why . . . Why not? I'd love to," Emily said impulsively, breaking the rule she had set for herself about no more men in the immediate future. Oh, well, she thought. She had never followed the rules anyhow.

"Pick you up at eight. Where are you?"

Emily hesitated. "I can meet you."

"No, I insist."

"All right. The Royale. Forty-fifth between Ninth and Tenth."

"You *are* full of surprises. A struggling actress who lives in Hell's Kitchen who sings like a star and looks like she belongs on Park Avenue. I *do* want to get to know you, Miss Emily Stanton." Amory shook her hand again and hailed a taxi.

Emily went into H. B. Greene's and bought the google-eyed doll to add to Jessica's collection. Then she began walking west to Hell's Kitchen.

4

"What's a date?" Jessica asked her mother.

"It's when a man takes a woman out to a restaurant and they talk and get to know each other," Emily said.

Jessica stroked Midnight, the name she had given to the stray black cat she had found at their new apartment and adopted. "Do they kiss on a date?"

"What do you know about kissing?"

"Aw, Mommy. I know. Do they kiss? Is that what they do?"

"If it's a good date," Emily answered.

"Can I go on the date?"

"Not tonight," Emily said.

"Come on, Mommy. Please."

"Not tonight. It's too late for you."

"Next one?" Jessica asked, eyes open wide.

"We'll see."

"Is he rich like Daddy?"

"Jessica!" Emily scolded her. "Don't be rude."

"But is he, Mommy?"

"That's not a nice question to ask. He's very sweet. That's all that matters."

"I'm sorry, Mommy." Jessica hung her head. "If he was rich, maybe he could take you someplace nice."

"Aw, darling. He will." Emily looked lovingly at Jessica, who had big blue eyes and her mother's fiery auburn hair. The little girl was finally adjusting to her new life. At first she had cried so much, wanting to go back to Park Avenue. She had missed her big room with its windows looking out at the skyscrapers. She missed playing with her nursemaid, Cora, in Central Park. She missed the big kitchen and the refrigerator stuffed with delicious things to eat. For Emily, perhaps the most difficult aspect of leaving Warren was to take Jessica away from all the privileges he provided. Now Jessica's only view was a dingy exposure of the next-door Salvation Army kitchen. She played in the barren corridors of their apartment building. She ate a lot of food from cans.

Although they no longer had Park Avenue, Emily and Jessica still had each other. In their newly reduced circumstances, their love had grown even more intense, their time together more precious. They had their rituals: the big pancake breakfast Emily would make for Jessica every Sunday, the morning walk together to Jessica's school on Fiftieth Street, Emily's clipping Jessica's favorite comic strips from the paper every morning for Jessica to see when she came home from school—Gasoline Alley, Casper Milquetoast, Little Mary Mixup. Their favorite ritual, and the most indispensable, was bedtime. With Jessica cuddling one or more of her stuffed dolls, and Emily cuddling Jessica, Emily would tell her little girl a bedtime story and then softly sing her to sleep with "Lullaby and Good Night." No other performance in Emily's life ever gave her as much satisfaction.

Emily was delighted at how resilient Jessica was. She came to enjoy the new neighborhood. Before long, she developed a taste for the calzone, the souvlaki, the gelati. She made friends with the ragamuffin kids she had met in the first grade. Jessica was learning her way around her new life. So was Emily. It was an adventure for both of them. They shared great times together. They didn't *need* Park Avenue. Emily was proud of Jessica. She was proud of herself. She could be an actress *and* a mother.

"What's his name?" Jessica continued.

"Amory."

"Amory?"

"Amory Longworth. Isn't that pretty?"

"Is he handsome, Mommy?"

"Very." Emily still felt funny about going on a date, her first in more than six years. She felt a bit risqué. It wasn't motherly to go on dates. Stop it, she chastised herself. She was only twenty-four years old. She was entitled to have men in her life. One date didn't make her a Jezebel, a fallen woman. She remembered what Cassie had said about not having to be a saint, but some of the lessons of the convent school seemed to die hard.

"Will he be my new daddy?" Jessica wouldn't stop the interrogation.

That was a hard one. And vastly premature. But it was an interesting idea. Emily wanted more children. Look how well the first one had turned out. She wanted to be in love. And she wanted a companion. Just because her first marriage didn't last shouldn't forever stigmatize her. What she had to get over was the notion that divorce was an evil, a scarlet letter. A bad marriage was nothing but a big mistake, she kept telling herself. You deserve another chance. You're not a bad person, no matter what your father said and your husband said. You're entitled to have the best life you can make for yourself.

The phone rang and saved Emily from answering Jessica's last query. Cora was on the line. She was sick, and couldn't baby-sit for Jessica tonight. Emily was crushed. Maybe someone was telling her something. Maybe she shouldn't go on dates. Maybe it was wrong. "No more date," Emily said.

"Why not, Mommy?"

"Cora got sick. She can't come."

"Let me go with you. Please, Mommy. I'm not sleepy."

"No. We'll stay home. I'll call him," Emily said, very disappointed.

Jessica could sense it. "What about Alex?" she suggested. "I like Alex. Maybe he can baby-sit for me."

Emily went downstairs and found Alex Foster answering calls on the switchboard in the large mirrored lobby of the Royale.

"How's the Yale man?" Emily greeted him.

"On the verge of literary immortality, if only this damned phone would stop ringing," Alex said. The beginning pages of his first play, *Fly by Night,* lay on the table next to him.

"You know, you could have a corps of secretaries answering the phone for *you*," Emily said. "With your education, you could be a big businessman."

"You sound like my folks," Alex said.

"I sound like *my* folks," Emily caught herself.

"I told you how much I hated numbers," Alex said in his quiet voice, with its slight drawl from his native Charleston, South Carolina. "Adding up all that money would have bored me silly. This is the perfect job for a playwright. I can write all day and my rent's free."

"Then how would you like an even more perfect job? I've got one for you," Emily said.

"And what could that be?" Alex asked.

"Baby-sitting for Jessica tonight. You can write all night and I'll make you dinner tomorrow."

Emily liked Alex, who was a most unusual desk clerk. Today he was wearing blue-and-gray-diamond golf socks, baggy knickers, a blue tweed jacket, and a jaunty red bow tie. With his dimpled face, blond hair parted down the center, his ready smile, Emily could imagine him in a raccoon coat with a flask of gin in the rumble seat of a Stutz Bearcat, and had she been younger, she could imagine riding off to the football game with him. Alex was flaming youth, and because of her early marriage, flaming youth was something Emily missed having experienced.

There was a lot about Alex that Emily didn't know. In truth, he had once wanted to go down to Wall Street with his classmates from New Haven. But he had been caught in a scandal and expelled from Yale. That was almost two years before, yet he still wasn't able to face it. The writing career thus came about by default; nevertheless, Alex now loved the idea of being a writer. The trick was to succeed.

Fly by Night was a comedy about two gold diggers, a man and a woman, each pretending to be rich, each out to marry a millionaire, who picked the other as his best prospect. They get involved for all the wrong reasons, but once they find out their respective charades, they fall in love anyway, for all the right reasons. Alex had told Emily the plot. She told him she couldn't wait for him to finish it, so she could star in it.

When Emily asked Alex to baby-sit because of her upcoming date, he stifled a rush of jealousy. He was good at dissembling. "Who's the lucky guy?" he asked, not directly responding to her request.

"He's one of the investors in the *Scandals*."

"So you're selling your soul," Alex joked.

"Only for top billing," Emily joked back. "If he wants to help me get a part, I won't stand in his way. Not that I'm lying in his path." She smiled.

"Take your breaks where you find them. You're good anyway."

"Oh, Alex, how do you know?"

"I just know," Alex said. "Once you're in the show, you can prove yourself. Getting in is the tough part. Until you make it on Broadway, business comes way ahead of pleasure."

"Yes, but . . . would you baby-sit for me tonight?" Emily asked in a breathless way that indicated to Alex that pleasure, rather than business, might be the stronger force driving her in this instance.

"Only if you promise not to fall for any outrageous lines," Alex said.

"I promise. And I promise to be back at a very decent hour," Emily assured him. "Alex, you're an angel."

Perhaps if he were more of a devil, Alex thought, he might have a chance with her. Admiring Emily's long legs and perfect derriere as she strode away to the elevator, he began conjuring up ways, deliciously devilish ways, to break the ice between them.

Although Prohibition had fairly well killed off the *restaurant de luxe*, not all speakeasies were tin-ceilinged, checkered-tablecloth affairs. The Ringside was a lavish basement operation run by the brother of the retired lightweight champion Benny Leonard. There were luxurious red leather banquettes, shining silver, and white napkins, tuxedoed waiters. The focus of the place, and its inspiration, was its dance floor, which looked exactly like an outsize boxing ring. Ex-champ Leonard would frequently enter the ring between sets by the jazz band, seated behind the ring, to announce celebrities. The celebrities were often Broadway people like Fanny Brice, sports people like Babe Ruth, or political people like Jimmy Walker, but they were just as often underworld people, gangland leaders with names like Kid Dropper and Johnny Spanish, and these latter were just as wildly and drunkenly cheered and saluted as the leaders of the overworld.

Emily was worried she would run into some of Warren's Tammany friends at the Ringside. After a few glasses of champagne, and no one she recognized appeared, she began to relax. The band played "The Sheik of Araby." She was with the handsomest man in the room. His total attention to her made her feel secure. Amory had on an expensive charcoal-gray suit, Emily a white beaded silk evening dress with a full skirt for dancing. Amory noticed her dress, her pearls, her hair. "You're the most graceful woman I've ever met," he said, running his finger up the sleeve of her dress to her neck, sending with it an electrical jolt of excitement.

Over a delicious grilled squab and a fine wine, she told Amory about how she grew up and about her martinet father, the warden of the Stateville Penitentiary in Joliet, Illinois, and about her mother, as quiet and yielding as her father was harsh.

"You're the last girl on earth I'd ever imagine would end up in the theater," Amory said. "Your father, warden at Joliet. Amazing. How'd you ever talk him into it?"

"I didn't. And we're still not talking," Emily said.

"That's too bad."

"It hurts me a lot, but as much as possible I try not to think about it."

"You'd think being a good Catholic, he'd be more compassionate to you," Amory said.

"We're not Catholic."

"But the convent school? The nuns?"

"He did that for the discipline. When you're a prison warden, I think discipline is your religion."

"I imagine Broadway's his idea of hell."

"You're so right," Emily said. "To leave the convent to come to Broadway was one cardinal sin. To leave my husband and to go back to Broadway was even worse. I wish my father would understand. Even a little support would go a long way. No matter how grown-up you get, you still want to please your daddy."

"And your husband. He just doesn't sound like he was right for you," Amory ventured.

"He seemed pretty terrific at the time. I was seventeen. He was twenty-nine, a man of the world, and I was basically a convent girl who had never really gone out before. I was incredibly flattered." Emily felt so relaxed. She loved having Amory to talk to.

The waiter cleared their plates and poured more wine.

"I bet he was a swell dancer," Amory said.

"How'd you know?"

Amory merely winked.

"He really was. He taught me how to tango and to waltz."

"Was that why you married him? He swept you off your feet?"

"No. I'm not sure I really wanted to get married. Then Emily blushed, realizing the wine had made her tongue too loose. "I'm so embarrassed. I'm talking too much."

"I like you when you talk. Don't stop now. Why did you marry him? How does a man win someone like you?"

"Oh. He was just persistent. Was and is. He likes to win. He has to win everything. It's all a game. I was one of his games. Warren Matthews is the most determined man you could ever meet. He's a fantastic salesman. The same way he sells tiles, he sold me on himself."

Emily was ashamed to tell Amory that the reason—the main reason—she had married Warren was that he had gotten her pregnant. She had been having fun going out with him. Nothing serious, but a good time. And one good time, after too many tangos and too much champagne, Emily had gone back to Warren's apartment. Thus her first boyfriend became her first lover. However, despite the vociferous informational campaign of Margaret Sanger and her American Birth Control League, Emily had known nothing at all about contraception. The nuns never told her, and all Warren had told her was not to worry.

Some of the other girls in the chorus gave Emily the name of a place in Staten Island where they went if they got into trouble. Emily agonized over an abortion, which was dangerous, illegal, and finally, in her mind, terribly wrong. The baby was a living thing. It was hers. She wanted it. At first, though, Warren didn't. When he finally relented and agreed to marry her, Emily was so grateful and relieved over having a father for her child that putting her career on hold seemed to be a sacrifice worth making.

"So, after six years of raising this magnificent little girl, you decided to go back onstage," Amory said, now over a chocolate soufflé.

"Where was your husband?"

"Warren was never home. He was always out being successful."

"And you wanted to be successful too. On your own. You had come to New York to be an actress, not to be a Park Avenue housewife. You wanted to get back on the track."

"Amory. How come you understand things?"

"I put myself in your place. It's simple. You gave him six years. You're entitled to some time for yourself. You're entitled to grow, to have your own life. How could he argue with that?"

"He took it personally," Emily told Amory. "He wanted me in the Junior League, not in a chorus line. He had some very fixed ideas about what a wife should and shouldn't do."

"You'd have thought he'd be incredibly proud of you." Amory gazed at her admiringly. Emily was warm from the food, the wine, the charm of this man.

"Proud? He was ashamed. 'Wives don't act,' " Emily repeated Warren's line.

"Any woman can cook and serve. You have a tremendous talent. How could he deny that?"

"I don't mean to brag, but I thought that until we got our maid Cora last year, I was a pretty good housewife. I really worked very hard at it. I just thought that I could do that and the theater too, but Warren felt very strongly that one career in the family was enough. He let me try some shows, but he just couldn't stand it."

"What did he do?"

"He got really crazy," Emily said, not wanting to tell Amory how crazy. She couldn't talk about the unharnessed temper, the screaming, the terrible beatings. Emily knew that Warren's abject apologies, his make-up gifts and flowers, didn't alter the reality that she was in a dangerous, volatile situation and that the marriage could not go on, even as a pretext. "The Broadway thing poisoned our relationship, and because of it we simply couldn't get along."

"Irreconcilable differences," Amory said, shaking his head in sympathy. He seemed to know everything, even the horrors that she was holding back from him. "Well, your daughter sounds wonderful, and you've *got* to keep her, and keep doing what you're doing," Amory said. He was interested in Jessica and very protective when Emily told him about Warren's demand for custody and his battery of attorneys. "A friend of mine's a top divorce lawyer. I want you to meet him. He can help. The right lawyer can make all the difference."

"I can take care of it," Emily said. "I don't think he really wants Jessica and all that responsibility. He'll calm down."

"Your husband doesn't sound like a white-flag guy. He won't give up so easily. You'll need someone like my friend."

They talked and talked. Amory told Emily more about his business, about how all the Pennsylvania speakeasies were stocking the Polar brand, and about how little all his business success meant to him. "As I told you, the business runs itself," he said. "So I look for ways to amuse myself. Basically, I'm awfully lonely. The Broadway thing is really a way, my way at least, to find someone to be with. I've met a lot of women in the theater, but, you know, most of them don't have . . . substance."

"I thought you were looking to be amused," Emily said, testing, trying to figure out how serious Amory really was.

"Sometimes I am. Sometimes I want something more. You know, I'm almost thirty. That scares me. What have I got? Business, money, friends to go drinking with. But when they go home to their wives, I realize how all alone I am. That really scares me. I think it means I'm growing up, getting ready to settle down. I do want a family."

"What's stopping you?" Emily asked.

"I'm my own worst enemy. I'm too fussy. Unless I meet someone who's really special, I pull away. It's all or nothing."

"Maybe you're just not ready."

"No. I'm just particular. I'm looking for someone special." He gazed hard at her.

"What's special to you?" Emily knew she was flirting and couldn't wait to hear what he would say.

"Someone with courage. Someone with character. Someone as beautiful within as she is on the surface. Someone. . . ." He paused. "Like I think you are."

"Amory." Emily blushed this time. She was glad the room was bathed in the smoky, rosy glow of the candles off the red banquettes, but she was blushing so much that she imagined he could notice over the light.

"I admire you," he went on. "I really do. How many women in the theater can raise a child? I've met lots of actresses. All of them are so vain, so self-absorbed, so me, me, me."

"Maybe you *have* to be that way to really make it."

"Look at you."

"Look at me?"

"I love looking at you. But aside from that . . ."

"I'm struggling. Every day . . ."

"The *Scandals* are going to be your big break. I'm seeing to that."

"But, Amory, you don't know me . . ."

"I heard you sing. I have ears. I have eyes. I know you're right."

Emily almost started crying.

The band, after a slow ballad or two, launched into "I'll See You in My Dreams," but the saxophone riffs and horn improvisations, together with the stepped-up tempo, made the song seem completely different.

"I thought you had to go up to Harlem to hear music like this," Emily said, fascinated by the sound of jazz.

"You really have to go to Chicago," Amory said. "After they closed up Storyville at the end of the war, all the great Negro players left New Orleans and went north. Reason this band's so good is that Benny brought them in from there."

"There's this wonderful Chicago band called the Wolverines Warren took me to hear at the Cinderella Ballroom last year."

"I know Bix," Amory said.

"Bix Beiderbecke, the cornet player?" Emily replied.

"Best white jazz musician I ever heard," Amory said.

"I like jazz," Emily said. "But I kind of agree with people who say that it's outlaw music, just right for the speakeasies. It's . . . almost revolutionary."

"Makes me want to dance. Shall we?" Amory said as he led Emily out onto the floor. He was a wonderful dancer, strong, sure, and he smelled so good. Here was her white knight, something she had never expected. As they danced, and the room spun, Amory leaned down and kissed her lips softly, then pulled back. "I've been wanting to do that all evening," he said with an almost boyish shyness so at odds with his dashing appearance.

"Me too," she said, and kissed him back.

At midnight, they stood outside in the cold, on Twentieth Street, waiting for a cab, in front of McGuffey Firearms, the basement of which housed the Ringside. A giant model revolver hung in front of the store. No one could miss it. Amory had his arms around Emily. He seemed to understand her, to know so much more about her than she had told him.

"Would you be terribly offended, Emily, if I invited you to my hotel for a nightcap?"

"I'd love to, but my daughter." It was the first time she had thought about Jessica for hours. She was flooded with guilt. "It's so late. I'm sure she's missing me terribly."

"I'm sure she's fast asleep." He held her tighter. "I have ulterior motives."

"I'm sure you do," Emily said playfully.

"I have this other play they're nagging me to invest in. I'd love you to read it."

"What about your etchings?" She winked.

"They're home in Philadelphia. Please. The play's for real. So am I." He kissed her again.

Emily didn't want to be "fast" or "loose." "Amory. Better next time."

He pulled back politely. "Of course. I don't want you to feel like a bad mother. It's just that I may not be back for a month or more, and that time's going to seem like an eternity for me."

Emily hated standing alone. "Amory," she sighed, "that's very sweet."

"I don't want this night to end. It's like a dream. I dread waking up." He grasped her hand, then kissed her once more, more passionately than she had ever been kissed before. "I'm sorry," he whispered in her ear. "I can't help myself. Please. One more hour. You'll make me the happiest man on earth."

"One quick nightcap," Emily gave in. She wasn't ready for this dream to end either. "Just one."

Amory positively lit up with satisfaction. He held her again and helped her into the sputtering taxi that had stopped beside them.

The Longacre Hotel stood hard behind Pennsylvania Station, in an Egyptian neighborhood. The Port Said restaurant was next door, reeking of garlic, sounding like a seraglio, as a clarinet oozed out a belly-dance casbah melody that lured in fat men in red fezzes from outside. Men around the hotel by day sold brass and rainbow silks and carpets, creating the aura of a bazaar. Exoticism aside, the Longacre was hardly romantic and hardly the kind of place Emily would have guessed Amory Longworth would be staying.

"Every place in town's booked up," he said, as if reading her mind. "Some big convention. I normally stay at the Waldorf, but . . . well, this is really more amusing." Inside, the Longacre was a tired, decrepit hotel. The three men she saw in the musty lobby were all with ladies of the evening, heavily painted, in tight dresses. She saw two other ladies by themselves. "Local color," Amory laughed.

"You'll never get lonely here," Emily joked.

"The emperor suite," Amory said as he unlocked the door and flicked on the light. A lone bulb illuminated a dingy room whose cracked plaster walls were bare except for a cheap oil of a sailing ship. There were two chairs with their stuffing coming out, and a narrow cotlike bed. The room smelled of leaking gas and overlooked the Port Said. The belly-dance music could be heard below. Surely there was something else between this and the Waldorf, Emily thought, but she didn't want to be rude.

Amory helped her out of her coat, and showed her a chair. When he opened the closet, she didn't see any other clothes. There was no luggage in the room. Odd, she thought.

"Here, this could be your ticket to the big time." Amory smiled as he handed her a script that was lying on the bedspread. *The Merry Month of May*, by Stephen Wallace. "I want you to be completely candid."

He wasn't kidding about the play after all, Emily thought, relieved that his motives in inviting her back with him were honest. But she also realized that part of her was disappointed. As quick as a swallow's change in flight, the warmth, the romantic glow of the evening, had vanished the moment they reached the hotel.

"*The Merry Month of May*," Emily read. "Is it a musical?"

"Just read it. The first act. That's all. Then we can talk. I don't want you to prejudge it."

As Emily sat down to read, Amory took her purse and set it on a chipped wood table behind the chair. "I want you to concentrate," he said, almost like a hypnotist.

"I will," Emily assured him, and began reading as quickly as she could. Maggie, an innocent small-town girl, of Centerville, USA, has a normal life with her church choir, corner soda shop, and the like, until one day Griffin, an eccentric man, arrives in a fancy black Rolls-Royce. He turns out to be a Hollywood director. He is so armed by the rusticity of Centerville that he decides to make a movie about the town with Maggie as the star and her family and townspeople as the rest of the cast. Naturally, the town is thrown into bedlam. Emily liked Maggie. She could see herself in the part. She was excited.

While Emily was immersed in the script, Amory took out his room key and went over to the door, which had a special lock that he deftly turned, double-locking it from the inside. The noise from the street and from the Port Said obscured the clicks. He put the key in his pocket.

"It's very interesting," Emily said, getting more involved with every page.

"Keep going," he urged her.

"You're not bored?"

"Please. Go ahead."

She read on. Amory went into the small bathroom for

a few minutes. When he came out, she was reading intently. Stealthily he stepped over to the table behind her, opened her purse, and dropped a wad of bills inside, closing it carefully. He walked around in front of her, staring at her for a few moments. Sensing his presence, Emily looked up. She was beaming.

"I love Maggie," she said. "I just love her. I could do it. I know I could. It's a swell play."

Amory made no response.

"Who's the playwright?" Emily went on. "Stephen Wallace? Has he ever done anything else? He's very funny . . ." She was talking now just to hear herself talk, hear somebody talk.

Amory stood over her, staring, silent. He turned and went over to the bed and sat down, eyes always on Emily, who crossed her legs nervously. A look of apprehension crossed her face like a shadow.

"Amory? What's the matter? Are you all right?"

No answer.

"I guess you're all talked out. Sometimes you just talk so much, like we did, you just run out of words and have nothing . . . Oh, Amory, please say something. Please. You're giving me the jitters."

He just stared.

Emily was frightened now. She hadn't known silence could be so terrifying. Warren had yelled at her, beat her, burned her, but he'd never scared her this much. "Tell me. Please. What's the matter?"

No response.

Emily knew she had to flee. She got up, didn't even bother to get her coat, and instinctively went for the door. It wouldn't open. She twisted the knob, to no avail. She looked back at Amory. He was picking up the telephone. "What are you doing? Let me out! Please! Please let me go."

"Operator . . . Lackawanna 4-2880," he said in a perfectly modulated voice.

She hoped he might be calling her a cab. But no. She knew she wasn't that lucky. "Amory. Let me out of here. What's come over you? Why are you doing this?" Emily tried again to open the door.

"Ninth precinct, yes . . . yes . . . Officer McNaughton

here . . . yes . . . that's right . . . let me have Sergeant Gilman . . ."

Emily knew something was terribly wrong, worse than anything that had ever happened to her.

"Joe . . . McNaughton . . . yes . . . I want you to send a car over to the Longacre Hotel . . . bringing someone in. That's right . . . fifth floor . . . room 507 . . . Right . . . Prostitution."

5

At one o'clock in the morning, Alex Foster was playing "All by Myself" on the piano in Emily's apartment when he passed out on the keyboard. Awakening, he had dragged his body over to the couch and fallen fast asleep.

The knock on the door was loud and insistent, but it took a few moments for Alex to hear it. He pulled himself out of his deep sleep and staggered to the door. At least she was back, he thought. He would be happy to see her. Maybe they'd have a cup of coffee, and she'd tell him about the high life.

"You must have had a wonderful . . ." Alex stopped short. A tall, well-dressed man stood in the doorway.

"I'm Warren Matthews. Jessica's father."

"Is something wrong with Emily?" Alex asked.

"I'm here for my daughter." Warren ignored Alex's question.

"What's the matter with Emily?" Alex asked. "Where is she?"

"Where is Jessica?" Warren Matthews said in a steely, resolute voice.

"Emily didn't say anything about your coming here. What's going on?"

"I don'ave time for this," Warren Matthews said, entering the apartment. He sniffed the air of the flat, and contorted his face into a sneer of distaste. His daughter was too good for this. How could Emily have taken her here?

Alex stepped in front of Warren. Although he was smaller than Warren, he was determined to keep him out. "I'm sorry! Jessica's my responsibility."

38

Warren flushed with fury. He grabbed Alex, to swat him like an annoying flea, but Alex was possessed. He hit Warren as hard as he could, and knocked Warren into the hallway and onto a dusty balustrade, which smeared Warren's camel-hair topcoat. Alex came out of the apartment after Warren, who pulled himself together and shook his head at Alex. That confused Alex even more. Why wasn't he fighting back?

Then they hit him. Two six-foot gorillas in leather jackets. With their pockmarked faces and squashed noses, they looked like boxers, from what Alex could see in that split second in the dim hallway. "You little fuck!" one of them said, and crashed a fist into the side of his head. The other said nothing and buried a powerful blow into Alex's solar plexus, knocking the breath out of him, as the first thug kicked him in the groin. Alex crumpled to the floor. A kick to the head sent him into unconsciousness.

Warren Matthews found Jessica lying in her bed. She looked like a little cherub in her tiny red flannel nightgown. She hugged Barney Google in one arm and her cat Midnight in the other. He picked up Jessica and held her.

"Mommy?" Jessica said, opening her eyes.

"It's your daddy," Warren said.

"Daddy?" Jessica yawned. "What are you . . . where's Mommy?"

"We're going home now."

"Where's my mommy?"

Warren did not answer that question. "Everything's going to be fine, darling." He wrapped her in a blanket. The cat scampered out of Jessica's arms. Warren's men entered the room and began emptying Jessica's drawers into some suitcases they had brought. "We're going now."

"Midnight," Jessica cried out as Warren began to leave the room. It took him a moment to figure out what she wanted. "Midnight."

"The cat," Warren ordered. "Take it. The doll too."

"Got them, sir."

They took Jessica, Midnight, her dolls, and her clothes down the steps into a waiting black Packard that took them uptown to Park Avenue.

6

"The only thing I care about is getting you out of here as fast as possible." The lawyer inspired confidence. He was squat, with a pug nose. A tenacious little bulldog of a man, the kind of lawyer that wins cases, Emily thought. The only thing that was disconcerting was his carnation boutonniere. It made him look as if he were going to a funeral. Then again, the flower was the only sign of color in the iron-gray monotony of Emily's cell in the Women's House of Detention on Eighth Street. There were no windows, no fresh air, only bars. The lawyer's name was J. Nicholas Collins. He was Emily's glimmer of support in a flagrant, incredible injustice, and she reached out to him.

"I specialize in helping women," he said when he entered her cell. "We see this all the time. The vice squad's no damn good," he said, with outrage.

It was the morning after her arrest, but Emily wasn't sure whether it was day or night. She had been up so long, she had undergone so much. None of it seemed real. She thought back to the night before, reconstructing the horror. First, there was the ride from the Longacre to the precinct house in the padded and barred police van. "Classy piece," she heard one of the officers say at the precinct, gazing at her white evening dress. "Nice one, Mike."

Amory Longworth was really Officer Michael McNaughton of the NYPD vice squad, she found out as she was being booked, fingerprinted, having a mug shot taken. "Top man," someone said about him.

"But I didn't do anything," she had pleaded to one smirking face, to one forbidding blue uniform after another.

"What they all say, lady. What they all say. Tell it to the judge."

And Jessica? Was she all right? No one told her. No one cared. She had tried to keep her composure, and she had almost made it. But when McNaughton, *Officer* McNaughton, had come to sign the complaint against her and offered as evidence one hundred dollars in marked bills that he must have planted in her purse while she was engrossed in *The Merry Month of May*, she had lost all control. She didn't know which emotions were pulling the strongest. Her concern for Jessica? Her anger at McNaughton? Her fear for herself? Whatever, she knew that she had to get out of jail before she could deal with any of it.

The bail was extortionate. Five thousand dollars. She couldn't even pay the bail premium of five hundred dollars. She didn't have it. She wouldn't dream of letting Warren know about what had happened. And she was too embarrassed, beyond embarrassed, mortified to ask any of the show people she knew for help. And her family? Wouldn't her father love this? No, she had to hope it was an enormous error, and standing before her now, J. Nicholas Collins was a godsend. He was going to get her out of this awful mess.

"I just want to get back to my daughter as soon as possible," was the first thing Emily could say to Collins.

"Exactly. That's my objective," Collins said. He had a Brooklyn nasal twang. He spoke the language of the local constabulary. He could get her out, Emily kept thinking to herself as she outlined every detail of the frame-up.

"Why do you think he did it?" she asked.

"Do I look like Sigmund Freud? Why does anybody do anything? Why are you wearing white and not red?" Collins was short with her. "I don't look for motives. I look for results."

"When can I get out?" Emily pressed.

"As soon as we get to court."

"When can that be?"

"Could be weeks. The courts are all backed up."

"No." Emily's heart sank. Weeks? She couldn't take hours more of this.

"No good, huh, Mrs. Matthews?"

41

LULLABY AND GOODNIGHT

"Miss, please." Emily restrained her irritation. What difference did labels make? "I'm sorry. I just want to get out of here."

"Me too. That's why I want to recommend that you waive a jury trial. Let a judge hear your case."

"Waive a jury?"

"Yeah. Give up your right to a jury trial. That's what takes so long. I think I can get you before a judge in a coupla days. I got connections with the clerk. The sooner we get to court, Mrs. Matth . . . Miss Stanton, the sooner you get outta here."

Emily tried to recall things she had heard about people in trouble. "I sort of thought you were safer with a jury. They'll understand what happened."

"A jury probably *wouldn't* understand, Miss Stanton. If you will listen to me, juries are not particularly sympathetic to actresses. I tell you, if you were a nurse charged with prostitution, I'd say wait for a jury. Or a schoolteacher. Juries really like them, because nurses help sick people and schoolteachers help little children. But actresses, well, people may like to go see actresses, but you know, they all think actresses lead a pretty wild life and, you know . . ."

"But I was framed," Emily said. "That man is so sick . . ."

"Listen, lady. I've been goin' to court for twenty years, and you know what? In your case, you're better off, just you and the judge."

"Why?" Emily asked.

"The judge is more likely to grasp the whole issue of entrapment."

"But I didn't *do* anything!"

"I understand, Miss Stanton, but with a jury, the word of Officer McNaughton that you are a prostitute is very damaging. Trust the judge."

"The man is a monster."

"Damn right he is, but he is the smoothest monster I've ever seen. Star of the Vice Squad. He's taken credit for cleaning up Broadway. Juries love him."

"I can't believe a jury would take his word."

"*You* did," Collins said.

42

7

The courtroom in the Criminal Courts Building on
Centre Street reminded Emily of one of the immigrant
holding pens on Ellis Island she had seen pictures of. The
paint was peeling. The portraits of several eighteenth-
and nineteenth-century New York jurists that provided
the room's decoration were peeling, as was a frieze around
the ceiling repeating the motif of a blindfolded Liberty
holding the scales of justice. An American flag stood
beside the raised bench. Across the room, to the right of
the bench, the jury box was empty. There were a few
rows of wooden benches. They were empty.

"The law moves a lot faster when you keep it simple,"
J. Nicholas Collins told Emily when she expressed a
misgiving about waiving a jury trial. And here she was, a
mere twenty-four hours after Collins came to her, in
court.

The judge's name was Stanley Renaud. He was about
fifty-five, small, wiry, with a waxed mustache and bulging
eyes. He looked somewhat like a ferret. Emily didn't like
him, but Collins assured her he was a "smart one" who
would understand what was going on.

Emily was already planning what she would do when
she was released. No one needed to know about the
entire episode. But, of course, there was no reason to be
ashamed. She could tell Cassie, who was away on tour.
The most important thing was to get Jessica back. Collins
told her she was being kept by her father, whom the
police contacted after her arrest. What did they tell him?
Would he believe she was guilty? she asked herself. Maybe
she should talk to Warren. He had loved her once, said

43

he still did. Maybe he could pull some of his Tammany strings to have this monster McNaughton thrown off the force. Warren was gallant, if nothing else. But then she'd have to explain why she was dating Amory Longworth.

No more dates for a long time. Emily was sure of that. She couldn't wait to see Jessica. She couldn't wait to take a hot bath.

"How long will the whole thing take?" she asked Collins.

"Couple of hours," he said gruffly, but somehow nicely. When she had asked him earlier about his fee, he was so unconcerned. "Pay me when you have it. I just wanna get you back to your little girl." It was a big, impersonal city, but there were lots of nice people with heart, she thought.

"How long have you been on the vice squad, Officer McNaughton?" asked Ethan Gross, the young assistant district attorney, an intense, self-righteous sort in a cheap suit with a shiny seat and elbows.

"Five years, sir," McNaughton said from the witness stand.

"And how many prostitution arrests have you made?"

"Twenty-five hundred and thirty-four, sir."

Emily was astonished. He was a sexual bounty hunter. Were they all innocent? Were they all falling for Amory Longworth? He was dressed in a blue serge suit, navy tie. He looked like an Arrow Collar advertisement. He sounded so mellifluous, so honorable. What an evil bastard!

"How many of these arrests have resulted in convictions?"

"Ninety-nine-point-one percent, sir."

Emily's heart sank. Collins patted her hand reassuringly.

"How did you know Emily Stanton was a prostitute?"

"On information and belief, sir. I had heard it around Broadway. Went with a lot of big producers, that kind of thing."

Emily was livid. Collins squeezed her arm to still any outburst. "You'll get your say," he whispered. "Save it for the judge."

"I had heard of her, but I only knew for certain, of course, when she requested money for her sexual . . . favors, sir."

"How much did she ask you for?" the prosecutor asked.

"A hundred dollars."

"A hundred dollars. Wasn't that unusually expensive?"

"She said that was her price. That she was worth it."
McNaughton stared straight at Emily. She wanted to
jump up and go at him. "If she didn't get it from me, she
said she could get it from someone else."

"How did you pay her?"

"In the marked bills the Vice Squad uses."

"Your honor, I have here the subject bills. May they
be marked People's Exhibit A?" Ethan Gross said, stepping forward toward the witness stand to have McNaughton identify the bills.

Emily could sit still no longer. "It's a lie. A dirty lie.
He planted the money," she cried out.

Judge Renaud, whose eyes were half-closed, came to
life and banged down his gavel twice. "Please! Sit down,
Miss Stanton."

"It's a lie," Emily persisted. Collins stood up to try to
pull her back to her seat, but he was unsuccessful.

"I want your client to sit down, or I'll have to hold her
in contempt," the judge said to Collins.

"Don't ruin it for yourself," Collins said to Emily
under his breath, and she sat down and clenched her
teeth as McNaughton went through his litany of lies
about Emily's high-priced immorality.

After a half-hour, Emily took the stand in her own
defense. Collins led her through the entire story. Amory
Longworth, theatrical investor, the Ringside, the Longacre,
The Merry Month of May. Emily felt she had made it as
clear a case of a frame-up as could be made. It worried
her to see that Judge Renaud seemed completely indifferent to her entire testimony, and McNaughton seemed
completely unperturbed and as self-confident as ever.
Still, no judge could convict her on this testimony.

Then, on cross-examination by the barracuda Ethan
Gross, Emily was really placed under fire.

"He said he was an investor—"

"So you wanted him to invest in you," Gross said
snidely.

"I object, your honor," Collins spoke up.

"Sustained." Judge Renaud yawned.

"Miss Stanton, what did you earn the week before you were arrested?" Gross continued.

"Why, er . . ." Emily hesitated. "Nothing. My last show had closed." Damn, she thought, he was going after the unemployed-actress angle.

"Would you say you had a steady job?"

"When I work—"

"But you weren't working, were you, Miss Stanton?" Gross was heavy on innuendo. She glanced at Collins for help. He just shrugged.

"I was trying to find work," she said.

"But you weren't working. Yes or no?"

"I was looking for a new job that would pay a lot—"

"Yes or no?" Gross repeated. "Yes or no?"

"Would you please answer the question?" Judge Renaud interrupted.

"Would the prosecution please repeat the question?" Collins said, standing up.

"Were you working at the time of your arrest, Miss Stanton? Yes or no."

"No!"

"And you hadn't been working for how long?"

"What does that matter?" Emily asked, exasperated that Collins wasn't getting her off this unfortunate line of questions.

"Answer the question, please, Miss Stanton," Judge Renaud snapped.

"About six weeks."

"What," Gross asked, "did you do for money during that period, Miss Stanton?"

"I had savings."

"She had savings," Gross mocked her. Why wasn't Collins objecting? "Why didn't you take a regular job, Miss Stanton? Why not?"

"Why should I?" Emily shot back. "I'm an actress. I can make do."

"With what? Tell me. How do you supplement your income, Miss Stanton?" Gross's shrill voice reverberated in Emily's head.

"I didn't supplement—"

Gross wouldn't let her finish. "I'll tell you how. With earnings from prostitution. That's how. Isn't it, Miss

Stanton? You sold *yourself*, didn't you?" He pointed his bony accusing finger straight in her face. "Didn't you? Didn't you?" he repeated loudly, as if this were a first-degree-murder case, not a case of prostitution.

"I did not!" Emily yelled back.

After a five-minute recess, Judge Stanley Renaud returned from his chambers with his verdict. "The court hereby finds the defendant, Emily Stanton, guilty of the crime of prostitution."

Guilty! Despite all of McNaughton's testimony, despite Ethan Gross's vituperative attacks, Emily had been sure Judge Renaud would find her innocent. She had been framed. It was so clear.

". . . and sentences the defendant to a term of not less than twenty-four months at the Bedford Penitentiary for Women," Judge Renaud continued in a monotone, his eyes still half-closed.

Emily turned to Collins. His eyes were downcast.

"But you said . . ."

He didn't look at her. "Jesus, who would've known? I guess they're trying to crack down—"

"Crack down? I'm innocent."

"I'm really sorry, miss. Honest I am," Collins mumbled.

Emily looked up at Renaud. She saw Ethan Gross, smiling, shaking hands with McNaughton, who looked past her as if she weren't there. All the sweet things he'd said, all the promises, and now she was nothing to him.

"This is madness," Emily cried out to unlistening ears. "You can't do this. I didn't do anything. He framed me. Can't you see it? He's the one. He's the criminal. Get him!" She was screaming. She was crying. She was seeing her whole life being snatched away from her. "Madness!" she screamed. "No! No!"

"Take her away!" Judge Renaud banged his gavel. A bailiff stepped forward and grabbed Emily. Renaud turned his back on her and departed for his chambers. McNaughton left with Gross. Collins sat there stuffing papers into his briefcase, blindly watching the bailiff lead Emily out of the courtroom.

"My daughter. I'm a mother. I'm not a whore. I'm a mother. I want my child. My baby."

LULLABY AND GOODNIGHT

The bailiff took Emily downstairs, down the marble halls, past the statues of Alexander Hamilton and Robert Fulton and John Jay, through the Corinthian columns, down the vast courthouse steps, and into a padded van that would take her to Bedford.

8

The men of Tammany Hall braved a ten-inch March snow to assemble at the Wigwam on Fourteenth Street. The special occasion was the ninety-fifth birthday of Grand Sachem Joseph B. Van Dam. It was a stag affair. There was a brass band. There were giant rounds of beef sliced by black chefs in white toques. There was more high-quality whiskey than anybody had a right to have, even Tammany, during Prohibition. There was a twenty-foot-square birthday cake with a hooded white-bearded Father Time who popped out, stripped, and was revealed to be a statuesque exotic dancer named Fiona Flame. She gave her business cards to several dozen of the pie-eyed braves.

Chief White Eagle, the famous Osage Indian whose stone face decorated the heads side of the buffalo nickel, was brought in by train from Oklahoma to present Van Dam with a war bonnet, declaring him an honorary chief of the Osage tribe. Van Dam had held half the posts in city government. Among others, he had been dock commissioner, excise commissioner, police commissioner, and elections commissioner. He still smoked cigars, drank Scotch for breakfast, and pinched as many pretty girls on their hindquarters as he could. He was never one for humility. A reporter for the *Times* asked him who he thought was the greatest living American. "I am," he answered.

"This is one of our outstanding young members," Charles Sullivan said, pushing through a crush of other sachems to reach Van Dam, who had just accepted the felicitations of Tammany leader and New York Governor

49

Al Smith, while the band played Smith's anthem, "East Side, West Side." "Mr. Van Dam," Sullivan addressed the self-styled great man, "I want you to meet Warren Matthews."

Van Dam shook Warren's hand. "What's so outstanding about him?"

"He's full of money and he's full of ideas," Sullivan said.

"Well, he can keep the ideas," Van Dam said, lighting a cigar.

"What's your secret?" Warren said, trying to make obsequious conversation. "How do you keep it up?"

"I don't keep it up. That's no secret." Van Dam chortled, one eye on Fiona Flame across the room.

"I want to look half as good as you do when I'm your age," Warren said, not giving up.

"Then keep living, young man, or you won't get there. Keep living." Van Dam darted off to eat some birthday cake.

Warren had another drink. He smoked a cigar. He said hello, exchanged pats on the back, toasts, bracing handshakes with the men who ran New York. He felt very important. He had everything he wanted. He was definitely getting his contract with the city, he had his daughter, he was building a new home in New Jersey for her, and he was able to get a divorce now. Emily's prostitution conviction carried with it the presumption of adultery. Now he could go back on the town. He was heavily courting Isabelle Millbank, who was giving him enormous sympathy for having been deserted by a wife who was secretly a fancy prostitute. Poor Warren! How sad! How could any woman be so rotten? But that was all behind him.

Across the room, two other Tammany men were talking.

"I hear they call you the Lone Wolf of Broadway," said Jimmy Walker to Michael McNaughton, who had been initiated into the Hall nine months before. They were the two best-dressed men in the room. Walker looked like a Broadway Beau Brummell, not a state senator. McNaughton looked like a Wall Street tycoon, not a vice cop. Walker had heard about McNaughton's phenomenal record and wanted to meet him. Besides, he admired any man with an eye for style. "Where d'ya get that name?"

"It's because I work alone."

"You've got admirable restraint, my boy. I couldn't do it."

"What do you mean, Senator?"

"All those pretty girls. All that temptation. You could be putting them in bed, not in jail. I don't see how you can hold back."

"You wouldn't, would you, Jimmy?" Terence McCarey cut in. "It would be all vice and no squad if you were in blue."

"You know," McNaughton said with a great deal of gravity, "when you get to know these women, and what they're all about, they don't seem pretty at all. I'd arrest every one of them if I could."

"At the rate you're going, you will," McCarey said.

"But who'll be left for me?" Walker moaned.

"You're doing a helluva job," Charles Sullivan said, joining the cocktail circle. "Helluva fine job. We can bring our families down to Broadway because of what you all are doing."

"Nobody in the whole country's got a vice squad like ours." McCarey beamed. "Nobody."

"I'm damn proud to be a part of it," McNaughton said.

"And we're proud that you're part of us," Sachem Sullivan toasted the young brave.

9

Stanley Renaud called the Penitentiary for Women at Bedford "the finest girls' school in the country." Certainly the location was right, in the wooded, rolling hills near the Connecticut border, where landed people rode horses and played golf and drank the nights away at their country clubs. From the outside, the green manicured lawn and brown Tudor buildings of the prison didn't look all that different from those of Miss Porter's or Ethel Walker or any of the finishing schools in the area. There were no walls, no towers, no electrical fences, no signs announcing the prison's identity. This certainly wasn't Alcatraz, or Joliet, for that matter. At worst, Bedford, as the prison was known, could be an orphanage. The institution was kept up so well for the sake of its rich neighbors in the town of Bedford, whose property values might go down if it were widely known that a *prison* was in their sylvan midst. Nevertheless, in the evenings, if you were close enough and listened carefully, you could tell what Bedford was. You could hear the anguished cries of the women inmates piercing the moonlit serenity of the forest night.

The cries and the coughs. They were Emily's first impression of Bedford as she lay on the hard cot of her little square cell looking at the cold concrete floor and the cold steel bars. She had been "dressed in," outfitted in the prison wardrobe of a coarse denim dress, scratchy muslin underwear, and a pair of prison-made shoes that pinched her feet and didn't give at all.

"You!" a loud voice echoed down the row of cells that

faced each other on the four floors across a bleak open atrium. "Open your mouth."

"I don't have no fever," the woman cried. "I swear."

"Open that trap," the deeper voice ordered. "You're all sick." There was an influenza outbreak at the prison, but the sick ward was already full. The coughs were continuous. "I'm going to take your temperature if I have to shove this down your throat."

Emily lifted herself up to see what was going on. Across the atrium, Louise, the huge, lumbering prison matron, was standing over the inmate, holding her mouth open as Goldie, Louise's little black inmate assistant, also known as the "stool pigeon," jammed the thermometer in. "Normal," Goldie mumbled after a minute, and moved on to another cell. Emily couldn't understand why the prisoner had been so afraid of having her temperature taken until she saw that Louise was using the same thermometer, without disinfecting it, on each prisoner. The matron wasn't concerned in the slightest about contagion, only about following the rule that during epidemics, the prisoners' temperatures had to be monitored. More frightening than this blind bureaucratic lockstep, though, was the element of sadism.

"Don't make me sick. Please!" the next women cried. "I don't want no flu."

"Open your mouth!"

"I don't want that thing in my mouth!"

"Wanna go to the hole?" Louise barked, referring to solitary confinement, bread and water.

"But I ain't sick."

"Open it!"

The woman cowered and gave way. As Louise and Goldie worked their way around the cellblock, Emily became increasingly apprehensive. Many women were wheezing with the flu. Others were even worse off.

Emily may have felt like dying, but not this way. She had been humiliated, degraded, framed, imprisoned, but somehow she retained her raw instinct for survival.

"Here's the new one," Goldie said to Louise as they opened Emily's cell. "Stanton."

"Well, well. What are you in for?" Louise stared hard

at Emily, looking her up and down. "Singing too loud in the church choir?" Louise cackled.

"Prostitute," Goldie answered for Emily.

"You don't say," Louise said, running her tongue over her lips more lasciviously than any sailor Emily had ever seen outside the peep shows at Times Square. "Well, let's see what you got, honey." Louise stepped forward, brandishing the dreaded thermometer.

"They took my temperature when they dressed me in," Emily said. "I'm okay."

"*I* didn't take your temperature. You may have picked up something. Open your mouth."

"It's not necessary, and that's not sanitized."

"Don't you worry. Let me just put it in your mouth."

Louise edged closer. Emily opened her mouth and touched Louise's hamlike hand. "Let me," Emily said softly, and Louise allowed Emily to take the thermometer and guide it in. At the last second, before it touched her tongue, she managed to simulate an accident. The thermometer fell to the concrete floor, shattering in countless slivers. "Oh! I dropped it," Emily feigned apology. "I'm sorry."

"Why, you little . . ."

"I didn't mean it."

"She broke it on purpose," Goldie said.

Louise seized Emily's arm. She was furious that she had been tricked. She was going to strike Emily.

"Louise! Stop it," an authoritative voice from the next cell called out. "I'll trade."

Louise let Emily go. "Later, baby," Louise growled to Emily, and left. Emily didn't see that Goldie had taken one of the two pairs of stockings Emily had been issued, as a form of tribute. It didn't matter. For the moment, she had been spared.

The next morning, over an inedible breakfast of a hash of unknown origin and tepid, metallic coffee, Emily met her unseen benefactor.

"Thank you," Emily said to her neighbor. "Thank you so much. What did you mean when you said you'd trade?" she asked quietly, so that the other inmates, and the guards, would not hear.

"I bribed them with some chocolate cookies my family

sent me." The strong voice of the birdlike, fragile woman in her mid-forties made her seem much more imposing than she looked. "I'm Alice von Kiel."

"Emily Stanton," Emily said, touching Alice's hand under the table. "That was so kind."

"That's not a word you use around here," Alice whispered back.

They continued their conversation in the prison yard, where the inmates got their fresh air, danced by themselves, smoked, shuffled, or, as the majority did, stared aimlessly at the trees in the distance.

"You're too pretty for your own good," Alice warned Emily.

"I don't feel pretty."

"You don't want to be noticed. The idea is to blend in. A week or two of the food, and you'll look like the rest of us. Doesn't take long."

"I'm sure. Have you been here long?"

"Five years," Alice said.

"Five years!" Emily grimaced.

"It's nothing. I'm here for life. Don't be so horrified. I'm used to it."

"That's . . . What . . . what did you do?"

"I killed my husband."

"Oh." Emily couldn't imagine this woman killing anyone. "You said you had a family."

"Two daughters. One son. He's at Cornell. Older girl's engaged, nice boy, back home in Binghamton. Other's with my folks. They're taken care of," Alice said matter-of-factly. Emily couldn't even *think* of Jessica without breaking down, but Alice was totally in control. That was what the years could do. For the moment, Emily was grateful that her sentence was only two years. Alice's life sentence gave Emily at least some perspective on what, until now, had seemed like eternity to her. "He was loaded," Alice continued.

"He?"

"Husband. Had a Ford dealership."

"You . . . killed him? On purpose?"

"I put rat poison in his whiskey," Alice said, almost boasting.

"Oh!" Emily was dazed.

"Emily, I miss my children, I miss all my kids. That's what I really miss. I was a kindergarten teacher. I had a wonderful school."

"But why did you . . . kill him?"

"Because I couldn't take it anymore." Alice glossed over the subject in a way that closed this conversation. Emily didn't pursue it. In any other area, however, Alice loved to hold forth. She seemed to enjoy talking to Emily. It made her animated. Likewise, Emily found Alice a minor salvation in this hell she had been cast into. Alice was articulate, intelligent, and despite her crime and her hardness, she was an oasis of reason and sanity to Emily. Alice believed Emily implicitly when Emily told her how she was framed.

Their next time on the yard, Alice gave Emily an introduction as to who the inmates of Bedford actually were.

"That's Janet." Alice pointed out a big woman with a haunted expression. "She burned down her husband's factory in Poughkeepsie, for the insurance. Wanted to be rich."

"What about the husband?" Emily asked.

"Sing Sing for ten."

"Any kids?

"Yes, they're with relatives."

Emily was sorry she had asked. For the thousandth time, she thought of Jessica. How was she? She hadn't heard a word, except that she was with Warren. She hoped he had Cora. She hoped Jessica was eating. What did her daughter think, to wake up and have her mother gone? What did Warren tell her?

"See that redhead? Mary. Bank robber."

"No," Emily said, surprised.

"Hit a bank in Westchester with her boyfriend. Got fifty thousand. He was shot."

"*That* woman?" Emily said, gaping at the redhead.

"Women are doing a lot these days. See her? Big forger. The other gal next to her was a subversive, worked for the Germans during the war. She's stuck here for life," Alice told Emily. "Betty Scott there, she ran a ring that stole cars. Only fancy ones, Rolls-Royces, you know, and Hispano-Suizas."

Emily found it hard to believe that these average-looking, sad women could be such ambitious lawbreakers.

"Of course, not everyone's a big shot," Alice said. She showed Emily a proper, spinster type with her hair tied into a neat bun, her face buried in a book. "Bess Horton. She killed her baby. Talk about bad luck. I think she had been a virgin. This was her first real romance. She gets pregnant, expects to go to the altar, but the guy's a rat and bolts. So she gets caught and ends up here."

"You mean she had an illegitimate baby? And she killed it?"

"She was desperate to be respectable. Look at her. You can see how straitlaced she is. Poor fool."

"That's terribly sad."

"We're all sad, Emily," Alice said.

About half of the four hundred women at Bedford were poor blacks sent away, as Alice explained to Emily, for petty crimes such as shoplifting. Almost a third of all the inmates were prostitutes. Emily was both amazed and abashed to be part of this group.

"You weren't the only one who was set up," Alice said. "See her? Bridgit Lund."

A bubbly strawberry blonde was trying to flirt with a stone-faced male guard who was passing through. "Eunuch," Alice said, watching the guard move on. "Bridgit needs flea powder, she's so itchy. She's here for two. She couldn't afford the bribe."

"Bribe?"

"You pay and you go. Bridgit spent all her money on clothes. The police thought she was rich. When she couldn't pay, tough luck."

"I don't understand," Emily said.

"You ought to. It happened to you."

"But I don't. Do they do this to call girls a lot?"

"All the time," Alice said. "The whole vice squad's on the take. Call girls are good targets because they have the money to pay off, but I hear what the cops are doing now is framing innocent girls, secretaries, nurses, actresses . . . I still don't get why you didn't just pay them.

You really thought you could get off? In this system? Ha!"

"Pay them? Nobody asked me for any money," Emily said.

"What do you mean?" Alice said, puzzled. "That's why they framed you, sweetie, for the money. They always ask for money. That's all they want."

"But—" Before Emily could go on, the bell rang three times, summoning the prisoners to the workshop.

"Back to the salt mines," Alice said.

10

Ever since the thermometer incident, Emily had been very wary of the matron. With her painted red lips and her billy club, Louise was a frightening creature. She had the face of a throwback, but she decorated this face with rouge and mascara. Strangely, she was often reading women's magazines like *House and Garden*, but would just as often use the journals to whack recalcitrant prisoners. Somewhere under the brutish form a woman may have been struggling to get out, but she couldn't, and the attendant frustration made Louise infinitely more difficult than the most frustrated, strict sisters at the convent. Louise hadn't really bothered Emily. However, she was constantly eyeing her. "You're feminine, the way she always wanted to be," Alice warned Emily. "Lie low."

Emily was surprised, then, when Louise came by her cell with a smile on her normally glowering face.

"You shouldn't be all alone as much as you are," Louise said in an uncharacteristically solicitous voice. "You don't talk to the others."

"I don't have anything to say."

"Come on, Stanton. You need to make some friends."

"I'm not feeling very sociable," Emily replied.

"You're going to be here awhile. The time goes by, but you might as well make the most of it. It'll be easier with some gals to pal with."

"Maybe in a couple of days," Emily said. "I'll try to get out and talk."

"Come with me now," Louise urged her. "Meet some of the gals. It'll pick you up."

"Now?"

"I got some nice 'uns for you. You'll like 'em. Come on, Emily."

Louise's addressing her by her first name worked. That made Emily feel human. She didn't want to seem like an aloof snob. "Blend in," Alice had counseled her.

"Why not?" Emily said, standing up from her cot. "Thank you, Louise."

"Just tryin' to help."

Louise led Emily down a flight of cold stone stairs to the end of the lower cellblock. She unlocked the steel door to a room where three women sat together in the dark, smoking.

"Here she is, gals," Louise announced with an odd pride. "Here's Miss Emily Stanton."

Gradually, Emily adjusted to the lack of light and began to see their faces. "All right," a large blonde said eagerly. "All right." She would have been pretty, except for her mouth. One of her front teeth was silver. The other was missing.

"Nice to see you," a second, skeletally skinny black woman added. Emily saw a deep scar across her neck and became a little frightened.

"Why don't you all get acquainted," Louise said in a kind of laugh. "Show her the ropes."

"You betcha," the big blonde said.

"Have fun," Louise added, and clanged the door behind her, locking it from the outside.

"Well, well, Miss Emily," the blonde rasped. "Sit yourself down. Smoke?"

Refusing the cigarette, Emily nervously took a seat on the cot beside the third prisoner, who had the freckled face of a tough Irish choirboy.

"That's Mike," the blonde said.

"Michelle," the freckled girl snapped back.

"Puttin' on airs for the company?" the blonde taunted her, then turned back to Emily. "See how much Mike likes you already. I'm Queenie. That's Coco."

"Sure is pretty," Coco, the black woman, said, admiring Emily. "Ain't she?"

Emily wasn't sure why Coco expressed her compliment in the third person. "Thank you," Emily said anyway. That was all that Emily could say to these women. What else was there? Where are you from? How long have you been here? Whom did you kill? What was the etiquette of prison dialogue? Emily decided just to let them talk, but now all they did was stare at her for an uncomfortably long period of time.

"They said you were in the life," Queenie broke the silence.

"No. Two years," Emily replied.

The three women started to laugh. "Not in *for* life. *The* life," Queenie explained.

"I don't understand."

"Hooker," Mike said.

"Oh." Emily understood. "Yeah. They said I was. They framed me."

"No shit," Coco said. "I thought they only did that to us negro girls. That's awful, ain't it?"

"Yeah."

"Awful. Terrible," Queenie added.

"Well, we're all in the same boat now." Emily wasn't looking for much sympathy. She didn't want to seem too helpless. "What are you all here for?" she ventured.

Queenie paused, looked at the other two, then spoke. "I forged some bad checks. Coco here was a shoplifter."

"Yeah. I got some nice stuff, though." Coco smiled. "Macy's *and* Gimbels."

"Mike got a little worked up at this girlfriend of hers, cut her up. But at least when we get out . . . Hell, that prostitution stuff's bad news for your reputation."

"Don't nobody want nothing to do with you when you get out," Coco added.

"Oh, don't say that," Emily said.

"That was real shitty, to send you up," Mike said, breaking her silence.

"Those cops are bastards," Queenie went on. "You're a classy lady. To do that to you. They got no shame. None."

Emily was surprised at the outpouring of support. These women had heart. She let herself relax on the cot, putting both of her legs up under her.

"You know," Queenie said, "there're a lot of hookers in this place. They are the scum of the earth. You watch out for them."

"They'll roll you. They'll hurt you," Coco said. "They're bad."

"How could they ever think you were one?" Mike asked.

"I don't know. This guy was crazy, this vice cop."

"Yeah, but you're too classy to be a whore," Mike said.

"Thanks. But it was his word against mine," Emily said.

"Bastard!" Coco said. "That pig."

"The last thing I could ever be is a hooker," Queenie said.

"I would hate that," Coco seconded her.

"Me too," chimed in Mike.

"But you know, sometimes I get to thinkin', bein' alone here without a man. Maybe I could. Maybe it wouldn't be so bad. But then, I was raised real religious, so I know I couldn't," Queenie soliloquized. "What about you, Emily? I know you didn't. But what if? We got a lot of time for 'what if.' Do you think you could do it? Say the guy was handsome and gave you a lot of dough?" Queenie asked Emily.

"Or if he was a movie star or a senator or a famous baseball player?"

"Yeah," Queenie said. "What if Rudolph Valentino asked you?"

"No," Emily said. "But I'd say yes to President Harding. He's the only one for me."

"But he died," Coco interjected.

"That's why I'd say yes. He'd be an easy date." Emily tried to be funny, and the other women broke up. Even the humorless Mike smiled.

"She's a card, ain't she?" Coco said.

"You're a hoot, Emily," Queenie agreed.

"But honestly." Emily turned serious. "I could never do that. Never. Sell my body? I don't see how any woman could. It's so . . . you know, if you sell your body, you're selling your soul at the same time. You know what I mean?"

"I do know it. I just couldn't let some strange man . . . *use* me. Treat me like I was a . . . *toilet!*" Queenie said indignantly.

"It's like rape. Paid rape," Emily said. "I don't even know why men would want to do it. What pleasure would there be with a woman who probably didn't even . . . care . . . for them? Who didn't even *like* them?"

"And what does the poor girl get?" Queenie said. "Some bucks. Some diseases. Any girl who'd be a whore is crazy. And any man who'd use a whore is sick."

"Sick as a dog," Coco said. "That's a bad business. You sure got a bum rap, Emily."

"I know it."

"So if you weren't no hooker, what'd you really do?" Coco asked.

"I was an actress."

"Ooh-whee, an actress!" Coco exclaimed.

"What parts did you play?" Queenie asked.

"All kinds. I started in vaudeville, in the chorus. I was working my way up. I was auditioning for this Gershwin—you know, George Gershwin, the composer—this new show he was doing, when it all happened."

As she talked, Coco got off her cot and sat next to Emily on the other side of Mike. "You know, baby," Coco interrupted Emily, "I'm an actress, too."

"Really?"

Then Queenie started over to the cot and stood before Emily.

"Me too."

"What do you mean?"

"Me too," Mike said, taking Emily's arm just a little too hard.

"You know what part I played?" Queenie asked.

"Wh-what?" Emily was shaking now.

"I played a whore. We all played whores!" She let out a witch's laugh and slapped Emily hard across the face.

"What's wrong with being a whore, bitch? Are you too good to fuck?" Coco grabbed Emily and ripped her prison dress open. "Look at this white skin! Look at this bitch."

"Hold her down!" Queenie ordered the other two, who, with depraved grins, seized Emily tightly.

"I didn't mean anything," Emily cried, knowing she had been caught in a vicious trap, tricked by these deranged women who hated her as much as they hated themselves.

"We like whores! We *are* whores!" Queenie declared, unbuttoning her own dress as the other two tried to take Emily's dress off.

"Stop it! Help! Help me! Guards!" Emily screamed out.

"Save *this*, you little bitch," Queenie said, naked on her knees, yanking off Emily's underpants. Queenie held the panties as a trophy and pinched Emily's pubic area. "Look at little Miss Redhead. The cuff matches the collar." The other two roared with glee.

"Leave some sugar for me," Coco yelled.

"This is sweet!" Mike said as she licked at Emily's breasts. "She's clean. Umm!"

Queenie stood up and thrust her pelvis into Emily's face. "Kiss me, bitch. Love me!"

"Never!" Emily spat. "Never! You crazy . . . Let me go!" she screamed at the top of her lungs, and rammed her head into Queenie's crotch, knocking her back. She loosened an arm and walloped Mike in the head.

"Get her!"

"Fix her!"

"Leave me alone," Emily screamed. "Stop it. Don't!" she cried, fighting and scratching and biting as hard as she could. But she was no match for these three. She managed to get free for a moment, but was knocked breathless down onto the floor by Queenie's ham fist in her gut.

"I want her!" Coco yelled, jumping on Emily on the clammy concrete. Queenie held her down. The dirty fingers of Coco and Mike probed, pummeled, abused her. They pried her legs apart and licked her with their hot tongues.

"My God! Help me! Please! Help me!" Emily cried out. Then Louise's face appeared at the open bars of the cell door. "Louise! Help me!" But Louise did nothing. An evil leer brightened her painted face. This was her welcoming party for Emily. If she couldn't have her herself, because she might lose her treasured matron's job, she would have her vicariously.

Queenie buried her huge gaping silver mouth into Emily, and the pain and horror exploded into unconsciousness.

11

For weeks following her "initiation" to Bedford, the sexual assault caused Emily terrible nightmares that made her afraid to fall asleep. While she was awake, she had to force herself to crowd out the horrid memories of the attack by constantly thinking of other things. Her first natural focus was on Jessica, but she felt that the mere juxtaposition of her daughter with this abhorrent event was in a way sacrilegious. The passage of time gradually dulled Emily's pain, but the grave psychological scar remained.

Emily had been at Bedford for two months before her mother came to see her. The months almost seemed like years. The monotony made Emily lose all track of time. Three terrible meals a day. Six days a week in the workroom. Seven walks a week in the yard. Sunday in chapel, listening to the platitudes of the chaplain. "You are fallen women, deep in sin, but God loves you still." Choral singing Wednesday, cell cleaning Thursday, Friday-evening bath, Saturday-afternoon radio show. Once a month they showed a movie. That was the best part. That was escape, watching the stories, reading the titles, imagining what the stars sounded like when they mouthed their breathless lines.

The scratchy phonograph in the recreation cell playing Fats Waller's "Birmingham Blues," was a reminder to Emily that the jazz age was burgeoning in the world outside. And where was she? Locked in prison, her youth, her energy, her hopes fading away with each dreary day, each pair of overalls she sewed, each wretched meal. To be back on Broadway, Emily dreamed, just one brief stroll through Times Square, one egg roll, one splash of perfume, one silk scarf, one taxi ride, one red rose. So little would mean so much.

As the prison experience shrank Emily's expectations, it also drained her spirit. Where was the old Emily, she tried to ask herself, the Emily who escaped from the convent into the wilds of Michigan, who made her way to New York, who forged a Broadway career out of nothing but pure spunk and willpower? Sometimes these recollections would engender the most lurid fantasies. She would strangle Louise, lead a prison break, go to New York, get a gun, and shoot Michael McNaughton to death. But Emily knew she would never give full vent to her wrath. Any rash move would keep her from Jessica forever, and no amount of revenge was worth that.

"How's my baby?" was the first question Emily put to her mother in the cheerless, olive-drab visitors' room. They held hands across the rickety table. Around them several other prisoners were talking to loved ones. A guard stood by, indifferent to all the emotion pouring out. "Is she all right?"

"She's fine, darling. Just fine." The tears were rolling down Mrs. Stanton's face, though she was trying her best to be calm. Mrs. Stanton was a wisp of a woman, very soft-spoken, timid, with the saddest eyes. "Cora's living in," she tried to reassure her daughter. "Warren was so nice . . ."

"Nice?" Emily was surprised.

"He was shocked at what happened. He said he couldn't imagine your doing something like that. He said at first he was angry at you for it—"

"I didn't do anything, mother. I was framed."

"Let me finish, dear. Please."

Emily held her tongue.

"—but when he thought about it, he couldn't imagine it, so he talked to some lawyers he knew, but they said it was too late, but that maybe you could get out early on parole. I have to say Warren was very understanding."

"And Jessica. What did you tell her?"

"We told her you were sick and were away in a hospital."

"Do you think you should take her, Mother?" Emily asked.

Mrs. Stanton frowned. "Warren loves her so much. She's doing so well in school. It might not be good . . ."

Emily knew this wasn't the real answer. "Father doesn't want her, does he?"

Mrs. Stanton lowered her eyes. She didn't answer.

"And he didn't want to help me, did he? No. He didn't. Did he?"

Her mother kept looking down.

"With all his connections, I can't believe it. No, I guess I can." Emily felt betrayed. Her own father. "Actresses. Whores. What's the difference? Serves her right. I know him," Emily went on, her betrayal turning to anger and rage.

"Please, Emily, please. I'm so sorry. I begged him. I cried. Believe me. He's so hard."

"He could have gotten me out," Emily said bitterly. "This isn't the convent, Mother. I'm not learning to be a lady here. No matter how much he thinks I disappointed him, I don't deserve this. No. I don't deserve it." Emily pulled herself together. Emily felt her mother's love, her frustrations, her fear of her father. Emily couldn't be angry at this kind woman who had taken her as a little girl to Chicago to the theater to see Sarah Bernhardt, had taught her to sing, given her dancing lessons, bought her the Hollywood magazines she used to escape with on those endless gray, snowy afternoons in Joliet. Her mother was her friend. What kind of life had she had, teaching piano to local children, conducting the prison chorus, but, first and foremost, ministering to the endless demands of Emily's father, who hadn't forgiven Emily for wanting to become an actress? Likewise, Emily could never forgive him for his puritanical rigidity.

David Stanton was an austere man who decried frivolity and any kind of pleasurable pursuit. Emily always thought that H. L. Mencken was writing about her father in his magazine *The Smart Set* when he railed, as he so often did, against Puritans, "whose haunting fear was that someone, somewhere, may be happy." He had spent his entire adult life in penology, having worked his way up the prison circuit, beginning at Leavenworth. There his father—the grandfather Emily never met—One-Eyed Jack Stanton (his left eye had been shot out by Wyatt Earp), had achieved some note as a frontier marshal. David Stanton was a small man, at five-seven barely taller than Emily. But he seemed large. A big, distinguished head, a deep, booming voice, a glowering presence that never allowed a smile to creep through, all combined to give him stature. He had always put Emily on the defensive, making her think she had done something wrong even if she hadn't, making her feel like apologizing. David Stanton was all business. Some of the nation's most violent criminals were inmates at Joliet. Riots, escapes, murder, mutinies would have become routine had he not run the tight ship he did. If David Stanton was criticized as humorless and heartless, Emily had to concede that his job did not permit many amusing moments.

Emily's father was not amused when his daughter left Warren Matthews and brought Jessica back to Joliet for the Christmas holiday. Emily hadn't been home since she ran away from the convent in 1916. She hated the place and always fought with her father. Her last visit was no better. She tried to make peace with her father, if only for her mother's sake, but he was intransigent in his position that she should return to Warren Matthews.

"First you run away from that wonderful school," he had told her, raking up a past she wanted to forget. "Most people in life wouldn't get a second chance. With your marriage to this fine man, you did. And what do you do, you want to toss that away too. You won't get a third. You're very spoiled, Emily. I don't know where it comes from."

"Spoiled?" Emily remembered how she had tried to argue. "Is wanting an identity spoiled? Is wanting a career spoiled?"

"You bet it is!" Her father's stentorian voice was that of a judge, final. "You married a successful man. You have a child. Taking care of them is all the identity a girl could ask for. Don't expect miracles. Nobody said marriage was easy. You read too many storybooks, girl. Go back to him, I tell you. You'll regret it if you don't."

Her father's words still rang in her ears. She recalled

her last look at Joliet, the guards with their machine guns, the snarling Dobermans that policed the prison perimeter, the high stone walls and electrical fences, and most of all, the searchlights that reminded her of Broadway premieres and transported her back to New York. And now here she was in her own Joliet, and because she had disobeyed her father and hadn't accepted his advice, he would never try to get her out. No, Emily couldn't blame her poor, submissive mother. Emily knew what her mother wanted to do; she knew what she was able to do. She reached over and kissed her. "Oh, Mommy. I'm so sorry. I love you. I really love you. I miss you so much." She began to cry.

"Darling, Emily, you're so thin," her mother said. "I brought you some food."

"Thanks, Mom. I'll eat it later. I'll be all right."

"What can I do? Let me do something."

"You just be strong. Be strong, Mom. I'll be out of here. You'll see. I'm going to clear my name. I'm going to get Jessica back. . ."

"Yes, dear. I pray so. I pray for you every night."

"And, Mother . . ."

"Yes?"

"I'm going to get even."

12

Emily was allowed to write three letters a week. She wrote to her mother, to Cassie Laverne, and her other actress friends, to the young man at the Royale, Alex Foster, to everyone she knew, trying to explain the frame-up, looking for help in getting out. She wrote to the governor, the mayor, the congressmen, the parole board, searching desperately for a way out of Bedford. She never got a single response from anyone. Was she that tainted? she worried. Was this conviction of prostitution the ultimate scarlet letter? Was there no appeal to anyone? Didn't anybody believe her? Emily was so deeply hurt and embarrassed by her absence of mail that she didn't even complain about it to Alice, who quickly had become her best, and only, friend at Bedford.

The worst part of the prison, Emily decided, was not the cells, not the blast-furnace heat in the workroom where they made men's overalls, not the clanging opening and shutting of the cell door ten times a day, but the food. The food was unbearable. The mess hall was depressing enough, with its drab walls, its splintery wooden tables, its flat tin plates and utensils, and its drafts. Actual0, the women would joke, better the drafts to air the room than the rank odors of what was being cooked and served. The food was unredeemingly bad, and the diet never varied. Greasy hash for breakfast engendered almost erotic dreams of bacon and eggs, which were sometimes promised but never served. Lunch was always some kind of gray sausages, cabbage cooked so long it stank, bread and water. Dinner was mutton stew, more cabbage, some old fruit stewed to hide the frequent rancidity, and watery coffee.

One afternoon the sausages were cold and more gristly than usual. Emily was too disgusted to eat any more. She slammed her fork down so hard that Louise noticed and stalked over.

"Eat up, you," Louise barked.

"I can't eat this."

"You'll miss your vitamins."

"Vitamins? There're no vitamins in that."

"Not good enough for you?" Louise bore down on Emily, spewing her foul breath in Emily's face. "It's good food. Eat it."

"Would you eat it?"

"Don't get smart with me, Stanton. Eat it!"

"No, I won't. I'm not going to."

The other women at the table, heartened by Emily's spunk, began grumbling as well.

"Mine's rotten too."

"It's bad."

"Disgusting."

"We won't eat it."

"Shut up." This sort of insubordination was precisely what Louise was there to quell. She hammered her nightstick on the shaky table, rattling the tin utensils as if there were an earthquake. The entire dining hall went silent. Then Louise turned on Emily.

"You eat this food, you little whore!" she shouted. Even in this cesspool of little whores, big whores, murderesses, drug addicts, Emily felt humiliated. Louise then grabbed Emily's arm and twisted it behind her back. She shoved Emily's face into the sausage. "Eat it, whore! Eat it!" Emily couldn't. Louise yanked her away and threw her on the floor, kicking her. Then she picked up Emily's bowl, kicked Emily in the ribs, dumped the food on her face, and laughed triumphantly. "Now, that's what happens to picky eaters. Okay, girls. Back to lunch!" The other women didn't dare help Emily up, for fear of incurring Louise's ire. They went back to the dismal meat, washing it down with the dead coffee, as Emily lay on the stone floor doing all she could to hold in her sobs and not give the matron any more satisfaction.

71

That night, by the dim, flickering electric light in her cell, Emily wrote her allocated three letters for the week, outlining the day's atrocities. Even though she had not received any replies, she felt she had to keep trying. She rationalized to herself that the bureaucracy one day *had* to answer her, that justice moved at a snail's pace, but that it *did* move. The letters were the only salve she had. They made her forget her bruises, her aches, her empty stomach. Emily sealed her letters, addressed them to the State Board of Corrections and the New York Courts Administration and a state representative whose name she had seen in the newspaper in the prison library. She left her cell and put the letters in the out box, where they would be stamped and mailed. Back in her cell, the lights were turned off, the guard slammed the doors shut. Emily closed her eyes and dreamed of Jessica, of real food, of Broadway, of revenge.

13

Month after month vanished in the grim regimen. Emily had no real sense of how the world was passing her by, only that it was. From newspapers she read in the prison library, she had some idea of what President Coolidge was doing in Washington. She knew that Lenin had died in Russia, that Woodrow Wilson died in Washington, that in India, Mahatma Gandhi was fasting to protest that country's religious wars, that in Chicago two well-to-do boys named Leopold and Loeb were sentenced to life imprisonment for kidnapping and killing fourteen-year-old Bobby Franks. There had been no trial because their lawyer, Clarence Darrow, had Leopold and Loeb plead guilty. Though the outraged citizenry was demanding a death sentence, Darrow, in an historic argument, had succeeded in convincing the judge to spare his clients' lives.

If she only had the great Darrow, Emily thought. He could set right what had happened to her. But first she had to get out. After months of letters to the parole board and others in authority went unanswered, Emily began to conduct a more local campaign at the prison to get her sentence reduced, sending letter after letter to the warden, asking for consideration. Finally she was called for an interview.

Warden Dorothy Lloyd was frumpy and pompous and dressed in tailored suits. There was an artificial chipperness to her voice, an all's-right-with-the-world quality that was incompatible with the realities of the world over which she presided. Yet Dorothy Lloyd was an ideal front woman. The inmates rarely saw her; she was too busy doing public relations with the horse breeders and golfers of the town of Bedford and the politicians of Albany to worry about the day-to-day horrors of her "finishing school," as she wanted the outside world to think of it. "It's a finishing school, all right," one of the inmates had said to Emily. "A girl comes here and she's finished."

Dorothy Lloyd was sipping tea from a Wedgwood cup when Emily came in. The office smelled of sachet. It was like an English manor house, not a prison. What hypocrisy, Emily thought, but kept it to herself. She also kept her father to herself. Dorothy Lloyd probably knew of him, but his lack of assistance was damning. Emily didn't want to be more damned than she already was. Instead, she repeated her story—an independent woman, a self-supporter, a mother (all of these things that Dorothy Lloyd would have extolled about "progressive" women at a society luncheon), a woman, a good woman, who was framed. Dorothy Lloyd offered her tea. It was rich, good, a reminder of the world she had been snatched from. Dorothy Lloyd's blue eyes blinked with what Emily hoped was the understanding of an educated, sensitive woman.

But it was all false hope. "I'm terribly sorry, Miss Stanton. May I call you Emily?"

"Yes, Miss Lloyd."

"I'm terribly sorry. I really am. We did have your record examined very closely. It went down to New York before the administrative board."

"You did?"

"You're a very determined young lady, Emily, and your conduct here at Bedford has been, with a few exceptions with the matron, fairly exemplary, so we did want to hear you out."

"And?"

The warden shook her head. "The board says that you had a fair trial."

"Fair!" Emily was outraged. "What was fair about it?"

"I wasn't there, Emily, but the board is quite impartial—"

"So you think I've sat here and made it all up. You think I'm lying to you. Is that it?"

"My dear, I'm not a judge. That's not my province,"

Warden Lloyd said in her best above-it-all posture. "That's not for me to say."

"Why not? Can't you have an opinion?"

"It wouldn't make a bit of difference."

"But what do *you* think? Do you think I'm crazy? Do you think I'm a liar? Or do you think I was framed? What do you think?"

"I think you're a fine young woman who's had some bad luck. I know you're going to get back on the right track when you're released," the warden said. "Would you like some more tea?"

"No, thank you." Emily despised the false politesse. "I don't belong here, Miss Lloyd. You must believe me."

"The best, the very best—and mind you, we can't guarantee anything—but the best you can hope for is an early release based on your continued good behavior."

"What does that mean?"

"Maybe we could take three months off your sentence."

"But that still would leave me almost a year," Emily said, the tone of desperation and fleeting hope strangling in her voice.

"The time goes by," the warden said. "You'll be surprised."

"But my daughter. She's so young. She needs a mother."

"She's got a mother," Warden Lloyd said, smiling the most insincere smile Emily had ever seen.

"What?" Emily couldn't believe what the warden said.

"Mr. Matthews has remarried. We've made inquiries. See, we do think of you, Emily. She's an excellent woman. Fine family. Old New York, I believe. I can assure you, your daughter is in extremely capable hands. She's very happy."

Emily was silent. This was another body blow, another dream extinguished. Emily had received a sheaf of legal papers, power of attorney, that sort of thing, waiving any objections to granting Warren a divorce and giving him custody of Jessica. She had wanted the divorce. As for Jessica, she assumed that since she was in prison, Warren would have to have custody anyway. The point was thus moot and not worth contesting, even if she had had the energy and wherewithal to do so, which she didn't. Furthermore, Emily's mother had told her how kind Warren

75

was being to Jessica. Rotting in prison had given Emily the sense that the outside world, just like her own, was in suspension. But it never occurred to her that Warren would move ahead so quickly and remarry. She had hoped that Warren and Cora would keep Jessica until she was out of Bedford, and then she could get her daughter back and pick up the pieces of her life. But now a new wife. Maybe this woman would never give Jessica up. This was the worst news yet. Emily was nauseated.

"Why, dear," the warden said, "you look so pale. I think what you need is some more tea."

14

Jessica was having a field day at FAO Schwarz, the toy store on Fifth Avenue. Her new stepmother, Isabelle, had just picked her out a dollhouse, or doll palace, as it were, modeled after Windsor Castle. The Queen of England was the doll, complete with scepters, crown jewels, and a real ermine doll's stole.

"Are you a queen?" Jessica asked Isabelle.

"No, dear. I'd like to be, but we don't have queens in America."

"Yes we do," Jessica insisted. "What about Daddy's new stations? They're Queens."

"That Queens is across the river. It's a place. This queen is a person, a very important person, with diamonds and robes, who comes from a very, very old family."

"But Daddy says you come from a very, very old family too. Why aren't you a queen?"

"Because my family isn't that old, dear," Isabelle said. "I did meet the queen once, when I was sixteen years old and my parents sent me to England to ride the horses. It's so divine. I can't wait to take you."

Warren Matthews, who had never been west of Pittsburgh or south of Baltimore, was mightily impressed with his new wife's background and sophistication. Still, he didn't want her to get the upper hand in their relationship. Thus, not to be outdone, he insisted on buying Jessica *his* gift, a train set, a *Twentieth Century Limited* with a transformer housed in a model building that looked like Grand Central Station.

"She hasn't the vaguest interest in trains," Isabelle objected to Warren as Jessica listlessly watched the *Limited* click around the store track.

"Trains are my business. She'll learn to love them," Warren said.

"Aren't you overdoing it?" Isabelle asked in the intolerant patrician drawl that betrayed her occasional disappointment in, as well as her family's disapproval of, Warren. He wasn't the lawyer or banker they had wanted her to marry. He was in trade. Still, having fallen on hard times, they had no real choice in the matter.

"Where my daughter is concerned, there's no way of overdoing it," Warren replied.

"*Our* daughter," Isabelle corrected him.

Isabelle couldn't have children of her own, and she was crazy about Warren's smart, pretty little girl, who was unformed enough, Isabelle thought, to make her own. Hence the "our" daughter, which recognized not only Isabelle's stake in the marriage but also Warren's eagerly professed willingness to forget altogether his first wife. "We can't do too much for her," Isabelle said, "but let's do the right things. Warren, darling, I think this train set is all a bit much. Spoiling children is so . . . nouveau riche, don't you think?"

"Was lending your father ten thousand dollars to keep his Harlem property out of foreclosure nouveau riche?" Warren shot back. "Was buying your mother that Queen Elizabeth, Queen Anne, whatever it was, chair, was *that* nouveau riche?"

"I'm sorry, darling," Isabelle retreated. "You're absolutely right. I want Jessica to be happy every bit as much as you do." She grasped Warren's hand and he knew he had made his point. He was in control. He had everything he wanted. He was doing favors for his newly poor Hudson River Valley aristocratic in-laws. He had a handsome, tweedy, refined wife who had come out at the Grosvenor, learned to dance at de Rham's, studied at Miss Chapin's, a classy true socialite wife who didn't work, loved to shop, dress up, entertain his friends, and raise his daughter. Of course, Isabelle didn't have Emily's beauty, her talent, her energy, but those things, in

Warren's mind, had backfired on him. They weren't for wives. He had the right kind of marriage now.

"Got enough toys now, sweetheart?" Warren asked Jessica as they left FAO Schwarz.

"Yes, Daddy. Thank you very much." There was a fearful, robotic quality in Jessica's voice. She had seen her father's temper the night he burned her mother. Her mother? Where was she? Whenever Jessica would ask—and at the beginning she asked over and over again—her father would say only that she was away and wasn't coming back. Then he would quickly change the subject. Though a child, Jessica sensed that she wasn't supposed to irritate her father by questioning him any further. Her mother wasn't coming back. That was all. Isabelle was her new mother. Jessica thought Isabelle was nice. She played with her and took her to the zoo and to ride ponies. But Jessica couldn't stop thinking about her other mother, her *real* mother. She cried to herself for Emily every night. But she didn't dare let her father see her tears. He didn't like her crying, because he seemed to know what she was crying about, and it made him mad, and Jessica didn't want to make him mad. "I love my toys. Will you play with the train with me? Will you fix it if it breaks?" Jessica asked.

"Yes, Jessica. We'll have a lot of fun," Warren said.

"Can Mommy have some fun now?" Isabelle asked. "Mommy wants to go to Saks and buy some toys for herself. Is that all right with everyone?"

Warren reached into his pocket and handed six twenties to Isabelle. "Your turn, darling. I have to go to a meeting."

"All these silly meetings." Isabelle faked a pout. "What do you meet about?"

"That's how Daddy has his fun," Warren answered Isabelle's question. "Now, you and Mommy go spend all Daddy's money and buy Isabelle a new dress. We'll meet for dinner at Childs at six. Okay, my two sweethearts?"

"Okay, Daddy." Jessica had difficulty whenever he called Isabelle Mommy. She instinctively looked up, hoping to see Emily.

Isabelle took her hand. "Pip, pip," she said, something

she'd learned in England. And they were off, climbing the treacherous steps of a double-decker Fifth Avenue bus, which disappeared into the traffic.

Warren got into a cab and went downtown. He stopped at McGuffey Firearms, the gun shop with the giant revolver hanging outside. He didn't go into the shop, however. He went downstairs into the Ringside. The club was fairly deserted in the afternoon. Only a few indefatigable tipplers at the bar. A few smoochers at the tables. Without the noise, the music, the dancing, the smoke, the Ringside could have been a roadhouse in Schenectady. Warren nodded at the bartender and went through the dance-floor ring to a red banquette in the dark, far corner of the room, where a couple was sitting with a bottle of Scotch, drinking it from coffee cups to maintain the marginal facade of respectful disrespect of the Prohibition laws.

"Hello, Warren." Michael McNaughton stood up from the shadows.

"Hello, Mike. And hello to you," Warren said with special gusto to one of the most ravishing women he had ever seen. She was a creamy-complexioned brunette, five-nine, full lips, voluptuous figure, a showgirl, yet not at all cheap, no, very expensive. Only this man McNaughton had women like that. "You two should be outside," Warren said. "Incredible day." And then he realized McNaughton's woman probably never went outside. She was smoking and looked lazy with languorous eyes that he couldn't resist. She was a flower that bloomed only in nightclubs. One had the sense that if she were exposed to sunlight, she would wilt, or even vanish.

"Warren Matthews, meet Lucretia Morgan."

She smiled enigmatically.

"You're looking good," Warren said to McNaughton. "And if you judge a man by the company he keeps" —Warren winked at Lucretia, who remained enigmatic— "you're doing splendidly."

"Good to see you, Warren. How's the family?"

"Couldn't be better."

McNaughton poured some Scotch in a coffee cup and pushed it over to Warren. "To your family."

"I'll drink to that." Warren smiled.

Before Lucretia could sip her drink, McNaughton quickly cut his eyes to her. On the unspoken cue, she stood up. Warren marveled at how seductive she was.

"Please excuse me," she said. "I'm going to powder my nose."

"Don't be too long," Warren said, admiring her as she swayed to the powder room. "She's fabulous," he said, turning to McNaughton.

"She's yours," McNaughton said.

"When?"

"Whenever you want it."

"Who is she?"

"She works for me. You know the best way to meet women is with other women."

"You don't need any help, Mike."

"Sometimes I do. Lucretia's very dependable. Women trust her. They're as taken by her looks as the men are."

"Can you trust her?"

"She's here, isn't she? You'll like her, Warren. She'll like you."

This McNaughton was an amazing fellow, Warren thought, full of surprises. He could accomplish anything. The women he knew! McNaughton had introduced him to one other stunning courtesan. Warren rationalized that this wasn't cheating on Isabelle, just a diversion. She was the right wife, the perfect wife, the only wife for him, but sex with her wasn't exciting. He didn't have the mad, passionate craving for her that he had for Emily. Emily could have had it all with him, he thought. Her ambitions had ruined her life. She did it to herself. She was selfish and headstrong and would have kept Warren from *his* life and *his* daughter. "If you love that little girl bad enough . . ." McCarey had said to him. Warren loved her enough, and that resourceful old magician McCarey had found him a way. That was a friend. That was Tammany Hall.

Warren looked furtively around the room. The drinkers were drinking. The smoochers were kissing. Warren took a thick white envelope out of his coat pocket and handed it to McNaughton, who coolly placed it in his breast pocket. "Your final installment."

McNaughton flashed an accommodating smile. "I thank you, Mr. Matthews."

"I thank you," Warren said, returning the dishonorable glint. "I thank you for everything."

They raised their coffee cups to each other.

15
1925

The only visitor Emily had had for over a year was her mother. She had given up writing letters. No one ever answered. No one seemed to care. She had resigned herself to serving out her sentence and then starting a new life. Everything would have to wait, and if Emily learned one thing at Bedford, it was how to wait. Therefore, she was completely surprised when she was told someone had come to see her in the visitors' ward.

Although she wasn't allowed makeup, she combed her hair and washed her face to try to look fresh. The cells had no mirrors, so she couldn't see what she looked like. But she knew it wasn't good. She was skinny as a rail, her complexion was a mess, she was haggard. She had completely forgotten what it was like to be pretty, to feel feminine, to have any vanity whatsoever. Prison did that to all the women. They had nothing in their lives to remind them they had any sensuality whatsoever, save perhaps the gingham dresses they were issued to go to church services on Sunday.

Thus it was an enormous lift when Alex Foster stood with a bouquet of orchids in the visiting room and said, "You're still beautiful." Emily could tell he meant it. Why had he come? They had met only a few times. Yet he was the last link to her past. He was the last person she had seen with Jessica. She always wondered what he thought, so much so that she had written to him twice at the Royale. When he never replied, she assumed he had rejected her, too.

"Alex. I can't believe it." She reached out and shook his hand. She was trembling. She wasn't accustomed to having callers. She wasn't sure how to talk, what to say. "It's good to see you. I thought . . . you hated me."

"Hated you?"

"You know . . . when you didn't answer my letters."

"Letters?" he said, perplexed. "What letters?"

"I wrote to you. Two letters. To the Royale. Did you move?"

"Yes, but they forward my mail. I never got anything."

Then it dawned on Emily. "I bet no one got them."

"Got what?" Alex was confused.

"My letters. I wrote so many letters. Other than the ones to my mother, I bet they never mailed them."

"Who?"

"The people here," Emily said in a whisper. "They're horrible. I can't believe it. All my letters . . . It was Louise. Louise! Oh, Alex, I'm sorry. It's just one more horror."

"How could they throw your letters away?"

"To punish me, Alex. She's so evil, this matron. She's so . . ." Emily tried not to cry. She was happy to have a visitor. She didn't want to scare him away. "At least you got here. Thank you. You're so kind to come. I wrote you two long letters. I wanted to explain. You were so great with Jessica, and I wanted to become good friends. I knew we could. I wrote all this. Thank God I have the chance to say it now," Emily sighed. "Oh, Alex, what happened that night?"

"Your husband came and took Jessica."

"I thought the police had come and taken her to him."

"No. He came."

"The police must have called him," Emily said.

"I guess," Alex said. "I tried to stop him, but he had these bodyguards and they were a little rough—"

"Bodyguards? Maybe they were police."

"Maybe. No badges, though. They were rough."

"Did they hurt you?"

"I needed the exercise."

"Poor Alex. You're so sweet. How's your play?"

"I finished it. Three others, too. Can't sell a one. Broadway's tough," Alex said. "This guy ahead of me about five years at Yale, Cole Porter, he writes musicals and his stuff is just starting to catch on. Maybe if I keep at it. Meanwhile, I got a job—a real job—at an advertising agency. I try to write at night, but forget me. How are you?"

"How am I? You can see. I'm here. I'm alive. I'm okay. Alex . . ." Emily had to ask him. There was no time for niceties, evasion. "Alex, I was framed. Don't ask me why, because I don't know, but I was. You didn't believe what they said about me . . . did you?"

"No."

Emily knew he wasn't telling the truth. "But you didn't come for so long." Although she knew she was being pushy and inquisitorial, she had to test him. He was a friend, the beginning of a friend. If they could convince him she was a prostitute, what chance did she have with the rest of the world? "Alex, when you didn't come, I thought maybe you believed them. Like everyone believed them."

Alex was silent. He didn't have an easy answer.

He had waited so long, but he had decided he had to see her. Getting the job at the small agency that didn't check references had boosted Alex's self-esteem. He started calling college friends, who fixed him up with girls. He came out of his self-exile. But of all his blind dates with private-school teachers who had gone to Bryn Mawr and social workers who had gone to Barnard and would-be poets who had gone to Radcliffe and secretaries who had gone nowhere, nothing had worked out. Of course, he had little money and less success. He wrote copy, but little was used, and what was used wasn't at all notable. What could you say about screens other than that they kept flies out, or scissors, other than they cut paper? Maybe one day he would be promoted to writing copy for cosmetics—"lips an incendiary red that sets your nights on fire"—that sounded good. But he had only one ambition, to sell a play and become famous and wipe out his past, and then meet all the really outstanding women of New York, the Algonquin Round Table types, the wits, the beauties, the artists, the women he read about in *Vanity Fair* but never even laid eyes on. Whenever he went into the Algonquin to buy cigarettes, the Round Table was empty. On the other hand, in her own very different way, Emily was the most interesting woman he had met in New York, and she was in prison. That made her even more interesting. "My Crush Behind Bars," he could see the short story in *College Humor*. But whomever he met, his thoughts always went back to Emily, who now had even more in common with him than the theater. So he screwed up his nerve and took a bus up to Bedford.

"Oh, no. Not you too, Alex," Emily gasped, after his long silence. "You did believe them."

"I didn't at first," he said. "Oh, hell, I'm lying. I believed them. All that authority. You believe authority. And then when I didn't hear from you, I thought maybe you didn't want to see me, that maybe . . ." Alex was at a loss.

". . . that maybe I was too embarrassed by what I had done to write to you?" Emily filled in the answer, and she knew she was right.

"Yeah. I guess . . . something like that."

"But you changed your mind."

"I decided it didn't matter whether you had done it or not. I still liked you . . . I wanted to get to know you. I wanted to see you. I know you loved Jessica. I knew you didn't want to lose her. I knew you were nice. That's all. We never got to know each other. I felt cheated."

Emily clutched Alex's hand and kissed it. "If I wasn't such a fright, I'd insist on kissing your cheek."

"There's something else," Alex said. He wanted to tell her about himself. He thought it might be some consolation to her. "I never talk about this, but I thought you'd understand, given all this . . ."

"What is it, Alex?"

"Remember when you asked me, what was a Yale man doing at the desk of the Royale?"

"I was only . . ."

"Why didn't I go down to Wall Street with all the other college boys? Well, I wanted to. I would have. But I couldn't. I didn't have the choice. Emily, I was expelled from Yale. I almost went to prison myself."

"Oh, Alex. You? For what?"

"For stealing twelve hundred dollars. You see, most of the boys at Yale were rich, and you really felt it. You felt awful if you weren't. I was on scholarship. My whole family had been going up to Yale since the early 1800's, when they had all this money from their rice plantations. Yale was popular with Charleston people. After the Civil War, we lost everything, but Yale never forgot us. Until I fouled it all up."

"They gave you a scholarship?"

"Yeah. They'd've given one to any Foster who could read and write. But the scholarship didn't pay for much and it made me feel like a poor relation. I was surrounded by rich kids from the Fence Club who drove their Bugattis up to Cambridge to go sailing with their heiress girlfriends, and just to get by, I was waiting tables at this old hashhouse away from campus so no one knew. It was hard. I wanted to dress like them, live like them, be like them."

"I can see why, Alex," Emily empathized. "It must have been hard at a place like that, the stranger at the party."

"That's what it was. Anyhow, there was this millionaire freshman named August Biltmore down the hall. The guy was crazy. He had a pet tiger. He had his own airplane. He had his own bar in his room. And he'd always leave money lying around like his dirty clothes. It was nothing to him. It was something to me. One weekend, when everyone was away at the Princeton game and I was feeling sorry for myself, I took it."

"How did he catch you?"

"That's the bad part. He never did. He never missed it. A year went by. I got new clothes. People started accepting me. Instead of being a ratty plebe, I was now a Southern aristocrat. I was a new man. And then the only guy who knew about it, my old roommate—and he only knew because he had gotten some girl in trouble and I lent him a hundred of what I took to help him out—well, he was picked for Skull and Bones and so was Biltmore."

"Skull and Bones?"

"Fancy secret society. And one of their rules is that the members can have no secrets from each other. So my old roommate told Biltmore, and Biltmore turned me in."

"What did he care?" Emily asked. "It was in the past."

" 'I thought you were a gentleman, not a thief,' he told

me. 'I cannot tolerate a thief,' " Alex mimicked his accuser's patrician tones. "Neither could Yale. They threw me out. Biltmore pressed charges. I got a suspended sentence. A year on probation. I couldn't get into another school. I was ashamed to apply for a job. I had a criminal record. So I came up with a new career. Playwright. The audiences don't care where you went to school if you can make them laugh or cry."

"Oh, Alex, I didn't know. I'm so sorry," Emily said.

"The Royale was my prison. I just got out."

Alex's sad confession made Emily feel strong, supportive. For that second, she didn't feel helpless. "You're going to be a great success, Alex," she said. "And it'll be a lot better than Wall Street."

"Thanks. I really wanted to tell you. You're not the only one who's gotten into trouble, but you didn't even deserve yours."

"You didn't either. It's all going to work out for the best for you." Emily leaned forward and kissed Alex's cheek.

"You're beautiful, Emily. They can't take that away from you."

"They think they can."

"You won't let them."

"Oh, Alex. It feels so good to have a friend. This is the only time I've felt good since . . . since . . . back then. Thank you for doing this. Thank you for coming to see me."

16

At the head of State Street in Albany stood the Capitol of the State of New York. Its construction had cost twenty-three million dollars and was completed in 1871. The statehouse looked like one of the Fifth Avenue grand châteaus of the Belmonts, the Vanderbilts, the Goulds, except it was far bigger and more grandiose. Jimmy Walker loved to climb the breathtaking two stories of stone steps leading into the building, less for the physical stimulation than for the adulation he knew was forthcoming once inside. He was the most popular orator in the Senate, with his bons mots, his witticisms, his rousing delivery.

Today, as Walker spoke, the sachems of Tammany were sitting in the gallery. They watched him stride gracefully into the vast Senate chamber, down the red-carpeted aisle to the speaker's dais. The room was handsome, with its granite columns, its tiles and panels of Sienese marble and Mexican onyx, the huge fireplaces and the great flags of the Union and of New York. The latter was distinguished by its royal-blue field, its proud coat of arms, and its motto "Excelsior." The spring sunlight cast its beams through the cathedral stained-glass windows, bathing the chamber in rich shades of ruby red, aquamarine, and gold. The stage was right, the lighting was right, the audience was right. Now it was time for the showman to perform.

Today he was speaking about Prohibition. Although the Eighteenth Amendment was a national issue, Walker was urging the state to use all its influence to bring about its repeal. It was a typical Walker speech, a crowd pleaser, a victory of style over content. What Walker said was unremarkable. How he said it was something else.

"Prohibition is a joke," he declaimed, cocking his head and tugging at his waistcoat. Then he raised his brow. "But the joke is on us. There is a fortune to be had in tax revenue on liquor, a fortune. But do we get it?" He paused, one of his perfectly timed pauses. "No!" Another pause. "Do the people who are in desperate need of public services get it?" Pause. "No!" He held the "no" for a long time. "Who gets it? I'll tell you who. The gangsters get it. That's who. The gangsters." Rousing applause from the listeners in the gallery, all eager to get out to the nearest speakeasy and have two rye highballs with their corned beef and cabbage for lunch. "The fat cats of the underworld are getting fatter and fatter on the profits of illegal alcohol. But there's one way to skin these cats, and that way is to repeal Prohibition!" The thirsty crowd cheered. The thirsty Senate cheered. Walker lifted his palm to quiet the noise and beamed at the audience. "I say let us break the stranglehold of the lords of crime have over us. Let us vote out this absurd and unenforceable law. Let us drink again. Let New York drink again!"

There was a deafening ovation. The normally stuffy senators with their walrus mustaches and drooping lids stood up from their leather swivel chairs and shouted, "Hear! Hear!" Jimmy Walker knew precisely what buttons to push. They loved him. Walker looked up and scanned the galleries. It wasn't the senators' love that mattered. It was the people's. Walker loved to play to the masses. He was so good that the Broadway impresario David Belasco often sent his actors up to Albany to learn by watching the politician he called "the little master." Walker was so good that the sachems of Tammany, watching calmly in the gallery, were thinking of making him the next mayor of New York.

It was 1925. The incumbent mayor, Warren F. Hylan, known as "Red Mike" for his flaming hair and flaming temper, was nearing the end of his second four-year term of office. He wanted to run again. But as he was now known to be William Randolph Hearst's man, as opposed to Tammany's, the Hall would not give him its blessing. It wanted a real Tammany man, and Walker was that. Accordingly, the Hall sent a delegation headed by Charles Sullivan, and including Terence McCarey and Warren Matthews, up to Albany to scout this prospect.

After the session, the Tammany delegation met in a large suite in the Hotel Ten Eyck to discuss the pros and cons of their potential candidate. Warren Matthews felt inordinately important to be one of the group, even though he was a junior member. He saw himself as a kingmaker, a political boss. He had another drink from the well-stocked suite bar to further inflate his confidence. All he needed was a cigar, but he decided to wait until after dinner with Senator Walker.

"I think he's definitely mayoral," Warren Matthews asserted.

"Mayoral," Terence McCarey repeated. "I like the ring of that word."

"Sounds like a horse," another elder said.

"Gentlemen, this isn't English class," Charles Sullivan said, raising his hand. "This Walker, I just don't know. He laughs too much. Important politicians don't laugh."

"Lincoln laughed," a sachem ventured.

"He was a Republican," Sullivan said, on which rare occasion he elicited laughter. "No, Walker's a bit frivolous. Those clothes. Sharpie clothes. And the women. Is that true?"

McCarey answered. "He's a Broadway man. He has an eye for the showgirls."

"More than just an eye." Sullivan arched his brow.

"He did have an affair, I believe," a portly sachem with an Irish lilt chimed in, "with Vonnie Shelton."

"From the *Follies?*"

"Yes. That's the one," McCarey said.

"The cute French-Canadian. The one he called Little Fellow," Warren Matthews volunteered. "She called him J.J."

"Warren ought to know. Night owl," McCarey teased him.

"No more," Warren said. "I'm a family man now."

Charles Sullivan was not amused. "Is Walker still seeing this . . . Little Fellow?"

"They're finished," McCarey said. " It's over. Besides,

he was pretty discreet. The only place they ever went was to Leone's, and to the private room on the third floor."

"So private half of Broadway knew about it."

"It's over," McCarey defended Walker.

"There's only one thing worse in a public man than telling jokes," Sullivan said, "and that's to go after other women when he's married."

"Jimmy's sowed his wild oats, Charlie," McCarey pleaded. "He won't act up when he's mayor."

"Besides, he's the best man we've got who'll get the vote," Warren Matthews boldly spoke up. "You can find purer candidates, but you can't find better. Jimmy Walker can win next year. That's what really matters now. He's somebody we can get out the vote for." Warren thought he might have been speaking out of turn, but then McCarey seconded him, and he felt relieved.

"Warren's right," McCarey addressed Sullivan. "We need a winner. Otherwise, Hearst'll kill us. And Jimmy'll play ball. He's a team man all the way."

"But what has he accomplished in the legislature? He legalized boxing. He legalized professional baseball on Sundays. What other laws has he sponsored?" one skeptical sachem asked.

"Leave the laws to us," McCarey said.

"He's not a statesman, he's a front man."

"We need a front man," McCarey exhorted the others. "We'll take care of the rest. The key is, he's somebody we can trust and do business with."

Charles Sullivan, as was his wont when he was about to agree to something that wasn't his idea to begin with, said nothing. He went to the window of the Ten Eyck, lit his pipe, gazed up State Street at the great Capitol, and tried to imagine what New York City would be like with a playboy as its mayor.

17

"He weren't that pretty, but that Isaac, he could last. He could go all night and still fix me ham 'n eggs the next morning and then go back some more. He wasn't no man. He was a love machine," one prisoner was telling another in the yard.

"If he was so good, what'd you go kill him for?"

"I never said nothing 'bout him being *good*."

"I bet you misses him now."

"I miss *that*. I don't miss him."

"Any man could do what you say he could do, he could be all kinda bad, and I woulda still kept him 'round."

"Not Isaac."

"Girl, he wasn't no worser than *this*." The second prisoner motioned around the yard. "I'd put up with a lotta bad for some good lovin', yes ma'am."

Emily turned away, pretending not to hear, and walked around by herself. All the women at Bedford seemed to talk about was men. Men and sex. Much of the dialogue was coarse and vulgar. Despite her having been raised on prison grounds, Emily had had an overly protective mother who shielded her from such obscenities, and despite her time on Broadway, Emily had never gotten inured to the dialect of obscenity, or "fuck-ese" as some inmates dubbed it. After her experience with Queenie, Coco, and Mike, Emily tried not to get involved with any of the other prisoners—except Alice. She didn't want to seem haughty or stuck-up, for that might have engendered resentment and other reprisals from the prisoners. So she simply tried to keep quiet, keep to herself, and be friendly when necessary.

The truth was that sex had become terribly intimidating to Emily, certainly after the horror with Queenie, Coco, and Mike, certainly after Warren. In her marriage she had seen it as something for Warren's pleasure, not her own. She never felt she was making love; she was letting Warren make love to her. He did covet her. In fact, he was wildly passionate about her. He insisted on sex almost every night. At the beginning of the marriage, Emily had enjoyed it, but her satisfaction was not only of no concern to Warren, it actually made him nervous, putting pressure upon him he did not desire. Thus Emily learned to stifle the excitement she sometimes felt, to keep her passions from going out of control the way Warren's would. As Warren saw it, and as Emily had learned it, real ladies didn't "enjoy" sex. That kind of pleasure was an emotion of the basest, most animal sort. It wasn't proper. It wasn't feminine. It was the preserve of "bad" women like the ones at Bedford, whose cage Emily had been thrust into. Small wonder she kept her distance. These women were sexual creatures, and sex made Emily more than nervous, for she knew that she had a sexuality, however repressed, and that she possessed powerful sexual feelings. And, after all, wasn't it sex that had drawn her to Michael McNaughton? In this sense, she saw herself as being punished for the same inner longings the inmates so readily sang the blues about.

Emily reflected on which kind of sex was worse—the sex of prison or the sex of marriage. In the last months with Warren, Emily had come to equate sex with fear and pain. Her scars had faded, but she couldn't forget the night she told Warren she had begun to audition. He had just finished making love to her. She was wearing a white silk peignoir he had bought, lying in the Irish linen sheets of their vast bed on Park Avenue. They had just had a drunken dinner with the subway commissioner. Warren was on his way to getting the contract. She didn't think she could have picked a more opportune time to bring up the subject of her own ambitions.

"Are you happy, dear?" Emily stroked her husband's broad, hairy chest after he had finished.

"I think I'll get it," Warren said. "My bid's not that much higher than Federated Ceramic and the Quigley people. Besides, they're Republicans, so forget it." There was no postcoital glow whatsoever. Their feeling of intimacy had no more permanence to Warren than a breath upon a mirror, and was as quickly forgotten. "Besides, I didn't give McCarey stock for nothing. I think it'll be all right."

"You gave him part of the company?" Emily said, surprised by what she heard. "Why?"

"Because that's the way it works."

"It's your company. Why should he have stock? Do you have to bribe him to get the contract?"

"That's the way you do business in this town," he said patronizingly. He lit one of his expensive Havana cigars and picked up some contracts to look over. "If I get it, we can move out to the country. Raise Jessica the right way."

"Why leave New York when you'll own the town?"

"The hell with New York," Warren mumbled. "Get a big estate, horses, a swimming pool, all for what an apartment on Fifth goes for."

Emily stroked Warren's back. She kissed his neck. She didn't want to leave New York. Then she'd never have any career. The time had come. She couldn't hold back.

"Warren, do you love me?"

"What do you want? A fur coat?" Warren turned to face her.

"No, silly. I don't want anything. Not like that."

"What is it, then?"

"Promise not to be mad at me?" Emily nuzzled Warren's cheek.

"Depends."

"You won't believe what I did today."

"Stop the suspense, Emily," Warren said. "What is it?"

"I went on an audition."

"You did what?" Warren pulled away from Emily, sat up in bed, and stared at her with a sense of betrayal that couldn't have been greater if she had told him she had put strychnine in his nightly glass of warm milk.

"I went on an audition. For a Broadway show. For a part."

"Broadway," Warren intoned incredulously. "Broadway show. Emily, what the hell . . ."

"Don't worry. I didn't get it. But I want to keep trying."

"Emily. Are you crazy? You don't need—"

"It's not need. It's want. I want to do it."

Warren held his head. "This is like a bad dream."

"We have Cora. Jessica's in school all day now. You're always working, making your deals. You hardly have time to talk to me. You know that. I understand your business. I just wanted to *do* something."

"Join the Junior League."

"Warren!"

"I don't intend to be married to a chorus girl."

"Who do you think you married?"

"You were a kid."

"I'm an actress, Warren. I want to get started again."

"Don't be insane. I think you drank too much tonight," Warren growled, taking the dominant tack. "Go to sleep."

"Please," Emily said, putting her arms around him, eager to avoid any confrontation. She believed she could sell him on it. "I'm the luckiest woman in the world. But, sweetheart, I've given you six uninterrupted years. Now I want to do something for myself but it's for you, too. I'll be more interesting. Think of all we can talk about at your business dinners. You saw McCarey. Your friends love all that theater stuff. It's fun. Oh, Warren, please."

"Don't fool yourself," he said coldly. "You can't be an actress and a respectable wife. What you want to do is unheard of."

"I know I can do it." Emily kissed him.

He didn't respond.

"Watch me. I'll be better at both. Come on, let's enjoy being young before we get old. Let's don't act like some stuffy old couple. If I'm back on Broadway, it'll make our life fun."

Warren wasn't interested in fun. "Chorus girls don't make good mothers."

"Stop calling me a chorus girl."

"What's the difference?"

"Ambition. Success. Come on, darling. You've got your ambition. You've got your success. Why can't I?"

Warren gave Emily a look that froze her from saying another word. "Because you have mine," he said, slipping Emily's white lace negligee off her shoulders and appraising her body in the most measured, mercenary way, as if she were a pedigreed cat or a prize cow, not his wife. "Because you have mine," he repeated.

Emily could see Warren was getting an erection as he stared at her, puffing on his glowing fat cigar. He put the stogie in the ashtray and grabbed Emily. "You have mine. What else is there? Mine!" He pinned her to the sheets and forced himself into her again. But this was an act of dominion, not affection. Once he was inside her, and she was gasping and sweating, not from pleasure but from sheer anxiety, he sneered at her and said, "Don't talk about the theater anymore."

"I'm gonna do it, Warren," she gasped. Emily didn't know what made her say this, whether defiance, stubbornness, pride, a mixture of all of them. Maybe because in his arrogant demand for control he reminded her of the father she had run away from. "I'm not your slave."

"You're my wife," Warren snapped with fury, forcing himself roughly into her, over and over. "I own you." He squeezed her arms so hard that they throbbed. "You're mine!" he declared. Before Warren could reach another climax, Emily, with all her strength, managed to slip out from under him. "You little bitch!" he shouted. Leaping from the bed, Warren grabbed his still-smoldering cigar and stalked Emily into a corner. Then he branded her on her right breast. Emily screamed in agony as the fire of the burning stogie seared through her. Warren wouldn't stop. He was possessed. "Don't deny me!" He hurled Emily to the carpet and tried to wedge her legs open. "I want you!"

"Stop! Stop!" Emily cried, but Warren would not have if Jessica, followed by Cora, had not come into the bedroom and seen her naked father trying to force himself into her naked mother.

"Daddy! Daddy! Oh, Mommy!"

LULLABY AND GOODNIGHT

Jessica's cries had sounded the bell on that first round and saved Emily, who somehow managed to pull herself together enough to sing her trembling daughter to sleep with "Lullaby and Good Night." Emily did her best to pretend to Jessica that all was well so that the little girl would forget the terrible scene she had witnessed. Warren, of course, later apologized with almost superhuman penitence, sending flowers, a new fur coat, encouraging Emily to go ahead and audition for *Dollar Signs* and even take the tiny chorus part in *Bicycle Built for Three* when she got it. He blamed alcohol, business pressures, jealousy, possessiveness, anything. But despite his outward apologies, the inner rage would not be extinguished, and the brutal sex, beatings, and brandings resumed, usually each time Emily got another show. Though the outbursts were punctuated by remorse and protestations of love, Emily knew the differences over her career were irreconcilable and that Warren's reprisals—always in the bedroom—would continue.

Of course, there were many moments at Bedford when she longed for her silk peignoirs and Irish linens, and yes, even the warmth of Warren's body. She often reflected on whether the brutality of the bedroom was any worse than the brutality of the prison, and in the course of these deliberations on the lumpy cot of her clammy cell, as day faded to night and there was nothing to do but think, the memory of Warren Matthews on Park Avenue seemed less and less distasteful.

18

At the beginning of her sentence, Emily had been vociferous in claiming she had been framed, but the many real prostitutes in prison resented her for it. She was denigrating their profession. Others, who had been sent up when they couldn't pay the bribe demanded of them, were so broken by the experience that they had nothing to say. They had said it all before, to deaf ears.

One who would talk, and wouldn't stop talking about herself, was the bubbly blonde Bridgit Lund, who was always trying to seduce the guards but never quite succeeding. Emily found Bridgit cheap and sleazy. She didn't like being placed in the same category as Bridgit and stayed away from her. One day, however, Alice insisted that Emily have a talk with Bridgit.

"I've got nothing to say to her," Emily protested.

"I think you do."

"What? We were both set up. Sure. But she's the real thing, Alice, and I'm not. I'd just as soon—"

"I just found out something else. You've got something very significant in common."

"What is it?"

"Michael McNaughton."

The three women met in the yard that noon. Bridgit seemed thrilled to meet Emily. "I always thought you were the prettiest girl at Bedford," Bridgit said to her. "Stuck-up, but sure pretty," she said in a breathless little-girl voice. "I've been wanting to talk to you, but you scared me off."

Emily was eager to get to the point. "Alice told me you were framed by Michael McNaughton."

"So to speak," Bridgit trilled, speaking as if she were describing not an atrocity but a high-school field trip. "He charmed me out of my pants. And then, the nerve, he demanded that I pay him three hundred dollars for his trouble. God, is he gorgeous." Bridgit spoke almost wistfully, as of an old boyfriend.

"Where did you meet him?"

"At the Astor Bar. I had just come to town. Imagine a little girl from Fargo, North Dakota, at the Astor Bar. All these rich guys. Usually I'd hook, but sometimes I'd go straight, depending on the type. You know, if they had a ring, they were married, so take the cash, but if they weren't, take the guy."

"You and Bridgit are coming to the same place from totally opposite directions," Alice said.

"Yeah, I'm a sinner, and you're a saint," Bridgit added. "But that's okay."

"Bridgit, please go on. This is important to me," Emily said.

"So there he was."

"What did he call himself?"

"You know, I don't remember. I'm bad with names. Maybe it was Gerard. That was his name."

"Oh." Emily was disappointed. No Amory Longworth. "Go on."

"So he was real sweet. You know, I really liked the guy. Knew everything about Hollywood. I'm a sucker for that."

"What'd he say he did? A producer—"

"I never asked. What'd I care? He looked rich. Even if he wasn't, I wouldn't have charged him. But he had these real nice cufflinks. My mother said always look at the cufflinks. They were solid gold, at least they looked like gold—"

"Bridgit, the bell's gonna ring soon," Alice prodded her.

"Okay. So I thought: Hello Daddy Warbucks, good-bye work. We went to his room—"

"At the Longacre?" Emily pressed.

"No. He took me to the Cherokee. What a dive, especially for a guy like that. But, you know, most of them are cheap when it comes to hotels . . . at least hotels for sex. Anyway, we get there and he whips out these handcuffs, and I think to myself: He doesn't seem the type, but if that's his kick, I've put up with worse."

"Did he try to get you to charge him?"

"Charge *him*? Charge *me*. I tell ya, I liked the guy. No way would I insult him for money. He told me he was a cop, he had me all staked out, and knew exactly what I did for a living. I could pay him three hundred bucks to drop the case or I'd go to prison. And I laughed, until I saw he wasn't joking. I didn't have dough like that. I said: Look, let me show you the time of your life. We can be friends. Come see me anytime. He didn't buy it. Three hundred or bust. So here we are, girls." Bridgit giggled in a way that was disconcerting to Emily. "You woulda thought he woulda had me first. Very weird."

"But you told all this to the court. I'm sure—"

"They gave me this lawyer."

"J. Nicholas Collins?"

"I don't think so. Maybe. Naw. I don't remember names. But he told me if I gave him two hundred he'd get me off. But I was flat on my tail. I had bought these clothes, and the stores wouldn't take them back. I offered the lawyer my clothes, that maybe he could resell them. I only wore them once. I offered him everything but dough, but he didn't want it."

"So what did you plead?" Emily went on.

"Innocent. But because I didn't have a job, you know, and I had done some tricks . . ."

"You admitted that?" Alice said.

"I was under oath," Bridgit said earnestly. "I am a very honest person."

"I still don't understand it." Emily stared out over the wall at the gathering storm clouds. Thunder began to rumble.

"Understand what?" Alice asked.

"Why nobody asked me for a bribe."

"Listen, somebody was paid off. Had to be. That's the way law and politics work," Alice said.

"I thought you couldn't pay," Bridgit said, wide-eyed.

"No, I didn't have the chance."

"I figured something was strange about your case," Bridgit said. "You look pretty rich to me. It's your teeth. My mother told me rich people had better teeth." Bridgit smiled, to Emily's annoyance.

"Look, it's obvious to me," Alice said in her all-knowing, weary tone. "Somebody set you up. The only reason they didn't hit you for a bribe is that someone else was giving them a bigger one."

"Who could that be?" Emily asked.

"Somebody trying to beat you out of a part?" Alice asked.

"I'm not that big. My parts weren't worth it. No."

"Don't get insulted," Bridgit said, "but were you cheating with someone else's husband? You've got the looks to lure a big fish."

Emily laughed. How far from the truth that was. The mere thought that she could be a femme fatale amused her. Despite Warren's ardor for her, she had no idea how to use seduction as an instrument of her ambitions.

"Didn't you say your husband wanted custody of your kid?" Alice continued her questioning.

"Custody? Yes. But it was more of a contest with me. I don't think he really wanted that kind of responsi . . . He *did* want to see her."

"Well," Alice said, an accusatory look on her face. "Doesn't that ring a bell?"

"That Warren would have . . . No, come on."

"Why not, Emily?" Alice was annoyed with her. "Look what he did to you. You told me how he beat you."

"That was . . . that was . . . It was his temper. He was really sorry . . ." Emily found Alice's insinuation about Warren terribly jarring. She didn't want to hear it.

"You sound like you miss him," Alice attacked her.

"We just couldn't get along. The marriage was wrong. But he. . ."

"Yeah. Wrong enough to get rid of you."

"Alice! That's crazy. He couldn't . . . He couldn't have done that."

"Why not? If he hadn't, you'd still be with your daughter. He couldn't have gotten a divorce, and he couldn't have gotten her from you," Alice said, raising her voice. "He has this ritzy new wife. He couldn't have ever gotten married again unless he sent you up here. It fits. It all fits. What happened to you finally makes sense. He's the one."

"But you don't do things like that for . . ."

"For his daughter. You don't think he wanted her pretty bad?"

"Not that bad." In a bizarre way, Emily was still thinking of Warren as family. She leapt to his defense. "I was married to him for six years," she said. "He wouldn't do anything like that. He's a straight arrow. He's a businessman."

"This *was* business," Alice asserted. "McNaughton wasn't doing this for fun."

"He doesn't buy those fine threads on no cop salary," Bridgit added.

"Maybe McNaughton just wanted one more arrest," Emily suggested, ignoring Alice's hardened attitude. Alice was a cynical, distrusting person, Emily thought. Alice had been at Bedford too long. Emily never wanted to become that way. People weren't vicious animals. She paused. McNaughton, yes, but not her husband, not Warren. She had married him. He had loved her. No. It wasn't Warren. "I think what moves McNaughton is the whole frame-up thing. The thrill of the game," Emily said.

"Jesus," Alice almost spat. "Listen, Emily," she said firmly, as if Emily were a small kindergarten child in need of a lesson. "If I've learned one thing, it's not to put anything past anybody. Your husband's the only person you know who had a motive to set you up. If you come up with somebody else, fine. Honey, you better wise up. Your husband's not the guy you thought he was. That's why you left. He's the man who—"

"No!" Emily suddenly screamed. The other inmates in the yard stopped their exercises, their free-form solo dances, their pacing, their moping, and looked in her direction. "It's not true." Emily lowered her voice. "He couldn't do that to me."

"Then don't nag me about it anymore. I've wasted enough breath today."

The work bell rang. Alice turned to go to the shop without a word. Bridgit shrugged and followed. Emily stood behind for a moment. She didn't want what Alice told her to be true. That would be the most horrible news yet. But deep inside, she knew she had to confront that possibility.

19
July 1925

There were tigers everywhere. Tiger skins on the walls. Mounted tiger heads. Tiger fangs as bookends. Tiger rugs. Even a tiger skeleton. Tammany was tiger crazy. But they were even more crazy about their candidate for mayor, Jimmy Walker, as they rallied for his nomination in their main banquet hall, the Tiger's Lair.

Walker was at the podium, adjusting his waistcoat, touching his handkerchief, cocking his head, giving the Hall what it loved hearing.

"This was the only place where my immigrant father found help and assistance when he landed in this country," Walker exclaimed. "It is the home of an organization which has done more to fight the good fight for the City of New York than any political organization that you or I have ever heard of."

The sachems and the braves stood, clapped, began to chant their war cry, "Tammany! Tammany! Swamp 'em. Swamp 'em. Get the wampum. Tamanee!"

Get the wampum. That was the idea foremost in Warren Matthews' mind as he stood and cheered. Michael McNaughton was there next to him, and they smiled at each other.

"Well, you got your man, Warren," McNaughton said.

"He's your man, too," Warren shouted back, and McNaughton knew he was right. McNaughton was thinking about the wampum as well, for Jimmy Walker was a laissez-faire politician, the kind of man who would give the vice squad an even freer rein than it now enjoyed. Walker's words that night—Republican words being voiced by a Democratic mouth—rang in McNaughton's ears:

"The least government is the best government. Ninety percent of the people want only to be let alone to enjoy freedom in safety. . . . I am ready to admit that I would rather laugh than cry. I like the company of my fellow human beings. I like the theater and am devoted to healthy outdoor sports." McNaughton laughed to himself. He knew what sports the frail, unathletic Walker was devoted to, and they didn't take place outdoors. "But let me allay any fear," Walker continued to bluster, "that because I believe in personal liberty, wholesome amusement, and healthy professional sport, I will countenance for a moment any indecency or vice in New York." McNaughton smiled to himself. He was going to have a field day. "If elected, *when* elected," Walker corrected himself with a wink and to rousing applause, "New York will be an open city, a free city, a fun city, but the safest city in the world!" McNaughton joined the standing cheerers in the smoky ballroom with tigers everywhere. This was his kind of town. This was his kind of man.

Jimmy Walker was Warren Matthews' kind of man, too. For Warren, Walker meant money. One of Walker's campaign issues was the subway. Walker wanted new lines to the Bronx, to Queens. He wanted the city, not the private traction interests, to run the subways. And with the city, which meant Tammany, in control, Matthews Tile would get even more business. One of Walker's campaign slogans was "Say It with Shovels." He began wearing little crossed shovels in his peaked lapels, like the keys of a concierge, and in a way, Walker was Tammany's concierge. He was going to get the honored guests of his Tammany Grand Hotel anything they wanted.

20

Delighted as she was with Alex Foster's continuing visits, Emily was caught between fury and despair over her letters. Would they have made a difference? She wasn't sure. Well over a year had gone by. An explanatory note to all the people she had written to saying "I know you didn't get my mail, the prison threw it away, but this is how it really was"—no, that was too late. She felt certain that Louise, who had the key to the letter box and collected the mail to give to the postman, was the guilty party, but she was afraid to make a scene. What was the point? Louise would love it, because it would give her a chance to stick Emily for misconduct, and then she'd never get an early release. Still, whenever Emily saw Louise smirk, she wanted to strangle her.

One Friday night Emily and Alice stood wrapped in coarse, itchy towels, waiting their turn in two rusty metal bathtubs. The room stank. Open toilet stalls stood across from the bathtubs. The women were permitted no privacy, no dignity, not even a curtain for modesty. The cracked tile floor was ice cold on their bare feet. Cockroaches scurried about. More chilling was the woman cleaning the tubs between bathers, a sad, scraggly new arrival, a young woman with jaundiced skin covered with open sores.

"Syphilis," Alice whispered. "Street prostitute from Buffalo."

"What kind of man would use someone like that?"

"The kind of man who gave it to her to begin with," Alice said.

Emily shivered as she watched the poor woman on her knees, scrubbing, gasping for breath as she worked.

"Move it," Louise's voice echoed through the cavernous bathroom area. The matron had followed Emily into the bathroom, eyeing her with her usual carnal leer. She liked to come in when Emily bathed and stare at her, naked. "Hurry up," Louise yelled at the syphilitic woman. "Miss Stanton wants to take a bath."

"Please, I'm sick. I don't have the strength . . ." the woman begged Louise.

"Miss Stanton wants to take her bath," Louise barked, and whacked the woman across the back. "Scrub it."

Louise was about to strike her again when Emily stepped between them. "I'll do it. Let her go. She shouldn't be working."

"Well, well, well," Louise cackled. "What do we have here, the sisterhood of whores?"

"We ought to have some common decency, for once. She's not well." Emily faced the hulking martinet, who cradled her stick in her hand, stroking it, getting it ready in the most menacing way. Then Emily took the sick woman's sponge and disinfectant from her trembling hands and leaned over to clean the tub. She had barely started when Louise's stick cracked down on her knuckles.

"If you like her so much, I think I should put you two slimy whores in the tub together." Louise snickered.

Emily wheeled around. Her hand ached. Blood oozed from the knuckles. "You're the whore! You're worse than any whore. You're sick, sick." Emily was screaming, exploding, turning deep red. "You threw away my letters, you sadistic bitch!"

At that, Louise whacked Emily across the shoulder with her stick, and then went at her head, out for blood. Emily dodged her. The stick clanged on the tub like a gong. All the inmates stood back watching, expecting their gladiator Emily to be devoured by the lion Louise. The matron began to pound Emily again, but Emily grabbed and began wrestling the behemoth. Emily felt a dragon was bearing down on her. Luckily, the floor was slippery and soapy and Emily was able to upend Louise. With all her strength, Emily grabbed the hulk and sent her splashing into the cesspool of the tub. The dirty water flooded out like high tide as the matron floundered and flailed. The crowd of inmates who had gathered cheered. Emily was bloody and, for a brief, giddy moment, a great hero. The women hugged her. They kissed her, as Louise, a dripping seal, rolled out of the tub onto the bathroom floor.

"You did it!"

"You showed her."

"Hooray, Emily."

For a flashing second they all were alive. They had energy. They had unity. They had hope. Then the guards came, put Emily into a straitjacket, and locked her in the hole, a solitary, dark, eight-by-eight iron pit, for a week. All her hopes for an early release were extinguished.

"I'm nobody. Who are you?" Alice read the lines of the poem to Emily. "Are you nobody, too?" The women were enjoying a period of lax discipline in the cellblocks, the inmates having bribed the night guard to leave the cell doors open after lights-out so they could visit each other. Alice was lying on Emily's cot in the dark, reading Emily Dickinson poetry to her. To Emily, it was very warm and cozy, lying there together, if prison could ever be warm and cozy. Emily had always dreamed of curling up with Warren that way, having him read to her. He never had. This was the really special Alice, the Alice she liked best. Not the tough, savvy Alice, but the soft, wise Alice, the big sister she'd never had.

Alice stroked Emily's hair. Without saying a word. She didn't read any more either, just stroked, and ran her finger down Emily's face, tracing her nose and lips. Emily was too surprised to say anything. She wasn't sure what was happening. "You're very special to me," Alice said.

"You too," Emily responded, uncomfortable.

"I love you," Alice said, and kissed Emily on the lips. At first, Emily gave in. It was warm, sensuous, enveloping. Then she realized what was happening, and she eased away. Alice pulled her back and kissed her again.

"Alice!"

Alice held her tighter, wouldn't let her go. Emily could

feel Alice's labored breathing. She felt her passion, and it scared her.

"Alice, please stop," she whispered, embarrassed that the other women might hear them.

"We can't stop. Give in. Relax. I love you." Alice kept going, kissing Emily, caressing her breasts, stroking her between her legs. Emily found herself flushed, excited. Her pulse quickened. She could feel the temptation, the possibility of release, of abandon. But she stopped at the edge. Refusing to give in, Emily forcibly shoved Alice away.

"Alice, no, stop!" Emily stammered. "Please. I don't . . . I'm not . . . that way."

"It's the only way we have," Alice said, sitting up. Her face showed both surprise that Emily was rejecting her and humiliation at the rejection.

Emily shook her head, ashamed to look at Alice.

"I don't long for men. How can you?" Alice asked.

"I don't long for . . ."

"Look what men did to you. How can you ever think of a man again? Men don't care. I care."

Emily reached out to touch Alice. "I love you, Alice. I really do . . . but not like that."

Alice turned away. "Then you don't . . . can't . . . love me at all."

"You're my friend. My best friend."

"No. I'm more than that. I have to be more than that."

"But why? We've been together so long, and now, all of a sudden . . ."

"It's not sudden. It's been building up so long. I kept waiting, thinking it would happen. That you were ready. I can't wait anymore. It's the way I am. It's the way we all are."

"Alice, I can't be your lover," Emily said. "You can have anything else . . ."

"Then you can't have anything," Alice said, rising. Her face was hard, angry, not the Alice of moments before, but the Alice who killed her husband. Her way. Or no way.

"Please, Alice." Emily reached out. "I need you . . . I'm not rejecting you."

"Yes, you are," Alice retorted. "I need it all or nothing. So it's nothing. We've got too much pain, honey. Way too much."

"Alice, don't leave me."

"You're on your own," Alice whispered icily, and went back to her cell.

Emily was alone, all alone. She buried her face in her lumpy straw pillow and sobbed for an hour until she fell asleep.

21

Many Wall Street law firms represented more well-known clients, more *Social Register* names, more companies on the Stock Exchange. But none accomplished more for its clients than Sullivan and Sterling, the Tammany law firm. It did not represent the House of Morgan, Grace Line, the New York Central, U.S. Steel, any of the blue-chip, silk-stocking clients. Instead it represented firms like the Swartzman Brothers, who were planning to build two fifteen-story apartment buildings in a residential area of lower Fifth Avenue and needed zoning variances from the antiskyscraper codes enacted in 1917 to preserve light and air for Gothamites. The firm was expert at obtaining such variances. Many of the major builders were its clients, and the continued boom in high-rise construction was a testimony to Sullivan and Sterling's effectiveness.

Not all the firm's clients were making dramatic architectural statements on the New York skyline. Most, in fact, were working far below, though no less profitably. For example, Sullivan and Sterling represented Stuyvesant Trust Company, a bank for which the firm had recently secured a major arrangement to handle the payroll for the Departments of Sanitation and Transportation. It represented O'Brian and Gilhooley, a firm that had an exclusive janitorial supply contract with the city schools through the Board of Education. It represented Kenner Construction, which was repaving the Henry Hudson Parkway. Sullivan and Sterling was the firm to see if you had, or if you wanted, business with the City of New York.

Sullivan and Sterling, then, was predominantly a politico-business firm, securing zoning variances, preparing bids for city projects, drafting contracts, that sort of cut-and-dried commercial work. However, the firm would also handle the messy personal matters of its clients, when the need arose. Warren Matthews, whose tile company the firm represented, was with senior partner and Tammany sachem Charles Sullivan, concluding the paperwork on a new tile contract. Sullivan's offices were situated on the top two floors of a Gothic skyscraper on Wall Street that looked down upon the more venerable Gothic spire of Trinity Church. Whether God or man was in charge of this kingdom at the tip of Manhattan was a matter of debate, but Charles Sullivan, with his laurel-wreath fringe of curly white hair, his meerschaum pipe, his starched white clerical collar, and his gold watch on a chain, was definitely one of the high priests of the realm.

Sullivan's office smelled old—old wood, old books, old smoke. Age inspired confidence, and though Sullivan didn't need the props, he had them all—the Currier and Ives lithographs, the fine leather chairs, the high walls of law books. The only bit of judiciana that normally adorned senior partners' law offices on Wall Street that was not in evidence was the obligatory law degree from Harvard, Yale, or Columbia. Charles Sullivan didn't have one. He had passed the bar by apprenticeship, not bad for a poor Irish immigrant. Today he was as grand as any of the Ivy League lions of the bar, but he had done it the hard way. Charles Sullivan didn't need degrees. He practiced Tammany law, which was much less a matter of court ruling and statutes than of power and connection.

"You know," Charles Sullivan said, puffing on his pipe, "if Frank Waterman gets in, there won't be any more of these." He pointed to the thick contract.

"He can't beat Walker," Warren said confidently. "He's got nothing."

"He's got a cause. Listen." Sullivan picked up the *Tribune* and read, " 'Tammany control of our subways would mean Tammany was free to give, without competition, contracts for subway cars, contracts for steel rails, contracts for equipment, contracts for all kinds of favored Tammany suppliers.' " Sullivan put down his bifocals and stared straight at Warren.

"Frank Waterman makes fountain pens," Warren said. "He's got nothing."

"He's got money, old money, big money. He's got integrity. He's self-righteous and angry as hell. We can't take him for granted," Sullivan said, rolling his R's in his commanding Irish brogue.

"He'll beat himself."

"No, Warren. *We'll* beat him. I want you to get to work."

"I am working on the campaign, sir."

"No. I want this to be your special task. It's your vested interest at stake. I want you to find Waterman's Achilles' heel. I want you to find it, and then I want you to hit it."

"You want me to dig up some dirt?"

"I want you to get the job done."

"Isn't this sort of thing more in Commissioner McCarey's line, sir?"

"The commissioner is busy."

"But I'm not in that kind of business."

"You're *not?*" Sullivan arched his brow at Warren, who thought about Michael McNaughton and knew exactly what Sullivan was getting at. McCarey must have told him. Warren had no room to back out. Having made his point, Sullivan stared out his window at Trinity Church, at the soaring Woolworth Building, at the Staten Island ferry zigzagging across the harbor.

Suitably chastened, Warren went hard to work, and, as was his mode, immersed himself in the task. When Warren realized all his pens were Waterman's, he threw them away and replaced them with Estabrook pens, Waterman's arch commercial rival. Diligently researching Waterman's vast holdings, Warren surveyed the Waterman empire, looking for a soft spot, something to discredit him to the electorate. Finally, after weeks of business lunches and intelligence-networking and cross-checking corporate accounts, Warren found his quarry—outside of Palm Beach.

One of Waterman's many properties was a resort hotel in this swank area of Florida, not known for its religious tolerance. On a hunch, Warren wrote a letter to the hotel, the Fountain Inn, requesting a reservation. He signed the missive Mrs. Esther Rabinowitz, Grand Concourse, the Bronx, the exact address of a Tammany cohort. A week later came back a reply that made Warren Matthews Tammany's man of the hour. "Our clientele," the hotel manager wrote, "is such that the patronage of persons of the Hebrew persuasion is not solicited." Warren passed the letter on to a Tammany man who was an editor at the *Morning Telegraph*. On October 30, the letter was reproduced in the paper. Waterman, in that one swoop, lost the Jewish vote.

It was the kind of accomplishment that gave Warren Matthews even more stature in Tammany Hall than mere money alone could. "This man can actually think," Walker jested, putting his arm around Warren for a photograph.

As would be expected, Walker used every show-business technique to attract attention to his campaign. Broadway, naturally, went all-out for him. Irving Berlin wrote a song, "We'll Walk in with Walker." The hit Walker himself had penned in 1905 when he was working as a lyric writer, "Will You Love Me in December as You Do in May?" was played incessantly by every orchestra, in every speakeasy. The cast of the musical *Gay Paree* threw Walker a block party in Shubert Alley. Rudolph Valentino, in from Hollywood for the premiere of his newest film *The Eagle,* shook hands with Walker for the press. George M. Cohan announced at the Friars Club, with the importance of the grand chieftain of Broadway that he was, that the theater "owed it" to Jimmy Walker to support him.

But more than the theater crowd threw their endorsement behind the Tammany candidate. On October 31 William Randolph Hearst, the foe of Tammany, caved in and gave his blessing to the singing Democrat. Frank Waterman announced that he had fired the manager of the Fountain Inn, but it was too late. On November 2, Jimmy Walker was elected the one hundredth mayor of New York by a landslide plurality of over four hundred thousand votes. He had campaigned so hard that his normal weight of 130 had dropped to 115. Still, he looked fit. The slimness became him. He had a confident, almost regal air.

At the Tammany Wigwam, Walker strode in at ten that night to claim victory. Waiting on the platform were the leading sachems, men like Sullivan and McCarey, Governor Smith and, finally, important men "on their way up," the sachems of the future. Warren Matthews was there, and when he shook the mayor-elect's hand, he knew he was part of the inner circle.

Isabelle was home with Jessica on this victory night, as were all the Tammany wives, including Allie Walker, the long-suffering spouse of the new mayor. Allie was tubby, frumpy, the diametric opposite of the leggy showgirls Jimmy Walker fancied. Mrs. Walker and her husband were both in their early forties, but Jimmy had a boyish appearance, and Allie could be mistaken for a matron in her fifties. Actually, Allie too had been a former vaude-ville player, but this life seemed so far behind her that it might as well have never existed. She had been slim, a top dancer, when Walker met her. Once they married, Allie gave up both on the theater and herself. She gained weight and sat at home and grew old, while Jimmy Walker, forever young, went to Broadway and had his own way. On election night, some reporters managed to get an interview with Mrs. Walker as she stayed alone, having no one to celebrate with. "Was there ever a wife with her husband on election night?" She smiled, putting on her characteristic supportive front for her husband. "If I see him by five o'clock in the morning, I will consider I am doing well."

Mrs. Walker didn't do quite as well as she had hoped. With Warren Matthews in his victory party, Jimmy Walker hit all the nightspots on the Great White Way. He got home at seven.

22
1926

In January 1926, a week after Jimmy Walker took office at City Hall, Emily Stanton, having served her entire sentence, was released from Bedford. It was a bitingly cold day as Emily stepped out of the Tudor administration building in the early-morning fog. Snow and ice covered the ground. The guards stayed huddled inside. It might as well have been an ice station in Greenland. The moisture in the air froze on her lashes and in the corners of her lips. She lugged a little suitcase containing the few possessions from her old life that the police had given her from the Royale. That was all she had. Shivering, penniless, tattered. Yet she felt wonderful. She was free. The deathly cold was exhilarating, reminding her that she was no longer in hell.

"Emily!" Alex Foster's voice cut through the foggy chill. He had written to her faithfully, promising that he would pick her up when she was free, and here he was, good as his word. She ran over to him, and he ran to her, oblivious of the ice sheets and the dangers of slipping. "You made it," he said, hugging her warmly. Ex-convict, dispossessed mother, fallen woman with a need for revenge—all these negative-sounding things made Emily the most romantic figure Alex could imagine. But Alex constantly reined himself in on the possibility of romance. Emily didn't even know him. She had so much business to attend to, a whole life to start again. And he himself was still a long way from being self-confident. He could barely take it when his plays were refused. Extra cautious about rejection, Alex elected the route of waiting. Waiting and hoping and looking for a sign from her.

"My dear, dear Alex," Emily said, hugging him for a full minute in the cold. "You came, you really came. Thank you. Thank you." She felt so lucky that Alex was her friend.

"Let's get in the car before we freeze to death," Alex said, shivering. "I borrowed it from a friend." He pointed to a battered black Ford. "It's not a Duesenberg, but it runs. Come on."

"Oh, Alex, just one more minute out here. Oh, I'm free." She drank in the sharp air, which cut through her lungs. The sensation was wonderful. Everything was heightened, the pine scent, the smoke from distant chimneys, the rustle of the trees in the wind. "It's so different, Alex. Outside that place. It's the same air, the same trees, but it's so different. I'm so thrilled to be alive."

"So am I, but neither of us will be much longer if we keep standing here," Alex joked. He took Emily's suitcase and led her to the car.

They drove to a diner for a real breakfast of bacon and eggs and orange juice and waffles and syrup and hot coffee. "I've never tasted anything so good," Emily said.

Alex was unable to take his eyes off Emily, the way she ate, the way she talked, her mouth, her soft lips. Even though it was the depth of winter, to Alex, Emily was as beautiful as a morning in spring. He held back from telling her how he felt about her, but it was hard. Instead, he told her about his job, the ad agency, the boredom, the rejections of the plays, and no matter how mundane what he told her sounded to Alex, it sounded exciting to Emily, merely by dint of its not being in prison.

After breakfast they drove along the Hudson, filled with giant floes of ice, toward Manhattan. Emily pressed her face to her window of the car like a little girl on her first Sunday drive. Nature amazed her. She was discovering the world again, as if her sight had been taken from her and miraculously restored. "Look at this. Look at that," she marveled, and Alex was caught up in her excitement. He had worried that prison might have ruined her, made her hard, unfeeling, a zombie. His fears were unfounded. And then Manhattan came into view, the dream city, the clusters of monoliths glittering in the midday winter sun.

They drove through the streets, down Fifth Avenue, where Emily was surprised at how many of the great private châteaus and palazzos of the city's millionaires had been demolished and replaced with huge apartment houses in a mere two years. Finally they reached crowded Times Square. "I'm home, Alex. Home. I'm back," Emily kept repeating. She made him stop twice, once for an egg roll, then for an ice-cream soda. She wanted to taste the foods she'd missed. She was so happy, seeing the theaters, the mobs of people. The deafening screech of the elevated, the honking taxis, the roaring buses were all music to her. The skirts were so much shorter, what would she wear? She was thinking about living. This was a new world for Emily, and Alex loved being her guide.

Emily spent her first night in Alex's apartment in a brownstone in Chelsea, across from the ivied campus of the General Theological Seminary. He had moved there from the Royale after taking his advertising job. The area reminded Alex of Yale, and he liked having God across the street, in case he needed help. More important, the rent was dirt cheap. A picture of Edgar Allan Poe on the wall was the highlight of the decor. Books were everywhere. Alex had done his best to straighten the place up for Emily's arrival, but he realized that the task was hopeless.

"Sorry about the place," Alex puffed after carrying Emily's suitcase up the long four flights of stairs.

"It's wonderful," Emily said. "Everything is wonderful today. It feels like the Waldorf to me."

"I guess anything without bars . . ."

"Not just that, Alex. It's yours. It's very warm."

Alex laughed as he listened to the air ringing in the ancient radiator's pipes. "Then by all means, stay as long as you want."

"Thanks, Alex. You're so kind, but I have to find a place of my own."

"No. Stay here. *Mi casa, su casa.*"

"No. I have to. Besides, you must have girlfriends," Emily said.

That hurt Alex, but he wouldn't show it. "No seductions here. It's just a place to collapse."

"You've got your own life to live. The one favor I'll ask is that you take me out to see Jessica tomorrow."

"Sure. Of course I will."

"I wonder if I'll recognize her. I wonder if she'll recognize me. It's been so long."

"Sure she will. Don't worry."

"Alex, I'm so worried. I'm so scared."

"Just get some rest. It'll work out. This has been a long day."

"It's been a great day, Alex."

They ate Chinese food in a neighborhood chop-suey parlor, and came home to listen to Jelly Roll Morton on the radio. When Emily undressed in the bathroom to go to bed, she saw that the only thing in her valise she had to sleep in was a filmy low-cut silk negligee Warren had bought her. So ironic, dressing for seduction when she felt anything but sexy.

"Alex," she said, sticking her head out the bathroom door. "Do you have an old shirt or something?"

"Why?" Alex asked, looking up from the middle of a new Scott Fitzgerald novel, *The Great Gatsby*. He had read three pages and hadn't absorbed a thing.

"All I have to sleep in is this silly thing." Alex caught a glimpse of the black negligee reflected in the mirror. Oh, if only she would come out in that, he wished. "I'll get you a shirt," he said. He gave her a Yale baseball shirt.

"I didn't realize you played baseball," Emily said, coming out with the blue shirt over her negligee.

"I was a great reserve shortstop. I should have stuck with it. I'd be on the Yankees by now. You look funny."

"I know," Emily sighed. "Maybe it'll be a new style. Alex, where should I sleep?"

He cleared away a pile of books and pulled a Murphy bed down from the wall. "Presto."

Emily hesitated. Where would Alex sleep? She felt awkward about dispossessing him.

"I'll sleep on the couch," he said.

"No, let me," Emily said, darting in front of him.

Alex held up his hand in refusal. "You deserve a good night's sleep. I want you to look your best for Jessica."

"Okay, for Jessica, but not for me." She smiled and dropped down onto the Murphy bed. "This is paradise."

"Should I turn out the lights?"

"No, you can stay up all night. A freight train wouldn't wake me. Come here."

Alex wasn't sure what she wanted. He stepped over to the bed, dreaming of things he knew were too good to happen.

Emily hugged him and kissed his cheek. "Thanks. 'Night Alex." She stretched out, rolled under the covers, and closed her eyes. She was out.

Watching her, Alex admired the long, graceful neck, the sculptured fine bones of her face, the slight hint of white cleavage he could see through the top button of his baseball shirt that she hadn't closed. A sleeping beauty, if there ever was one, he thought. He retreated to the couch and tried to read Fitzgerald. He couldn't. He kept staring at Emily, sleeping so serenely. He'd never wanted anyone more, but he had absolutely no idea how it was going to happen. Then he returned to *Gatsby* and read until three in the morning.

23

The Model T rattled through the Holland Tunnel. The sign at the end read "Welcome to New Jersey. The Garden State." Alex and Emily drove through the industrial cordon, a Maginot Line of belching smokestacks. The Statue of Liberty, framed by the towers of Wall Street, was visible across New York Bay in the distance, her arm bearing the torch of freedom. The scene gradually changed from marshy meadowlands into lush undulating hills dotted with houses that grew increasingly grand, as if an evolving species. By the time they reached Bernardsville, the houses had mutated into palaces. The picket fences were now ornamental gates and walls. Many of the estates had horses and cows grazing in the fields. The estates had English names—Runnymeade, Sherwood Forest, Windsor, Blenheim—grandiose names that made Emily feel she was in a different world altogether, the world of rich country squires. These squires, however, were uniquely American. They toiled by day selling stocks and bonds on Wall Street. Only on weekends did they ride to the hounds and pitch hay.

The Matthews estate had no name except Matthews on the mailbox. Two granite pillars with globes atop each of them stood silent sentinel before a long driveway leading to a Tudor house with gables and shingles and beams and red brick. A new black Cadillac and a sporty red Buick cabriolet stood in the house's porte cochere. Otherwise, there was no sign of life. Warren had always wanted to live in the country, she recalled. Now he had his wish.

"How can I compete?" Emily wondered to Alex. "What

comforts can I offer my daughter, what advantages next to this?" Alex and Emily waited in the car parked across the road for about half an hour. Isabelle emerged first, in a long Persian-lamb coat, looking very rich, her brown hair windswept. She belonged out here, Emily thought, with the horses and the English names. Then Jessica came out, in a blue school blazer and gray skirt and high white stockings, carrying a lunch box. A black maid, not Cora, wearing a white uniform, followed.

"There she is," Emily gasped. "My baby . . ." She went for the door of the Model T, but Alex held her back.

"No. Not here. You don't have any rights yet."

"I want to—"

"They won't let you see her."

Emily couldn't take her eyes off her daughter as she got into the Cadillac. "She's grown up. I want to go up to her."

Alex held Emily's arm. "Wait till we get to the school. It'll be better."

The Cadillac drove down the driveway through the gates. Alex started the Ford and followed. Emily was crying. She wanted to be strong, but seeing Jessica, seeing the new wife, seeing the wealth and comfort that she seemed light-years from, she didn't feel strong at all.

About four miles down the road, near the Bernardsville town center, with its post office, grocery store, bridle shop, and gas station, was a quaint sign that read "Miss Draper's School." The Cadillac turned into the spacious grounds and dropped off Jessica at a gingerbread-cottage schoolhouse in a grove of poplar trees. Jessica kissed Isabelle good-bye and went inside. Emily dried her eyes. She wanted to pull herself together before recess.

"It's been two hours," Emily complained to Alex after what seemed an interminable wait.

"I know. They should be breaking soon. It won't be long," he assured her.

The bell rang, a mellifluous ring compared to the strident fire-alarm sound of the prison bell. Emily knew she had to stop comparing everything to prison, but it was only her second day of freedom.

Jessica came out in a cluster of girls. Some of her classmates, all in Miss Draper's blue-and-gray uniforms, began running, playing hopscotch.

"Funny how rich people *look* rich. These girls could be playing in the streets of the Bronx, and you'd still know they were rich," Alex noted. He could tell from their shimmering hair, their fine skins, their carefree smiles.

"Yeah," Emily said. "I see." She watched Jessica eschew a group game. She grabbed a rope and began skipping it alone.

"There's your opening," Alex said.

"Here goes," Emily said. She took a deep breath and opened the car door.

"Good luck."

Emily walked onto the school grounds in her thin wool coat. She was acutely aware of her not looking like Isabelle or the other girls' mothers from the nearby estates, but that didn't matter now. Emily's heart thumped louder and louder. This was worse than her first audition, this was worse than her first role. Worse than running away from school. She was scared, really scared about the reunion.

"Jessica," Emily said, coming up behind her daughter, who was counting to a hundred as she skipped the rope.

"Eighty-one, eighty-two . . ."

"Jessica."

"Eighty . . . Yes, ma'am?" She thought it was a teacher and let the rope fall. She turned around and saw her mother, pale and trembling.

"Mom . . . my," Jessica sighed in a very low breath. She stood staring at her, not sure what she was seeing. Emily looked at her. Was she happy? Was she sad?

"This is my school," Jessica said distantly. She looked around self-consciously to see if the other girls were watching. They were preoccupied with their games.

"I know. It's your school," was all Emily could say. She didn't want to embarrass Jessica.

"Daddy said you left. He said I would never see you again." Jessica maintained a cool, faraway tone.

"But here I am, honey." Emily couldn't control her tears of happiness. "Oh, darling, here I am. Your mommy's back.

Come here." She held out her arms. "Let me hold you."

Jessica shuffled uncomfortably, darted her eyes around the playground to see who was watching. "But, Mommy, this is my school."

Emily understood her discomfort. She saw a quiet, unoccupied area around the side of the schoolhouse. "Come over here and let's talk. Come on, angel." Jessica followed, shrugging her little shoulders. "You're so big. You're so beautiful," Emily said, stepping forward to hug her, but Jessica dodged backward.

"They said you left me."

"I would never leave you."

"Where did you go? Where?"

This was the hard question. Emily didn't want to try to explain, not now, perhaps not for years. "I had to go away," she said. "I was sick. Very, very sick."

"Are you sick now?" Jessica asked, not necessarily out of concern, but rather out of inquisition.

"No, I'm fine."

"You look . . ."

"Yes, darling?"

"You look different."

"I'm fine. I'm fine now. Are you all right? Are you happy?"

"But why did you leave me, Mommy Why?"

"I'd never leave you. I . . . Someday, honey, I'll explain to you why I was unable to see you, even though I missed you every, every second of the day. Oh, honey, come to me. Kiss me. Please."

Jessica held back and lowered her head shyly. Emily started crying again. She hated this. This was the worst rejection. "Please. Please let me kiss you, baby."

The school bell rang again. Emily could hear the rustle on the playground. "I have to go," Jessica said, staring at her mother as if she might have been a creature from another galaxy.

"How's Midnight?" Emily gasped, making one last effort to connect.

"He got run over," Jessica said sadly. "He shoulda stayed in New York." The bell rang again. "I have to go." Jessica turned, leaving Emily alone.

"I love you. I missed you, darling . . . Please say something. Please."

" 'Bye," Jessica said under her breath, but Emily didn't hear her. Jessica was so confused. She had no idea what to say. She had thought her mommy loved her, but when she had abandoned her, she thought her mommy didn't love her anymore. And now her mommy was back, but there was a new mommy now, who was so nice to her. Jessica had so many questions. All she knew was that if her first mommy ever came back again, she wanted to ask her some of them.

"We should have expected it," Alex said, trying to console Emily as they drove back to Manhattan. "After all, they had two years alone with her, two years to indoctrinate her."

"Yes, I guess," Emily said. "But it's so hard, Alex."

"She has to be incredibly confused," Alex said. "You know she loves you. She just has to get used to the fact that you exist. It's a shock, like seeing an apparition. I saw the expression on her face."

"What do I do, Alex? Please help me."

"You've got to keep going back . . . regain her confidence. But first you've got to get a lawyer. This custody thing's a tricky business. They're not going to want to give her up."

"What if I talk to Warren?" Emily asked.

"It's not just Warren. Your husband's new wife will probably want to keep Jessica."

"But I'm her mother."

"I'm sure she thinks she is, too."

"Warren would want to be fair," Emily said, still not believing for a moment that he had had any hand in her frame-up.

"This isn't a matter of equity," Alex said. "It's a matter of emotions. She's the new wife. She's got tenure now. It's only normal that he'd back her up. They've got this perfect life they're living out here. They're not going to be too thrilled if you try to break it up. You have to play it very straight here. What you need is a smart lawyer."

"You're right." Emily exhaled. "Alex, you're a real friend. But I'm not going to let this take over your life . . ."

"I don't mind."

"I do. It's my problem. I want to solve it." Emily assumed new resolve when she glimpsed the spires of Manhattan ahead. New York always gave her a rush of confidence. "Today was just the beginning," she said with fervor, "of a lot of things."

24

Emily walked up the steps of the Park Place IRT station into a blizzard of ticker tape. Mayor Jimmy Walker was throwing one of his parades. The placards read "Welcome, Queen Marie," and the throngs of office workers testified less to the allure of this minor celebrity than to the alacrity with which they took any excuse to get away from their jobs. After a few queries, Emily ascertained that the queen, whose motorcade slowly inched up Broadway, was the monarch of Rumania and the granddaughter of Queen Victoria, hardly reason enough to warrant the confetti blizzard. The main attraction was actually Mayor Walker, in his silk hat and morning coat. When she saw the nifty little man in his finery beside the buxom queen in the open touring car, Emily changed her route and followed the parade to City Hall. She recalled having met Walker once. A block later, as the band struck up "Will You Love Me in December as You Do in May?" she remembered where. He was a Tammany man she had been introduced to years before with Warren, playing the piano at Blackstone's. Or was it Rector's? She wasn't sure of the place, but it was the same song. And now he was the mayor. Amazing. Emily hadn't read a paper in her last few months at Bedford. She had no idea what was happening in New York politics. A piano-playing mayor who gave parades for obscure Balkan royalty. What was New York coming to?

Emily was early for her appointment with the attorney Alex had helped her locate, so she tarried in the mob at City Hall to watch the mayor formally welcome the queen. Walker could not stop making wisecracks. He made a running joke of Queen Marie's ample bosom. When he was about to pin her with a medal, he delighted the crowd by saying, "Your majesty, I've never stuck a queen," and leering at her bulging bodice, "I hesitate to do so now."

"Proceed, your honor," the queen replied in her regal tone. "The risk is mine."

"And such a beautiful risk it is, your majesty." Walker grinned lasciviously.

Absurd theater masquerading as government. Emily wondered how far the giddy flapper era from which she had been snatched had pervaded public life. If Mayor Walker was doing low burlesque on the steps of City Hall, what was President Coolidge doing at the White House? The Charleston? And Warren living with his socialite wife in a New Jersey Camelot, with Emily's daughter in a gingerbread Hansel-and-Gretel school? And where was Emily? She had left Alex's and found a tiny room for ten dollars a week above a pickle shop on Essex Street on the Lower East Side. On the door was a mezuzah, or Jewish good-luck charm. The decor was an engraving of Moses and the Ten Commandments. Emily's most indelible image of the neighborhood was of one Hasidic Jew in a brand-new Ford blowing his horn at another Hasidic Jew pushing an apple cart. Slowly but surely, these Russian and Polish immigrants were finding prosperity and becoming Americanized. Emily's landlord wore a long black frock coat, studied the Talmud, yet also liked to quote Shakespeare. When she told him she was in the theater, he motioned to the din outside the window and said, "Theater. You got theater right here. All the world's a stage, *bubbeleh*." She had a pickle-barrel bard and Warren had Camelot. Incredible.

Emily hoped that Hiram Hogan, the lawyer Alex had found, would be able to set things straight for her. Hogan's office was in an old Victorian building on Park Row. Alex had asked some friends of his, and Hogan's name kept coming up. His specialty was women. In a man's world, a business world where everything was male, a lawyer whose specialty was women was a rare commodity, and Emily wanted to meet him.

Hiram Hogan didn't seem to be a ladies' man. Around

sixty, he was a grizzled old warhorse who, with his rolled-up sleeves and fraying vest, appeared more like a tender of a bar than a pillar of one.

"Look," Hogan said to Emily in a gravelly, whiskey-rotted voice after she had laid out her case. "A lot of Bedford girls come see me, and I've been able to help a few, but you've got a big problem, young lady, that you don't seem to have addressed."

"What's that?"

"To have any chance to get that little girl back, you've got to prove you're a fit mother."

"What do you mean by fit?"

"It's spelled m-o-n-e-y. That's what I mean. Your first order of business is not to come here, but to go get a job that pays money. Money to support a child, and money to pay me."

"I'm going to get a job."

"Well, don't say that so fast. It isn't going to be easy, not with a prison record."

"That's another thing I wanted you to help me with."

"You sure want a lot, young lady. I take hard cases, but I don't do charity, I'm sorry to tell you. And I know you've got nothing now."

"No, but—"

"If you can't afford my fee, how in God's name can you support your daughter?"

"I'll find a job," Emily said. "I will. And I'll be able to pay you. What I need to know from you now is how I can get my daughter back. The other thing is, I've got to clear my name. What are my chances for overturning that conviction?"

"Let me turn the last question around on you. Other than your word, what evidence do you have against McNaughton?"

"There were other girls at Bedford he set up."

"You try to get them to talk. Just try. Your problem is, you don't have any evidence."

"And that Judge Renaud, how could he have heard what I said and—"

"He's considered a reputable judge."

Emily wanted to wring her hands at this stone wall she

would have to get over. Was this the right lawyer? "Whose side are you on?" she blurted out.

"I want to be on your side," Hogan said. "But right now, it's your word against theirs, and sweetheart, you're a convicted felon."

Emily hated those words. "Can't we go back to court?"

"Not without some new evidence. Without it, the Court of Special Sessions—that's where we'd try to go—always affirms in these prostitution cases. You need hard evidence, but I'm a trial lawyer, not Sherlock Holmes."

"Then I'll have to get it myself."

Hogan smiled, not quite condescendingly, but with a sense of futility. "What are you going to do, put on a wig and a mask and wait for McNaughton to do it again to you while I'm standing in the corner? Look, get a job, concentrate on yourself, make some money, bring me a retainer, and then I'll go to work trying to get your daughter back to you. Clearing your name, that's another matter. That's tougher. Let's worry about the present right now. If you take care of yourself, you can put the past behind you."

"There's one other thing."

"Yes?"

Emily didn't want to say it, but it had been nagging her for a long time. "One of the girls at Bedford said"—Emily couched it as a suggestion from someone else, to avoid suggesting it herself—"that my husband, my ex-husband, might have bribed McNaughton to set me up. That's not possible, is it?"

"When you've been practicing law for forty years, you know that anything's possible. Sure it's possible. Not likely, but possible. You didn't have any money or property he was after. You weren't trying to blackmail him, were you?"

"No. Of course not."

"And the woman he married. Think he was seeing her on the side when you were still together?"

"No. I know he wasn't."

"So he didn't want to get rid of you for her, as far as you can tell?"

"No."

"So the only thing you had that he really wanted is

your daughter. Now, that's something. That, and the adultery thing to free him to remarry, but only you know if your husband is the kind of man who would destroy you."

I'm not destroyed, Emily thought, and Hogan sensed her resilience.

". . . try to destroy you," he corrected himself, "to get her away from you. I wasn't living with you. I don't know what went on. But from what you say, your husband sounds pretty straight. And McNaughton, despite what you say, gets decorated every year. He's a cop's cop. I don't think your husband would risk attempting to bribe a man like that. If it backfired, he'd have gone to prison."

Emily breathed easier. "Just wondering. At Bedford you have a lot of time to wonder. Thank you very much for your time, Mr. Hogan."

"Don't thank me. Pay me," Hogan laughed. His coarse frankness engendered trust. He wasn't some slick lawyer with promises he couldn't keep, like J. Nicholas Collins. "Get a good job and get back here. Best of luck to you." Hogan lowered his bifocals and waded back into his black-and-white hodgepodge of forms and motions.

25

"Is that you, George?" the woman comic asked on the stage of the Gaieties.

"It's me," the male comic said, waddling out from behind the curtain on stage right.

"Where have you been?"

"Out celebrating."

"Celebrating what?"

"My friend," the man said, "has just been elected mayor."

"Honestly?" the woman asked in a high pitch.

"What does that matter?" the man deadpanned.

The theater had about fifty people, mostly old, in for the matinee; mere specks in the expanse of fading red velvet in the orchestra section. "They're handcuffed," Howard Price, Emily's old producer, described the apathetic crowd as he and Emily stood at the railing in back of the theater. "Or they're sitting on their hands. Or maybe the act's all wet. What does it matter? Vaudeville's dead."

The comics were followed by an underfed young stripper who performed to the three-man band's rendition of "April Showers," using an open umbrella to tease the spectators. As the layers of satin and ruffles and bustles came off, the audience saw that under it all, there was practically nothing there. They were handcuffed for her, too.

"A fish," Price apologized, meaning an act that stank.

"When did you start with the strippers?" Emily asked.

"When the people stopped coming. So you see, Emily," Price said sadly, "what can I do for you when I can't

133

even do anything for myself?" The years and the change in the public's taste had broken this once confident man. He had a stubble. His tie was stained. His voice shook. "I don't want to put you up there taking your clothes off."

"No, but I can still sing."

"Not on the big stage. Unless the person's famous—and I can't afford famous—they don't want to pay to hear singers anymore."

The comics had returned. "I'll never eat another one of your mother's pies," the male comic said.

"How dare you say that!" the woman comic fumed indignantly. "My mother made pies before you were born."

"That's when she musta made the one I just ate."

Minor guffaws, but hardly a wow. Another, more voluptuous stripper came on, powdered and robed like a geisha. The band played "Nagasaki."

"We're a morgue today. Nights are better. The only way I can get anyone in here," Price observed, pointing a shaky finger at the stage, "is by getting younger and younger girls. But they got laws about that, too. I don't know. I'm sorry, Emily. I know you'll get something. You had a swell pair of pipes. Nice gams too. You'll work. Just keep trying."

Emily couldn't have tried harder. But the initial thrill of walking down Broadway, making the rounds, being back in show business, quickly deteriorated into the vicious reality of rejection. She heard "Million Dollar Baby" playing loudly in a record store. The theater marquees glittered. Katharine Cornell in *The Green Hat*, Helen Hayes in *Caesar and Cleopatra*, Ethel Barrymore in *Hamlet*. The movies were booming: *The Gold Rush*, *The Phantom of the Opera*. Yet Emily was alone on the streets, going from one rejection to another.

Emily hadn't called Cassie Laverne or any of her old theater acquaintances. She knew that Louise had discarded all of her letters to them. Besides, she wasn't sure any of them would even want to see her, not the way she was now. Emily was ashamed of what had happened to her, and horrified at the thought that her old friends probably believed that she actually had been a prostitute, and would therefore want nothing to do with her. Of course, she could explain it all, but she didn't have the heart to do it now. Maybe after she started working again, then, like her similarly discredited friend Alex, she could hold her head up and call these people. But when would that be? Where was the work?

"I understand you've been in some trouble, Emily," said a producer who had praised her audition three years before. "A knockout," she rememberd him saying. "Can't wait to use you." A high-stepping chorus line practiced onstage to rousing music while Emily sank on hearing that the producer knew about her background.

"Er . . . I can explain," she gulped, off balance, not really even wanting to have to explain. She scanned the faces of the long-legged beauties. All smiles, all their energies put into their work. No prison records to expunge, no daughters to retrieve, no problems like her problems. How could she compete with them? How could she even get a chance? "I need the work."

"I'm sure," the producer said. "I'd like to help you, but I run a clean chorus line. I don't want any trouble."

"It's not what you think. I was framed."

"I'm sorry," the producer said. He turned away from her and returned to his chorus line.

Emily was able to get a reading for a role in a new show. It wasn't important, but it was a speaking part.

" 'Oh, Derek, let's forget about Samantha. Let's think about that night in Sorrento when we met. We'll always have that,' " Emily read in the director's office.

"Not bad, Miss Stanton. Not bad." The director was dressed in a sharkskin suit and a white silk scarf. She had waited two hours for the reading. Thirty other aspirants were warming the benches in the hall outside, pacing the floor, praying for the few moments onstage that might lead to longer moments onstage and, one day, maybe to stardom. "Not bad." The flashy director looked her up and down.

"Thanks," Emily said, trying not to seem as hopeful as she was.

"Let me see your legs."

"Huh?"

"Your legs. That dress leaves too much to my imagination, and my imagination isn't working."

"But this is supposed to be a dramatic part," Emily said.

"Come on. Let me see your legs. There's drama in good legs," the director said.

"What does that have to do with this role?"

"Everything," the director said, shaking his head and opening the door for Emily. "Thank you, Miss Stanton."

Another week of hiking up and down Broadway, living on doughnuts and hot dogs. The "clean-chorus-line" remark still rang in Emily's head, haunting her, sapping her energy and her confidence. The two-year hiatus at Bedford was hurting her far more than the six-year hiatus of motherhood. She was afraid to use her old references, because Bedford might come up and nobody wanted "trouble." So for a twenty-six-year-old would-be actress to start a career without a portfolio, the task was more and more hopeless. Her one remaining hope was a casting agent she had been referred to by other rejectees she had met in the waiting lines. He was supposed to be good. He knew all the producers, all the directors.

Arthur Jaffee liked her looks, liked her voice. He seemed like he could do something. No more than five-two, he wore spats and a gardenia and kept the fingers of his right hand above his heart inside his coat, the same ay Napoleon did. The walls of his office, overlooking the bustle of Times Square, were covered with photographs of Arthur Jaffee with Ziegfeld, Cohan, Chaplin, Barrymore, all the great names of entertainment. But after he sent her out on several calls, Arthur Jaffee quickly lost interest in Emily. In fact, she annoyed him immensely for turning down his suggestions, most of which involved removing some if not all of her clothes.

"I don't get it. You're a great-looking broad, but you wanna keep it to yourself. You won't strip, you won't show your ass. You some kind of nun or something?"

"I have no interest in being a stripper."

"Why not? You still look pretty good for your age."

"Thanks."

"Come on, baby. Learn to take a joke."

"Mr. Jaffee, I'm an actress. I'm a singer. I'm good. I want to do what I'm good at."

Jaffee paged through some files, paying little attention to Emily's plea. "If you're so good, why did every producer I sent you out to turn you down?"

"Probably because I wouldn't go to bed with them."

"You want work, don't you?"

"Work. Not sex."

"Miss Stanton," Jaffee said in the most exasperated voice, "in this business unless your family backs the show or owns the theater, sometimes you have to do one to get the other. Don't look at it as sex."

"What should I look at it as?"

"As your way in. You won't have to put out forever. It's the name of the game."

"Not for me."

"Then go into another line, baby," Jaffee said. "This ain't for you. You don't want to pay the price, you don't have to be here. Nobody's twisting your arm, but hey, these are the big boys. I sent you to Carr, to Miller, to Ferguson, they coulda put you over the top, any one of 'em. Give the guys a break, they may give you one. Best I can do."

"I'm sorry, Mr. Jaffee. It's not worth working if that's the only way." She wanted to say that she hadn't had to use her body the first time she tried to get on Broadway. Had New York changed that much?

"Come on, Miss Stanton. You ain't fooling no one with this Goody Two Shoes bit. They all know you did time."

Emily was stunned. Why hadn't he told her he knew? Why did he keep up this charade? Now she understood why all the producers he had sent her to see had been so aggressive, so vulgar. He was just a procurer, sending her out for sex with his cronies. There was never a chance of any part. "You knew? Why didn't you—"

"You want to pretend, so pretend."

"There were no parts!"

"There are never parts. You make your own parts! I introduced you."

"You're nothing but a . . . pimp!" Emily yelled at him.

"That's what you need, honey. You were doing good hustling on Broadway before. You could come back."

"You're disgusting!" Emily said, standing up to leave.

"Dame really hates guys," Jaffee mused as Emily slammed the glass door. "How the hell did she get as far as she did?"

Emily walked out into Times Square and said good-bye to it. She realized her career in the theater was over.

26

The Ringling Brothers Circus was at Madison Square Garden. A few blocks away on Eighth Avenue, a greasy spoon named Demos Coffee Shop was a sideshow in itself. On one side of Michael McNaughton and Luis Quito at the counter sat a strong man, on the other, a bearded lady. A group of bullet-faced pinheads from the freak show filled a table, devouring hotcakes. McNaughton liked to meet his contacts at Demos. Here in the city's lower depths, no one cared what went on. No one cared about anything. No one noticed, even against the circus freaks, that two of the handsomest men in New York were hatching an evil plan.

Luis Quito was, if anything, even handsomer than Mc-Naughton. He bore a distinct resemblance to Rudolph Valentino. When McNaughton had arrested him two years before as a pimp in Spanish Harlem, he saw Quito's potential instantly.

"You sure she's all alone, *jefe?*" Quito asked in a low voice that contained both the charm of the Spanish court-yard and the urgency of the New York street. "I don't like taking chances."

"She's all alone," McNaughton said coolly.

"I don't know why we don't stick to the hookers. Why do we need these secretaries?"

"Because they have money, and they don't want any trouble," McNaughton said.

"But they've got friends."

"Not the ones Lucretia finds. Out-of-town girls. Way out of town. This one's from Nebraska. She's got no one."

139

"How can Lucretia tell?"

"That's her line, Luis. Has she ever been wrong?"

"No, but that was suckering hookers. These are fancy bitches."

"Lucretia can be as fancy as they get. She goes to the beauty shops, the stores. She finds out who's who. Women trust her. They talk to her."

"I don't know. I don't like this new territory."

"You're jumpy, Luis. Not like you."

"It's these freaks." Luis looked around. "They give me the jeebies."

"You believe in ghosts back in Guatemala?" McNaughton said.

"Yeah, we did. Zombies and things. Creepy."

"You don't want to go back there, do you, Luis?" McNaughton said in an I'm-holding-the-cards tone to his illegal-alien accomplice.

"Never, *jefe*."

"Then shut your mouth and get to work," McNaughton said, smiling.

Michael McNaughton was diversifying. Shaking down prostitutes was one good way for vice cops to supplement their income. Setting up shy young single secretaries from out of town was another way, he had discovered, to nourish his insatiable greed. Framing the innocent was a far more elaborate, more malicious enterprise than simply extorting a bribe from a call girl or a street girl or a bar girl so that she could continue her illicit sexual commerce. But Michael McNaughton didn't want to be a cop. He wanted to be rich. Everyone else was making the big money. Why shouldn't he? In the vice squad, he had found an unorthodox yet quite efficacious route.

McNaughton's motives were not solely fiscal. He had a reason to hate prostitutes. When he was six in Boston, his dockworker father had been murdered by one in the notorious cribs of Scollay Square. The assailant was never found. The trauma made McNaughton want to be a cop, to settle the score with the painted women of the night who had taken his father away from him. But two years later, when his mother, alcoholic, destitute, and unable to care for him, placed him, her only child, in a squalid public orphanage and disappeared from his life, Michael

McNaughton's hatred of whores began to metastasize into a full-scale, rabid misogyny. He never married, and his desire to avenge his father's death mushroomed into what was now a crusade, a holy war against women. No one could be more charming. No one could be more seductive. No one could disguise his true feelings better. No one could hate women more.

Peggy Holden was alone in her little apartment on Downing Street in the Village, listening to Jessica Dragonette crooning on the radio while she read the latest issue of *College Humor*. Peggy didn't have a boyfriend, sometimes she got lonely in the evening, and she hadn't even been to a Broadway show. Nevertheless, she was thrilled to be out of North Platte, Nebraska, and even more thrilled to be in New York City. She had gone to business college, had a good job at Cunard Lines, which had even promised her a free trip to Europe if she stayed with the company two more years. A knock at her door roused her from her reveries of all the wonderful things ahead of her.

Cracking open the door proved to be a reverie in itself. Here was such a good-looking man. "Yes?"

"My name is Charles Salas," Luis Quito said. "I'm with Mark Luxor Beauty Products. I was wondering if you had a moment for me to show you our new Crème d' Elysees. It's the latest beauty cream, with some special ingredients you won't find in the stores."

"Why . . . all right. Do come in." Peggy unlocked the chain and opened the door. Door-to-door salesmen were as much a fixture of city life as the morning milkman or the house-calling doctor. Salesmen were always dropping by, selling vitamins, magazines, Bibles, kitchenware. But none ever looked like this one.

Peggy was very sorry she had taken off her makeup. She looked so plain.

"I'm sorry, but I don't think I can sell you anything," Luis said hesitantly as Peggy opened the door and the electric light revealed her face.

"Oh? Why not?" Peggy was curious.

"You don't need it. You've got beautiful skin, Mrs. . . . ."

"I'm Peggy."

"You could be selling this cream, not buying it." Luis smiled.

"You're a wonderful salesman." Peggy smiled back. "Would you like some tea or coffee?"

Luis entered the neat apartment and looked around. "I won't be taking much of your time, ma'am."

"No, that's all right. Wouldn't you like something to drink? It's freezing outside tonight."

"You must be from the south," Luis said.

"No. Why?"

"Your hospitality. You're very kind, Peggy."

"I think everyone from a small town is naturally more friendly. Sit down. Cofffee or tea?"

"Coffee will be fine."

While Peggy went into the kitchen, Luis opened his sample case, took fifty dollars in fives, and placed them in a drawer by her sofa.

She came out and, all business, Luis began his sales pitch. "Crème d'Elysees is the latest in beauty treatments. It's made from fluids that are almost identical to the ones in your own skin, so you never get that greasy feeling. Can I demonstrate?" He opened his case, took out one of the many jars he had stocked up from the beauty-supply wholesaler, and, while touting its emollient qualities, began rubbing Crème d'Elysees into Peggy's hand. Then a terrible banging at the door interrupted them. Startled, Peggy jumped up. It was Michael McNaughton, flashing his badge and demanding entrance in the name of the law. He came in and immediately pounced on Luis, cornering him against a wall. Peggy stood by, terrified. She thought that perhaps she had let in a criminal. Thank goodness this policeman was here to save her.

"Came here for a good time, huh?" McNaughton said. "Huh? Tell me," he commanded.

"Y-yes, officer." Luis feigned trembling.

"How much did you give her?" McNaughton growled, and suddenly Peggy realized that this officer was not here to protect her at all.

"N-nothing, sir."

"Don't lie to me, greaseball." McNaughton grabbed him by his tie. "Did she offer to commit prostitution?"

"N-no . . . no, sir."

"Tell the truth, or you're going to jail, too."

"She . . . she did, officer."

"Did you pay her the money?"

"Yes, sir."

"How much?"

"Fifty."

"Where'd she put it?"

"There." Luis pointed to the drawer with the bills. McNaughton opened the drawer, glared at Peggy with the cold satisfaction of a hunter who has cornered his prey, and marked the bills for evidence.

"You wait here!" McNaughton handcuffed Peggy to a heavy cabinet and strong-armed Luis downstairs. "You're going down to headquarters to make a statement," McNaughton barked to Luis.

"I'm sorry, sir," Luis apologized. "We weren't hurting anyone." McNaughton slammed the door. What Peggy imagined was a waiting police car was actually a taxi.

"Wasn't that easy?" McNaughton asked him as they shook hands.

"Easier than with the hookers. *Jefe*, you're a genius," Luis said, speeding away to a speakeasy called the Toledo while his chief, McNaughton, went back upstairs to bring Peggy Holden in for prostitution.

"But, officer, I swear, I'm not a prostitute. That's the last thing on earth I'd do," Peggy pleaded with McNaughton.

"Then how do you account for the money?" McNaughton kept playing straight. He would not seek any bribe from Peggy. He would get his cut later. His role was that of stern authority. His function was one of fear.

"He planted it. This whole thing is so crazy. I have a good job. I work. I'm not a—"

"Then can we call your boss as a character witness? Where do you work?"

"At Cunard Lines. Wait!" Peggy said. "Don't call them. Please. They'll get the wrong idea. Please don't."

"They wouldn't approve, would they?"

"No, of course not. Oh, help me, sir. I don't know what's wrong with that man, why he would say that I took money from him."

"He did. And you have the money. You'll have to tell it to the judge. I'm sorry. I'm just doing my job."

"You won't call my office, will you?" Peggy asked desperately. "I don't want anyone to know about this."

"It's all a matter of public record, miss. Can't help that."

"But I didn't do anything. This is going to ruin me. Oh, no," Peggy wept. She was in a panic. She would do anything to get out of this situation. She was precisely where Michael McNaughton wanted her.

At that point, Peggy's nightmare had just begun. At the Toledo, Luis Quito placed a call that activated the second phase of the vice squad's venal infrastructure—to a bail bondsman named Jack Dunphey in his office on West Tenth across from the Jefferson Market Women's House of Detention, where Emily Stanton had been taken. In fact, Dunphey shared his office with the lawyer who had represented Emily, J. Nicholas Collins. Their quarters had a big plate-glass window and a dramatic red seal advertising bail bonds and notary services. There were no law books in the office other than a volume of forms and the Criminal Code. There were many similarly spare storefront offices on West Tenth Street, which was known as the Ladies' Bar, because most of the lawyers here practiced across the street at the Women's Court. Most were also on the take.

Jack Dunphey rushed over to the House of Detention, where McNaughton had booked Peggy Holden. "Terrible bit of luck," he lamented to Peggy, playing guardian angel to the hilt. "We can't change your luck, can we, lass, but we can get you out of here."

"How? Please, tell me."

"You can fight the charge, mind you, but you'll be stuck here awhile."

"I don't want any publicity. I have a job, a good job."

"Don't need any questions, do you?"

"No, sir. I can't have this on my record."

"Listen to me, my lass. I have a friend, a top courthouse lawyer. I think I can get him to take care of this."

"But a trial could be so embarrassing. I might lose my job."

"Who said anything about a trial? A good lawyer never

goes to court. My friend can take care of this in short order, wipe it clean, and you can forget it even happened. The only problem. . ."

"What?" Peggy said, anxious.

"He's pretty expensive."

"How much?"

"First, there's your bail bond. That'll be five hundred dollars there. Then, the lawyer's fee. That's one thousand."

Peggy frowned.

"I'm sorry it's so high. Like I said, you can always stand and fight."

Peggy thought of her savings, almost two thousand dollars in the Chase Bank. She had been so proud to amass this much. She was going to buy clothes, to travel, to enjoy life. Then she thought of what had just befallen her. She looked at the bars. Where her freedom and her future were concerned, price was irrelevant. She was so distraught and humiliated that she signed over her passbook to Jack Dunphey.

The wheels of justice, thus properly oiled, rolled smoothly and swiftly. The next morning, J. Nicholas Collins appeared before Magistrate Stanley Renaud. Because Michael McNaughton did not appear, Collins moved for a dismissal and Peggy Holden was discharged and given the small balance in her Chase account. Her savings gone, her equanimity shattered, Peggy was, nonetheless, so relieved to be free that she would tell no one for fear of future reprisals. She called Cunard Lines, apologizing profusely for getting the flu, and was back behind her desk the next day, with no one the wiser. Meanwhile, Michael McNaughton and his cohorts would divide the spoils.

The next time McNaughton and Luis Quito met at Demos, the circus was gone. Now a horse show was at the Garden. The coffee shop was filled with grooms redolent of hay and dung.

"Listen to this, *jefe*." Luis was reading a *Mirror* article on the three-hundred-man vice squad and how pleased the mayor was at its recent upward spiral of arrests. What the article did not mention was the spreading rot behind the figures. The majority of the members of the vice squad were involved in the system of framing and shakedowns, through which they earned multiples of their five-thousand-dollar-or-less annual salaries. "This makes you guys sound like God," Luis said. McNaughton did not respond. Luis read aloud, " 'Mayor Walker boasted that because of the squad, "New York is the cleanest, safest, finest city in the world. Our police are second to none." ' How long can this go on, *jefe?*"

"In ten years I imagine I can retire. I always wanted to manufacture something, have a big plant. Maybe I'll make you a foreman, Luis."

"Hell, I like Broadway too much. But aren't you worried these *chicas* might get together and fight this thing?"

"I'm not worried about anything."

"Why not?"

"We've got the judges, Luis. It's all covered."

"You got it made, *jefe.* I wish I was on the squad."

"Be happy you're on the team, Luis," McNaughton said.

27

The Matthewses were informed by Miss Draper that a strange woman was coming to visit Jessica on the playground. Who was this woman? When Jessica told them the woman was Emily, Warren knew he was going to have a fight on his hands, a fight he was well prepared for. Although he had legal custody and despite the permanent taint of Emily's conviction, it was clear to Warren that she had no intention of giving up.

"Why didn't you tell us she's been coming to the school?" he asked his daughter over dinner in their baronial dining room, whose formality intimidated Jessica even under normal circumstances.

"I was . . . afraid," Jessica replied.

"Afraid?"

"I know you don't like her," Jessica said.

"It's not that I don't like her, sweetheart. I don't like it that she ran away from us, from *you*."

"She said she didn't run away," Jessica said, very confused. "She said she was sick."

'She *did* run away. She *was* sick, sick in the head. So sick that she left us. Left you and me to go and be an actress. She ran away from us. She has her own life. I don't know why she's doing this. It's not fair to you. I want you to stop talking to her," Warren said.

"But she's my mother," Jessica said tentatively.

"Isabelle is your mother," Warren said to Jessica. Isabelle came over to the girl and stroked her hair, a gesture of affection that made Jessica pull away.

"But she isn't my *real* mother."

That infuriated Warren. Isabelle spoke for him, repeating to Jessica what Warren had just told the child. "Emily left you, dear. She doesn't want to be your mother. She wants to be an actress. When she comes to see you, she's only acting." Both Warren and Isabelle had discussed telling Jessica about the arrest. They decided that would be too much for her. The actress logic, they concluded, would make sense to an eight-year-old.

It didn't. "She's not acting. She says she wants to take care of me."

"Nobody can take care of you better than we can, dear," Isabelle said.

"But she says she loves me."

"We love—"

"Then where was she the last two years?" Warren cut Isabelle off. Now was the time to be firm with his daughter. "She ran away from you, and now she wants to come back and be your mother again. Don't believe her."

"Daddy, she says she loves me. She swears she does." Tears filled Jessica's eyes, even though she knew her father didn't like her to cry.

"Emily is very disturbed. I know this is hard, Jessica, but please trust me. Trust us," Warren said, turning to Isabelle, who took his hand and tried to smile understandingly at Jessica. But Jessica knew it wasn't the same look her real mother gave her. She *felt* something with Emily. Isabelle was more like a nice teacher at school. She didn't *feel* anything with her. "Trust your daddy," Warren continued. "Look at your home. Look at your toys. Look at your pony. Look at your clothes. Isabelle and I do everything for you. What did Emily do? Emily left me. Emily left *you,* and she'll do it again. You can't trust her. She may seem nice, but you can't trust her." That frightened Jessica. Whom could she trust? "Look what we do for you. Look what she does. Then tell us who loves you the most. Tell us."

Jessica couldn't tell them anything. All she could do was lower her little head. Despite all her efforts to hold them back, the tears fell.

After Jessica had left the room, Isabelle lit into Warren. "I find this whole thing rather distasteful, Warren. I thought she had left Jessica for good. I had no idea she'd come back into our lives."

"I'll take care of it."

"You told me she didn't want anything to do with Jessica."

"She didn't."

"So why is she coming back?"

"Because she's . . . she's crazy."

"That . . . that filthy prostitute," Isabelle hissed in her overbearing society voice in a way that made Warren feel doubly guilty for what he had done. He'd never told Isabelle what had really happened. He could never tell her, or anyone else. In Isabelle's mind, Emily was a whore, the lowest species of womankind, the unfittest of unfit mothers.

"I guess she's still a mother," Warren said, unable to quell his compulsion to speak. "She had a lot of time in prison to think." Sometimes when he let it, the guilt would corrode his insides. Warren had made his deal with the devil. He had his heaven on earth, but he also had hell to think about. Now Emily was back to remind him.

"She's not a mother. She's a whore. Jessica is ours. And I don't want our daughter exposed to that whore," Isabelle proclaimed.

"I don't either," Warren agreed.

"Mummy told me never to marry a man who was divorced. Mummy always warned me about these other wives."

"I don't want to hear about 'Mummy.' "

"And here the other wife was a . . . a whore! Mummy said it was simply mad of me to marry a man who was married to a whore."

"Then why did you do it? Because your mummy had run out of money? Because you were all desperate?"

"Money," Isabelle sniffed. "Is that your only trump card? Is that the only way you can bully me? Money? Is that why you were married to a whore? Is that the kind of woman your money can buy?"

"Did I know what she was? How could I know!" Warren yelled at Isabelle, hating himself for having to keep up the lie for the rest of his life. "Don't you think I suffered?"

"Mummy was right," Isabelle said.

"Then go home to your drunken 'Mummy'!" Warren lost his patience. "Go get a job and support her. Get out!"

"Oh, Warren, darling." Isabelle looked shocked. She hadn't intended for this to go so far. "Don't say that. I'm sorry. I didn't mean . . . I'm so scared. I love you. I love Jessica. I love our life."

So did Warren. Isabelle needed Warren, but Warren needed Isabelle as much. "I'm sorry, too," he said. "I'm sorry she came back."

"Can't you keep her away? She was your wife. I don't want her to become my curse, my awful curse. Oh, please, darling. I'm not strong. I can't take this. Keep that evil woman away from us." Isabelle was weeping. "Keep her away. I'm so scared of her. Please promise me, please."

"I promise," Warren said.

28

Although she had never envisioned herself as a salesgirl, Emily was beginning to enjoy her work. To begin with, it was a job, providing not only a living but also a charge account for clothes, to get her hair done, and to buy other things she needed, and Wanamaker's had everything anyone could ever need. The great emporium on Broadway and Ninth Street was the grandest store in New York. Just going to the place made Emily catch her breath, with its open well of marble staircases illuminated by the light streaming in through the stained-glass skylights. A string quartet played classical music. A marionette theater entertained the children. The place was fragrant with the aroma of perfumes and powders sold from the elegant cosmetics counters on the main floor. There were more flowers than in a botanical garden. Customers dressed up to shop at Wanamaker's. Going there was an event.

Wanamaker's did its best to make its employees feel as special as their environment. An elite corps of "merchandise specialists," not clerks, the management called them, serving an elite clientele. Emily's "specialty" was young women's dresses, on the third floor, what the salesgirls called the "flapper shop." Here the customers were college-age girls who didn't have to work for what they bought. And what they bought were the most abbreviated silk chemises, shorter every day, hoyden dresses they accessorized with long slinky strands of pearls, cloche hats, and rolled-up stockings. These were dresses to tempt their boyfriends, dresses for wild dancing, dresses that wouldn't get in the way—of anything. Emily was amazed how anyone could pay so much for so little, but where fashions of the Jazz Age were concerned, less cost more.

Emily decided she was good at selling because she was honest. Remembering the pleasures of dressing up, keen memories which fanned her enthusiasm, she sold each dress as if she were buying it herself. She wasn't that much older than her customers, and they all thought she was so pretty. Looks talked. The flappers listened to Emily, who had their looks but not their privileges. And she listened to them talk about the Harvard-Princeton games, the midnight rides in Hispano-Suizas, the all-night swimming parties in Southampton. She envied how carefree they were, their nonsensical fun, the heady amusements of a life she had never had.

Emily's sales were the highest on the floor, which meant her commissions were rising, and if she saved enough, she would someday be able to retain Hiram Hogan. As for Broadway, she tried not to think about it, tried not to be bitter. Perhaps one day, once she had Jessica back, once she had figured out a way—and she knew that there *had* to be some way, someday—to clear her name, the stage might open up for her again. But now, now she had to sell.

The flapper twirled in the three-way mirror, flinging her pearls this way and that, admiring every profile of the black sheath and white flounce dress, with its dramatic dust ruffle. She adjusted her imitation-jewel-encrusted headband with an Indian feather in it, vamping for the mirror.

"Think it's hot enough?" She turned to Emily. "I want to be sexy."

"It's scalding," Emily said, trying to sound like her customers. "But not *too*. You could be Daisy Buchanan."

"Daisy who? Do I know her from Southhampton?" The flapper was confused.

"No. The Scott Fitzgerald heroine. In his book—"

"Who reads anymore?" The flapper laughed.

"Too many parties?"

"Too many hangovers. I can't keep my eyes straight." She pirouetted around in the dress, did a slight shimmy, kicked out her leg as if she were dancing.

"Take it," Emily urged. "It's you."

"Sold," the flapper said. "What was that Fitzgerald thing again?"

After Emily wrapped the dress and sent her customer on her way, Mr. Brand, the floor manager, who had been watching the transaction, walked over. Wearing his cutaway morning coat and boutonniere, he could have been dressed for a fancy horse race. Emily thought it was a little too much, but it was the Wanamaker way.

"Hello, Mr. Brand. You know those black dresses? Well, I'm glad you didn't mark them down."

"Miss Stanton," he said gravely, "could you step into my office for a moment?"

She thought he was going to scold her for being too friendly with the customers, for not having enough of the reserve that was the hallmark of the Wanamaker style, but she had a ready answer—her results. She was surprised, then, when he praised her. "You're doing a good job here. You communicate well with the younger customers. Your sales are the highest on the floor."

There. He'd said it for her. "I like the job, Mr. Brand." Maybe retailing was her métier. Maybe she would rise in the store, become a buyer, even a department head. Maybe she could start her own small specialty store someday. "I like the job a lot, and I'm going to get better and better."

"Yes . . ." He paused, and the corners of his mouth turned down. "I feel terrible about this."

"What?" Emily asked.

Brand opened a drawer and held up Emily's job application. "This," he said, and her heart broke. "Miss Stanton, on your employment application you didn't mention that you had a criminal record."

"No," Emily choked, searching for an explanation she knew was too late. "I didn't say anything because—"

"We're very careful here, you see," Brand went along. "We check everything. Sometimes it takes months, but we check everything. You shouldn't have lied to us, Miss Stanton."

"It wasn't a lie."

He raised a dubious eyebrow. "What was it, then, an omission?" he said, hurling the word at her. "You were in prison."

"If I had put it down, you would never have hired me." Emily decided all she could do was tell the truth.

"But you didn't put it down." Brand paused. "And we can't keep you."

"Please, Mr. Brand," Emily begged him. "I'm trying to start a new life. I'm doing a good job. You said so yourself. I'm selling a lot—"

"You lied to us, Miss Stanton."

"It didn't hurt anyone. Please let me stay on, Mr. Brand. This job means so much to me."

"You lied to us." He held the line.

Didn't Wanamaker's ever lie? About dresses with Italian labels that were made in Staten Island, about "French" perfume bottled in laboratories in Queens, about charging fifty dollars for a skirt that cost the store only five and calling it a bargain? The quality may have been there; the provenance sometimes wasn't. Wanamaker's may have been grand, but wasn't much of its grandeur a matter of packaging? Didn't the clerks lie, telling old women how young they looked, telling fat women they were sleek, sallow women they were radiant? Wasn't the art of selling just one big lie? But Emily kept these thoughts unsaid. What good would their utterance achieve? This wasn't a court of law. Court of law! Even in a court of law there was no justice. "Mr. Brand, have a heart. You won't be sorry," was her final plea.

"I am sorry. Wanamaker's is sorry. Sorry to lose you. We have our rules."

29

Having collected her final paycheck, Emily virtually limped out of Wanamaker's. The blow had been so heavy that for a whole week all she did was sleep and drift up and down the streets of New York like a fallen leaf in the wind. She didn't have the fortitude to look for another job and face the likelihood of rejection. Nor could she bear the reality that she had nowhere to go. So she wandered, in a daze. On this early April day she was on Fifth Avenue. The weather was breezy, with a foreshadowing of spring. The buds were on the trees, the robins were chirping. To Emily it was the darkest December. She was cold. She clutched her light coat to her neck. What now? she pondered, as she had all week. What now? And she didn't have a single answer.

She loitered up the avenue, past antique shops, china shops, toy shops, all symbols of the life of comfort and security she used to have. She stared into a jewelry shop. The windows were a blaze of baubles. Inside she watched a blond woman in a full-length mink coat examine one trinket after another as two fawning clerks waited on her, attempting to connect with one of her whims. The woman was probably as worried about gems as Emily was about food, Emily reflected. People would always worry about something. What she would give to worry about new clothes for Jessica. Those worries, she felt, would never come now. Suddenly the blond woman in the mink coat turned around to look at some diamonds in a case by the window. However, rather than look at the jewels, she stared directly at Emily. Why is she looking at me? Emily wondered, and then realized why. The blonde was none other than her old friend Cassie Laverne, staring at the image outside as if it were some apparition, trying to locate in the past whom the image conjured up. Leaving Cassie puzzling, Emily ducked away and ran down the street and sought shelter in Woolworth's five-and-ten. She didn't want Cassie to see her, not now, not like this.

Emily lingered for a while around the different counters —kitchenware, bathware, gardening. This is where she belonged, not Wanamaker's. Maybe she could even get a job here, she thought.

"My million-dollar baby," Cassie said triumphantly, coming up behind Emily, embracing her lost friend. "Emily!"

"Cassie!" Emily hugged her back. "Oh, have I missed you!"

"If you did, then you've got some nerve running away like that!"

"Do you really want to see me?"

"Bad enough to follow you down here. Emily!"

"You never got my letters, I guess."

"Lost letters." Cassie threw up her hands. "I've heard that one before."

"I did write. Really. But my letters . . ." Emily wasn't sure how to, or if she should, explain. "I guess when you didn't hear from me, you must have gotten mad."

"I was mad as hell. But I figure show people, easy come, easy go. Damn, I missed you, honey. And why the hell didn't you come to me if you needed help? That's what really hurt. I was your friend."

"You knew?"

"Of course. I found out when I got back from the road. That kinda gossip's too rich to keep covered up. I thought you were this innocent little sparrow, a step away from a virgin. And instead you were this hot number. You sure had me fooled."

"Cassie, it's not true. Not at all. I was framed." Emily spoke in a low voice, so the other shoppers, already curious about Cassie's mink, wouldn't overhear. "And I did write to you, but they threw away all my letters. I swear."

"Come home with me. Come right now. We got years

to catch up with." Cassie took Emily's hand and pulled her toward the door.

"Cassie." Emily stood back, admiring Cassie's hair, her makeup, her clothes, even her perfume that smelled of money. "You really made it. You look wonderful. You're rich. What were you in? I've been out of it so long, I have no idea what the shows were."

"This didn't come from Broadway, kid," Cassie said.

Cassie Laverne was a fallen Southern belle from New Orleans, blond, blue-eyed, fair, with a boyish figure that had become the ideal flapper look, the goal of fashionable women. Men adored Cassie. They were captivated by her Southern drawl, her easy laugh, her come-hither sexuality. The fact that she never said no also had something to do with it. Her real problem was that while she never said no, men never said yes, not when it mattered. Cassie was loved and left more than any woman Emily ever heard of. Yet it had never made Cassie hard, only more vulnerable, sweeter, funnier in an ironic way.

Cassie sometimes liked to affect the style of someone who was plantation born. She was, in a sense, but not in the main house. Her mother was a maid to one of the old Creole families with a sugar estate on the River Road along the Mississippi. Her father was a cane farmer who had abandoned her mother. Cassie grew up in the servants' quarters, in awe of the rich planters with their fine antiques and glorious memories of the antebellum mint-julep life. Cassie had been far too low in the still-enduring Southern caste system to even hope to marry up and out of her thrall of poverty. In New Orleans, her prospects were to become a waitress or a factory girl and the mother of ten Catholic children. So she left. New York was the land of opportunity. The stage was a democracy. Nobody cared who you were, where you came from. If you were good and if you were lucky, anything could happen. Cassie wasn't worried about the good, only the lucky. Two years ago, at twenty-seven, Cassie had told Emily she felt old. She was getting desperate. But now she seemed to have it all.

Cassie lived in a lovely apartment with a doorman on a tree-lined block on Seventy-fifth Street betwen Madison and Fifth. There were bay windows from which you could get a glimpse of Central Park. There were bright flowers, cheerful chintz sofas, and mirrors everywhere, especially in the bedroom, where Cassie slept in a vast canopied bed that, she said, reminded her of the master's quarters of the Louisiana plantation. After taking a cab back from Woolworth's and showing Emily around, Cassie poured sherry from a decanter and listened, with full sympathy, to Emily's story.

"It makes my skin crawl. That's the most horrible thing . . . What can I do?"

"Be my friend again," Emily said.

"That's easy."

"Now you must tell me about you and . . . all this." Emily looked around her at the nice furniture, breathed in the fragrance of the flowers. "Imagine, you and I sitting and sipping sherry in luxury." Emily was getting a little tipsy. It was the first alcohol she had drunk in years. "If you weren't in a hit show, what did you do, marry a millionaire who died?"

"Guess again." Cassie smiled naughtily.

"When I last saw you, you were struggling, living in that little room. How can you go from there to Fifth Avenue—"

"—in one wave of the mink. Neat trick, huh?"

"What unconscionable acts did you do? No. Don't even tell me," Emily joked with her friend.

"I became a hostess," Cassie said.

"A hostess?"

"In a speakeasy."

"Hostesses can't live like this."

"The ones at Texas Guinan's can. You can, too."

"Texas who?"

"Texas Guinan runs the greatest speakeasy in New York. It's like Rector's and Reisenweber's and Blackstone's used to be before Prohibition, but wilder. Everyone who goes there is either rich or famous or notorious or gorgeous or something, but nobody's dull. And everybody wants companionship. Look at this." Cassie went to a dresser drawer and showed Emily a jewelry case overflowing with sparkling, expensive keepsakes. "Nice, huh?"

"Cassie, what do you have to do for all this?" Emily asked.

"Be my sweet self." Cassie winked.

"What happened to Broadway?"

"Didn't work. Six years. I gave up. There are better ways, my friend, and I finally found one. I only have to work three nights a week. It's a cabaret, and I get to sing and dance, just like on Broadway, except this time I get discovered. All the time. And we play to a very select audience. Very!"

"What kind of people are they?"

"Men like I never thought I could meet. Not like the old days. Remember the fat sophomore from Rutgers with the thick glasses who didn't want to bring me to his fraternity party because he was embarrassed that I was too old? Well, those dog days are over, honey. These are the salad days. Now I get respect."

"What about proposals? I thought you wanted to get married."

"Me? I'm having too much fun."

"I see. These . . . men," Emily said, fingering one of Cassie's many trinkets, "they're very, *very* generous."

"I'm playing in a different league from the Elysium days. I was lucky to get a wilted flower from those tightwads. It's all who you meet. When I was a second-string showgirl, all I met were second-string losers. With Texas, it's all nobs and swells."

"Texas—what is it?" Emily asked.

"Texas Guinan's."

"Sounds like a rodeo."

"Texas Guinan's a person. More than a person. She's become a legend. But her place, in a way, *is* like a rodeo. It's the wildest party in New York."

"But these men. You meet them there, and . . . they ask you out. What if you don't want to . . . ?"

"I beg your pardon." Cassie feigned indignation. "What kind of girl do you think I am? I'm very hard to get, as you can well see," Cassie said, waving her hands, proud of her domicile. "These gentlemen are the crème de la crème, my dear"—Cassie faked a society accent—"but you don't have to go out on any dates with them. You ought to, but you don't have to. I mean, if Mr. Rockefeller meets you and falls madly in love, you have a perfect right to break his heart."

"Cassie, you make me laugh," Emily said, having fun, like old times.

"In all seriousness, if you want to, I'll send you to meet Texas. She'll love you. Start as a hostess. You can sing. You want to sing? You can sing there. It's better than selling dresses. And I promise you it's the best place to meet rich men I've ever seen."

"I'm not interested in rich men . . . or any men, for that matter."

"Emily, sweetie," Cassie said, pouring more sherry, "I know what you've been through. But face it, you're an ex-con. How else can an ex-con live like this? How else are you gonna pay that lawyer? You need money, honey."

"I need a job."

"This is a job. Come on, Emily, why don't you try it? Let's get rich together," Cassie said. "You deserve it."

30

Partially out of curiosity and partially out of desperation, Emily allowed Cassie to set up an interview with the legendary Texas Guinan.

Emily would never have noticed the brownstone on West Forty-fifth Street off Sixth Avenue if there hadn't been so many fancy automobiles parked out front. She spotted the place by two of the exiters—portly, prosperous drunks in black tie draped around chauffeurs in livery and caps coming down the steps. The chauffeurs somehow managed to angle their charges into the back seats of, respectively, a big Lincoln and an even bigger Daimler, adjust their caps, and drive away. A third besotted celebrant was escorted by a distaff farewell party. Three incredibly striking young women in very short spangled flapper outfits assisted a chauffeur and planted good-bye kisses on the reveler, tattooing his face with red lipstick marks, which somehow rendered the parting less traumatic. Knowing this indeed must be the place, Emily passed through these departing fun lovers into the town house.

The jazz band was playing "Toot, Toot, Tootsie, Goodbye" through the smoky haze as a farewell serenade to a white-bearded tippler who, had he been dressed in red, white, and blue instead of black and white, could have been a dead ringer for Uncle Sam. Three more short-skirted stunners in high heels surrounded the man, singing the song to him, picking up where the band was leaving off. The tempo of the instruments slowed to a halt. The black musicians, also in black tie, began packing up their instruments. It was seven A.M. Closing time, quiet time, and the only time when Texas Guinan would interview new applicants.

"Get that bum outta here," a booming cowhand's voice cut through the torpid party's end. The voice had that Southwest twang, rough and ready, but it was slightly too high to be a man's. "I don't give a pig's ass how many oil wells he's got. Get him outta here before your eggs get cold."

The chorines stopped singing. Two large bouncers picked up the man and conveyed him through the jungle of palms to the door.

Emily nervously walked past several tables where some of the most attractive women she had ever seen were sitting down to breakfast of champagne and scrambled eggs. The proprietor was sitting by herself at a table in the back of the room. "You must be Texas," Emily said.

"Well, I ain't Oklahoma." A full gilt moon rose above a gilt-paper river decorating a wall behind her. The tackiness of the place was part of its charm, a charm epitomized by Texas' greeting each of her guests with a boisterous "Hello, sucker!" Texas was in her mid-forties, as buxom as a Hellenic statue, with yellow—not blond, but yellow—hair to match the moon and palms, heavily mascaraed blue eyes which seemed almost black due to the dense lashes, and pale white skin that lived by moonlight. The overample Texas stood in sharp contrast to her showgirl charges, but her size gave her the authority requisite to reign over her night court, her Garden of Allah. Emily's first instinct was to dash out. She was way out of her league. These were glamour girls. Big-time good looks. "Don't look so shocked," Texas said, eating her eggs and caviar.

"I'm Cassie Laverne's friend. Emily Stanton."

Texas swigged some champagne. "Emily Stanton?" She considered the name, then smiled with recognition. Half the back of her mouth was gold. "Oh, yes. The little jailbird. Hi, honey, welcome to the big time. Sit down."

Emily sat, abashed by Texas' comment. She didn't want anyone to hear. Little jailbird.

"Don't be 'shamed, baby. Bedford's my kind of finishing school. Adds a little spice to your résumé."

"I'm not proud of it," Emily said in a low voice.

"Always be proud. I ain't 'shamed o' nothin', and I got plenty that normal folks might be 'shamed of. Hey, if I kept *customers* out of here 'cause of prison records, I wouldn't have enough business to pay for toilet paper. These days, to get the big money, you got to be a crook. The honest dollar died with Prohibition." Texas caught Emily's hungry eyes fixed on her breakfast plate. "You look like you need some chow."

"That does look good."

"Gloria," Texas called to a black maid in a black uniform, "get Miss Stanton here some bacon and eggs. 'Less you want caviar?"

"No. Bacon's fine."

"Pronto, Gloria." Texas pushed a fluted glass in front of Emily. "Champagne?"

"It's a little early."

"Early?" Texas laughed her hearty ranch laugh. "Hell, it's late, honey. We only see morning from the tail end. Cassie told me to hire you. Said you sing and dance real nice."

"I used to be pretty good."

"Don't give me that used-to-be. This ain't no history class."

"I was on Broadway before all—"

"Well, don't get any fancy notions here, and you won't be disappointed. This ain't no legitimate stage. Fact is, there ain't nothing legitimate about the place. That's why everybody likes it." Texas looked Emily up and down. "You've got a great face if you'd just smile."

Emily forced a smile.

"And you'd have a great shape if you held yourself up straight. Yeah," Texas said, sizing Emily up head to toe. "Yeah. With a little bit of work, you could be something. Yeah! I like it! Wanna be something?"

"Sure I do." Emily knew she had to be positive around this dynamo. Then she scanned the room, all the polished beauties, better-looking than any chorus line. "But do you really think I could fit in here?"

Texas didn't even answer. She had called the maid over for further instructions. "Gloria, you get me the beautician and the dressmaker, you know, Mrs. Spinelli. We've got an overhaul to do."

163

31

The jazz band played "Runnin' Wild." The hostesses in blinding silver lamé chemises, far above the knee, did the shimmy on the dance floor with a wide range of partners—pitchers from the Yankees, financiers from Wall Street, mob bosses from Mulberry Street, colonels from Kentucky, tool-and-die moguls from Ohio. Texas Guinan was putting them all through their paces. Who else could make a Belmont leapfrog, an Astor skip rope? At the tiny tables one party blurred into another, all into one big party, where the revelers ordered Pol Roger champagne at fifteen dollars an illegal bottle, Havana cigars at a dollar apiece, and Red Flannels, the house specialty of steak tartare on rye, for a dollar-seventy-five. One hostess did nothing but sell rag dolls for five dollars each. No man was a gentleman unless he bought his date one. Another hostess sold flowers. A real rose was two dollars. A paper carnation, gardenia, or magnolia went for a dollar. Again, every gentleman had to buy one.

"Are ya havin' a great time?" Texas Guinan loudly asked an Indiana pharmaceuticals manufacturer, for the whole room to hear.

"Why, yes."

"Ya sure?"

"Of course."

"Then add twenty bucks to his tab," Texas announced, and the club roared.

What most of the gentlemen had in common was money and an eye for pretty women. No one ever dropped less than fifty dollars a night at Guinan's. Some dropped much more. Whenever Al Capone came in from Chicago, he would organize soirees at Guinan's, where he left a hundred-dollar bill under each hostess's plate as a party favor. The bottom line was that these plutocrats from around the nation were making Mary Louise Cecilia Guinan, from Waco, Texas, a plutocrat herself. She had banked well over a million dollars on the strength, or rather weakness, of the Volstead Act outlawing liquor.

Texas had tried to make a career in films. At one point she was known as the female William S. Hart, but she wasn't known widely enough. Her failure in show business explained her empathy for her two dozen hostesses, most of whom shared her thwarted ambitions but weren't above using the speakeasy as a stepping-stone to being discovered. Texas was very cordial to "show people." She knew them. But to her, anybody could be a show person in her club. Men loved being on her stage, kicking up their heels, letting down their hair, raising hell until the sun came up.

There were eighty-eight theaters on Broadway in 1926. When they let out, the elite of these theatergoers knew that their night had only just begun. They headed straight to Forty-fifth Street, some with their wives or girlfriends, others, who were in the majority, unencumbered and looking for new friends. Texas' ability to throw a fabulous, exclusive party for her "friends" every night had made her richer than all the westerns could have. Texas was New York's undisputed Queen of the Night.

After working at the club for a week, Emily invited Alex to visit. "There's the police commissioner," she said, pointing out George Garrity, who looked like a banker and in fact had previously served as state superintendent of banking.

"But this place is illegal," Alex Foster said. "How can he be here?"

"Alex," Emily said. "Who's going to arrest him?"

"Look," Alex exclaimed. "There's Babe Ruth." The Yankee slugger was belting back straight whiskey, encouraged by four of the prettiest athletic fans Alex had ever seen. "Isn't that Douglas Fairbanks?"

"Yes. He's been here before. He seems to be a nice person."

"And, look, W. C. Fields. Jesus, Emily, I've never seen so many famous people."

"Aren't you glad you came?" she yelled over the jazzy din.

"The lady at the door wasn't," Alex shouted back. "Before you came and got me in, she told me to come back after I'd robbed a few banks."

"That's their idea of charm around here."

"Serve 'em, Emily," the bartender said, shoving out a tray of drinks.

"Make yourself at home," Emily told Alex, and carried the tray over to a table of men in tuxes.

Alex stood at the bar surrounded by other hostesses. The women, ranging in age from twenty to thirty, would serve drinks, flirt with the customers, dance with them or dance by themselves in energetically impromptu performances on the tiny raised stage opposite the bar. The girls had talent and liked to show it off.

Alex watched Emily. He couldn't believe how glamorous she had become. Her hair was bobbed, with a radiant sheen, and set off by a black beaded headband with a white rose in it. She was made up so well that the prison pallor, the gaunt look of Bedford, had been obliterated. In her black high heels and silk stockings and lamé dress, a showcase for her graceful figure and bathing-beauty legs, Emily was delectable, totally sexy.

Emily knew the men were ogling her. After all the terrible rejections, she had to admit she liked being noticed. She liked being a woman again. She liked the silk on her body, the perfume, the makeup highlighting her eyes and lips, the ritual of bathing and dressing. She was wearing all silk—silk stockings, silk panties, a silk brassiere.

"What does the underwear matter?" she had protested to Texas. There was something sinful about the lingerie. "No one sees it."

"It matters," Texas had shouted back. " 'Sides, I'm payin' for it. It makes you special. The wrappin's jest as important as the gift."

The men kept winking. No, being ogled, being appreciated, wasn't so bad, not after being dehumanized and brutalized for so long. Emily didn't hate herself for dressing to tempt, to excite, to charm. She needed the attention. She decided that she liked the job. She liked it very much.

At about one-thirty, there was a great commotion. The band broke into "Will You Love Me in December as You Do in May?" and in came the mayor of New York.

"Hello, sucker," Texas Guinan greeted him. She squeezed the tiny politician into her all-enveloping bosom. Extricating himself, he moved from table to table, working the room. Trailing in his wake was a pretty young woman with bobbed black hair.

"I didn't know Mrs. Walker was so cute," Alex said to Emily, who had returned to the bar to place another drink order. "You never see her."

"Neither does he," Emily said. "Two manhattans, one old-fashioned, and a cuba libre," she told the bartender.

"Huh?" Alex didn't understand what Emily meant.

"That's not his wife, silly. That's his mistress. Betty Compton. She's an actress."

"Only in New York would the mayor do this in public," Alex said.

Alex ordered a real Scotch on the rocks. Most speak-easies sold the most adulterated spirits, things that could make you blind, or worse, if you weren't careful. This was the best liquor he had drunk since Prohibition began.

Emily went to serve her tray of drinks, passing a round table where Cassie Clayton was in a group with three other blondes dressed in varying depths of décolletage, sitting with an intense man with impeccable English clothes, a diamond stickpin in his cravat, and a star sapphire on his finger. He was slightly balding and somewhat jowly and fleshy. He reminded Emily of a Turkish sultan, decadent, yet powerful. The three blondes were his, not Texas'. They weren't fine enough to work as hostesses. They lacked the spark and the beauty that Texas wanted. However, they seemed completely docile, completely servile to this master, and not exactly bored. They didn't seem intelligent enough to be bored, but totally without a single interest of their own other than pleasing this man.

"Emily . . ." Cassie pulled Emily over. "I want you to meet Arnold Rothstein."

"Hi," was all Emily could say. She wanted to gasp, but Guinan girls were never to gush over celebrities. She knew about Arnold Rothstein. Everyone knew. He was supposed to be one of the most powerful men in New

York City. Rothstein was Manhattan's gambling czar, as well as its "big fixer." He was known as Mr. Fixit, and was reputedly able to fix anything, including the 1919 World Series, on which he was said to have put up the money to persuade the Chicago White Sox to lose in Cincinnati, resulting in the Black Sox scandal. Although Emily didn't see him speak to Jimmy Walker—he, if not Walker, was too discreet for that— Rothstein was rumored to work hand in hand with Tammany, which, for the right percentage of Rothstein's illegal deals, would make sure its elected city officials would be looking the other way.

Rothstein looked straight at Emily with his compelling dark eyes. "Hello, Emily," he said. "Why don't you join us?"

Emily surveyed the table of blondes and shook her head politely. "I think you've got a full house."

"There's always room for the queen of hearts," Rothstein said in his deep, nasal, vaguely Brooklyn accent.

Emily had forgotten she was talking to one of the foremost card players in the city. Now that she rememberd, she shot back, "I'm not quite ready to show my hand." She smiled, turned, and went back to Alex at the bar.

"I like her," Rothstein noted to Cassie, and said no more.

"How do you say no to Arnold Rothstein?" Alex asked.

"No." Emily laughed. "It's fun, isn't it?"

"I'll say," Alex said.

Every few sets a hostess would get up and sing. Cassie Clayton sang "I'm Just Wild About Harry," improvising her own choruses, walking around the room, leaning on the tables, crooning personalized choruses to Babe-y, Arnie, Jimmy, and so on.

"Give the little lady a hand, gents," Texas Guinan rasped out afterward, and the gents stood and cheered.

Then when Emily least expected it, Texas stepped up to the microphone and said, "We have a lovely little lady who's just joined us. Why don't you give a big hand to Miss Emily Stanton."

Emily nearly dropped the tray of drinks she was carrying from the bar. "But . . . I'm er . . . not . . ." she tried to demur, but couldn't raise her voice high enough to be heard. Before she backed out completely, Alex took her arm and guided her into the spotlight.

"Break a leg," he told her, and gave her a give-'em-hell smile.

Emily tentatively stepped toward the stage. Texas reached out and pulled her up. As the eager gentlemen who had been eyeing Emily all night applauded, Texas asked Emily, "What ya want to do?"

Hide behind the bar, Emily thought. "Bye Bye, Blackbird," she said, and Texas relayed instructions to the bandleader, who struck up the tune.

Emily began slowly. She was shaking. Her heart was about to jump into her throat. She thought she was going to forget the words. She thought she was going to black out. She thought she was singing the wrong tune. She thought no one was listening. The men were busy with other girls.

But the men *were* listening. Emily gained strength with each line, and by the final chorus she was scanning the room, locking eyes with all the men, and knowing she had them, every one of them. They stopped flirting with the other hostesses. They stopped babbling about the stock market, the Yankees, the weather. For that moment, Emily was the boss. She was in control. For that moment, she felt like the biggest, most important star in the world. The audience, this powerful audience, was all hers.

"Give the little lady a big, big hand," Texas said, hugging Emily on the bandstand. "Yes. Give it to her."

Alex took Emily home at six o'clock. The day was just starting to break over Essex Street, this first-light glow of spring sun that would bring the city to its screaming, boisterous life. Now was the halfway time between light and darkness, the only time when the city was truly serene. The night city had closed. The day city had not yet opened. There were no shouting vendors. No roaring subway. No honking cars. The silence was almost pastoral, though there wasn't a tree or blade of grass anywhere in the concrete wasteland where Emily rented her room.

"Back to reality," Emily said, getting out of the rumbling taxicab, though the harshness of the reality didn't really hit her. She was high, both from the champagne she had drunk and from the reception her song had gotten. This was her coming-out, her back-to-life party. She wanted to keep dancing till she dropped. "It's like 'Cinderella.' "

"You'll always be a princess to me," Alex said, paying the driver. He was high, too. For once, he felt confident. He felt like the rich men in Guinan's. Besides, he was one better. He was with the prize they all wanted.

"You're sweet," Emily said.

"You were the star tonight. I'm so proud of you."

"Alex, I'm not worried about anything. I feel too good. Is something wrong with me?"

"Nothing is wrong with you."

Emily could see her breath. It was still cold. "Brr," she shivered. "Alex, why aren't you dressed more warmly?"

"Warm me up," Alex said, drawing Emily to him. First he hugged her. Then, unable to resist anymore, he kissed her, really kissed her, for the first time. Her lips melted into his. Alex lost himself for a moment. When he came to, he waved the cab away with one hand while holding Emily with the other.

"What did you do that for?" Emily said, pulling back as the cab rattled off down the cobblestones.

"I'm going to walk home. After I take you safely to your door."

"Alex, you're so . . ."

"Yes?" He smiled, putting his arm around her as they approached the door of the building.

"Well," Emily sighed, "it's been a great evening . . ."

"No good-byes till you're safely locked in your place. There're strange men in the neighborhood." Alex grinned, and they went inside.

They kissed again at the top of the stairs. The dank, dirty hallway didn't matter. Nor did the absence of a light bulb. The dark made it better. Emily backed off, opened her purse, and took out her key.

"Well . . . Alex. Good night . . . again."

He couldn't stop kissing her.

"Alex . . ." Emily smiled. She didn't want him to go, but didn't know how to say it without being too unladylike.

He took care of it. "You're not going to send me out into that cold, uncaring world without a nightcap." He grinned.

Emily grinned back, opened the door, and waved Alex in. She knew he was there to stay. He was a great friend. He was cute, charming, kind. He kissed wonderfully. He was crazy about her. For the moment, for Emily, too, the past was behind her. She wasn't worried. She wanted to be desired. "I wouldn't dream of it," Emily said, locking the door behind them.

32

Emily felt guilty about having gone to bed with Alex. She wanted to dismiss it, writing it off to alcohol, to impulse, to excessive euphoria over her successful singing performance at Guinan's. She enjoyed it at the moment, being kissed, being held, being loved by a man again. The next day, however, in the depths of her hangover, she hated herself for having given in to pleasure, and perhaps thereby leading Alex on, when there was so much unresolved pain in her life that had to be her first order of business. She wanted to be with her daughter. She wanted to clear her name. Those were her priorities.

Furthermore, she was furious at herself for having led Alex Foster on. He was her true friend, but she wasn't ready for what she knew he wanted. She knew she was going to have to hurt him, and shuddered at, and shrank from, facing the moment of doing it. She kept making lunch dates and excuses not to see him at night, to avoid the inevitable.

Emily worked at Guinan's five nights a week, and although tips were generous, she never made over sixty dollars a week. This was more than at Wanamaker's, but after living expenses, not enough to pay Hiram Hogan the thousand-dollar retainer he required. She calculated that it would take her over two years of scrimping to amass that sum. And that was just the retainer. She'd have to pay Hogan even more money later on. She had asked around about Hogan. Everyone said he was good, and he was honest. Besides, there weren't that many lawyers who were interested in cases like hers. But the money. "There are two kinds of justice," Hogan had told her. "Good justice and bad justice. I get good justice, but good justice costs money." He told her that her custody case was as hard as he'd ever seen, that it would take a lot of time, and that his time was very expensive.

"Please find it within you heart to help me," she said. Emily had entreated him to get started without the retainer.

"If I had a heart, it would have been broken into smithereens from what I see," Hogan had said, refusing in as nice a way as he was capable of. Law to him was a business, not a duty.

Emily, then, needed money, more money than she could possibly make at Guinan's. But where?

Emily had thought the tiny woman was a decorator. At least, that's what it said on the Tiffany embossed business card she had handed to Emily one night at the club. "Polly Adler, Interior Design. BU 8-6996."

"I don't have that kind of apartment," Emily said when the diminutive lady in red, barely four-ten, said, "You're very special, dollink," and pressed the card in her hand. She had seen her around the club once or twice. She had a Russian accent, an unruly mop of bleached brick-red hair, and the keen eyes of a horse trader. She was always with two or three very pretty girls a head taller and at least a decade younger than she. Men came by her table to kiss her hand. Emily initially thought she was an eccentric show-business impresario, but there were so many eccentrics at Guinan's, she hadn't bothered to keep track. "Call me," the woman urged, but Emily put the card aside. One day she came upon the card again and quickly figured out who Polly Adler really was. She and Cassie discussed the matter over sodas at Rumplemayer's.

"Gee, Cassie. I knew there was no other way for you to make the money you did. I just couldn't face it," Emily said.

"I couldn't face it either. That's why I didn't ask you to live with me. I didn't know quite how to come out and say it. If I had, knowing what you went through, you probably would have run off in the opposite direction. And since two years was too long not to see you, I said nothing."

"Interior designer," Emily laughed, but sadly. "I guess she is, of a sort. Oh, Cassie, poor Cassie."

"Not poor, honey." Cassie stayed light.

"I wanted to believe that you had rich boyfriends who lavished you with presents."

"That's only in the movies."

"I wanted to believe the movies. It's so much easier. Dammit," Emily said.

"It's all acting," Cassie explained. "It's a natural progression from Broadway. You're just performing on a . . . er . . . more intimate stage. You get paid a whole lot more and you never get rejected. I like that part, the no rejections."

"Polly Adler, the biggest madam in New York," Emily said. "And she was trying to recruit me, too."

"Be flattered. She only wants what she considers the very cream of Texas' girls. Guinan's is kind of a showcase for us. The men see us there, then they call Polly."

"What made *you* start?"

"I wasn't making it on Broadway. I was getting old. Nobody was rushing me to the altar. Now I have money. I feel secure. And I'm going out with men I'd never have met otherwise."

"But for what?" Emily said. "To let them"—she paused—"use you."

"I'd go out with them for nothing. Just for fun. I'm getting paid to do what I'd do for free. You know I'm an incurable romantic."

"Maybe just incurable." The two women laughed. Emily realized she shouldn't get upset. She shouldn't be moralistic. If Cassie wanted to do it, that was her decision. But the revelation that her best friend was a prostitute made Emily very uncomfortable.

"Honey, you act like you thought you were walking into a fairy-tale cottage that turned out to be a haunted house," Cassie said.

"Cassie, I'm sorry. I don't mean to seem like such a prude. I just have these terrible images of . . . You see, I worry about you being used."

174

"Don't you worry your head, baby," Cassie assured Emily in a strong voice. "I'm using *them*. I'm building my own security. I have *their* money in *my* bank. Talk about used. You were married. *Married!* And look what happened to you."

"I know," Emily said. "I know." Then she called the waiter over, deciding what she really needed right now was another soda. Any bigger decisions than that were impossible to contemplate.

33

Emily waited on the school grounds at Miss Draper's for the recess bell to ring. It was her fourth surprise visit to Jessica, and she couldn't wait for her daughter to see her. She was wearing all her makeup, a new white wool suit, and a frilly gray blouse. She felt very country-clubby today. She felt like she belonged out here with the society women in the hunt country. She was dressed every inch the sophisticated lady. For the first time, she wasn't ashamed of herself anymore, and she knew that Jessica wouldn't be ashamed to tell her schoolmates this was her mother, her *real* mother. She could hold her own with Isabelle today. She could finally face Warren. She was even thinking that rather than go through a legal battle with him, perhaps she should just go to see him and talk, like old times, and tell him what had happened to her. Maybe he could help in clearing her name. He had connections in Tammany. Then she thought about Jessica and realized that Warren and Isabelle would never give her up, not now. Still, she felt awkward about the idea of being totally estranged from the father of her child, and wished there was a way to have some sort of dialogue.

Emily had a gift for Jessica, a beautiful, expensive Clara Bow doll she had found at a store on Madison Avenue. It was early May, and the trees were blooming, that rush of new green that broke the long winter monotony of gray and generated thoughts of boat rides and balmy strolls, and yellow butterflies, and lazy picnics in the grass, all the wonderful summer things, moments Emily was looking forward to sharing with her daughter.

"I'm sorry," a shrill female voice shattered Emily's daydreams, "but I must ask you to leave the school grounds."

Emily turned to see a tall, prissy matron in her fifties with bifocals hanging around her neck from a chain. Very authoritarian, she reminded Emily of the librarians back in her elementary school in Joliet, who would never let you even whisper or have the slightest fun exclaiming at the pictures, giggling at the passages, whispering secrets.

"I've come to see my daughter. I hope you don't mind." Emily tried to be ultracordial. "I'm Emily Stantion, Jes—"

"I know exactly who you are and I do mind," the woman said in a clipped, forbidding voice. "I'm the headmistress and I've been instructed by Jessica's parents not to let you see her."

"I *am* her parent."

"I *know* who you are, Miss Stanton, and I also know you have no legal visitation rights."

"I have a moral right to see her. She's my daughter."

"Miss Stanton, you have no right to talk about anything moral. Stop meddling in Jessica's life. It's very bad for the girl. You've caused enough trauma for her already. Now, leave her alone."

"That's not true," Emily said, angered. "She wants to see her mother."

"You're no mother," the headmistress growled. "This is private property. Don't come here again. Ever!" She turned on the heel of her brogues and walked back to the gingerbread schoolhouse.

Emily, furious, stamped toward the door. She would go in and tell that woman something. She didn't want her daughter entrusted with someone so narrow, so unkind, so dictatorial. And Warren. She would have to face him now. Surely he would understand how unfair this was. He would want to work something out. As Emily turned the knob on the door, a large hand came down on hers.

"The lady asked you to leave," the brawny man said. Emily recognized Mac, one of Warren's plant foremen, now in cheap sharkskin rather than overalls. She was

177

relieved to see him. He had always been so nice to her, moving furniture, carrying sacks of groceries. She used to feed him milk and cookies.

"Mac." She smiled. "Don't you remember me? I'm Emily. Mrs. Matthews. Mac, it's good to see you."

There was a moment of recognition. Mac seemed to be smiling but his mouth contorted into a sneer of non-acknowledgment. He and his partner, the same men who had beaten up Alex Foster years before, had been sitting vigil here on and off for two weeks waiting for Emily. They had their instructions from Warren. There was no time for nostalgia. "The lady asked you to leave," he repeated, squeezing her hand.

"Mac, it's me. You've got to remember."

"Do what da lady said," Yuri, the other man, a broad-beamed Serb with a Mongol countenance, said. "Move it. Now!" Yuri grabbed Emily and began dragging her away from the door.

"Leave me alone," Emily yelled. "Mac, please. Please. You were my friend." Mac joined Yuri in grabbing her and dragging her off the school grounds. "Stop it. Stop it." Emily struggled. She dug her daintily painted red nails into Yuri to break loose.

"Ya little bitch!" Yuri snarled, and struck her across the face with his left hand. There were three rings on his fingers. As she crumpled to the ground, she could sense the warm, wet blood dripping down her nose and lips, onto her new white suit. Her eyes blurred, she tried to get up. "Mac," she begged for mercy. But there was no mercy, and Yuri had hit Emily so hard that she blacked out.

In the scuffle, Jessica's gift box had torn open. Yuri saw the doll and crushed it with his foot. Jessica would never see her gift. Only the head with its bobbed hair remained intact. Yuri put it in his coat pocket as something to juggle. They picked up Emily, covered with blood and grass and soil, and put her into a waiting taxi, paid the grateful driver twenty dollars, and told him to deliver her back to New York, no stops. When Emily came to, near Newark, her first consciousness was an epiphany that seared and burned far more than her cuts and bruises. Could Alice at Bedford have been right?

Looking out at the brown factories, and the Wall Street towers across the Hudson, and the Statue of Liberty beckoning boldly in the bay, Emily realized that it could have been Warren, after all. The man who had once loved her might also be the man who had destroyed her life.

34

"We could file assault charges," Hiram Hogan said.

"I want more than that," Emily told him. She had tried to cover her injuries with makeup, but the black eye and the swellings were impossible to hide.

"Don't jump to such wild conclusions. Just because your husband had you beaten up doesn't mean he had you framed."

"Why not?"

"Miss Stanton, you had no legal right to see your daughter. Now, your husband had no legal right to have you beaten up, either, but it's not clear these men were working as his agents, or for the school. And you were technically trespassing on the school grounds."

"That's outrageous."

"That's the law."

"You mean I can't go back?" Emily was as frustrated as she was battered.

"Not if you don't want to get thrown back in jail. The school can get a restraining order against you. They probably will."

"This is so unbelievable. Not to let me see my daughter. It's evil."

"That's their right. Put yourself in his wife's place. You wouldn't want you around either. It's hard enough to raise a kid."

"She doesn't raise her. Her maids do."

"Please, Miss Stanton. What this all amounts to is your former husband doesn't want his daughter's life disrupted any more than it has been. If he believes what the court believed about you, he has no reason to want you around. He's being a protective parent."

"Disrupted? What about my life? What about taking my daughter away from her natural mother?"

"Whatever was done, at least on the face of it, was done strictly by the book. If you want to see your daughter, if you want to do anything, you've *got* to go through the proper legal channels. New York may be corrupt, but vigilantes belong in the Wild West, Miss Stanton."

"*Want* to see her? I've *got* to see her. Do whatever you have to do. Please, Mr. Hogan. You're a lawyer. Help me."

"You remember our previous discussions?" Hogan asked.

"Yes, yes, the money," Emily said. The cursed money. "I promise I'll get it for you somehow soon. I promise. Can't we get started now? Please."

Hogan shook his head adamantly. All the black eyes in the world were not about to move him. Emily only hoped he would show Warren as little mercy once he got started. "If I've learned one thing from this business," Hogan said, "it's never to work for promises. If you expect nothing, you're never disappointed."

Emily and Alex had gone out to Coney Island, riding all the way under Brooklyn on the D train, jammed with pale straphangers flocking like lemmings to the beach, the first day of the year it was warm enough to go swimming. When the subway emerged from the ground and became an elevated and the blue ocean and silver strand and Ferris wheels came into sight through the soot-stained windows, the riders gasped and cheered. Winter was over.

Although it was only May, Coney Island that Saturday afternoon was as gay and alive as the Fourth of July. No one was alone. There were families. There were lovers. Everyone seemed happy. Alex and Emily rode the roller coaster. They ate saltwater taffy and hot dogs with mustard and sauerkraut at Nathan's. They took off their shoes and went for a long walk, inhaling the clean salt air as the gentle surf lapped at their bare feet. They held hands and Emily tried to be happy, but she didn't feel it. Being surrounded by happiness and mothers with their daughters and people with real jobs and real security, people she couldn't imagine having the problems she had, made her jealous and uneasy. Alex won a fat teddy bear for Jessica by knocking down milk bottles at a boardwalk game of skill. Alex knew about the schoolyard incident and had suggested this outing to help Emily put it behind her. Alex wanted so much for her to be happy. He was having his dream, being with this gorgeous, lovely woman, and he didn't want to wake up. His mood was heightened by the old Italian organ grinder playing "Sorrento" while his little monkey in his jockey outfit held out a cup for donations. Alex gave him a penny. The monkey bowed.

Later, Alex and Emily spread their blanket out on the sand far in front of the boardwalk to watch the sunset. They had a quiet spot. No one was around them. It was the first time Alex had been alone with Emily since the night they had spent together. He couldn't help himself from getting close to her and kissing her.

"Alex, not here," Emily resisted.

"That's what beaches are for," he said, wrapping their other blanket around them, holding her tight, kissing her again. For a moment she gave in. She knew she wasn't in love with Alex. She couldn't be in love with anyone. Not now. But she gave in anyway, letting him kiss her, explore her body, grow excited by her. As she gave in, she pretended that this wasn't Alex at all but rather a complete stranger, and she tried to imagine what it would be like for a stranger to be intimate with her in this way. She gently withdrew from Alex's heated embrace. "That was nice," she whispered to him, trying to be as kind as possible.

"Yes. But don't stop," Alex sighed, and reached out for her again.

"Not out here," Emily said, sitting up and distancing herself.

"Emily . . ." Alex looked affectionately at her. "I don't know how to say this, but you're the best, bravest, nicest person I've ever met . . . the only person I could ever imagine spending the rest of my life with. I love you, Emily." He kissed her again.

"I love you, too," Emily said after the kiss. She stroked his cheek tenderly, straightened his windblown hair. "But not that way." His words of affection stirred up the worst guilt in Emily. Best, bravest, nicest. These were superlatives she didn't believe she deserved, not with what she was thinking about. She was thinking about money. She was thinking about Polly Adler. "Not that way," she repeated.

"But . . . but . . . that night . . ."

"That was . . . impulsive. It was . . . was . . . nice, it was . . . great," Emily said, searching for words not to hurt him, and she hated herself for it. How often in life does someone who is really this good a person propose to you? How she cursed the timing! "But I didn't want to set up any expectations . . . I guess, maybe, we shouldn't have . . . Alex, please understand. I'm not ready for anything like this. I'm not fit to be your girlfriend. I'm not fit for anything."

"Don't be crazy. I love you, Emily." Alex persisted. "Let me make you happy."

"I can't be happy. Not now. Alex, you're my friend, and I love you dearly, but right now my happiness doesn't matter. The only thing, really, that would make me happy is to get Jessica back. I've got to do that."

"We could make a home for her."

"I'll never get to that point. Not unless I can earn enough money to hire this lawyer."

"I can chip in . . ."

"It's not enough. You're struggling to make ends meet just like I am."

"If I were rich, would it be different?"

Emily didn't want to say that it might. Didn't that negate the whole idea of love? So cold-blooded, so practical. She wasn't like that, though now perhaps she had to be, in order to survive. Besides, Alex was somehow like a boy with a schoolboy crush. Being with Alex was great fun, but their night together notwithstanding, it was not the sweep-you-off-your-feet, romantic, bowled-over, incomprehensible passion that Emily had come to equate

with true love. She had never known it, not even with
Warren. Maybe it was only in movies, novels. Odd thing,
the man who had come closest—Emily wanted to incinerate the very idea—was Michael McNaughton. No, Alex
was right in many ways. But he was wrong for her. And
above all, the time was wrong.

"Alex, I don't think I'll *ever* get involved again. It's
not you, it's me." She took his hand. She saw he was
almost crying. "Don't get so wound up over me. I'm a
bad risk. I don't want to hurt you. Never."

"I can't keep myself from being wound up. You're all I
ever think about."

"I'm a mess now. I can't handle anything. I just can't
be in love. Not the way you want it. I just can't. Please
try to understand."

She knew he couldn't understand. When you're in
love, you can't. Alex was so crushed, he couldn't even
look straight at Emily. He stared out at the tiny waves
rippling onshore. The organ grinder on the boardwalk
cranked up "I Wonder Who's Kissing Her Now." The
sun had begun its descent. The dying day turned a melan-
choly, deepening purple. The roller coaster roared in the
distance. The Ferris wheel's colored lights began to twin-
kle. Yet the amusement park held no joy. In her own
way, Emily was far sadder than Alex was. Making love
with him had raised the ante of a game that she shouldn't
have been playing. She could see by the way he stared
out to sea that he couldn't come back, that their relationship would never be the same, not when he'd opened his
heart and been turned down. The reasons didn't matter.
Emily had lost her friend.

"I haven't seen Alex around for a while," Cassie said
to Emily at the bar one night at Guinan's a week after
the outing at the beach.

"Two martinis and two orange blossoms," Emily ordered from the bartender. "We're not seeing each other
anymore."

"It was nice having a little of that college cheer around,"
Cassie said. "Was his father anybody?"

Emily shook her head.

"How did he get to Yale?"

"Scholarship."

"Then don't worry about it," Cassie said, cold-bloodedly mercenary, but always in the most lighthearted way. She was what she was, and Emily couldn't dislike her, even if she tried.

"He was so sweet. I wish . . ."

"A mere child. And a poor child. You need a man, my dear. A very rich man."

That night Emily did dance with a rich man. He was, however, not interested in giving her his money, but rather in investing hers. James "Wiz" Radlow was of average height and build and had a pleasant face that would have looked boyish had not his curly brown hair begun to thin out on top. But Radlow's assets were not in his looks but in his supreme self-confidence. He was divorced and the girls at Guinan's considered him a catch. "Wiz" was short for "Wizard." The Wizard of Wall Street, he called himself, with more moves than a chess champion. He saw himself as a future Harriman or Rockefeller. He drove in a British-racing-green Rolls-Royce, dressed in Savile Row tweeds and Oxford scarves, and spoke very fast and very sure in a New York vernacular that sounded to most people like the King's English. His firm, Radlow Securities International, Limited, was going to be up there with the giants soon, he would tell the hostesses, up there with Morgan, with Brown Brothers, with the Huttons. When the girls asked him what he actually did, he simply said, "I make people rich." He was dazzling. His self-assurance made him sexy, and he was a great dancer. But he wasn't at all interested in Emily. Only money.

"Give me your money," he told her. "I'll make you ten times your investment."

"My money?" Emily laughed. "You've got the wrong girl."

"I've got the right girl," Radlow said, leading her into a smooth fox-trot. "Texas' women are highly touted for their initiative." He gave her a knowing wink. "Ten times your investment. I guarantee."

"Unless your math's better than mine, ten times nothing is nothing."

"My math's better than anybody's, so you give me your money and I'll do magic tricks with it."

"Have you ever loved a poor girl?" Emily flirted with him.

"Never," he said without hesitating, and spun her around the room. She was living in a world of money, money, money. All that mattered was money, and she had none, and no great prospects. The world was dancing by. Her daughter was out of her hands. As she spun around the floor, she saw the faces of several Tammany politicians, which, because of an article she had just read in the *Journal American*, had now become death masks to her.

It was a small piece about an honors ceremony at the Tammany Wigwam. Five policemen had been decorated by sachem Charles Sullivan for "meritorious service." One of the names was that of Michael McNaughton. She read the tiny blurb a dozen times. It had never occurred to her that Michael McNaughton could have had anything to do with Tammany Hall. She thought he was just an officer on the take. Perhaps the police commissioner was a Tammany man, but not Officer McNaughton.

Emily knew that being *inside* the Hall was something very, very special, a kind of political blood brotherhood that would create a *de facto* relationship between Warren and McNaughton. Emily remembered quite well the blind loyalty Warren held for Tammany and its braves. She was sure that, for McNaughton, the loyalty was reciprocal. McNaughton's being a Tammany man, in Emily's mind, vastly increased the likelihood that he and Warren, and possibly other Tammany men, had colluded to frame her. She made an excited call to Hiram Hogan, who was unimpressed by her discovery.

"All the top vice cops are Tammany men," Hogan said over the phone. "So what?"

"Warren, my husband, was, still is, I'm sure, very big in Tammany. There must be a connection between him and McNaughton."

"Miss Stanton, I have a very sweet dentist who's a big man in Tammany Hall. Do you think he was in on it, too?"

"But my husband and McNaughton. It's one more thing."

"The police force is Tammany. The courts are Tammany. New York is Tammany. What's the big surprise? Let's try to lay off the conspiracy theories and concentrate on the custody thing. I don't mean to be hard on you, but I want you to be realistic."

"I'm sorry. It seemed so . . . so . . . like they may have really teamed up. Through the Hall."

"Anything else, Miss Stanton?" Hogan droned impatiently.

"I'm working on the retainer."

"I hope so, Miss Stanton," he said. The line went dead.

Emily's mind began working overtime. Since the incident at Miss Draper's, when she began to suspect that Warren could be her enemy, she had spent long hours reconstructing his life, remembering how it revolved around Tammany Hall. "It's the way we do business," she recalled Warren cutting her off when she asked about why he had given a kickback to Subway Commissioner McCarey. "The way we do business." She had more than a slight inkling now that Tammany Hall— which controlled the courts, the lawyers, the police— might have had something to do with what happened to her. Every time she saw a judge, a sheriff, a senator, a city official florid and drunk and wenching at Guinan's, every time she saw Mayor Walker with his mistress, every time she heard about Arnold Rothstein's illegal deals, or Cassie's illegal dates, or every time she sold an illegal drink, Emily was reminded of what a terminally corrupt city New York was. The law was made to be flouted. The heroes, the legends of the town, were criminals. In this atmosphere of decay and license, a man like Michael McNaughton had to thrive. Just the way a man like Warren Matthews, who might have conspired to frame and ruin her so he could get Jessica, marry his socialite, and live in his little England, would also thrive. Emily had to have money to fight these forces. She could not do it on moral indignation alone.

She wanted to strike back, but she knew she would first have to take the dreaded, drastic step that she had been considering ever since that day on the sand with Alex Foster.

35

The tasteful limestone town house was on a steep block of Ninety-third Street between Park and Lexington, near where Emily used to live with Warren. The apartment monoliths ruled Park Avenue. The side streets were human scale, a reminder of the nineteenth century. Down the block was the huge Ruppert Brewery, shuttered by the Prohibition laws. The owner, Colonel Jacob Ruppert, was concentrating his energies on his baseball team, the Yankees. Farther down was the East River, with its busy traffic of tankers and tugs.

Emily loved the neighborhood. Ninety-third was a charming, homey block, with playful children on their summer holidays and their lawyer and banker parents getting ready to evacuate the increasingly stuffy city and its upcoming dog days for the coolness of Long Island, Maine, the Berkshires. Emily could have been one of them. She had been. How easy it was to be a Park Avenue housewife. Then her ambitions got in the way.

And now she was back, not to go to a meeting of the Junior League or the Daughters of the American Revolution or a charity function with the other East Side wives. She was back to visit the neighbor no one, save the most well-connected husbands, knew about, the best-kept secret on the East Side. Emily was going to see Polly Adler.

Ringing the bell, Emily was nervously perspiring as she was received by a black butler in a green-striped tunic. The downstairs was all black and white marble, elegantly simple, but generally more lavish than the other town houses. The butler led her up in a small elevator to

Polly's office, which, with its vast mahogany desk, piles of ledgers, and prints of old New York, could have been, except for its crimson walls, that of a senior brokerage partner on Wall Street. Emily looked out a small window to the room below, which also had a distinctly masculine cast. The remarkable living room was nearly empty this quiet afternoon. It looked like a proper men's club, with its moose heads, stuffed swordfish, and other hunting and game-fishing memorabilia, its deep leather chairs, its backgammon tables, its copies of *Country Life* and the *Wall Street Journal* and the *Harvard Alumni Monthly* lying about. What set the scene apart from a club like the Racquet and Tennis, however, was what Emily saw at the other end, the dark end by the empty fireplace. Two banker types were playing cards with two stunning women in full makeup but wearing only the flimsiest diaphanous nightgowns. One of the bankers lost, or won, as the case may have been. He laid down his cards. The woman opposite him stood up, took his hand, and led him up a grand white marble staircase with a crimson velvet runner, a stairway to paradise, judging from the anticipatory smile on the banker's face.

"They can't see you," Polly Adler said. "The glass is only one-way." With her fright wig of dyed hair, her matching nails, all matching the walls, her incongruously sedate Chanel suit, the tiny, thirtyish madam was an uneasy amalgam of the stately and the grotesque. The dark, slightly slanted eyes had a satanic leer. That this was her entrance to hell ran through Emily's mind as she lit a rare cigarette, both to seem more sophisticated and to calm down. Polly ascended a platform to the chair behind her desk. "I'm glad you came, dollink," she said, in the accent of her native Russia.

"I'm not so sure." Emily smiled politely.

"They're in from Detroit." Polly waved out the window.

"Car manufacturers?"

"Bankers who lend money to the car manufacturers."

"I thought they were bankers."

"Bankers, brokers, who can tell them apart? A banker from Michigan, a broker from New York. They're all alike. They all want the same thing."

"Sex."

"That's right, dollink. You're a smart girl. I can tell."

"Not smart enough. This all shocks me."

"What?"

"The whole thing. These men, these women, what goes on here. I guess you can take the girl out of Catholic school, but you can't take the Catholic school out of the girl."

"I got lotsa Catholic girls work for me. I like Catholic girls. Good girls. High moral standards. Don't you laugh. What I mean is, they don't lie. They don't steal. They know they have to answer to a higher source."

"Miss Adler . . ."

"Polly."

"Polly. You know, Polly, I was framed as a . . . prostitute."

"I know, dollink," Polly said, her red-nailed fingers paging through a ledger. "Cassie told me all about you."

"When Cassie told me that she did this, I thought that was one of the worst things I ever heard. And now, just a couple of months later, I'm here myself. When I told her I was coming to see you she joked that my reputation was already ruined anyway, so what'd I have to lose. And I said, my dignity. Or at least whatever is left of it."

"There's no dignity in being broke, dollink," Polly said.

"But I don't want to do this. I *have* to do this to earn money for a lawyer to try to get me custody of my little girl. That's the only reason I'm here. I'm stuck. I can't make enough money any other way, Polly. What worries me is, if I ever get caught, then I'd really be ruined. I'd never get my daughter back."

Polly gazed at Emily with her trader's eyes. "You won't get caught. I'll bet my life on that."

Emily looked back out into the grand parlor. Another of the beauties in a gossamer negligee was leading the second banker upstairs. "You'd never have to do that," Polly said. "You're strictly dates, dollink. It'll be first cabin for you."

"What am I doing?" she blurted out. "Polly, this isn't me."

"What is you, dollink? You tell me."

"I don't know . . . I just want to get my little girl back and go onstage and be an actress again."

"Miracles can happen. It can happen. But you have to work. We all have to work for what we want."

Work. Emily thought of the "work" that lay ahead of her. Here was the ultimate irony for Emily. She had been *framed* as a prostitute and now she was *becoming* a prostitute to try to undo the terrible damage done to her *because* she was framed as one. Would more damage be done, she wondered, or would she finally begin to turn the tide? In any event, she was making a decision and taking charge of her life. She prayed it was the right one.

"You're beautiful, and I mean it," Polly raved over Emily. "Beautiful. Look at those bones. Look at that skin, those legs, those fingers. Those fingers were born to wear diamonds." Emily laughed. Polly went on. "And you've got talent. I saw you at the club. You can sing. You've got charm. You've got everything but luck, dollink."

"That's for sure."

"Emily, I tell you. I'm not running a whorehouse. I'm running a dating service. The most expensive dating service in the world. I've been to Paris. I've been to Shanghai. I've been to Tokyo. Nobody's got what I got. I got the best. The best girls, the best men. Gentlemen, let me say. I deal with gentlemen, Emily, gentlemen who can make you rich the way you deserve to be."

"I despise myself for doing this," Emily said, looking for a way out she knew now she couldn't take.

"Don't think so much about yourself. It's not healthy. Let me ask you"—Polly pointed her finger at Emily—"a much more important question."

"What's that?"

"Do you despise men?" Polly looked hard at her.

Emily pondered the question a long time. She now despised Warren. She despised McNaughton. Maybe she really despised herself, and the plight she was in. Maybe she rejected Alex because she was protecting him from herself. On the other hand, she was attracted to men. She had romantic notions. Maybe she just didn't know. "I'm not sure," she told Polly, as honest as she could be.

Polly smiled, the first smile Emily had seen on her. "Then there's hope, dollink. There's hope."

36

The first date Polly Adler arranged for Emily was with Arnold Rothstein. The gambler had been asking Polly about Emily ever since he spotted her at Guinan's. Because Rothstein was Polly's most favored client, the moment Emily became "available," as Polly put it, Rothstein was the first man Polly called. Although Rothstein could have called Emily directly, he didn't. He was married. Moreover, he was too insistent on total control with his women. Thus he always went through Polly. That was how he had met Cassie, whom he had seen several times. That was how he had met all his mistresses. Rothstein was one gambler who wasn't interested in games of chance where his physical desires were concerned.

Emily tried on four different sets of Cassie's brassieres and panties and six different slips before Cassie decided she was right for A.R., as she referred to Rothstein. And that was only the lingerie. They went through half the dresses in Cassie's packed closets before coming up with something that would work, a sporty pale lavender frock, that Cassie had paid seventy dollars for at Bergdorf's.

"Isn't this a little demure?" Emily hesitated.

"He likes demure," Cassie said, patting Shalimar perfume behind Emily's ears. "You're going to the races. It's just right. Besides, he'll be that much more surprised when he sees what you have on underneath."

"Don't say that." Emily shivered.

"What?"

"I was almost feeling like I was dressing up for a regular date. I hate to feel like a call girl."

"Come on, honey. This is your first date with a famous man. Look at it as your coming-out party. How many women get to go out with Mr. Big?"

"How many would want to?"

"Every one of them," Cassie said, holding a purple scarf up to Emily's outfit and discarding it. "Too flashy."

"How does his wife put up with it?"

"I'm sure she has fringe benefits. Think of what she can buy." Cassie selected a slate-gray scarf. "I believe this is it."

Emily looked at herself in the long mirror. Images of being defiled by a savage Mongol warrior, fangs flashing, a bloody scythe held to her throat, crossed her mind. "I feel like a sacrificial lamb being readied for the slaughter. A fatted calf."

"You and your images. You should be a poet. Now, do we like these shoes?" Cassie said, looking at Emily's purple pumps. "Or should we go with an open toe? Your toenails are nice. He likes feet."

"What does he make you do?" Emily ventured, asking the dreaded question.

"He's very conventional. Nothing outrageous, like hanging you from gallows or coating you in oil. Not with me at least." Cassie grinned.

"I can't do it," Emily said.

"He's like any other man. You're not a virgin."

"I feel like one. I'm so nervous."

"Where's the old Emily?" Cassie chided her. "When you were sixteen, you were daring. You weren't afraid of anything. Look what you did, ran away to New York, not knowing a soul. If you can do that, you can do anything."

"That was a long time ago."

"Not that long. Come on. You were the most resourceful girl I ever met. Now you're a little fraidy cat. Christ, you went to *jail*. You're supposed to be tough."

"It's all been knocked out of me, Cassie."

"You've got it. Just dig deep. Think about how sexy you are."

"Me?"

"Yeah, you. Don't be fishing for compliments, you hot little number."

Emily laughed. "How am I going to get through this? Tell me."

"By thinking of all the things A.R. might be able to do for you?"

"Like what?"

"Like straighten out your conviction."

"What do you mean, Cassie?"

"A.R. is very tight with Tammany Hall. He could get to the bottom of the whole McNaughton thing with one word to Walker."

"Why should he do that? I'm nothing but an expensive call girl for him."

"Don't sell yourself so short. If he liked you . . ."

"He might see me again. What a treat," Emily groaned.

"But if he liked you a *lot*, he might do something else. And if he didn't like you, at least you'd have some money to show for it all."

"The whole thing is horrible. How do I do this?"

"Emily, you always complained how mean your father was, that he didn't want you to have any glamour, that he thought you should marry some tractor salesman from Peoria. And you ran away to New York because you wanted to have a glamorous life. So now you've got it. You're going out on the town with one of the richest and most powerful men in this glamorous city, baby. You're dressed up in gorgeous clothes. You look gorgeous. You got your wish."

"It's one night. And it's a job."

"Only in your mind. It's a *date*. It's an introduction. The rest is up to you. Listen, I told you, Polly told you, one of her rules, you absolutely don't have to go to bed if you don't like him." Cassie lifted up Emily's skirt to the top of her rolled silk stockings. "Let's change these garters to match the scarf. I have this thing about colors."

Arnold Rothstein was the toast of Aqueduct Raceway. So many people knew him, waved, clamored to shake his hand, and he proudly introduced Emily to every one of them. She didn't feel like Rothstein's whore. She felt like his queen. He looked rather natty in his double-breasted navy blazer, blue bow tie, gray trousers, and white shoes, but behind the jaunty appearance was a seething, damned-up power. The supplicants who did everything but kiss his large, almost papal ring knew what Rothstein could do. No one dared cross this man. Of course, the horses didn't know who he was, and despite his fame as a gambler, every one of the horses he bet on lost— Pride's Crossing, Miss Liberty, No Bananas, Cheerio, Cannonball. Rothstein didn't say much to Emily, other than to smile politely, compliment her on her looks. The track was too noisy to talk. His "aide," Birnbaum, a Neanderthal in pinstripes, with a bulge on the side where his holster was, would place Rothstein's bets, return, and sit behind him and Emily in their box. In addition to Birnbaum, Rothstein's burly chauffeur, Greenblatt, stood a constant vigil outside the box.

"Can't be too careful," Rothstein said. "Lots of nuts out there."

After a few more losses, Rothstein folded his hand. "You know, there are a lot more horses asses at a racetrack than there are horses," he quipped good-naturedly.

From Emily's calculations, he had lost thousands, but he didn't complain, never showed any temper. He had a huge roll, from which he kept peeling off the smallest denomination he had—a hundred. "I think it's time to go to dinner," he said.

"I hope I'm not a bad-luck charm," Emily said.

"Horses come and go," Rothstein said. "But I'm the luckiest man in town." Emily wasn't sure he meant her, or in general. She didn't ask. They were chauffeured by Greenblatt in a bulletproof car to Gage and Tollner in Brooklyn, where they ate lobster by gaslight, served by courtly black Southern waiters who called him "Massa Rosseen" and made Emily feel like royalty.

At dinner, Rothstein said nothing about his business ventures. Polly had cautioned Emily not to ask, and she didn't. Polly also told her not to tell Rothstein about her own personal troubles. "No drama," was Polly's rule. "These men are paying not to have any problems. They got their own, dollink, as you can guess." So Emily told Rothstein she had just come to New York from a small Illinois town where her father ran a feed store and that she had great hopes of making it big on Broadway. "Texas is helping me get started," she said. No child, no ex-husband, no prison. How simple life would be for her if the charade were true.

"My father ran a store too," Rothstein said with relish as he discussed his childhood, his working in his father's clothing store in Brooklyn. "My father, God rest his soul, was called Rothstein the Just. He was the fairest man I ever met. He was as good as his word. That's all you need. Your word. So when a man wants me to sign a contract, I get suspicious."

Otherwise, they talked about women's fashions. Rothstein was very interested in how short women's skirts were going to get. He owned an interest in a fabric house. "If they get any shorter, we may go under." He said nothing at all about what a mobster he was, that his hit man, Legs Diamond, killed people for him regularly, that he owned scores of speakeasies, gambling houses, narcotics dens. To Emily, he had the disposition of a nice, fairly quiet Jewish businessman whose only vices were cards and horses.

For a man as feared as Rothstein, Emily thought he was incredibly soft, as soft as his fair white baby's skin. He did nothing for himself. Greenblatt drove and Birnbaum placed bets. The waiter even shelled his lobster for him. He was a sultan, with an array of courtiers to do his bidding. Emily remembered reading that Rothstein had shot and wounded two undercover detectives who had tried to arrest him in a crap game. She couldn't imagine him pulling a trigger. What other capacities was he holding in reserve? Emily dreaded the answer, which she knew was coming up imminently.

"My God, dresses are getting skimpy," Rothstein said as he reached under the table and ran his hand up Emily's leg, past her knee, stopping somewhere at mid-thigh, where her stocking ended. "How do you sit down?"

"You learn to cross your legs really fast," Emily said, worrying how much further he was going.

"You've got the legs for it," he complimented her, and then pulled his hand away. "And a face to match. Emily, did anyone ever tell you you look like Greta Garbo?"

"No . . . no, they didn't."

"They never told me that either." Rothstein laughed,

defusing the tension for a moment. "It must be something, being a beautiful dame."

"Let's ask Greta Garbo."

"You're okay, Emily," Rothstein said, taking her hand.

Emily continued eating, anxiously. She wasn't sure what to say, how much to flatter, how coquettish to play, so instead she just ate and tried to smile. "I even like the way you eat," Rothstein said, smacking his own lips over the strawberry ice cream.

"The food's good," Emily said.

"I like your mouth. Singer's mouth—lover's mouth. Your mouth's got it. Got it all." As the hour grew later, everything he said had sexual overtones. He didn't say much, only compliments, but Emily knew what the compliments were a prelude to. She really didn't know anything about this man, her first client. How could she make love, or let love be made to her, by someone she knew nothing about? What if she said no? Could she really? When was it all going to happen? Her mind was racing.

"Well," Rothstein said, looking at the big clock on the wall, which read eleven o'clock. "I think it's time."

"Time." Emily gulped. "Time for what?"

"Time"—Arnold stubbed out the butt of his Cuban cigar in an ashtray, which one of the stand-at-attention waiters rushed over and replaced with a clean one—"to take you home and put you to bed."

This was it. But Emily had had no idea that he would want to come to her place. Not Essex Street. Polly had never told her that. What would her landlord say? "I think you'd be more comfortable at your place," Emily said, her voice almost trembling. "I don't really have any—"

Rothstein started laughing, the first time all day, laughing so hard that two of the old waiters came over, thinking he was choking to death. "Massa Rosseen, Massa Rosseen . . ." They put their arms around him. "You all right, massa?"

"I'm just fine," he said as he waved them away. They scurried back to give Rothstein his privacy.

"What's wrong?" Emily asked. "Did I say something?"

"Yes. You're funny. I like you." He laughed again.

"Why?" Emily said, puzzled.

"You'll go to your place. I'll go to mine."

Emily couldn't believe what she'd heard. It was like a reprieve from the death sentence, but she did all she could to conceal her relief.

"Don't look so shocked," Rothstein said. "What kind of guy do you think I am? I'm not like that."

"I didn't mean . . ."

"I'm old-fashioned. I believe in courtships."

The next morning, Emily was awakened by a uniformed messenger with a huge bouquet of the biggest roses she had ever seen, compliments of Arnold Rothstein. The flowers belonged in a Fifth Avenue penthouse, not her Lower East Side room. She was almost embarrassed to display them, they were so lavish. As she unwrapped them to put them in a milk bottle she would use for a vase, an envelope fell out. Inside was a note. All it said was, "See you soon. A.R." There were also two hundred-dollar bills.

"He still hasn't done it?" Cassie was amazed. "After three dates?"

"He's been a perfect gentleman. Ouch!" Emily groaned, straightening herself up after hanging upside down on the rings of MacFarlane's women's gymnasium on West Sixtieth Street that Texas made her hostesses go to at least once a week. "Aren't we trim enough?"

"Not for Texas," Cassie said. "The more definition our bodies have, the better." Cassie continued doing her leg lifts, while the other women in the room were jogging in place and doing sit-ups on mats. They all wore jersey tank suits and stockings rolled below the knee.

Emily thought the whole exercise routine was silly. "What does this have to do with working in a speakeasy?" she said as she picked up a medicine ball and threw it at Cassie.

"It has to do with character," Cassie said, twisting the word to make it sound ridiculous. "Texas won't let us get sloppy."

"Only she can be sloppy."

"She's the boss. Ouch," Cassie gasped, falling backward from the weight of the ball. "Christy Mathewson, move over. You're strong."

"I wonder why he hasn't touched me." Emily was more than a bit confused by Rothstein's polite distance.

"It's really weird that he hasn't made a move," Cassie said. "Very weird."

"Cassie, you know what's even weirder?"

"What?"

"I'm beginning to like him. . . . I mean, when I forget who he is."

"You never ask me any questions," Arnold Rothstein said to Emily on the hot summer night as they sat in the trellised roof garden of the Central Park West penthouse he kept for entertaining his mistresses. He had his regular residence, with his wife, across the park on Fifth Avenue. "What do you want to know about me? How many millions I've got? What politicians I own? Who I've killed? Ask me anything."

Emily remembered Polly's precept and held back. "What do you think makes you so successful?"

"Hunger," Rothstein said. "Hunger and desire. I grew up a poor Jew around rich Italians. You know, the big Sicilians, big gangsters. My father sold them clothes. I'd help them pick out expensive silk ties. They were up from the streets, but they were kings. They had style. I loved the way they sounded, how they dressed, their haircuts, their broads, those big dinners with the lobsters and the spaghetti and the clams. Dinners where everyone was having a helluva time until some guy looked at another guy's broad and would get shot for it. They had style."

"You've got style," Emily said, referring to Rothstein's Old Masters and English antiques. These surroundings were totally at odds with his romanticized nostalgia for the deadly gangland bravado that had influenced his youth. "Everything you do is the best. I've never seen anyone live so well. You got what you wanted, A.R. And more."

"You know what really made these guys? They had guts. They had no fear. They weren't afraid to roll the dice. That's what gave them that style. I wanted to be brave, too. I didn't want to grow up and be some accountant. My father wanted me to be an accountant, said I was good with the numbers."

"I think he was right," Emily said.

"Yeah." Rothstein smiled at her. "Yeah. I didn't want to serve anybody. I wanted to run things. I wanted to roll the dice. Roll 'em and win. I always dreamed of being up here in the sky with a perfect lady like you." Rothstein's attention to Emily this evening gave her no indication that any other woman existed in his life, including his wife. The wind rustled the leaves in Central Park below. Candles lit the terrace. Rothstein's building was reflected in the park lake, the water was so still. His French cook had prepared an impeccable dinner of asparagus, veal with truffles, a chocolate soufflé, and lots of champagne for Emily. Rothstein drank straight seltzer. The phonograph reverberated with the langourous "What'll I Do?" The night was fragrant with the honeysuckle on the trellises. Emily was literally sitting on top of the world. As she looked out at the park, at the apartment houses in the distance on Fifth Avenue, the carpet of lights that lit up the greatest city on earth, Rothstein put his arm around Emily. They swayed to the music for a long time, and then he kissed her.

"You're nervous, aren't you?" he asked in a low voice.

"Uh . . . yes," Emily said. Remember, it's their party, Polly had told her. Their fantasy. Their bubble. Don't burst it.

"I'm nervous, too," Rothstein whispered, sliding his hand into her low V dress and cupping her breast adroitly.

"You're never nervous, A.R.," she said as she ran her finger along the nape of his neck.

"I am tonight." Now he was caressing her derriere through her dress, but again so suavely she didn't feel uncomfortable. There had been so many women, Emily thought, that he had this worked out to a science. But it was his party. She wasn't going to spoil it.

"You're very exciting. You're driving me crazy." He slipped one of Emily's dress straps off her shoulder, then the other. The dress fell to the ground. She was standing there in only her heels, stockings, and panties, kissing Rothstein, massaging his neck with his silk bow tie. "You're incredible," he said. His hands explored her. "You're driving me crazy."

These words excited her. She could hear his breathing deepen, his pulse pound. She could touch his hardness. "I can't . . . I can't . . . resist you," he gasped.

At last she had power, only in this way, and only for these moments. But now, for these heated moments, the King of New York was putty in her hands. That Rothstein had seen so many women, so many mistresses, but could be so aroused by her, gave Emily a new appraisal of her feminine allure. She had had so little experience with men. With Warren she had been totally repressed. With Alex she had been carried away by the moment. And now, the King was worshiping her. One of the most influential men in New York was on his knees, kissing her, up her thighs, above her stockings, as far as he could. She could have demanded anything from him at this split second and he would have given it to her. Polly Adler was right. She did have something, something that could give her leverage over even the strongest of men. The thought that she held this trump card provided Emily a fleeting rush of intense exhilaration. What power was this, though? The power that Warren beat her and burned her over?

They moved to a cushioned chaise longue under a blossoming cherry tree on the roof, where after teasing and kissing, and exploring each other, she let Arnold Rothstein, New York's Big Boss, make love to her, high above the city whose underside he controlled. The moment wasn't orgasmic. But it was Emily's loss of innocence. Rothstein made love to her again. The candles had burned down to nothing. The only light was the stars above and the buildings in the distance. Emily was glad of the darkness. Rothstein wouldn't be able to notice her tears.

37

Rothstein was the first. The second came soon after Emily's night on the terrace of Central Park West. She was at Guinan's, dancing the black bottom to the raucous strains of "Wild Man of Borneo" with a German dirigible pilot in New York for a layover while his experimental airship was being readied for its transatlantic return. She was enjoying his accented description of flying over the wastes of Greenland, the rocks of Iceland, the frigid dark of the North Atlantic.

"Miss Emily, you'se got you a telephone call," Gloria, the maid, interrupted.

"Take a message, please." Emily smiled and kept dancing.

At the end of the dance, Cassie and Rebecca, another hostess, stepped over. "Can I steal Emily away from you, Mein Capitan?" Cassie said, batting her lashes.

"But I met her only—" the captain tried to protest.

"I'm Rebecca." The new hostess smiled. "You are so handsome."

The German smiled back, giving in. He was in the city only for the night. The hostesses were all pretty.

"Polly's on the phone," Cassie insisted, leading Emily to the phone booth decorated as a Chinese pagoda. "She's got a job."

"But I'm on Texas' time."

"Polly comes first. It's okay. They have an arrangement."

Emily listened to her assignment from Polly, who was very abrupt. "Don't ask. Just go, dollink. He's a very important client."

"Judge Crater? The Criminal Courts Building?" Emily repeated her destination incredulously.

"Don't ask. Just go. I have twenty Japanese here. Oy vey. Talk about aggravation." Polly hung up.

"Judge Crater," Emily told Cassie, who waited outside the booth. "He's a big judge, right?"

Cassie nodded that he was.

"What about A.R.?" Emily held a bizarre loyalty toward her first man.

"This is business," Cassie said. "There's no such thing as exclusivity, Emily. A.R. has twenty girls. Forty girls. A hundred, who knows? The worst thing you could ever do is get hung up on one of your clients."

Clients. The word chilled Emily. She hated to think of it that way, so clinical, so mercenary, that she was one of a hundred, just another night. In fact, she was getting a bit attached to Rothstein. He had treated her so well. She didn't think about the fact that he was married, that he saw many other call girls. She only focused on the time she was with him, and that time wasn't at all terrible. Whether it was self-delusion or self-hypnosis, she treated Rothstein as a real date. That worked for her. But Cassie was right. She was applying romantic notions to what was a commercial situation. She had to stop, or she would get hurt, really hurt. Romantic notions could lead to expectations, and one of the rules of this game was that expectations were not permitted. "You go, Cassie. I'm not sure," Emily wavered.

"Remember," Cassie punctured Emily's fevered indecision, "Crater's one of the top Tammany judges. You want to find out about your frame-up, there's a man for you."

Emily was jolted away by the thought. She couldn't afford to be a romantic. She had a purpose. "A Tammany judge?"

"They're all Tammany, but he's a bigwig."

"Why would he tell me anything?"

Cassie threw back her head, amused. "I've got some general from Paraguay out there I'm dancing with, honey, and he's telling me half his state secrets. And that's just over some jazz and Scotch. If you can't get a man to talk in bed, you're doing something wrong."

*　　*　　*

The Criminal Courts Building in downtown Manhattan was the last place one would ever expect to be a spot of assignation with a call girl. Then again, Polly Adler's call girls always went far beyond the margins of the expected. Emily got out of the yellow cab. The side door next to the locked revolving one was open, just as Polly had told her. She entered through the Roman columns into the dark marble lobby. An eerie emptiness permeated the place. Mobbed with lawyers, clerks, stenographers by day, by night the halls of justice were still. Emily's footsteps echoed loudly down the long corridor. She walked up the end stairwell to the second floor, then down to the third door on the left. "Chambers of the Honorable Joseph Force Crater, Supreme Court" was on the door, which, as Polly promised, was open. Emily walked through a dark outer office toward a light in the inner officer. The door was cracked open.

"Judge Crater?" Emily called out.

"Come in. Come in," the deep voice replied.

Judge Crater, a large, balding man in his late fifties, his spectacles giving his eyes the aspect of an octopus, was leaning over, poring into a pile of casebooks pulled from the shelves of the library surrounding his desk. He wasn't the kind of man Emily would expect to use Polly's women, but as Polly said, "They all call me. All of 'em."

"Hello," he said in a cheery voice. "You don't know anything about common carriers and bailments, do you?"

"Sorry. Can't help you there."

"This is an impossible case." He took off his glasses and squinted up at Emily. "Jesus, you're pretty."

"You're working too hard." Emily took her coat off as she closed the door behind her. She walked over toward his desk, removed some law books from a chair and sat down. As she crossed her legs in front of the judge, she noticed his eyes traveling from her face to her thighs. "He's passive," Polly had instructed her. "Make it easy for him, but don't scare him. You're an actress. You want to act? Act!" Emily remembered Polly's exhortation and, against all her natural instincts, forced herself to cross her legs again.

"I've never seen you at Guinan's," Emily said.

"I'm not coming back till Texas gives me my old ringside table."

"I'll tell her. You should come by."

"Maybe I should," the judge said, stepping out from behind his desk and approaching Emily. He leaned over. Emily thought he was looking for some lost papers, but he was looking for something else. He took the heel of Emily's high heel and stroked it. "Maybe. But my wife isn't keen on it. Nice shoes."

"Thanks. I really think you're working too hard."

"This is the only place I can have any peace."

"It's cozy." The room smelled of leather and books.

"Where did you get these shoes?" He fondled the other high heel.

"Andrew Geller's." Emily gritted her teeth and crossed her legs again.

"Geller's has the best shoes," the judge said. He pulled closer to Emily and began caressing her feet, then slowly, very slowly, he started working upward.

It took two more midnight sessions with Judge Crater before Emily learned anything about Tammany Hall. Nevertheless, her desire to find out about her being framed gave her a reason to be working for Polly, a sugar coating on the bitter pill of being a call girl. Trying to clear her name through doing something that in itself sullied it struck Emily as almost self-defeating. Yet this was the only way she had, and the only way to raise money to retain Hiram Hogan for her custody fight.

"You know, this isn't really worth it," Judge Crater said in a drunken moment of self-deprecatory pique. A bottle of rum sat atop a mountain of motions. The complex case was impossible for him. His only response to it was to call Polly as salve for his frustrations. "Twenty thousand dollars for this. That would have bought you a lot of shoes." He kept sucking on Emily's toes, whose nails she had painted a provocative red for the occasion. "Beautiful! Beautiful!" he gasped.

"What did you say the twenty thousand dollars was for?" Emily asked him after he was finished and she was dressing.

"For nothing. Money for nothing."

"I don't get it."

"For this place. You have to make a donation to get to be here."

"I thought it was an honor."

"Honor has a price."

Emily didn't pursue the line of questioning, but she felt safe in assuming the purchase was from Tammany.

"An investment," Cassie told Emily, agreeing with her conclusion that Crater had paid the twenty thousand to buy his judgeship in the Tammany-controlled appointments process. "There's big money in being a judge. You get kickbacks for deciding the right way. He earned that twenty back real fast."

"I wonder if Renaud bought his post."

"Renaud?" Cassie asked.

"The magistrate who sent me to Bedford."

"Why not? How else do you get on the bench, honey?"

"Do you think Warren could have bribed him?"

"Who knows? Anything's possible."

Emily wanted to learn more from Judge Crater, but he stopped calling. She felt rejected, as if a suitor had dumped her.

"Stop thinking of them as *men*," Cassie tried to console her. "They're *clients*. They're *business*. Sometimes they may fall for you, but if they don't, don't take it all so personal. Does Texas get jealous when her people go to the Hotsy Totsy? It's a free country. They're free to love, free to leave. That's what they're paying for, their freedom."

"I hate it."

"You think too much, honey."

38

Listening to the surf crashing, the gulls squawking, and the calliope playing "A Pretty Girl Is like a Melody," Emily watched the ceiling fan and counted its lazy revolutions stirring up the briny sea air. She did everything she could to distract herself from what was going on in the bed where she lay nude in the Imperial Suite of the Chalfonte-Haddon Hall resort in Atlantic City. For the last hour her weekend client had kept attempting to make love to her, but was unable to sustain an erection. "Goddamnit," he said, rolling off her. "Let's just drink."

The man called the hall porter, who dispatched a uniformed bellhop to the suite with another bottle of bootleg gin and crystal goblets. The man gave the boy a twenty-dollar tip. He gave everyone a twenty-dollar tip. That was his trademark. He drank the gin straight. Emily added tonic to hers. There was no way she could keep up with him. Nevertheless, she was vastly relieved to be drinking instead of trying to have sex.

The man was a multimillionaire named Jack Phillips, who was fleeing the jurisdiction of a New York court. Emily had read about him in the papers. Phillips was the "Pipe King," having made his fortune selling pipe to the city. The fortune might have multiplied, had angry taxpayers in Queens, incensed over seemingly extortionate assessments for a new sewer line, not begun their own cost analyses. They discovered that of the ninety-dollar-per-foot cost of the new sewer, fifteen dollars was labor. The remaining seventy-five went to Jack Phillips for material, which, the residents proved, cost him only five dollars a foot. They went to the courts, and Phillips left town before his deposition could be taken. Polly Adler had sent Emily down to the Jersey shore to calm him down.

"Goddamn snoopers," Phillips railed about the taxpayers to Emily. A gaunt, bony Irishman whose drinking made him look a decade beyond his fifty years, Phillips wore his blue silk dressing gown with its insignia of crossed pipes. "Leave it off," he admonished Emily when she tried to cover herself with his monogrammed pajama top.

"It's getting cool," Emily said.

"It's summer."

"It's damp."

Jack Phillips stood up and closed the window. "I like lookin' at ya. I wanna get somethin' for my money."

Emily detested being on display. She detested Phillips' crass approach to her. There were no illusions, no pretensions here that this was a real date. This was a service, like room service, like the Japanese chauffeur who drove his Pierce Arrow. Phillips was used to giving orders. Emily was nothing but help. Temporary help.

"Let's try it again, baby," Phillips would say from hour to hour, when the gin had hit him in the right way and he had become aroused at the way Emily walked across the bedroom. They would go to the bed, Phillips would doff his robe, and endeavor, sometimes for minutes, sometimes more, to have sex with her. It never worked.

"I think you're drinking too much," Emily tried to console her client, who was paying her four hundred dollars to be the hostage of his impotence.

"I always drank too much. But I never had this before. It's not the booze. It's the goddamn subpoena messing me up. I'm worried, baby."

"Why don't we talk about it. Might make things better," Emily suggested. She slipped on Phillips' silk pajamas. This time he didn't protest. He knew, sexually, the cause was lost.

"We had it all fixed. I never thought these schmucks in Queens could add and subtract." He poured more gin into his glass. "What did they know? They're supposed to be stupid."

Phillips accepted Emily's invitation to rant and rave.

209

That was the best part of this lost weekend, for he ranted about Tammany, and that diminished the degradation Emily was going through. Through his gin-soaked haze, Phillips told Emily his life story, how he had risen through the Tammany ranks as a ward healer to a job as a city purchasing agent. But he lost his job when he was arrested for selling spoiled beef to an insane asylum. "If sane guys can't tell the difference in some ritzy food joint, how can a bunch of nut cases tell a bad steak?" he spat, with the characteristic Tammany contempt for the taxpayer.

After the beef scandal, Phillips had made his comeback, he told Emily, getting the New York franchise on a specially patented lockjoint pipe. "We fixed it with the city engineer so he said only this kind of pipe could be used. Hell," he laughed, "it was the same as any other pipe, 'cept it was mine and nobody else's. Made me rich."

"Was the city engineer from Tammany?" Emily asked, feigning innocence.

"Hell yes. We grew up together, but he wasn't doing it for love. We all got rich."

Wasn't Warren Matthews doing the same thing with tiles as Phillips with his pipes? Emily reflected. After more gin, she grew emboldened, knowing Phillips would never remember what they talked about. "Did you ever meet a Tammany guy named Warren Matthews?"

"Matthews. Sure. Smart bastard. You see him, too?" Phillips slurred drunkenly. "Don't tell him you saw me. I don't want people thinkin' I pay for it."

"Don't worry. Friend of mine knows him. Supposed to be a big shot in Tammany Hall."

"Thinks he is. He's McCarey's boy. Fuck 'em all. Where the hell are they when I need 'em?" Phillips yelled out, hurling his goblet across the room, splashing gin all over the sheets. "Where are they? *I* was the big shot. Now look at me. They want me for grand theft. I'm a goddamn fugitive."

"Can't Tammany fix it?"

"That's what I say. But now the feds are coming down on me. Tammany can take care of the city, sure, but revenuers want a million bucks in back taxes. I'm fucked, baby. Get me another glass."

"What about Mike McNaughton?" Emily asked a few drinks later into the night.

"The cop? You know him?"

"Met him once."

"Better watch out."

"Why?"

"He might get you. Stay away from him."

"Is he friends with Warren Matthews?"

"They're all friends. What the hell difference does it make?"

"Not much," Emily backed away.

"One last try," Phillips said as he touched Emily's bare leg and fumbled with the buttons of his pajama top she was wearing. "One last try before I go to jail."

Phillips never made it to prison. He died of acute cirrhosis two months later, before the Internal Revenue Service got him. After her weekend with Phillips, however, Emily began keeping a diary. Although she never heard any direct information on her own case—that would be too risky to press for—she heard a lot of damning information about Tammany Hall, information she knew she would have some use for in the battle she was planning to wage for Jessica, for herself. This knowledge was going to be her power.

Not all Emily's dates were Tammany men. They were an odd lot. In Emily's first two months, Polly Adler introduced her to two Wall Street brokers, a Bronx furrier, a California swimming-pool builder, a rich dentist fron Scranton, a Massachusetts boarding-school headmaster who wanted Emily to spank him with a riding whip he carried in his briefcase, and a French art dealer who gave her an etching of an artist named Chagall.

Some men, the hurried, married New Yorkers usually, were only interested in a brief assignation of an hour or two in some hotel or borrowed apartment. Emily tried to avoid these cash-on-the-barrelhead types, unless they were men like Judge Crater, who might tell her something she wanted to know. She preferred the out-of-towners, away from their wives and in Gotham to live the way they couldn't live in Akron or Fort Worth or Spokane. These men generally wanted to pretend what Emily wanted to pretend—that she was a real "date," a love affair in microcosm. These men, the "romantics," as Polly categorized them, courted Emily, flattered her, and wined and dined her so generously that she could almost forget, for her few hours together with them, what she was actually doing.

Occasionally Emily felt a possible romantic attachment. The first of these was a dashing Denver archaeologist named Steven Ward, who was stopping in New York on his way home from a dig in Aleppo, Syria. A true cosmopolite who was equally at ease in Legs Diamond's Hotsy Totsy Club as he was in the ruins of Chichén Itzá or Angkor Wat, Steven, because of his long absence from urban civilization on this past expedition, was smoldering with enthusiasm about going out on the town his first night in Manhattan. Emily got caught up in his zeal for a good time.

They did Manhattan right, dropping in to the Lido to hear Libby Holman, to the Trocadero to watch Fred and Adele Astaire dance, to the Silver Slipper to laugh at Jimmy Durante. All along, Steven, who was craggy and weather-beaten, but whose lined face seemed to hold the secrets of lost continents and buried treasures, regaled Emily with tales of his adventures. He told her about cannibals with blowguns in the Amazon while they played miniature golf at gangster Larry Fay's Club Intime, and about being buried in sand by Zulus while they listened to Helen Morgan sing "Bill" at Dutch Schultz's Embassy Club.

Steven was too wound-up to call it quits. They had one round of nightcaps at the Bal Tabarin, another at the Montmartre. There were so many French names, Emily could pretend she was on the grand boulevards of Paris, not the mean alleys of Times Square, where the glossy boîtes were secreted behind nondescript brownstone facades.

Finally Steven took Emily back to his room at the Piccadilly and made love to her. For these sparkling hours, Emily felt the potential for romance with him. Then, when they had finished, rather than continuing to hold Emily in his arms, Steven handed her a twenty-dollar bill and called it "cabfare" and apologized that he needed some sleep, by himself, to be alert for a lecture he was supposed to deliver at Columbia the next day. Emily almost cried. So she bade him good night, consoling herself that Steven had paid Polly, who took care of all the business, a hundred dollars for the pleasure of Emily's company.

She left the hotel and emerged into the Times Square night. All alone, she viewed Broadway as the lowest loggia of hell. These were the desperate hours, and everybody was hawking something. Slowly cruising cabbies, their flashing headlights soliciting a fare; the poor peddlers selling foil-wrapped "pure whiskey candies—three for five cents" to whatever lost soul had a drunken sweet tooth at that hour; the painted ladies of the evening with their red lips glowing like neon in the dark. These latter jarred Emily the most. They were her sisters, weren't they? she thought. The only difference was one of class. They were doing the same thing, simply on different plateaus, pushing for another score. Emily hailed a taxi home as the sun began to rise over the skyscrapers. The loneliness, after all the noise and the fun, was brutally deflating, as was the knowledge that for all her efforts and all her charm, she would in all likelihood never see Steven Ward again, and if she ever did, it would end the same way. But Emily learned to bear it. She was learning things, often important things. More significantly, she now had enough money to give Hiram Hogan his full retainer.

39

"Eat your corned beef, Warren. Eat hearty," Terence McCarey said to Warren Matthews.

"I've got no appetite," Warren said.

They were at McCarey's favorite restaurant, Dinty Moore's, on West Forty-sixth Street. McCarey loved the Irish food, the Broadway bustle, the sports figures. Jack Dempsey was across the room. The great fighter had stopped to slap McCarey on the back. McCarey was a political celebrity. He had made a fortune as subway commissioner. He was a leading light of Tammany. He knew everyone in town. "This is the life, Warren boy. This is the life." Warren never liked being called "Warren boy." He was almost forty, but whatever McCarey wanted to call him, he had to take it with a smile. McCarey was his guru, his adviser, his boss. McCarey had made him rich. "You're sitting on top of the world," McCarey said.

"I'm sitting on top of a volcano," Warren said glumly, twirling a strand of uneaten cabbage on his fork. "She's going to ruin everything."

"What can that poor little lass do?" McCarey said. "What's left of her."

"She's got a lawyer, Hiram Hogan."

"Hiram Hogan's not a bad bloke. For a Republican," McCarey chortled. "He is a pretty fair divorce man. I heard he stuck it to Al Gilhooley with a choker of an alimony. But hell, I'd pay it to get away from his missus. It would be cheap at any price."

"What's he going to stick me with?" Warren was worried. "That day at the school? He can't get me for that, can he?"

McCarey shook his head reassuringly.

"I didn't like hurting her, sir."

"You've got a soft heart, Warren," McCarey laughed.

"How do I keep her away now that she's got this lawyer?"

"What does she want? Tell me."

"She wants Jessica."

"Is that all?"

"That's enough, isn't it? Maybe she wants money, but he didn't say. Maybe she wants to get me."

"Get you for what? You didn't do anything to her. *Never* forget that. *Never!* You're clean. Clean as a whistle. Don't think dirty. Remember that," McCarey admonished Warren in a hard voice which, chameleonlike, turned soft again. "She's just a mother who wants to see her little girl. Perfectly normal."

"You're not suggesting . . ."

"I am, indeed, my boy. Let her see her."

"No."

"It's a crumb. Throw her a crumb."

"She could poison Jessica's mind against—"

"She loves the girl as much as you do. She's not going to poison anything. She just wants to see her. She wants to love her. She's a mother!"

"I don't like it."

"I do. Let her work for it. Let her think it's a whole loaf, but I tell you, Warren boy, it's nothing but a crumb."

"She'll want more."

"She'll be thrilled."

"Hogan'll want more."

"It's our court, my boy. He can't get more."

"I hate the idea of having to fight with her over Jessica. My daughter's not a football."

"Glory be, Warren. Look who's here. It's Tunney. Tunney and Dempsey under the same roof. Don't you love this town, Warren? Gene! Gene!" McCarey got up and waddled toward the entrance to greet the heavyweight contender.

40

The custody hearing was held on August 30, 1926, and Emily was an hour late in getting there. She couldn't help it. It was the same day as the funeral of Rudolph Valentino, who had died at thirty-one of peritonitis while in New York to promote his new film, *Son of the Sheik*. Over a hundred thousand grieving fans, mostly women, mobbed St. Malachy's Church near Broadway, where last rites were held, creating one of the worst transportation jams in Manhattan's history. Actually, Emily managed to beat Warren and Isabelle Matthews to court. They were delayed getting in from New Jersey nearly two hours. The hearing was further held up because three of the female court stenographers called in sick and a male replacement had to be found.

When Emily finally saw Warren and Isabelle in the courtroom, with their two very proper lawyers in their vested suits, she knew that whatever her case, the odds were against her. She hadn't seen Warren for years. The years had been good to him. Slightly graying at the temples, impeccably dressed, he wore his new life with Isabelle well. And Isabelle . . . well, once a debutante, always a debutante. She had that outdoor glowing complexion, the long hair that was born to be windblown while riding to the hunt. They belonged in their Jersey Camelot, in their country clubs, with their money. Warren was old money now. You could marry into pedigree and change yourself. He was quietly arrogant, no longer with the swagger that Emily remembered. No need for bravado anymore, once all the wishes had come true.

Emily felt cheap compared to Isabelle. Despite her

nice black dress, her pearls, her quiet shoes, she didn't feel Establishment. Even were she wearing Isabelle's tasteful tweeds, she still would have felt she was falling short. Isabelle had the sort of bearing an actress couldn't fake. Hiram Hogan didn't help, either, with his rumpled suit, his hulking frame so fat that his shirttail had pulled out and could be seen through the back flap of his jacket. Warren's lawyers were surely Ivy League men. Somehow Emily could tell. Hogan was from an entirely different school.

The American flag. The New York flag. Excelsior. The smell of the furniture polish on the benches. The courtroom summoned up to Emily the worst flashbacks, justice as a mockery. She feared she would be exposed as a call girl and railroaded back to Bedford. Emily didn't like being anywhere near justice, not in New York.

"What is your occupation?"

"Actress."

"What is your current occupation?"

"Cabaret hostess. Singer."

Isabelle smirked. Warren smirked.

"The motion for custody is denied," the judge finally ruled, after a blur of hours of testimony during which both Warren and Isabelle took the stand and provided a storybook image of the life they had created for Jessica.

Warren and Isabelle didn't even smile. They expected the result. But then the judge added, "The court, however, does grant the petitioner visitation rights of once a month." Then the Matthewses frowned and huddled with their expensive lawyers, who shrugged helplessly.

Hiram Hogan was pleased with this minor triumph. "At least you can see her now," he whispered to Emily. "It's a beginning."

The court's ruling wasn't the full custody she had dreamed about, but it did mean she was legally fit to see her daughter. Emily considered it a victory, too, a bit of a validation, a bit of dignity.

As they filed out of the courtroom, Emily came face-to-face with Warren. "You look good." She tried to be polite. Despite what she strongly suspected he had done to her, for the moment she had put it out of her head and was feeling strangely expansive, generous.

"You look good, too, Emily," Warren replied, under-stating the visceral attraction he still felt toward her. How dissatisfied sexually he was with Isabelle. How he remembered the nights with Emily. How he wanted her. How he hated her for defying him, for not being the wife she should have been, for making him do what he had done. "How are you?"

"Getting by. I never thought we'd meet like this, Warren."

"No. Me either." He stepped aside to speak to her.

"I thought about you in prison. A lot. I even missed you, thought maybe I made a mistake."

"You did?" If only, Warren wished, she had felt this way sooner.

"I wish you had gotten in touch with me at Bedford. It would have meant something."

"I . . . er . . . didn't . . . know." Warren had no idea what to say.

"Maybe we could have been friends. Maybe we can still . . . I mean, because of Jessica we'll have to be seeing each other now."

"Maybe. We'll see." Isabelle was glaring at Warren for speaking to Emily. He could feel the pressure in her look, telling him not to talk to her.

"Warren, why did Mac and that other man attack me at the school?"

"I almost fired them for that. I was furious. I don't know what got into them."

"I wish you had called to tell me that. I thought you were behind it," Emily said.

"I wasn't. They got out of control. I didn't want them to hurt you. Really." Warren cut his eyes shiftily. "Emily, I've got another life now, but if there's anything I can do . . ."

"There is, Warren." Emily decided to take advantage of his penitent attitude toward her.

"What?"

"My conviction."

"It's done with."

"No, it's not. It's always going to be there. I want to get it set aside."

"What can I do?"

218

"Warren, you're in Tammany. You've got connections. Help me get my name cleared."

"I asked—"

"Please, Warren. You can do it. It's all connections. Just one thing I ask, for a lifetime."

"It's not so easy."

"Please, Warren." She took his arm. "For old times' sake. One favor."

"Tammany won't do anything about this."

"Come on, Warren. Tammany can do anything it wants. Warren, I'm not a baby. I was married to you. I know."

"Then you know more than I do. There's nothing I can do. You've got a lawyer. Ask him."

"I'm asking you, Warren."

"I'm sorry, Emily."

Emily didn't like the way he was patronizing her now. "Could it be you don't want my name cleared?"

"That's not so," Warren said defensively. This was it, the accusation he knew was coming someday.

"You have to know I was framed."

"I had nothing to do with it," Warren blurted out quickly, too quickly.

"I never said you did," Emily said. "Wait a minute." She looked at Warren's face. She had lived with him for six years. She knew the nervous, twitching grin he usually displayed whenever he lied. "It *was* you, Warren, wasn't it? I didn't want to believe it, but it was you. You were in on it. You and McNaughton and Tammany. You were all in on it. I know when you lie. You're lying, Warren."

"You're crazy, Emily. I didn't do anything." He loathed her now for having trapped him this way.

Emily looked down the corridor at Isabelle and the blue-chip lawyers. "You did it, Warren. You dirty bastard. You had me framed. 'If there's anything I can do,' you say. You! You . . .!" Emily lunged forward and grabbed Warren's tie, one with tigers on it she had given him years before. Was he wearing it to flaunt it? More likely, he had forgotten where it came from. "I'm going to get Jessica back. You don't deserve her. You don't deserve to live." Emily found herself ripping at the tie, trying to strangle Warren.

"Leave him alone," Isabelle shouted, running down the hall, trying to yank Emily away. "You crazy witch."

"Leave me alone," Emily lashed back at her, at the same time trying to claw Warren with her nails.

"Stop her. Stop her," Isabelle called to her lawyers, who had to pry Emily away.

"Maniac," Warren choked. "Bitch."

She wouldn't let go. "You framed me. You. You. You animal."

Hogan interceded and broke Emily's grip. "Emily! They'll have you arrested. You'll lose it all." That made her pull back.

"You!" She pointed her finger at Warren. "You!"

Warren straightened his tie. Isabelle was crying. Her ordered life wasn't geared to such sordid interruptions. They looked at Emily as if she were worse than untouchable. The Ivy League lawyers were shaken by the outburst. So this was how ex-convicts behaved. They trotted out all the condescension they had ever learned. Emily was ashamed for losing control. She was living up to the reputation she had never deserved. Warren had his wish. He had reduced her to a screaming banshee. Now she wanted to apologize to the entire crowd that had gathered in the hall outside the courtroom.

"Come on," Hogan said, putting his arm around her. "Round's over."

"I can't believe you were married to that." Isabelle hugged her husband.

"Me either, darling. I didn't know."

"Are you all right?"

"Are *you* all right?"

"Yes, but Jessica. Our poor little girl. I don't want her to see her."

"What can we do? Just one day a month. Poor fool," Warren said as he watched with relief as Emily disappeared into an elevator. "She's not fit to see anyone."

41

Emily's first visit with Jessica was on a Sunday. She took the train to Morristown and took a cab from there to pick up Jessica, who was waiting with a maid by the gate of the driveway. They went back to Morristown to see a Greta Garbo movie and then to a restaurant called Larry's Turkey Farm. Jessica played with the birds outside, then, after a slight wrestling match with her conscience, ate the turkey heartily. The old farmhouse, with its wood beams and cuckoo clocks, was a wonderful place for children. The smells of fowl roasting, bread baking, hens clucking outside, was a wonderful antidote to the city. The purity of being here with Jessica put the compromises of the rest of Emily's life, the other thirty days, or rather nights, of the month, in high relief. She tried not to think of her date tomorrow. Today she was a mother, and nothing else. Only today mattered.

"They're different birds," Emily had said in coaxing her daughter to pick up the drumstick. Emily was happy to be with Jessica legitimately. She treasured every minute, though her normal desperation was gone. She knew in a month she would see her again, build her trust, develop their closeness. Prison had taught Emily patience, if nothing else.

"Will you be a famous actress like Mary Pickford, Mommy?"

Emily loved being called Mommy. "She's very famous."

"You're just as pretty," Jessica said, munching away on the turkey leg.

"Oh, thank you. You're even prettier, darling."

"Did you want to be an actress when you were little?"

"Yes, that was my dream." Emily gulped hard. She knew that dream was over.

"Why?"

"I thought it would be fun. It would be exciting."

"Weren't you scared?"

"Scared of what?"

"Being in front of all those people. Forgetting what you're supposed to say."

"No. I was never scared. Not of that," Emily said.

"What did scare you, Mommy? When you were like me."

"I was scared of your grandpa, my father."

"The way I'm scared of Daddy?"

"What way is that?" That Jessica was afraid of Warren concerned Emily. What was he doing to her?

"He gets mad."

"What does he do?"

"Nothing." Emily was relieved. "But I'm scared he might hit me. He gets all red like a balloon sometimes if things aren't okay. He looks like he could pop."

"Things you did?"

"No. Just things. His business, I guess. Things about money. But I'm still scared he could hurt me."

"You're too good, sweetheart. He won't do anything bad to you. He loves you very much."

"You know what else scares me, Mommy?"

"What?"

"That Mommy and Daddy might go away on a trip and never come back."

Jessica's reference to Isabelle as "Mommy" hurt Emily in the pit of her stomach.

"That won't happen, sweetheart," she managed. "Besides, I'm always going to be here for you."

"But you left before."

That wounded Emily. No matter what she said or did, Jessica did not fully trust her.

"I told you, honey, that will never happen again. I was sick. I'm well now. I'm going to always be here for you."

"But you live in New York," Jessica said. She was

right, Emily thought. What Jessica was saying was that, practically speaking, Emily was *not* her mother.

"Mommy?" Jessica continued.

"Yes?"

"Where did you get all these nice clothes?"

"I bought them," Emily said.

"Daddy said you don't have any money, but that you dress like a movie star." More propaganda Emily would have to rebut. "When you first came back, you didn't have clothes like this."

"I've been working really hard and I've made some money so I can dress up and look pretty just for you."

"What do you do, Mommy?"

"I sing."

"Do you have a record?"

At first Emily's heart sank. She thought Jessica was referring to Bedford. Had they told her? "Record?" Emily gasped.

"I want to play it on my phonograph."

"Oh." Emily breathed easier. Kids were so damn smart. "Not yet, but when I do, you get the very first one. It takes a long time to get a record."

"Where do you sing?"

"You have so many questions, Jessica honey."

Of course she did. They didn't really know each other anymore. Emily knew that a long period of reacquaintance, of selling herself to her daughter, of winning her confidence, lay ahead of her. She could see that her little girl had tremendous inner conflicts. Her comments about her fears of her father, of being alone, clued Emily that all was not perfect. Warren had conditioned Jessica not to confide in others, but Emily sensed that Jessica's life in New Jersey was not as storybook at it seemed at first blush. There was something too ordered and too perfect. Nevertheless, Emily didn't want to press Jessica to open up. Even if Jessica were to discuss whatever trouble she had, what could Emily do? Emily didn't want to destroy the precious little equilibrium her fragile Jessica had achieved. Thus Emily was resigned to stay on the surface, keeping things positive, waiting until Jessica felt comfortable enough with her to reach out to her. Emily would have to suppress her own impatience and wait in the wings for her daughter's love.

"Tell me, Mommy. Where do you sing?" Jessica persisted.

"In a nightclub."

"What's a nightclub?"

"A nightclub," Emily said, "is a big restaurant where people like me sing, and there's a band, and everyone dresses up in nice clothes and dances."

"That sounds neat! I want to go with my friends to dance and watch you sing."

"But you'll have to dance with boys. What about that?" Emily said, wiping the crumbs from Jessica's mouth.

"Oh. Maybe I don't want to come. Can I have some ice cream now?"

"Of course you can."

"Mommy never lets me eat this much."

The reference to Isabelle hurt again. Emily wanted to be Jessica's only "Mommy." Emily loved no one else. She had nothing else.

"She doesn't want you to get so fat you won't be able to wear your clothes."

"Then she can buy me new ones. Could I have a piece of cake too?"

Emily kissed her daughter. "If it will make you happy, honey."

"You're so nice, Mommy." Jessica smiled. "I'll go even if there are boys."

"Where?"

"To your nightclub. I'll bring all my friends and I'll say, that's my mommy. That'll be fun."

"I like it too." Emily beamed, looking at the big cuckoo clock on the wall tick away the only happy moments of her life.

42
1927

After a year of working for Polly Adler, Emily had saved almost thirty-five hundred dollars. She rented a new apartment in Murray Hill on Thirty-eighth Street off Park, in a beautiful new doorman building across the street from the staid Union League Club, where a number of Emily's dates were members. She never saw men at the apartment, though. The place was her refuge. She furnished it in the new art-deco style. She rejected the homespun of Joliet, the antiques of Park Avenue. The whites and blacks and chromes matched the ultramodern mood of the city and of the times, and of Emily herself, who grew sleeker and more sophisticated with every evening among the *beau monde* who reveled at Texas Guinan's. The room Emily had set aside for Jessica had a more rustic warmth, yellow carpets, bright summery flowered wallpaper, circus posters, dolls and stuffed animals, lush picture books. This fantasy room gave a method and a purpose to Emily, and a foreshadowing of the life she might lead if and when Jessica ever came to live with her.

For the moment, however, Emily was doing her job and growing increasingly successful at it. After the first agonizing months, she tried to stop flaying herself over the immorality of her occupation. She tried to look at it as if it were a terrible play she had taken because it was the only part in town for her, and the terrible play turned out to be a smash hit, a long run. But the rationalization never worked.

Sometimes, to buoy up her spirits and resolve, Emily would make mental lists of the things that she found good about working for Texas and Polly. First on any list was the money. Emily relished seeing her bank account grow. Those moments when three figures became four, and four became five, were immensely satisfying. It was the first time she had ever cared about money. It was the first time she had ever earned a lot. Now she understood, in a way, what made Warren so obsessed. For the first time since she had separated from him, she had a modicum of financial security. She had Hiram Hogan on retainer. In time he would try to expand her visitation rights. In a longer time, she hoped he would be able to litigate the bigger case of what Tammany had done to her and, somehow, some way, get Jessica back.

Looking forward to that day in court, Emily liked the idea of playing detective and filling several diaries with bits and pieces of information about Tammany Hall.

In addition to the virtues she could identify in the money and the mystery, Emily could not deny that she enjoyed becoming a sophisticated New Yorker. Wasn't that what running away from the convent and from her forbidding father were really all about? She wanted to dress up, sing before an admiring audience, dance the night away. And that was what she was doing. Furthermore, she wanted the attention her father would never give her. She wanted men to notice her, to make a fuss over her. And that was what she was getting.

Then there was the sex. The passion and lust that Emily's dates had for her were not without their gratifications. Those moments when the men were so helpless next to her, when they told her how beautiful and fabulous and perfect she was, when they laughed at her jokes or begged her to sing for them, those moments all made Emily feel part of an exciting world.

Her singing at Guinan's got better and better. She became friendly with the musicians in Texas' house band and helped improvise on special numbers the jazzmen would put together. In the years while Emily had been at Bedford, jazz was coming out from underground and becoming more and more a popular phenomenon. Most of the best jazz could be heard up in Harlem. Emily was frequently taken by her dates to places like the Cotton Club, Connie's Inn, and the Savoy Ballroom to hear the black bands of such jazz notables as Duke Ellington, King Oliver, and Louis Armstrong. But plenty of good jazzmen played downtown as well, particularly at Guinan's, and Emily enjoyed working with them.

Emily's signature piece came to be the song called "Easy Street," of which she was particularly proud, for she had gone to the public library, immersed herself in the encyclopedia, dictionary, and thesaurus, and written all the lyrics herself. She liked to sing the song late in the evening, when Guinan's was packed and she was a little tipsy from the sweet rum punches she liked to drink. The fruity alcohol concoctions put her in a tropical mood and negated what, in darker or sober moments, might have seemed to her the absurdity of the soaring spirit of the song. She was celebrating everything her life was not. Wishful singing. But Emily was tired of singing the blues. Maybe, she believed each time she sang it, "Easy Street" would come true for her. She always began the song the same way, stepping up to the stage, tapping the microphone with her fingers to call the room to order, and then going into the slow, sad prologue without accompaniment.

> I've trudged along the Via Dolorosa
> I've moped across the Bridge of Sighs
> I've cried my way down Bad News Avenue
> I broke my heart on the Boulevard of Lies

The audience thought Emily was going to do a weeper, but then she flashed a big smile and fooled them.

> But now I've hit my stride
> My eyes are open wide
> I've got a brand new beat
> It's Easy Street.

Now the percussion, brass, and keyboard rang in, and Emily started dancing on the stage as she sang.

LULLABY AND GOODNIGHT

Kickin' up my heels
Makin' lots of deals
Shufflin' my feet
On Easy Street.

Gathering momentum, Emily pranced off the stage among
the tables, serenading the assorted clusters of men, sated
with food and bloated with drink and titillated by the
hostesses, all primed for Emily's musical seduction. She
looked at each of them, if only for a note, but that was
all it took to put the men under the spell of her voice.

It's a Paris rue, a New York avenue
Just walkin' home with you
That's Easy Street
It's a Roman via
Every time I see ya
You make life sweet
You're Easy Street.

I can take the Appian Way
The Champs Elysées
And throw them away
To be here with you.

I've no need for State Street
I've got my own great street
Sunset Boulevard's
My own backyard.

Life's a state of mind
Now I'm doing fine
We'll hold hands together
And walk our street forever.

Emily jumped on one of the tables, did high chorus-
line kicks, took one man's monocle, unraveled another's
bow tie. She was feeling wildly rambunctious. She loved
the power of her music, of her performance. She had her
childhood wish as she sang her song. She was a star. She
went back to the stage, glowing and triumphant, and
belted out the final refrain.

LULLABY AND GOODNIGHT

Let's go home, *très vite*
You're so awful neat
You're my easy, breezy,
Teasy, take it, baby, very easy.
You are my Easy Street.

The men stood up and hollered. Their cheers and whoops drowned out Texas Guinan. There was no need to request a big hand for this little lady. Emily had turned the place into a rodeo, and she was its queen. The first time she did "Easy Street" nearly twenty men called Polly Adler within the week to ask to see her. The song was good for Emily. It was good for business.

Yes, Emily was getting some of her self-confidence back. But it was confined to the world she was locked into, and this world had its own severe limitations. With her criminal record, there was no escape from Texas Guinan's underground to the *terra cognita* of Broadway. And despite the adulation of her speakeasy audiences, despite some of the incidental benefits of his lifestyle, there was no hiding from the loveless and degrading Devil's Island that being one of Polly's girls exiled her to. But always, in the end, one thing kept her going. She simply could not lose sight of her long-term goals of getting even with the corrupt politicians of New York and getting Jessica back, and, once she had her back, enabling her daughter to live every bit as well as she did with Warren. And that was why Emily continued on.

43

"You're a smash, dollink," Polly told Emily one afternoon when Emily came to Polly's for their weekly ac-
counting. "They're all crazy about you."

"Business has been good."

"They love you, dollink."

"I try to be nice to them," Emily said.

"Nice, schmise. That's not what it is. What it is is
that they know this isn't you. This isn't what you were
born to do. I got gals, this is all they can do. It's natural
for them. You, you're something else. They're touching
the untouchable and they love it. No, dollink, you're the
ultimate conquest. Aren't you flattered?"

"If you say so, Polly," Emily said.

"And the best part is, they tell their friends. You've
got great word of mouth. The dream of this business.
Listen, dollink, I've got somebody I think you know
who's just starting with me. Needs a little fixing up, but I
think she's going to be very popular." Polly rang a buzzer.
Who could this be? Emily was curious. "Speaking of girls
who were born to this . . ." Polly said. In walked Bridgit
Lund, from Bedford, wearing a white chiffon jumper that
left nothing to the imagination. Emily was disappointed.
She felt proprietary about Polly's. How could Polly let a
floozy like Bridgit come to work for her? Didn't she have
high standards?

"Bridgit." Emily shook her hand. "You look good."

"You ain't so bad yourself, Emily. Wow! Nothing like
being outta prison to make a girl look good," Bridgit
trilled in her little-girl voice. "Unbelievable that you're
here."

"I feel the same way," Emily replied.

Polly excused herself to attend to some Chinese visitors downstairs. "You girls catch up on old times."

"You are a great actress," Bridgit said.

"What do you mean?"

"I believed that whole bit at Bedford."

"What bit?"

"About you being framed."

"I was framed!"

"Then what are you doing here?"

"I needed the money. I couldn't get a legitimate job with my record. This was the best I could do." Emily spoke abashedly.

"Yeah, I know what you mean," Bridgit said. "I still can't believe it."

"Believe what?" Emily asked.

"That I'm going to be working with the saint."

Emily continued with her Tammany diaries. One of her most prized entries was obtained one night at Arnold Rothstein's when their lovemaking was disturbed by a phone call from Mayor Walker.

"Only the mayor, the governor, and my mother would I let interrupt us," Rothstein said as he kissed Emily apologetically and slid across the Irish linen sheets to pick up the phone, leaving Emily to lie naked under a huge Canaletto painting of the Grand Canal in Venice. An English lord had given Rothstein the treasure to settle part of his huge gambling debt at one of the many casinos Rothstein operated in East Side town houses—mini Monte Carlos with baccarat, roulette, croupiers, and a diamond-studded clientele to match the magnitude of the bets. Who said gangsters couldn't have culture? Rothstein also had two Rembrandts, a Franz Hals, and a Raphael in his penthouse.

"Yeah, Jimmy. I was in the middle of something . . . You're funny, Jim. It's okay . . . Of course he'll pay. He's good for it. If I say he pays, he pays. No, no, no, it's all fixed . . . You're covered, Jim . . . No trouble . . . That's the deal . . . My word . . ." He reached over and stroked Emily's body while he talked. He kept winking at her. There is no risk, Jimmy . . . no risk . . . How's Betty? Give her my love. 'Night, Jimmy."

Rothstein rolled back over and began kissing Emily.

"I didn't know you knew the mayor." Emily feigned ignorance. Always play dumb, Cassie had told her. The dumber you acted, the more they told you.

"He's a dear personal friend."

"Must be to call in the middle of the night."

"That's when he works. That's why they call him the late Jimmy Walker. That and he's always late for meetings. There's a joke. If you make an appointment with him in December, he'll get there the next May."

"You should run for mayor, A.R.," Emily said.

"Why should I? The mayor runs for me."

Emily invested her earnings with Wiz Radlow. The perfect gentleman, he never asked her where she was getting her money. As a regular at Guinan's, he probably knew, though Polly Adler said he had never used her services. In any event, he didn't care where the money came from, only that it was there.

"The whole country has Wall Street fever," he told Emily on the Staten Island ferry. "Any idiot who invests is getting rich."

"I hope that'll include me," Emily said, holding on to the rail and watching the tugs crisscross in the bay. They had taken sandwiches for a lunch meeting this blustery fall afternoon. Staten Island was a symphony of oranges and yellows, a brilliant contrast to the grays and blacks of lower Manhattan. One island of steel, another of wood. "I never met anyone who lived on Staten Island," Emily said.

"No one lives on Staten Island," Wiz said. "It exists only as a place where the ferry can turn around. I think it's time for you to buy a car," Wiz suggested, always thinking of ways to marshal Emily's assets.

"Buy it with what?"

"With your profits from Atlas Tool and Radiator. The convertible debentures I put you in already tripled. And the New York Central I got you is at one-ninety-three today."

"Wow. Everybody must be traveling."

"Traveling to the bank. I told you I'd take care of you. Listen, I've got an even better one." The ferry clunked into the dock at Staten Island. No one got off, just a few cars heading over to New Jersey. This was a lunch cruise.

"Another stock?"

"But of course, madam." Wiz mimicked a Continental accent. "Equitable Coach Company."

"Never heard of it."

"That's why it's a hot tip."

"What do they make? Coaches, I guess."

"They make money. At least they will. Equitable Coach is a little bus manufacturer, tiny company. I'm not sure they've even made a bus before. But they're about to get the entire franchise to build buses for the new lines in Brooklyn and Queens. Hundreds of buses."

"How can they? Why not General Motors?" Emily asked.

"Because of Tammany."

"Tammany?"

"Might as well call it Tammany Coach. You see, there's this young state senator, Hastings, high-liver type, like Mayor Walker. Well, when Walker was majority leader of the Senate, he needed one vote on a bunch of issues. Hastings was laid up drunk. I mean really hung-over. One more drink and his blood would've been pure alcohol. Walker begged him to come to the Capitol and vote. Well, Hastings arrived on a stretcher and raised his hand up yes each time Walker needed him."

"I guess Walker owes Hastings," Emily said.

"You bet he does. And Hastings has a third of Equitable's stock. Of course, the company's worth nothing till it gets the franchise, but it'll definitely get it. I'm sure of it. This is all on the come. That's why you should get in now."

"And it's all based on Walker's debt to Hastings?"

"Walker always pays his debts. Besides, I'm sure Hastings'll give Walker stock, too, so he'll stand to gain more than just honor." Emily remembered Warren's giving stock to McCarey. "I'm telling you, it's gonna be worth a fortune."

"How do you have all this inside information?"

"Hastings. I invest his money. Trust me."

"Okay." Emily nodded. She didn't object to taking Tammany's money. Look what they had taken from her. Besides, it was more evidence of the endless sea of corruption. The one thing she was uncomfortable about was that here she was morally drowning in it as well.

Wiz was one man at Guinan's who had shown no sexual interest in Emily. She couldn't understand why. On one hand, she appreciated the respect Wiz showed for her. On the other, she felt somehow rejected by it. Emily had been treated badly for so long she was now going overboard in wanting men to like her, and anything less demonstrative than a romantic kiss she interpreted as disinterest, if not disfavor.

From the beginning of their friendship, Cassie had said the easiest way out was to marry a rich man. A man like Wiz. Then Emily would be ultra respectable. Then she could make a real bid to get Jessica back. But Emily would never marry for money. Moreover, she wasn't meeting anyone, rich or poor, who was even vaguely interested in marrying her. Cassie's aspirations and self-delusions to the contrary, Emily hadn't seen any nuptials being generated at Guinan's. Winning a Polly Adler client away from his wife was an even more absurd notion on Cassie's part. Nice men didn't marry whores. Emily wasn't about to fool herself. Listen to Hogan, expect nothing, and you'll never be disappointed.

The ferry glided over the waves past the Statue of Liberty and into the terminal at South Ferry. Rushing back to his office on Wall Street, Wiz left Emily with a polite peck on the cheek.

"I'm off to protect your investments," he said.

44

Even though Alex Foster had been expelled from Yale, the passing years and his increasing success in advertising had taken much of the sting out of that collegiate disgrace. He was still a Yale man and had a number of friends from his New Haven days whom he saw in New York. Two of these friends had talked Alex into going with them up to Connecticut for the big football game with Harvard. Yale had enjoyed a smashing victory. To celebrate, Alex and his friends drove back to New York and began barhopping.

First they went uptown to the Puncheon Club, at 21 West Fifty-second, and decided it was too dressy. Then they went down to the Village to Mlle. Petitpas' French restaurant on Bleecker Street, which served decent food but much better wine, but they decided that wasn't right either. They went back up to Fifty-third and Park to Matt Winkle's, which looked just like the Hasty Pudding at Harvard. Problem was that at Winkle's too many belligerent Crimson alumni were drinking there. As a last resort, the Yalies went up to Moriarty's at 216 East Fifty-eighth Street.

Moriarty's was two worlds under one corrugated-tin ceiling. The first was neighborhood Irish—off-duty cops from the precinct, doormen from the fancy apartments on Park, janitors from Bloomingdale's. The other world was the young Ivies—"gintlemin," as barkeep Dan Moriarty called them. The barkeep known as Ole Pete was less polite. He called them "no-good, boardinghouse trash." They loved it. Whatever their appellation, they were in their twenties, and they came here to recapture or perhaps improve upon the drinking experience of their days in New Haven or Cambridge or Princeton and relax from their long days in their brokerage houses, their banks and law offices, their advertising agencies. The Irish paid fifty cents a drink, the "gintlemin" a dollar and a half.

Moriarty's was a brownstone basement with a long redwood bar. There were only three tables, known as holding tanks, because no one ever sat down except the drunks. There was no menu, and the only food served was "Long Island duckling," otherwise known as a ham sandwich, prepared by the delicatessen down the block. Despite the absence of amenities, the place was a legend, and it was always jammed.

The only thing wrong with Moriarty's, and many would dispute that it was a fault, was that except for an occasional socialite date of one of the guys, a wisecracking writer from *The New Yorker*, some adventurous Bryn Mawr girls in town on Saturday for their first martini, there were never any women there. Although women weren't unwelcome, Moriarty's was a man's place, a true saloon.

Women were the only thing missing from the Yalies' night on the town, but that could be remedied. Alex Foster was drinking a martini with his college-freshman roommate, Army Armstrong, who sold commodities on Pine Street, while their friend Randolph Chase, who worked in his uncle's arbitrage house on Beaver Street, went off to make a secretive phone call. The crowd, many in shawl-collar tuxedos, were linking arms, swaying, and singing "Bulldog Eli Yale."

"Triumph!" Randolph Chase explained, returning from the telephone. "Triumph!"

"You should have been a cheerleader," Alex said, thinking Chase was referring to the game.

"Not that, you ass."

"What is it, Chase?" Army asked.

"I just got three incredible goddesses . . ."

"Who?" Alex asked. "They'd have to be pretty ghastly to make a date at eleven o'clock."

"They are incredible. They're handpicked by Polly Adler."

"The madam?" Army's eyes popped open.

Chase nodded with his best undergraduate swagger. "Nothing but the best."

"Chase, how the hell did you get Polly Adler's number?"

"Belated graduation present from Uncle Winthrop."

"I knew the old bat was good for something," Army said. "God! I just thought of something."

"What?"

"Can you imagine Uncle Winthrop getting laid?"

"Perish the thought," Chase said.

"Who did you tell her we were, the maharaja of Jaipur?" Alex asked.

"Uncle Winthrop's nephew and his two Yale classmates. Why pretend we're some bloody Indians? I told her you were a Carnegie," Chase added, flicking his cigarette ash in Alex's direction, "and you, you slovenly pig," poking Army in his beer belly, "were a Frick, which is far better than you deserve. And since I'm a Chase, that makes us the three most eligible swells in this town."

"Do you know how much this could cost?" Alex asked.

"Forget the lucre," Chase sneered. "When Yale beats Harvard, nothing is too extravagant. Besides, my good man, you just got a raise. You're the ad genius of Madison Avenue. You should be celebrating. Having fun."

Fun. Alex had had no fun for a long time. After Emily's rebuff, he had immersed himself in his agency and come up with a number of very successful campaigns.

"It's almost a miracle," one advertisement had a girl with freshly short-cut hair saying. "Dandruff is a nuisance when your hair is bobbed. You see it more. But not with Sanatine. Dandruff and Sanatine simply do not go together." Alex had thought of a new use for the mouthwash he worked for—a scalp massage— and sales had risen. That was his first big campaign. He followed that up with another for a rouge company called Etruscan Bloom, with the slogan "Did nature fail to put roses in your cheeks?" Then, for Parklant Facial Cream, "Beauty isn't forever."

LULLABY AND GOODNIGHT

The result was a raise for Alex and an office with a view of the nave of St. Patrick's Cathedral. He knew he was on to something in twenties advertising—anxiety. The time was one of high narcissism and higher self-doubts. Exploit these insecurities, offer to soothe them, and you could sell products, lots of products.

Even though the scandal of his college years was finally behind him, Alex was still unhappy. Neither *Fly by Night* nor any of his other plays had sparked the slightest interest. And he hadn't met any woman who could compare to Emily, none of the secretaries who doted on him as the boy genius, none of his friends' sisters, no one. He tried not to think about Emily at Guinan's, that pool of rich sharks in tuxedos. He tried to rationalize her away—her record, her child, her problems—she wasn't for him. Too many warning flags. But he hadn't found anyone else who could move him to dream.

Emily, Cassie, and Bridgit were waiting under the clock at the Biltmore Hotel, the most popular rendezvous in the city. To meet under the Biltmore clock was the "thing to do," as a matter of tradition, as well as one of convenience. The hotel was located at Forty-fifth and Madison. It was a crossroads close to everything—Grand Central Station, the theaters of Broadway, the offices of Madison Avenue. The lobby was warm and comfortable, and until Prohibition the Biltmore had served some of the most generous drinks in town. It was almost midnight. Emily, Cassie, and Bridgit were all dressed in short chemises, ready to go dancing. The average passerby would have thought that they were three very jazzy society wives waiting to meet their husbands after some stag Yale reunion.

Bridgit was humming the Yale fight song.

"Bridgit, you're giving me a headache, and we haven't even started drinking yet," Cassie groaned.

"I'm so excited," Bridgit said. "I love these Yale boys."

"I didn't realize you were so particular," Cassie said. "Frankly"—she mocked a Park Avenue clubwoman's tones—"I'd much prefer a Hahrvahrd man."

"What do they say," Bridgit asked, "for God, for coun-

238

try, for Yale. Don't you love the sound of that? It's so classy."

"This could be big tonight. One of the guys is the nephew of Michael Mellon."

"I thought it was Michael Carnegie," Emily said.

"What's the difference," Cassie laughed. "Steel is steel."

It never occurred to Emily to worry about who the dates were. Polly Adler took care of that. Anyone she dealt with was safe. These were rich boys out for a good time. Emily had seen so many older men recently, she was actually looking forward to going out, doing the Charleston, drinking from flasks, making puns, college stuff, feeling young again, as young as she was.

Alex, Army, and Chase walked arm in arm up Madison Avenue, in their raccoon coats, singing drunkenly—to the Yale football anthem "Boola Boola"—"Polly, Polly, Polly, Polly, send us girls and make us jolly." They approached the Biltmore. Every woman they passed excited them, increased their anticipation of the night ahead.

"First, we'll go dancing. Then back to my uncle's place on Seventy-ninth," Chase said. "He's down in Palm Beach."

"Is that the one with the wine cellar?" Alex asked.

"The one and only."

"God. They'll think we are fat cats of a high order." Army smacked his lips. "Who gets the main bedroom?"

"I do, you peasant ingrate. Plus I get first choice," Chase said. "It's my uncle."

"What about that *noblesse oblige* they taught at New Haven?" Alex chided.

"A gentleman's highest duty," Chase said, "is to himself."

Alex hissed at him and spun through the revolving door. The Biltmore lobby smelled of expensive cigars and a wild blend of perfumes, the scents of all the women who waited for their dates beneath the huge overhead clock.

"There they are, I bet," Alex said, spying three women in the distance.

"Paradise, here we come," Army raved, bounding up the steps.

239

"I get first choice," Chase asserted.

"Give me the little blonde," Army said.

"It's my connection, hog breath," Chase snarled.

"We'll work it out. Let's meet them first," Alex conciliated. As they drew closer, Bridgit was the first to turn around. She spotted the three raccoon coats. "Here come our bulldogs," she exclaimed.

"Look at her," Army said, gasping.

"I said she's mine," Chase insisted.

Then Cassie turned around. Not wearing her glasses, she couldn't see. She always said her shortness of vision was a great asset in dealing with men. She couldn't see what was going on half the time, and that was just as well.

"She's great, too," Army said.

Alex lost his breath. He had met this woman but he couldn't remember where. Then Emily turned around, and Alex knew exactly where. "Oh, God," he gasped. He stopped short. Army and Chase held their step to see what was the matter. Alex stared at Emily for an endless moment to make sure it was she. "Oh, God," he repeated to himself.

Emily was petrified when she saw Alex. The horror and revulsion on his face engulfed her with shame. She ran out of the Biltmore lobby into the night, into the faceless throngs of people, speakeasy crowds milling between their favorite gin joints on the Broadway fringes, people leaving the theaters, people walking arm in arm, or searching for companionship, or stumbling drunk on the streets. Emily wanted to disappear.

Alex went into the men's room. He was going to be sick. How could he have been such a wretched judge of character? He hated himself.

Cassie fled the lobby, searching for Emily.

Back inside the hotel, only Bridgit remained.

"Do you think it was these coats?" Army said, turning to Chase.

"What the hell went wrong?" Chase muttered.

Bridgit stepped over to the boys and took one arm of each. She wasn't about to blow the evening. "Hi. I'm Bridgit."

"I'm Randolph Chase." Chase cleared his throat, trying to sound important. "This is Army . . ." Army shot him a corrective look. "Armstrong Carnegie. Of the Carnegies, you know." Army smiled.

"I love these coats," Bridgit giggled. "You know, they say three's a crowd, but I never had any trouble with crowds, if you get my drift."

Chase and Army broke out into grins. They knew exactly what she meant.

45

"Mommy, you're not happy," Jessica said to Emily on their monthly outing two days after the Biltmore incident. They were in the ice-cream shop in Morristown where Emily always took her daughter for hot-fudge sundaes and banana splits.

"You know I'm happy, darling. I'm happy to be with you."

"But your eyes are red. Were you crying?"

"No, dear. I've just been working very hard."

"Singing?"

"Yes, dear," Emily said.

"You look like you were crying. Like when Daddy used to be mean to you."

Emily hoped that Jessica did not remember the screaming and the beatings. Jessica had never mentioned it, not even then. Emily had prayed that Jessica had put those horrors out of her mind. But how could she have? "Why did you say that, sweetheart?"

"Because he hurt you and made you sad. You look sad now. Did some man hurt you?"

"No, honey."

"Why did Daddy ever hurt you?"

"I don't know. He was angry."

"He never hurts Mummy." Now Isabelle was Mummy. Emily was Mommy.

"He was angry because I was an actress and I wanted to go to the theaters and do my job," Emily explained. "He wanted me home all the time. He got angry because I disobeyed him. . . . But honey, I want to talk about you. Are *you* happy?"

"School's fun. And I have some friends. Christian is my favorite friend, and Penny.

"I have a lot of toys and games," Jessica recited.

"Are you happy with *her*, your . . . ?"

"Mummy? She's all right. But she always makes all these promises, and then she forgets."

"What kind of promises?"

"She said she would get me a new pony. She said she would take me on the big boat to England, like when she was a kid."

"Those are big things."

"Little things, too. She said she would get me a new dress like my friend Susie has. And another thing, she's always out playing cards or buying that old furniture. She just loves furniture. It's like Eliza—Eliza's the maid—it's like she's my mummy. I spend most of the time with her. Mummy just talks to show off to her friends. My daughter this and my daughter that." This was the first time Emily had heard Jessica complain. "It's like a doll, Mommy. You know, when you first get a new doll, you think, isn't this neat, and you play with it all the time. But after a while, you get tired of it, and you never play with it anymore. Do you think Mummy wants another new daughter? A *real* daughter?"

"No, darling. She probably has a lot on her mind. You know, your daddy has a lot of things she has to do for him. You know, to go out with him and have parties for his friends."

"She used to be so nice. Now, when I try to ask her things, she says 'You're a big girl,' and goes away."

"Well, you can ask anything of me, my precious little angel. Anything you want."

"But I never see you." Jessica was now near tears, but between Isabelle's propriety and Warren's toughness, she had learned to hold them back. "Mummy always says, 'Go ask Eliza,' but all Eliza can do is cook. Eliza's not my mommy."

"I am, Jessica, my love. I am. But you should go and tell your daddy whatever problems you have. He wants you to be happy, too."

Jessica shook her head. "No, Mommy. That's okay. I

miss you, Mommy." Jessica toyed with her sundae. "I wish I could see you more."

"Me too."

"I wish you didn't work so hard so you wouldn't be so sad."

Emily forced herself to smile. "Stop saying that. I'm perfectly happy. And don't you tell your daddy that I'm sad."

"I don't tell them anything," Jessica said, and Emily knew that her daughter was probably no happier than she was.

46

The confrontation with Alex jolted Emily out of an insidious resignation with her life and work. She wanted permanent custody of Jessica, and she wanted it now. If she got it, she would take her daughter away from New York and go down South, out West, anywhere to start a brand-new life together. But how? The court had refused her custody. She barely had visitation privileges. She therefore knew she would have to go over the court. She reviewed all the information she had collected on Tammany Hall. Perhaps Hiram Hogan could go to the district attorney with her diaries. In return for her testimony about some Tammany racket, they would reverse her conviction and give her her daughter back.

Goaded by her own impatience, Emily went to visit Hogan, swallowed her pride, told him of her connections with Polly Adler, and showed him one of her diaries. As he read with great interest, she thought she was onto something, that this was her breakthrough, that the wages of her sin would finally prove to be more than damnation. They were going to be her ultimate salvation. Hogan closed the red leather book and opened his eyes wide.

"Whew. Fabulous stuff! I wish I was a publisher."

Emily assumed this was an opening. "What can we do with it?"

"Lock it in your drawer and never show it to anyone else," Hogan said.

"What do you mean?" Emily asked, surprised.

"Just what I said. Bury it. Or they'll bury you."

"But can't we use this to get my case reversed?"

"How do you want to use it?" Hogan asked gruffly.

245

"Is Judge Crater going to testify against himself? Will Arnold Rothstein be your character witness?"

"Mr. Hogan, I've got solid evidence of how incredibly corrupt Tammany is. Look at this. Selling judgeships. Protection rackets. Liquor payoffs. Stock swindles. Bribes, bribes, bribes. Millions and millions of crooked dollars. This city's being bled to death. I've heard it. I've seen it. I've written it all down. Right here!" She pointed proudly at her diary. "And there's a lot more."

Hogan looked at her and gave her a deflating "So what?"

"Tammany Hall can't afford to have this information released."

"Released to whom?"

"To the courts."

"Courts? You saw what the courts did to you. Tammany Hall *is* justice in this city. Whoever you go to with this will be just as crooked as the ones you want to report."

"Then I'll go to the press."

"Yeah? And then you'll really be crucified. How'd you get this dope? they'll ask you. As a high-priced call girl. You'll get the publicity, all right, but you'll never, never get your daughter back."

"So what do I do?"

"Be grateful for what you got. Be grateful that you're not in Bedford. Be grateful you're alive."

"What good is being alive if I can't have my daughter, if I have to be a prostitute to earn a living, if Tammany has turned me into something I'm not?"

"Then prove it. But you prove nothing by telling me how crooked Tammany is. That's old news. We know it."

"Does the public really know it?"

"Everybody knows it. Corruption is a fact of life in New York. If you don't like it, go live in Vermont. They're honest there, but you've gotta take the snow. No, if Tammany ruined you, you have to prove it, prove it directly."

"How?"

"By proving that Warren Matthews and Michael Mc-Naughton and whoever else conspired to frame you. And, frankly, I don't know how you do it. One will never testify against the other."

"What if I could get other women to come forward? Other women McNaughton framed?"

"Well, it would help, if you could get a court that wasn't a Tammany court—and there aren't many of them—to listen. But forget it. You'll never get anyone to talk. If the woman went to prison, then she won't have any credibility. Even if she did, she probably wouldn't want to dredge up her record. And if she paid off the vice squad out of fear, she'll always be afraid. Fear works. She won't talk. She'll never talk."

Emily appreciated Hogan's point. For all her sleuthing, she had not heard one word about the entire framing process. She had collected evidence of multiple forms of corruption, but not one word about what she wanted to hear. Nor did any of the women she knew at Bedford want to talk about it. The only one she was in touch with was Bridgit Lund, and she knew Bridgit wasn't about to testify about anything. Bridgit had a lucrative career as a call girl to protect. What women would talk? How could she find them? She didn't know.

"So there's nothing I can do?" Emily sighed.

"Go see your daughter. I got you visitation and we were damned lucky at that. I'm a lawyer. I'm not a magician. Remember one thing. New York is rotten to the core. The rot makes it exciting. That's why we're here. You can't fight Tammany Hall."

Emily thanked Hogan, took her diary, and left. She knew that, within the law, she had gone as far as she could go.

Outside the law, Emily continued to see Polly's dates, hoping that one of them might provide a special break for her. Her prime candidate was Arnold Rothstein. At the beginning, her main incentive for continuing to see him, other than for the money, was to discover incriminating evidence about Tammany Hall that might give her some leverage in getting Jessica back. But now that Hogan had told her that no matter what she had, Tammany was above and beyond incrimination, Emily began to think of her dates with Rothstein in another light. Perhaps, as Cassie had once fliply suggested, perhaps with all his power and his Tammany connections, he himself

could help her get Jessica back. He could prove to be the
way out of a life which seemed more depressing every
day after Hogan's shattering pessimism. Emily's problem
was that she had absolutely no idea how to pose the
question to him.

Rothstein was having problems of his own. He had
been looking bad. His ties were crooked, his collar buttons sometimes undone. He would forget to shave. His
complexion was sallow. He lived on bicarbonate of soda,
punctuating his sentences with belches. Rothstein was
under enormous pressure from a new business he had
entered, a business that took Emily a while to figure out.

One night when she arrived at the Central Park West
penthouse, the Chagalls, Rembrandts, and other European art were gone. In their place were flowered scrolls,
Buddha statues, painted screens, silver swans, Oriental
tapestries, and endless chinoiseries. The penthouse had
become Peking in the sky.

"What happened?" Emily said as she wandered through
the Eastern treasures, the jade figurines, the delicate
miniature junks decorated with jewels, the bonsai trees.

"I've gotten into the import business," was all Rothstein
would tell her.

These objects d'art were the best of the chinoiseries
that Rothstein's agents, under the business entity "Roth-
more Imports, Ltd.," were bringing through customs and
jamming into art galleries and antique shops from Lafayette Street to Madison Avenue. The real goods, however, were heroin, smuggled inside the antiques. Heroin
cost two thousand dollars a kilo and could sell for three
hundred thousand on the streets of Harlem and, through
Rothstein's agents, in the other Harlems all over the
country.

Emily found out about the heroin by indirection, overheard conversations, slips of paper. There were suspicious calls from men with names like "King" Solomon in
Boston, Warren Torio in Chicago, Yasha Katzenberg in
Shanghai. Rothstein never took drugs, other than bicarbonate, yet the words "kilos," "pure white," "cutting,"
and other phrases could mean only one thing.

Rothstein had gone into drugs because his other ventures had begun to falter. His "bucket shops," fraudulent

brokerage houses that would speculate on their own accounts against their customers' interests, had become the target of the authorities, as had his stolen-bond racket. Rum-running had made him one fortune, but now there was too much competition. Narcotics, however, was a new world for Rothstein; the pioneers were small operators and corrupt physicians. There was no one who ruled the field on a big scale. Rothstein saw himself as the kingpin, the Rockefeller, of narcotics. Yet the huge cash demands of this high-stakes drug trade were becoming his undoing. Rothstein gambled more and more heavily. Instead of taking Emily to horse races and fancy dinners, he took her to all-night card games.

Rothstein's favorite poker game was held at the Park Central Hotel apartment of his friend George "Hump" McManus. The living room, with the Chinese furniture Rothstein had given him, looked like a deluxe Oriental bordello, all black lacquer. There *were* always lots of paid women around. The men around the table this night were McManus, a bookmaker, two sinister men from Los Angeles— the first a dark Mexican named "Nigger Nate" Raymond, the second, Alvin C. "Titanic" Thompson, a golfer who won a fortune betting on the links—and three unsavory New York bookies, Martin Bowe, Joe Bernstein, and Meyer Boston.

The women lounged around the parlor, making telephone calls all over the country and drinking Bacardi cocktails. Emily felt degraded by the company. She read the *Times*, but that made her seem too snooty, so she began to drink and join the small talk about good hairdressers and fall styles. Meanwhile, the bets rose into the thousands in the smoky room. There was no cash on the green-felt table. Only white chits, IOU's, and almost all of them Rothstein's.

The game went on nearly forty-eight hours. Emily asked if she could go home, but Rothstein insisted that she sleep over in McManus' bedroom. "I need you, baby," he whispered in a nervous voice. She had never seen him nervous before. Emily's rest was interrupted by numerous groans. Some of the players would sit out a few hands to have sex with their girls in the bedrooms. Rothstein never left the table. Titanic Thompson came and made a pass at Emily. McManus took him aside and explained the rules. No one touched A.R.'s women.

By the morning of the second day, all the cocaine on earth couldn't keep the players up. As a last gesture, to salvage something, Rothstein bet fifty thousand against Nigger Nate Raymond in a high-card draw. Rothstein drew a queen, and gave a smile of relief. The California hustler drew an ace and laughed, sweeping a sea of white chits, little icebergs worth a fortune, into his lap. Rothstein, who had lost over three hundred thousand dollars, went into the bedroom and woke Emily.

Back in the living room, the Californians were demanding cash.

"I don't carry that sort of dough under my fingernails," Rothstein said.

The Californians knew better. Rothstein was known never to have less than two hundred thousand dollars in cash readily available to him. Despite their protests, Rothstein left with Emily. "See you in a day or two," he told them as he slammed the door. "See them in hell," he told Emily in his limousine. "I don't pay off on fixed poker."

Stiffing these alleged fixers seemed, in a curious way, to revive a despondent Rothstein. For his next date with Emily, he took her out on the town.

With his two bodyguards, Birnbaum and Greenblatt, one in front, one behind, the couple walked up Seventh Avenue to the Warner Theater to see Al Jolson in *The Jazz Singer*. There were lines around the block at the theater to see this first all-singing, all-talking motion picture, which was creating almost as much excitement in New York as Babe Ruth's sixty home runs. Rothstein and Emily, naturally, walked right in. Kings never waited in line. Rothstein was acting like the King again. They walked back home singing "Swanee."

After the movie, Emily sensed it was the time, if it would ever be the time, to ask the King for help. It made her so nervous. "Baby, what's wrong . . . you're cold as ice," Rothstein said as he was beginning to unzip Emily's black sequined dress.

"Nothing," Emily said. "Nothing's wrong."

"Don't tell me that." He sat up straighter and sipped

his nightcap of antacid. He couldn't eat late. He almost always had dreadful indigestion.

"I don't want to burden you with my problems, A.R." She did want to, but she wasn't sure how to go about it.

"Why not? You got a problem, I can fix it." He put special spin on the word "fix." It was his favorite word.

"I guess you can." Emily smiled. "How'd you like to help a damsel in distress?"

"If you're the damsel . . ."

"What about the distress?"

"What is it?"

"Feel like a bedtime story, A.R.?"

"Shoot."

"I never told you this, but I have a daughter . . ." Emily began her story. This was a new direction for her. If she couldn't beat Tammany, as Hogan had told her, she would join it. She was inside, in a way, already. She would work from the inside to get Jessica back. As Cassie had said, one phone call from Rothstein to Walker, and things could be immediately set right. She knew Rothstein liked her. Now was the test of how much. Of course, she was violating Polly's edict against dumping personal problems on her clients. But she had known Rothstein over a year now. He was more than a client, she hoped. She didn't believe, or want to believe, that their intimacy could be that superficial. He had to have feelings.

As she told her tale, she was delighted at Rothstein's reaction. His fist clenched. His jaw tightened. He did like her. At the end he simply said, "I'll talk to Jimmy."

"A.R.," Emily exulted, "you mean you'll help me? Really?"

"You're my baby. Damn right I'll help you. Just sit tight." He patted her derriere. "I'm going to England next week. As soon as I'm back, I'm gonna fix it."

Emily unzipped her dress and made love to Rothstein like she had never done before.

47
1928

Emily was singing "Blue Skies" when Michael McNaughton came into Guinan's. He was with Lucretia Morgan, wearing a fox stole, and a young aspiring actress named Annie Hunt, who had just come to town from Topeka. Annie was living at the Three Arts Club—for out-of-town singers, dancers, and actresses. Her father had a tool-manufacturing company back in the Midwest. He wasn't crazy about Annie's coming to New York, Annie had told Lucretia in the coffee shop across the street from the club. Lucretia scouted for prospects there. Like Emily's father, Mr. Hunt believed that nice girls didn't become actresses. Nice girls stayed and sang in the Methodist Church choir—that would get the dramatics out of their blood—and married nice boys met at a church social or the golf club or daddy's business.

But Annie was a little spoiled. Daddy had given her some money, told her to go east, take classes, get it out of her system. Confidence woman Lucretia said she was an actress. She saw Annie was all alone, scared, and had money. She was an ideal target. Accordingly, Lucretia said she would introduce her to her friend Adam Lovell, a big show backer. He had a weakness for well-scrubbed, wholesome, church-choir types like Annie. He was backing a new musical by a young man from Indiana named Cole Porter. He needed a Midwestern, all-American girl for a small singing part. He was charming and delightful. Annie would be his type, Lucretia told the wide-eyed innocent. Adam Lovell might even want to date her, as well as cast her. Adam Lovell was Michael McNaughton.

Given her background, Annie would pay and never tell

a soul. McNaughton had taught Lucretia how to spot the ones for whom the avoidance of the disgrace of a prostitution frame-up could have no price tag too high. They expected to get at least a few thousand dollars from Annie. A nice night's work.

When Emily saw them enter, she nearly choked on the words of her song. She recognized McNaughton immediately. The elegant suit, the wavy hair, the gorgeous eyes, the gleaming teeth. Who were these women? The shorter one was the mark, Emily decided instantly. The tall one was too sophisticated, too savvy. She was in on the sting, Emily knew without knowing. She had to save the other girl. But how? Somehow she finished "Blue Skies," took her bow, and stepped out into the swirling smoke and dancing tuxedos.

"Give the little lady a big hand," Texas called out, and dispatched another singer to the microphone.

"Hello, Michael," Emily said as she walked over to the tiny corner table where the trio were sipping pink ladies and toasting Annie Hunt's bright future on Broadway. Emily could see the romantic glaze on Annie's face. McNaughton had seduced her completely. The rest was a matter of execution. She had to stop it. "Michael!" Emily repeated, getting the table's attention.

McNaughton didn't recognize her. It had been too long. There were so many others. Emily looked quite different now.

"Uh . . . I don't believe we've . . ."

"Don't remember me, do you, Michael?"

"I'm sorry, it's Adam . . . Adam Lovell." McNaughton stood up gallantly. "There must be some confusion."

"Adam Lovell." Emily nodded. "Uh-huh. You don't remember me?"

"No, but I'd like to . . . Why don't you sit down? This is my friend Lucretia Morgan, and this is Annie, uh, Hunt, yes. Annie Hunt."

Emily sat down. She noticed the beautiful ring on his finger. A Tammany ring. She saw a place setting on the table. Her first thought was to grab the knife and plunge it into his heart. That's what he deserved. But that would be a pyrrhic victory. She would go back to prison, possibly to the electric chair. No, that would not accomplish her goal. There had to be another way to get revenge and savor the victory.

"You're a good singer," Annie said. "This is a great place."

"Absolutely," McNaughton said, clinking Annie's glass.

"Thank you," Emily said, and turned to McNaughton. "So, Michael, your memory's failed you."

"Adam. Adam," he corrected her.

"Can't remember who I am. Can't remember who you are. Can't even remember who she is."

"We just met," Annie politely came to his defense.

"I bet you're an actress," Emily said.

"Yes . . . how'd you guess?" Annie smiled. "At least, I want to be an actress."

"And you're an actress too?" Emily said, turning to Lucretia.

"Struggling."

"You're a great actress," Emily continued. "I can tell."

"Aw. Not really."

The tension was mounting, diffused only by the raucous party atmosphere. "He's going to get you your big break, isn't he . . . Annie, it's Annie, isn't it?"

"Yes. And yes. I mean, gosh, I hope so," she giggled. McNaughton beamed at her supportively. "I really hope so."

"He got me my big break," Emily said, her smile vanishing.

"Who are you?" McNaughton asked.

"Just another pretty face. Somebody else you were going to put on Broadway."

"What are you—"

"You gave me my big break. Except then your name was Amory."

McNaughton began to remember. He had used so many aliases.

"But my big break got me in prison, didn't it? Didn't it?" Emily rose from her seat and took Annie's hand. Lucretia, at the same time, grew very worried and placed her arm around Annie. A tug-of-war was brewing.

"This woman is crazy," McNaughton said. "I don't know you."

"I'm Emily Stanton, Officer McNaughton." Emily said

it at the crescendo of her voice, but not loud enough to disturb the band playing "Limehouse Blues." The fox-trotters dancing around the table didn't notice either. "I spent two years in prison because of you, you dirty, rotten bastard. Two years. I guess you've framed so many women, you don't remember. I'm just another statistic."

McNaughton stood up, acting unfazed. "Come on, Annie, let's get out of here." He gave Emily the same "you're-insane, beneath-contempt" glance Warren had given her at the custody hearing.

"Let's go, Annie," Lucretia echoed. "Sorry."

Then Emily raised her voice. "She's in with him. Run, Annie. Run for your life. This is Officer McNaughton of the vice squad. He's no backer. He frames women. He'll frame you as a prostitute. Run, Annie. Go home. He can destroy your life the way he did mine."

Texas Guinan came up behind Emily and grabbed her. "Hey, honey. What's wrong?"

"He's going to frame her." Emily pointed at McNaughton.

"She's crazy," McNaughton said to Texas.

"He's a vice cop," Emily yelled. "Run, Annie. Get away from him. Please. Believe me. Go."

Annie looked at McNaughton. She looked at Lucretia. She looked at Emily. She made up her mind. "It's really late. Thank you for a nice evening." She almost curtsied and then ran for the exit.

"Thank God," Emily cried.

Lucretia took McNaughton's arm. He gave Emily a searing glance and walked out. Texas gave the bandleader a nod. He struck up "Toot, Toot, Tootsie, Good-bye."

"What in blazes was all that about?" Texas asked.

"That was McNaughton. Officer McNaughton. The one who framed me," Emily told her.

"Over here . . ." Texas motioned Emily to the kitchen, away from the noise. "Are you out of your mind?"

"What?"

"Making a scene like that?"

"But that man ruined my life."

"Not good enough, honey."

"Good enough what?"

"Good enough excuse. Emily, in my establishment,

the customer is always right, even if he just murdered his folks." Texas breathed her gin-sotted breath on Emily. She was sweating like a pig; her makeup was beginning to run. She worked hard for her money. Sentiment had no place here. "I'm sorry, honey, but that's the way it is."

"He was going to frame that girl."

Texas became impatient. Her face had hardened. Its normal butterball, Kewpie-doll grin was gone. "I don't care what the hell he was gonna do to her. I don't care if he was gonna carve her up and sell the parts at Penn Station as souvenirs. That's *their* business, and this here's *my* business. Listen to me, sugar." Texas bore down on Emily. "If he was the one who you say framed you, I remember your story, that man was a Tammany man. I'm here because Tammany allows me to be here, and so are you. Any Tammany man gets the red carpet here. And a man from the vice squad! How dare you start up like that? Tammany can shut us down so fast, and you don't want that. It's only more trouble for you. Don't bite the hand that feeds you, sugar. You understand?"

"But, Texas—"

"Don't do it again. Understand?" Texas jammed her pudgy finger hard into Emily's stomach. She lost her breath. It hurt. It scared her. "Understand?"

"Yes, yes. All right. I'm sorry."

Emily was also sorry she had allowed Annie to leave Guinan's without even getting her address. Here was the first real evidence of the framing process Emily had encountered, and she had let the prospective victim, and a prospective ally for her, get away. Who knew how to find her? She would probably disappear into the vast anonymity of New York. Emily knew that in the blindness of her rage she had missed a major opportunity. Then in a flash of further reflection she rationalized it all away. Even if she found her, even if the girl were willing to talk, who in this venal city would even listen to them?

"I'm sorry, Texas," Emily repeated.

Texas swung back into the party outside the kitchen door as if nothing had happened. "Hello, sucker," she yelled in her best festive voice to an incoming celebrant. Emily forced a smile and prepared to follow.

48

One of Emily's most unusual clients was a teenager named Vincent "Mad Dog" Coll, who was perhaps the most feared killer in the entire city, no mean accomplishment for a nineteen-year-old in a league populated by some of the most vicious criminals in the world. "He's got absolutely no imagination," Polly Adler had told Emily. "That's why he's so dangerous. He can't imagine ever getting killed himself."

Tall, gangly, with freckles, the Irish-born Coll looked more like someone who would deliver groceries rather than murder sentences from his boss, Dutch Schultz, who paid Coll's tab with Polly as one of Coll's fringe benefits. "He's quick on the trigger," Polly told Emily to make her less apprehensive about seeing the child gangster. Polly's phrase had nothing to do with Coll's gunmanship. It meant that he was a prostitute's dream, a premature ejaculator, who would arrive and leave in the space of a half-hour. Coll usually used Polly's girls after hits, when he was very excited, often seeing three or four girls in an hour or two, with Schultz paying hundreds of dollars to keep his boy calmed down.

Actually, Coll had more imagination than anyone gave him credit for, at least in the mayhem department. He specialized in Oriental tortures, needles under fingernails, hot feet (burning toes and soles with lighted matches), and crucifixions. With Polly's ladies, however, he was shy and diffident and, in his own way, a gentleman. He would blush and apologize for ejaculating so quickly, when in truth, the girls couldn't thank him enough. He was fairly laconic, except with Emily, who intrigued

257

him. He decided they had a great deal in common. "So both of us got our lives ruined by Catholic schools," he said, lighting up when Emily mechanically responded to a question about her post.

"Immaculate Virgin Mission, I'll never forget the name. Immaculate virgin and me, that was some combine," he guffawed. This school tie made Coll comfortable enough with Emily to chatter about his upcoming trial for the murder of a four-year-old child killed by a stray bullet during a gang shoot-out in Italian Harlem. "I don't kill little kids," the kid protested to Emily, whose skin crawled, lying in bed with this jumpy, freckled teenager whose gangster boss was paying a hundred dollars an hour for this peculiar sexual baby-sitting. Emily couldn't wait to leave, but one of Coll's boasts intrigued her. "I kidnapped Owney Madden's top guy and got thirty grand ransom," he bragged, "so Dutch could get me the best mouthpiece in town. This guy never loses. Not for thirty grand, he better not lose. Or he loses big."

The thirty-grand guy who never lost, Emily found out from Polly, was a Brooklyn criminal attorney named Samuel Leibowitz. That's what Emily decided she needed, a criminal attorney who didn't lose. Hogan had told her to give up, but she would never do that. Rothstein had promised to help her when he returned from England. If he did, maybe she'd never need a lawyer again. And wasn't Leibowitz a pipe dream? He wanted huge fees and he seemed to represent only big-time criminals. Who knew, maybe he was a Tammany man, too. Nevertheless, Emily bought the newspapers every day, and when she saw the defense Leibowitz presented for Coll, she realized there was at least one magician at the bar, and she wished she could meet him.

The police had wanted Coll badly. Although internecine gangland warfare not only gave New York romance but also eliminated the mobsters the police would otherwise have had to deal with, killing children was another matter. That gave the city a bad name. "Coll had to go," was the word from City Hall.

The people's star witness was a man named George Brecht, who turned out to be an ex-con and a "professional" star witness who worked for police around the country in sealing the fates of unwanted criminals. It was widely known that Brecht had been a "guest" of the NYPD for months, being taken to speakeasies and Yankee games and boxing matches, always in the company of three police chaperons. On the witness stand, he testified that he had seen Coll fire the machine gun that killed the child. He knew it was Coll because of the dimple in his chin. That was the dead giveaway. Emily saw photos of Coll after Brecht's testimony. He was smiling. She found out why when Leibowitz cross-examined Brecht.

Brecht had stated that he earned his living selling Eskimo Pies. He, naturally, would not admit that he was the petty thief and professional witness that he was. Leibowitz sent out for fourteen Eskimo Pies, twelve for the jury, one for the district attorney, one for the judge. On cross, Leibowitz demonstrated Brecht knew less about his product than any salesman possibly could. He couldn't describe the label. He'd never heard of dry ice.

"How did you carry them?" Leibowitz asked.

"In . . . er . . . boxes."

"Cardboard boxes?"

"That's right," Brecht answered.

"And no ice, no dry ice?"

"No."

"And what month was this?"

"Er . . . July, I believe."

"July," Leibowitz boomed. "July. July was a hot month, as I recall, was it not?"

"Yes, it was hot."

"But you carried these Eskimo Pies around in the hot July sun with no dry ice." The Eskimo Pies were melting in the jurors' hands as they licked the chocolate coating. "And they didn't melt?"

"No, they didn't."

"How did you keep them from melting, then, Mr. Brecht?"

"They were cold. They stayed cold."

"I see. Their own coldness kept them from melting," Leibowitz intoned sarcastically.

"Yes."

"Those were very interesting pies." Leibowitz smiled, knowing Brecht's ignorance of the pies and of the laws of thermodynamics would win the case. Brecht's morale began to unravel. Leibowitz nailed him on lie after lie. Coll was declared not guilty.

"I shoulda gone ahead and shot some more people that day," Mad Dog Coll boasted when he saw Emily.

"How does Leibowitz do it?" she asked.

"It's the voice," Coll said. "He's got a voice like a priest. Like a real priest."

Emily read with interest about some of Leibowitz's other cases, all of which read like Damon Runyon Broadway stories—the Breadknife Murderess, the Vendetta Woman, Two-Gun Tilly Sachs, the Razor Slayer, the Insurance Death Plotter. He got them all off. And then, of course, there was Leibowitz's most famous client, Al Capone. But when she called his office and spoke to two secretaries about her case, their reply was, "We don't do custody." "We don't do civil cases, period." "He's taking only capital cases, dear, we're very sorry." Maybe if she had enough money, Emily wondered. Maybe if she had thirty thousand dollars. She didn't. Yet Leibowitz, the magician, Leibowitz, the king of criminal lawyers, stayed on her mind.

49

Walking down the hospital corridor, Emily was struck first by the smell, a pungent combination of perfume and ether. There were so many showgirls, call girls, party girls, outside the room that Emily might have thought she was at an audition for a Broadway show were it not for the white tiled halls, the stretchers, the transfusion bags, the doctors and nurses clad in white, rushing about with those grim, efficient faces. There were scores of others bodyguards, lawyers, gangsters, nightclub owners—mobbing the hospital lobby, swatting off reporters as if they were annoying mosquitoes. Rothstein's burly major-domo Birnbaum was sewing as the arbiter of visitation privileges. He knew who was really important. If the person was on his list, he would grunt approval to a gray-haired nurse, who allowed those who mattered an audience with the dying ruler.

Emily had heard about it while dancing at Guinan's. She hadn't seen Arnold Rothstein since he came back from his trip to England, although his promise to talk to Mayor Walker was etched in her consciousness. That promise was her great hope. When she heard he had been shot, she bled inside as well. Not only had she become close to him, she needed him.

The gun battle had taken place at the Park Central Hotel, Emily learned from the talk in the lobby. Rothstein had been eating cheesecake in his Broadway "office," a back table at Lindy's Restaurant, when a call came to meet a Mr. McManus at the Park Central. As he opened the door of McManus' apartment, he was shot several times in the chest.

261

Emily remembered McManus from that endless poker game. Rothstein had never paid off Titanic Thompson and Nigger Nate Raymond. In fact, he had smeared their names all over New York and, by implication, that of host McManus. The worst thing for a gambler's reputation was the charge that he ran a crooked game. The Californians had gone back West empty-handed. They continued their pressure on McManus, who had tried to threaten Rothstein into paying. That amused him. "Scare me?" he laughed heartily to Emily before he left for England. As Emily had known for months, Rothstein's real problem was cash flow. In the heroin trade, the drug dealers didn't take chits. He had property mortgages to pay. Tammany bribes. Rothstein needed all the cash he could get. Why pay some West Coast shysters?

Oh, why hadn't he, Emily thought as she waited in the corridor with the call girls and the detectives. Rothstein had gone to the Park Central alone. No Birnbaum, no Greenblatt. What a mistake. Rothstein, bleeding critically, had somehow made it to the street and hailed his own taxi to Poly-Clinic Hospital. Despite the persistent hospital-bed interrogation by the police, he remained true to his underworld code of honor. He would not name his assailant. While police and bodyguards stood vigil, the only people allowed in were Rothstein's wife—a plain woman, Emily thought—and the police. Carolyn Rothstein didn't seem upset by the other women. She, like Allie Walker, had given up on her profligate husband years before. Rothstein's real friends, his Tammany friends, had to be absent for purposes of discretion. They could not publicly acknowledge their umbilical cord to the underworld.

After numerous applications to the nurse at the door, Emily was recognized by Birnbaum and allowed into the room. The other girls in the corridor buzzed jealously. Emily was struck by how frail and helpless the forty-six-year-old gambler looked, a puppet strung to transfusion bottles and electric monitors. Arnold grunted to his lawyers in the room to get out. They looked at Emily and dispersed. Emily touched his cold, clammy white skin. His eyes were slits, his breathing a faint whisper.

"Poor A.R." She caressed him. He smelled of ether,

of rubbing alcohol, of death. "You've just got to get better."

"Dammit," Rothstein gurgled. He tried to breathe. "Dammit," he mumbled. "Emily, I wanted . . . to . . . to . . . to fix it . . . for you." He gave her what seemed to be a faint smile and closed his eyes. Emily left the room.

Two days later he was dead. A collective sigh of relief was breathed when the steel filing cabinet in Rothstein's home at 912 Fifth Avenue "disappeared." "That saved Tammany from mass suicide," one City Hall pundit observed.

All Emily had from her association with Rothstein were dozens of entries she could show to no one, entries about this Tammany judge and that Tammany senator, protecting this Tammany bootlegger and that Tammany racketeer, early-morning calls from Jimmy Walker, oblique references, but nothing at all that she, Emily, could use to prove she had been framed. She would trade anything else she had, easily, to have Rothstein back. He would have helped her. He was the most important man she knew. Besides, even though she at first felt betrayed to see all his other mistresses, she realized that this was his game— and hers. She knew she would miss him.

50
1929

"I know you want out of this," Cassie told Emily, "but there's only one way, and that's straight up the aisle to the altar." They had come up to Polly's this afternoon to collect their pay. They waited in her office.

In its way, Emily's life in New York had acquired a rhythm as slavish as that of Bedford—sleep, sing, date, sleep, sing, date. All her hopes to stop working for Polly had died with Rothstein. Hogan wouldn't help her. Right now, she couldn't afford Leibowitz. Her only course, then, was to keep working and save even more money, but Rothstein-type customers were rare, even in the boom economy, and with Polly taking half, Emily was no better than a comfortable wage slave, except she didn't have an office on Madison Avenue. Her tenure would last no longer than her looks.

With the unremitting nights she was keeping, she noticed the first evidence of purple circles growing under her eyes. All her trips to Elizabeth Arden's salon, with its massages and mud packs and emollients and lotions that promised eternal youth, could not withstand her abusive regimen. Age and sex were wearing her out. Cassie's exhortation to marry rich stung. In her two years working for Polly, Arnold Rothstein was the only client who she believed really liked her and whom she considered a friend. None of the others ever showed any serious interest in her. "They want variety, dollink," Polly explained. "What can I say? If they want the same one, they stay home with the missus." No, Emily hadn't met anyone at Polly's or at Guinan's who was interested in anything but a good time, his good time.

"What about Wiz?" Cassie asked.

"He's my broker."

"He's very respectable. I could go for him."

"All he's proposing is AT&T and Bethlehem Steel."

"I think you should expand your portfolio."

Perhaps, Emily thought. She had grown to like Wiz. Maybe there could be something more, but if there were, Wiz had showed no interest in pursuing it.

"Which of you is going to take him?" Polly said, breezing into the room.

"Take who?" Cassie asked.

Polly called the girls over to her window. Downstairs in the parlor was a chubby, overdressed young man with slicked-down hair, spats, and a morning coat. To Emily he resembled a walrus who had gone to a greedy haberdasher. "Henry Lamb." Polly beamed.

"Looks more like Henry Hog," Cassie laughed.

"You'd be high on the hog with him, as they say down South, dollink. You know the Lambs?"

"Only the wolves," Cassie said.

"Chicago Lambs. They own the stockyards. Real money, dollink. Real money. Beef. He's a nice boy."

"Stockyards? Hmm!" Cassie took a renewed interest after Polly's recitation of Henry Lamb's background.

"He's all yours, Cassie," Emily said. She couldn't face the thought of a date today.

"You're turning down more business than most girls get, dollink. Think of that giant meat business his family has," Polly said.

"I've been feeling vegetarian these days," Emily said wanly.

"Thanks, Em," Cassie said. "I guess I'll put off that trip to Altman's."

"There is one slight . . . well, I wouldn't say problem, but Cassie, keep this in mind," Polly said. "Henry has these ideas that he is—you won't believe this—Tom Mix. He has this fetish with saddles and lassos. I don't want to scare you . . ." Polly trailed off.

Cassie rolled her eyes in weary disgust.

Emily was already out the door.

Emily huddled with Wiz Radlow in a dismal rain under

a black canvas umbrella, listening to President-elect Herbert Hoover speak. Hoover stood in front of the Sub-Treasury Building on Wall Street, across from the Stock Exchange. The Sub-Treasury, with its Greek columns, resembled a temple, a temple of money. Wall Street itself was an acropolis, an acropolis of gold, of rising stocks, of dreams of wealth and power. There were brokers and lawyers in the crowd, to be sure. But there were others, just as optimistic. There were runners and cleaning women and short-order cooks milling about, smiling as the roundish little bulldog from California spoke out in the rain: "What a thrill to be here at the heart of American business. I can hear the heart beating. This heart has never been stronger." They cheered. Everybody, literally everybody, thought he or she was going to get rich. Maids knew all about the brokerage houses of Morgan Stanley. Convertible debentures were in the lexicon of every cabdriver. The A & P markets sold caviar on the shelves. Bespectacled bookkeepers danced until dawn in nightclubs. No one ever slept. Nineteen-twenty-nine was the year of the dollar.

"Only a fool works for a living anymore," Wiz Radlow said to Emily under the umbrella. "What would it be like without the stock market? We're going to become a nation of investors."

"Wiz . . ." Emily squeezed his hand as Hoover droned on. "You've been good to me. Thanks."

"The market's been fabulous," Radlow said rapturously. "With Hoover in Washington, it can only get better. Sky's the limit, Emily. I've got a new issue for you. Armacost Copper." Wiz leaned over to whisper, so none of the neighboring brokers would hear. "They've hit a vein in the Philippines, and before it's made public . . ."

"Do you think they've really found anything?" Emily was dubious. After all, she had been around Arnold Rothstein and his bucket shops, which made their fortune on phony issues with phony strikes—gold, copper, silver—whatever the precious metal in in which anyone gullible and greedy enough to invest might believe.

"We can buy at six and a quarter and get out at twenty-five," Wiz said.

"But is it copper or fool's gold?"

"What does it matter? In, out, you make a few easy thousand. A good rumor's better than a dull truth."

"No more new issues. I'm investing in real estate," Emily held back coyly.

"Emily!"

"No more paper. I want to own something I can touch." And *someone* too, Emily thought.

For the first time since she'd married Warren, Emily had begun to think about settling down, about long-term financial security, about a father for Jessica. Was Radlow a possibility? She wasn't sure. He *was* the first man who hadn't seen her as a pure sex object. Oh, there had been Alex, but that was impossible—and after the incident at the Biltmore, she was certain Alex would never speak to her again. At bottom, Emily sensed that Wiz Radlow could take care of her. After over two years of working for Texas and Polly, she felt beaten, fatigued. She wanted a protector. She wanted out of the losing game she had gotten herself into; out of her expensive velvet demimonde of smoky nightclubs, strange, unwelcome bodies, and forced, spurious passions.

One night Emily and Wiz went up to Harlem with three visiting British investors who wanted to go "slumming." Emily couldn't quite understand the word "slumming." The nightclubs in Harlem were far more luxurious and elaborate than Guinan's or most of the others downtown. Big bands. Duke Ellington, Cab Calloway, the stunning "high-yaller" mulatto showgirls, the shows, the pageants, the uninhibited dancing.

That evening, they went to the Plantation, where there were more French patrons than Americans, then to the Yeah Man, which was filled with white gangsters watching Josephine Baker. The Britons made an easy purchase of some reefer, or marijuana, from a dealer standing in front of a pink Cadillac on Lenox Avenue. Then they hit two spots—the Nest and Mexico's— in "Jungle Alley" on 133rd Street between Lenox and Seventh before ending the evening at a little boîte in an apartment house on St. Nicholas Avenue named Clinton Moore's filled with homosexuals in formal clothes dancing together. The main attraction here was the piano player, a fragile young black man named Joey who played obscene variations of popular tunes: "The Man I Love" became "The Gland I Love," and so on. Joey's main talent, the one the men packed in for, occurred when he turned the keyboard over to an associate and took the stage himself, carrying a flickering white candle in a silver candelabrum. As the pianist tinkled "I Can't Hold a Candle to You," Joey proceeded to strip off his tux, dancing around the candle and finally extinguishing it by sitting on the candle until the whole thing disappeared. The Britons loved it.

"Anything to close a deal," Wiz said early in the morning after dropping the Englishmen off at the Plaza.

"Clinton Moore's was disgusting," Emily said. She was tipsy from all the drinking.

"The Vanderbilts had Joey perform at one of their parties."

"Sing or . . . dance?"

"Both. He's the darling of high society," Wiz said as his Rolls-Royce cruised down a virtually empty Park Avenue. The only signs of life were a few limousines dropping off late-night revelers who moved like the living dead. Emily loved this hour. If only New York could be this quiet all day.

"I'll make you breakfast," Emily said as the Rolls pulled up to Emily's apartment house.

"I never eat eggs," Wiz said.

"Who said anything about eggs?" Emily said. "You never come up." She had danced with him, held hands with him, but he had never made a further move.

"I've got to get some rest. I have to be at the office tomorrow."

"It's Saturday, Wiz. Come on up. I'll light candles, if that's what you need."

"Is that what you think?"

"I haven't seen evidence to the contrary," Emily teased him. "You're guilty until proven innocent."

Spurred by Emily's good-humored challenge to his masculinity, Wiz leaned over and kissed Emily's neck, then lips. "Not guilty." He smiled, indicating he had proved his point.

"The jury's still out. Insufficient evidence," Emily insisted, and shut off the purring motor of his Rolls. Wiz surrendered and went upstairs with her.

Emily didn't bother with breakfast. They proceeded straight into her bedroom. She never brought her men customers there, but Wiz was not a customer. Everything about him was so confident, she couldn't understand his reluctance to go to bed with her. It intrigued her and caused her to become more aggressive than she had ever been. She couldn't deny to herself that she wanted him, and the only way it seemed she could have him was to take the initiative. If anything went wrong, she could blame it on booze. New linen sheets were on the bed. There were orchids in a vase. Emily wanted this to happen. Hugging him inside his tuxedo jacket, she moved his cummerbund around and unfastened it. The room smelled of Chanel, her favorite perfume.

Wiz was strangely tentative about taking Emily's clothes off as she was undressing him.

When she placed her hand inside his starched white shirt and stroked the hair on his chest, he took her hand.

"Emily, you're wonderful, but it won't work."

"What won't work?"

"I'm sorry. It's worse than being queer. At least queers have fun."

"What's the matter?"

"I can't do a thing. I've been . . . impotent . . . for years."

"No. You're not . . . at Guinan's . . . the women are all crazy about you."

"That makes it even worse. It's all a facade, Emily. I can't make love."

"Oh, Wiz, I'm so sorry. I didn't mean to hurt you by this. I've gotten so comfortable with you, it seemed right, it seemed natural to do this. I'm terribly sorry. Please forgive me. I wanted you to want me."

"I do want you, Emily. I wanted you the first time I saw you."

"But you didn't want to try?" she asked.

"I did. I did. But I knew what the end result would be. I didn't want to try and then lose you."

"You should have tried, Wiz. You wouldn't lose me. I thought you weren't attracted to me."

"How could anyone not be attracted to you?"

"I thought for sure you weren't . . . Do you know why, why this happened?" Emily asked solicitously.

"Work, pressure, the divorce. I don't know. It's been my curse. My job is my mistress. I'm too depressed to talk about it."

"Don't. Come to sleep." Emily motioned to the pillow beside her.

"Thanks, but I think I better go."

"Poor Wiz. Are you sure you won't stay?"

"I'm sure. I am crazy about you, though, Emily. I wish I could please you."

"You do please me, Wiz." Then Emily decided to make her move, her fall back position. "But you know what would be wonderful?"

"What?"

"If you gave me a back rub. That would put me right out. Would you, please? I'd love that."

"Of course I will."

"Great. Let me get undressed." Emily stood up and turned on a low light. She began to take off her clothes, flashing back and forth behind a Chinese screen Rothstein had given her. She didn't show Wiz too much, just a bit to, she hoped, excite him. She put "Ain't Misbehavin' " on the phonograph. She asked him to unhook her bra. She wrapped herself in a red silk kimono, again a gift from Rothstein, so Wiz wouldn't see everything.

"Emily," Wiz protested, "it won't work. I've had vitamin shots. I've tried it with girls from Guinan's. I've been to psychiatrists. I've taken—"

"Don't worry. It's all right. I still think you're great." Emily sat in her kimono, slightly open, and kissed Wiz. "Just a back rub, and I'll be out like a light." She took off her kimono, threw it on a chair, and fell on her stomach on the bed.

"You have the most beautiful back and a wonderful behind," Wiz sighed.

"Please rub my back, Wiz."

He knelt over her and began kneading her back, touching her derriere, occasionally slipping his fingers under her and touching her breasts.

"This is wonderful, Wiz," Emily said, not being at all aggressive.

Her shyness, her reticence, were starting to do something to him. He felt an urge of curiosity. He tried to turn her over.

"Keep massaging. Please, Wiz. I'm almost asleep. I'm almost gone. It feels so good."

The resistance was doing it. He decided he wanted to see her. He wanted to have her. He felt himself, for the first time in two years, becoming aroused. "Emily."

She didn't respond.

"Emily. Emily, you won't believe this."

She pretended to be asleep. Polly had taught her how to deal with impotence. "Oh, let me sleep, Wiz," she muttered.

"Emily. I can. I can do it now," Wiz said. He took his pants off and fell on her, kissing her all over her splendid white body. She turned over and opened her eyes with a delighted slow smile. "Emily, I'm crazy about you," he panted, and began to make love to her. She held him and was very pleased with herself.

51

"I've forgotten about Wall Street. I've forgotten about stocks. I've forgotten about money," Wiz said to Emily in the ornate bedroom of his Fifth Avenue apartment, which was at tree level with the emerald symphony of spring in Central Park. They were cuddled in his antique bed, in which, he proudly told her, Lord Byron had died in Greece. "With you now, Emily, I'm looking at life from a completely different perspective."

"Yeah," Emily laughed. "From under the covers." She tickled his stomach. "You're like a little boy who's just gotten a new toy."

"And what a cute toy it is," Wiz said, nuzzling Emily's cheek.

"And what a cute boy." Emily nuzzled him back.

"I'm mad for you."

"You're mad for sex," Emily teased him, seeing that he was getting aroused once again. "You're really something."

"No. I'm mad for you," Wiz insisted. He kissed her lips, down her neck. "Mad, mad, mad. It's more than sex. A lot more. Before you, it was all money, money for money's sake. But now you've given me a reason for it all. I want us to live. Live high. Fly!"

"You're sweet, Wiz."

"Without you I was a stockbroker. With you I'm a king."

Emily kissed him. Wiz kissed her back and held her, not like the others, who held her as if she were a commodity to be used and discarded. Wiz held her as a woman, the best and only woman, a woman who mattered greatly to him. It made her relaxed. It made her secure. It even made her excited. Once she had adjusted to the harsh truths of being a courtesan, Emily had held sex in reserve. She could put on a performance, of course, but she had anesthetized herself erotically. Her affair with Wiz, however, was changing that.

Wiz was breathing heavily. His heart was pounding. He wanted to make love again. Emily could feel that his desire had crossed the point where it could not be ignored.

"Shouldn't we start getting dressed?" Emily said. "The opera starts in—"

"I'll never be able to sit through Wagner without . . . Just once more."

"That's what you said two hours ago. You're bad!"

"You're making me bad!" Wiz sighed as he caressed Emily's breasts. "God! You're wonderful."

Emily wasn't altogether sure how she felt about Wiz, but she definitely enjoyed being appreciated.

The sexual breakthrough with Wiz turned him overnight into a mad romantic. He would send flowers, buy her little pins and jewelry, surprise her with expensive chocolates, and call every day, even though because of his hectic business schedule they were able to see each other no more than once a week. Wiz spoke as if he had discovered love for the first time with Emily, which made her feel very good. And whenever they would be together and spotted an imposing new town house, he would always say, "That would be perfect for us." He hadn't proposed, but everything he said spoke of permanence and alluded in one way or another to marriage. The more time she spent with Wiz, the more she liked him. Maybe she could fall in love with him, if only half as much as he seemed to be falling for her. He was warm, generous, crazy about her, although she didn't really know him very well.

"Tell me about your first wife," she would ask him.

"I'd rather talk about my next one." He would begin kissing Emily and avoid the subject. He would avoid most subjects dealing with his past. "Forget the past. All that matters is the future." Wiz never asked her about *her* past, either, and that was a great relief to Emily.

LULLABY AND GOODNIGHT

One of Emily's most enjoyable moments was taking Wiz out to New Jersey to meet Jessica. She was so proud to pick her daughter up in a Rolls-Royce, disappointed that neither Warren nor Isabelle was around to see this moment of triumph. They motored down to a pretty park near Morristown with cows in the meadows and tall grass and daffodils under a dappled white sky. Jessica wore a white sailor suit, matching the tennis whites Emily and Wiz were wearing. They were a family. Wiz rode Jessica piggyback. They played blindman's bluff. He was all high spirits. As with Emily, everything Jessica wanted was Wiz's command. She asked for root beer; root beer it was. He got into the car to go down the road to the general store.

"Thank you, Mr. Radlow," Jessica said.

"Call me Wiz, Jessica."

"Okay, Wiz. Wiz," she said flirtatiously. She was eleven now, and turning into a tall, radiant little beauty.

"Yes, Jessica?"

"While you're at the store, could you get some potato chips?"

"Jessica!" Emily scolded her.

"Pretty please with sugar on top."

"That does it. Potato chips!" Wiz saluted her. "Do my ladies want anything else? Your humble servant departs," and Wiz's Rolls roared away down the gravel path.

"Do you like him?" Emily asked, hoping anxiously that Jessica did.

"He's getting bald, Mommy. I don't like that."

Children could be so cruel. "Jessica, that's not nice. Being bald doesn't have anything to do with the kind of person someone is."

"Mummy said she doesn't trust bald men." Mummy and all her snobbish attitudes. Emily didn't want her daughter to turn out like Mummy.

"Honey, we have to spend more time together. Look at this," Emily said, showing her a diamond ring Wiz had given her. "See how nice Wiz is. He gave it to me."

"Wow," Jessica said, touching the sparkling stone. "Does that mean he wants to . . . marry you?"

Emily didn't know the answer. He had just given it as

a gift. He had said nothing about an engagement. "Oh, who knows. It's a friendship ring."

"It's big enough for both of us," Jessica said, pulling the ring off Emily's finger and trying unsuccessfully to get it on two of her own fingers. "Maybe I'll marry him."

"So you like him?"

"I like him, Mommy." She hugged Emily. "If you like him, I like him. Mommy," Jessica went on, this time in a more serious, not-at-all-playful tone.

"What, dear?"

"If you marry him, will you go away and leave me?"

"Of course not."

"Not like before."

"That was so different. I was sick."

"You promise? Promise you won't let him take you away from me."

"I promise, my love." Emily drew Jessica tightly to her. They snuggled in the grass, as the soft summer breezes rustled the leaves and stirred up the perfume of the hyacinths. "My darling, why are you so worried?"

"Because . . . because you're the only person who loves me."

"I do love you, darling, but you shouldn't say that."

"But it's true." Jessica was crying now. Just minutes before, she was so poised and strong and opinionated, and now she was a mess. Emily wiped her daughter's tears away. "I'm sorry, Mommy. I'll stop. I won't let Wiz see me cry."

"You can cry all you want. Get it out of your system, baby."

"I'll stop," Jessica sniffled.

"But don't say no one loves you, sweetie. I know your father loves you. And your . . ." Emily wasn't sure what to call Isabelle. She didn't want to call her Jessica's mother. Her pride wouldn't let her. ". . . your mummy. I'm sure she loves you too."

"Not like you, Mommy."

"In their own way."

"I'm so mixed up, Mommy. You know, like before, when I said something about Wiz getting bald and you said don't talk like that?"

"Yes. That wasn't nice."

275

"I was trying to sound like Mummy. Because that's what Daddy wants. He wants me to be like her."

"You just be like yourself," Emily urged her little girl. "And everything will be okay. You're doing just fine, my love." Jessica's deep confusion about her identity and about her divided loyalties to her assorted parents gave Emily the most profound discomfort. She knew Warren and Isabelle didn't approve of her and wanted to mold Jessica in Isabelle's image. Thus Jessica had to keep the love she felt for her real mother bottled up, all to herself, every day of the month but one. Emily didn't want to let Jessica go. She had premonitions that something terrible could happen to such a troubled child. She now wished she and Wiz could get married, and make a permanent, stable home for the one person in her life she loved unequivocally.

"I'd marry him so fast it would make your head swim," Cassie urged.

"He hasn't asked me yet," Emily said during the calm at Guinan's before the after-theater celebrants poured in.

"He's heading in the right direction. God, you could use it."

"But, Cassie, I'm still not really in love," Emily agonized. "I mean, I love Wiz, I really do, but it's not the really deep kind."

"What do you want, Emily? Everything?"

"Cassie, you're the only one I can talk to. Sometimes I ask myself: If he weren't rich, would I be with him? And I don't even know the answer to that. Between Texas and Polly, I can't even think about men without thinking about money. I hate being like that. What have I turned into?"

"A smart grown-up. At last!" Cassie said.

"That's not me. I always wanted to be in love, crazy in love. And now I'm just calculating. How can I learn to really love Wiz?"

"By loving yourself and what he can do for you. Oh, baby, when are you ever going to figure it all out? Forget about that teenage stuff. Radlow is big money. He's legit. He's Wall Street. When you go back to court with him on your arm, you're immediately transformed from unfit mother to mother of the year."

"You're right. I bet I could get custody. I bet I could." Emily inhaled her Camel, drank her rum punch. For once, she felt optimistic that things just might work out for her.

52

Broadway in August was a steamy haze of humidity.
The heat rose from the asphalt, poured from the rank
exhaust fumes of the trucks and taxis and buses in Times
Square. Seeking relief from the heat, tourists from around
the country and the world swarmed like locusts to the
open-air orangeade counters. They crowded into the newly
air-cooled movie palaces to see Norma Shearer talk in
The Trial of Mary Dugan or George Arliss in *Disraeli* or
King Vidor's all Negro musical *Hallelujah!*. Or they'd
settle for far, far less—they would see the silents that
were still showing— just to keep cool. Braving the ninety-
five-degree temperatures, Emily had come down to Times
Square to buy theater tickets for one of the early-
September openings, a show she didn't want to miss
under any circumstances.

Emily had seen the advertisement in the *Times*: "David Belasco presents *Fly by Night*. A New Play by Alex
Foster." She wanted to see Alex again. She wanted to
congratulate him. And she wanted to show him that she
was doing better, too. She had a respectable boyfriend
who could conceivably become her husband. Alex would
see that what Emily had been at the Biltmore was not
what she was now. That was another moment, part of an
unfolding drama that had started as a tragedy but was
going to have a happy denouement.

Emily was so pleased for Alex. The Shubert Theater.
The marquee. The thrill of opening night. All the limousines, the critics, the patrons in black tie. She spotted
some of the wits from the Algonquin Round Table. Dorothy Parker, Robert Benchley, Alexander Woollcott. They

seemed like piranhas, quick, smart, darting, vicious. She hoped they would be kind to Alex. Then she saw him in black tie, in the lobby, shaking hands with the white-maned Belasco and being fawned over by press agents. Alex was pale, nervous, as boyish as ever.

"Alex," she said, taking his arm from behind. "Remember me?"

"Emily," he gasped.

"I always believed in you," she said, and kissed his cheek. "I'm so excited."

"Emily," Alex stammered. "I . . . I . . ."

"This is Wiz Radlow," Emily said before Alex could say anything else. Alex shook his hand, not sure what was going on.

"Emily says you're brilliant," Wiz said. "A cross between Bernard Shaw and Eugene O'Neill."

Emily had said neither. That was what she liked about Wiz, his impromptu, shoot-from-the-hip charm. He always had a compliment.

"I don't know about—"

"Well, kid, I hope it runs forever," Wiz said. He took out his card and put it in Alex's hand. "If it does, let me invest your money for you. Let me check these," he said as he removed Emily's wrap and headed downstairs to the cloakroom. "Good luck, Al."

"Emily," Alex said, standing back and staring at her. The other people who passed and shook his hand, wishing him well, didn't even register. He stared at Emily. He saw the ring on her finger. She saw him looking.

"We're almost engaged," Emily answered his unspoken question. "He's very successful. I met him . . . he invested my money." Then she was ashamed she had mentioned money. Alex knew how she had earned it. "I've missed you, Alex. I'm glad you made it."

"How are you?" He wanted to ask so much more. This was all he could get out.

"Better. I'm a lot better."

"And Jessica?"

"Growing up. I see her every month. Maybe it'll be more now, if he and I get . . . How did all this happen?"

"College friend's sister was secretary to one of Belasco's angels. Some oil guy from Texas. He showed it to Belasco, and he liked it."

"Yale paid off."

"In the craziest way. I wish it had happened six years ago, when I wrote it, but that would have been too easy," he said.

Emily wished so, too. "It happened, Alex. That's what counts."

"So you're getting married," Alex intoned. "Wow . . . I guess . . . that would be great for you . . . I always hoped . . ." A long line of well-wishers was waiting for Alex. The houselights were starting to blink. Emily saw Wiz coming up the stairs from the lower lobby.

"I hope it's a hit," she said, kissing Alex's cheek again. "Best of everything. You deserve it."

"Th-thanks. Hope you like it." He nodded to Radlow, who put out his arm for Emily as they descended the red carpet into the orchestra. "Mr. Foster . . . Mr. Foster . . ." the well-wishers and reporters clamored. Alex went through the motions. He knew he should have felt triumphant. His name was in lights. He might never have to write ad copy again. No more preying on people's insecurities. No more Marmon ads, Pierce Arrows to extol. Or pink bathroom sinks. Or new refrigerators. Or dandruff remedies. This night should have been a celebration. But seeing Emily made it all turn to ashes. Even if *Fly by Night* was a hit, he felt like a failure.

53

Emily took an extreme interest in the 1929 mayoral elections. One afternoon she strolled up Park Avenue to hear the Republican candidate, Fiorello La Guardia, speak. She passed the rich children with their white-gloved nannies, and the toys—the silver hoops, the Russian dolls, the yapping Pomeranians—that only Park Avenue children had. How she wanted to have Jessica, and spoil her, but Jessica was getting too old for toys. She thought about having more children, starting fresh, and spoiling them. After all, she was only twenty-nine. She could do it. She could be a young housewife again. How pure, how simple, how nice that seemed.

Fiorello La Guardia stood on a reviewing stand in front of the old whale of an armory, in the midst of the luxury apartments. La Guardia was the complete antithesis of Mayor Walker, Emily thought. He had a high-pitched street voice. He was squat and fat and his suit was rumpled, the pocket flaps stuck inside the pockets, one of his collar points waving in the brisk wind. Despite his appearance, the small crowd of nannies and maids and curious housewives from the apartments seemed mesmerized by what he was saying. The sincere, righteous anger in his voice said to them this was no mere campaign speech; this was heartfelt outrage.

La Guardia railed against "that Pandora's box of corruption that we know as Tammany Hall. It takes more than a Duesenberg and a velvet overcoat to make a mayor. It takes more than a silk hat and a pair of spats to make a police commissioner. Tammany Hall has carved this city up like it was a turkey at one of their banquets.

The only laws they obey are not the laws of Albany, but
the laws of the political jungle, where they are the tigers,
and you, my friends, are the lambs."

Later that week, Wiz took Emily to one of La Guardia's
campaign examples of Tammany excess, the new Casino
nightclub in Central Park, a true crystal-palace green-
house in the center of Manhattan. The porte cochere was
filled with Rolls-Royces, Bentleys, Daimlers, Pierce-
Arrows, and, at the entrance, Mayor Walker's Duesenberg.

"This used to be nothing," Emily told Wiz. "A snack
bar."

"No more," Wiz said as the liveried doorman in a high
hat opened the door. "This is Jimmy Walker's new baby."
Inside, Emily could hear the discordant conflict of the
upbeat "Sweet Georgia Brown" with the gentle lilt of
"Am I Blue?"

"Am I hearing things?"

"They've got two orchestras. Leo Reisman's in the
main room. Young kid named Eddy Duchin's in the
other." A discreet sign announced a cover charge of
twenty dollars.

"A fortune." Emily winced. "It'll keep out everyone
except the millionaires."

"That's all they want," Wiz said. "They've got a big
investment here to earn back. Place cost four hundred
grand. Walker's got a private room upstairs, with a gold-
leaf ceiling and a sunken bathtub."

"Incredible," Emily said as she watched the dreamy
moonlight streaming into the candlelit ballroom. "This is
the sort of place that things like revolutions get started
over. The public has got to be up in arms."

"Are you kidding?" Wiz laughed. "This is New York.
You know they love Walker. They want him to enjoy
himself. He's like a sports hero. Nobody minds if Dempsey
or Ruth lives it up. Same with Walker. Besides, Jimmy
may steal a dime, but he'll let you have a penny of it. He
shares the spoils. Wants everybody to live it up."

"Somebody's getting cheated," Emily said.

"But they don't seem to mind, do they?"

Wiz and Emily dined in a way that was reminiscent of
the court of a French emperor *before* the deluge. They
had *coquilles St. Jacques, homard à l'américaine, île*

flottante, and other delicious things she couldn't begin to pronounce. Wiz told her that the chef had worked for the Rothschilds in Paris. They drank champagne, which was brought in from several laundry trucks parked among the Rolls-Royces. The laundry trucks served as a cover to foil nosy Prohibition agents. "It's not really necessary," Wiz laughed. "The feds can't afford the cover charge."

They ate and danced and drank, but Emily couldn't take her eyes off, not the decor, not the artistic plates of *haute cuisine*, but rather the dapper little mayor and his showgirl, as he waltzed her from table to table, from socialites to gangsters to politicians. The Casino was a monied melting pot of Biddles and Ziegfelds and Fishes and Zukors. It was like a much more formal, grander Guinan's, except here every man was with his wife or date. It was the grandest restaurant to open in New York since Prohibition, and the ringmaster was Jimmy Walker. Challenging Tammany was challenging this man. If Fiorello La Guardia, who was trailing badly in the polls, couldn't do it, how could she? Emily was glad she was with Wiz.

Despite her increasing involvement with Wiz, Emily continued to see Polly's men, if only as fiscal insurance in case Wiz didn't work out. Judge Crater called for Emily again, after a hiatus of over a year, and she made her way downtown to the Criminal Courts Building.

Crater was in unusually high spirits. "I'm rich, Emily. I'm one rich judge." He danced around the office, uncharacteristically tossing papers about.

Emily had stripped to her black stockings and high heels. She knew what the judge wanted. "I've never seen you so happy," she said, striding across the room slowly toward him, the way he liked, stopping to pretend to look at a brief here, a law book there, so he could get aroused by her seminakedness. "How did you get so rich?" She sat on his desk and stretched one of her legs out toward his swivel chair. He sat down and began stroking her thigh, where silk met flesh.

"Very nice," he murmured. "Very nice."

Emily pulled her leg away and crossed it over the other. Crater reached under her, removed her high heel, and held it on his lap. "What happened to you?" Emily continued.

"Give me your other shoe," Crater said, reaching out. Emily backed away. He kissed her stockinged feet. "Give me the shoe."

"I want to know how you got rich first."

"Why?"

"I'm curious." Despite her inability to find a lawyer who was brave enough to take on Tammany Hall, Emily had nonetheless continued keeping her diaries. One day, she hoped, they might, just might . . .

"Let's play first."

"Not till my curiosity's satisfied."

"What difference does it make?" Crater was shaking, he wanted her so much.

"Satisfy me. I'll satisfy you." Emily pointed her big toe at his nose and rubbed it.

"God! All right. You won't understand. It's just numbers."

"Let me try. I *love* numbers."

"The city just bought this old hotel on Canal Street, the Van Cleve."

"That fleabag. It's been closed for years."

"City's going to tear it down for the highway."

"Did you own it?"

"My old client did. He got it for seventy thousand. The city bought it for three million."

"What did you do?"

"I was the referee for the appraisal. I set the price."

"Three million? And he paid seventy thousand? He made out like a bandit. And you did too, you naughty judge." Emily sat down in Crater's lap, wrapping her long legs around him and loosening his sweat-soaked tie. He fondled her breasts, then tried to get the high heel from her hand. "Uh-uh," Emily teased him. She understood that Crater would be getting a huge kickback for his role in the hotel transaction. "How could something that cost seventy thousand sell for three million?"

"Tammany arithmetic," Crater laughed, and Emily gave him the other shoe.

The judge never had a chance to enjoy his windfall. One night he left Billy Haas's Restaurant on Forty-fifth

Street, where he had been dining with some of the show people who frequented the place. He got into a cab and was never seen again. A vast nationwide manhunt by local authorities as well as the FBI drew a blank. Some Republicans speculated that Tammany disposed of him to prevent disclosure of the Canal Street deal. The tabloids blamed sex. One showgirl came forward, saying that she was planning a breach-of-promise suit. Two others followed.

Tammany didn't like the adverse publicity generated by Crater's disappearance, because it was already under heavy fire from La Guardia and the Republicans. Shortly before the election, as a palliative action, Tammany's leader for the past five years, George W. Olvany, abruptly resigned "on grounds of ill health." What might have made him ill was the impending La Guardia revelation that Olvany's law firm had made over five million dollars in fees for appearing before the Board of Standards and Appeals during Olvany's tenure at Tammany. Its clients there were big builders who wanted variances from the antiskyscraper codes. Olvany's firm, like the other Tammany law firm of Sullivan and Sterling, got the variances, for a huge fee. All over town Emily could see and hear—the construction noise was deafening, and constant—the results of these variances. The Empire State Building at Thirty-fourth and Fifth was about to go up, replacing the old Waldorf Astoria, which was being torn down. At Forty-second and Lexington, the Chrysler Building was rising. The town was buzzing with excitement over the future erection of John D. Rockefeller's Radio City on Fiftieth Street.

Emily saw Walker campaigning all over town. He was in the soup kitchens shaking hands with the bums. He was at Yonah Schimmel's Knish Bakery on Houston Street shaking hands with the Hasidim. He was at a barbecue shop in Harlem kissing black babies and their flattered mothers. He drove his Duesenberg down Broadway as the theaters were letting out, blowing his horn, which ran the whole musical scale: do-re-mi . . . And then she saw him again at the Casino in the Park, and she knew that neither La Guardia, nor New York, nor certainly herself, had a chance.

LULLABY AND GOODNIGHT

On election day Emily voted for the "Little Flower," as they called La Guardia, and listened to the election results at Guinan's. At four A.M. it was all over. Walker had eight hundred and fifty thousand votes, La Guardia three hundred thousand. On the radio, Walker's voice bbbled and crackled, "Is somebody out there complaining? I don't hear any complaints tonight," and Emily couldn't tell whether the noise that followed was static or whether it was the mob cheering. What she didn't see were the people on the platform at Democratic headquarters at the Commodore. The sachems of Tammany were there, all right. On Walker's right, not far away, was Warren Matthews, who had made a contribution of ten thousand to the reelection fund. Down the podium, on the left, was Michael McNaughton. "It's a big night for me. It's a big night for Tammany," Walker shouted over the band playing "Will You Love Me in December as You Do in May?"

Emily left the hostesses at the bar radio. She went into the bathroom, sat by herself, and cried.

54

Emily didn't hear from Wiz for nearly two weeks after October 29. That had been the day of the stock-market crash, but nobody really quite believed it. October had been a bad month in general, with stocks slipping precipitously. Black Tuesday had been dreadful, but four of the most influential financiers met at Morgan Bank that day and announced that the crash had been caused by "technical rather than fundamental" considerations and that the "market was sound." This despite such plunges as RCA dropping from 505 to 28, General Electric going from a September high of 396¼ to 168⅛ and General Motors from 181⅞ to 36. Charles Mitchell, chairman of National City Bank, Albert Wiggin of the Chase, William Potter of Guaranty Trust, and Thomas Lamont of the House of Morgan all got together to calm the world. "There has been a little distress selling," Lamont said dryly after the meeting.

Emily decided everything was all right when most of Guinan's banker and broker regulars showed up at the club the following Saturday night and made jokes until dawn.

"I'm not well," one broker said.

"What's the matter?" the other asked.

"I've got heart trouble at thirty-five," the first said.

"That's nothing," the second laughed. "I've got RCA at twenty-eight."

They drank and danced.

Emily had a small portfolio. Most of Wiz's stocks—the "big-spread" issues he told her about—weren't even listed. They were over-the-counter. Emily wasn't quite sure where that counter was. Her listed stocks had shrunk to a quarter of the price she had paid for them. Nevertheless, she believed one starchily pompous investment counselor when he reassuringly patted her behind on the dance floor to "Crazy Rhythm" and said, "It'll come back up."

What bothered Emily more was Wiz's not returning her calls. That, and the fact that the market was definitely not coming back up. She was glad she had bought a small apartment house in Queens with some of her paper profits. Real estate didn't appreciate dramatically like those glamorous-sounding stocks Wiz put her in—Caracas Pipeline, Shanghai General, Luzon Mining—but she could at least get on the RR train to Jamaica and walk through her three-story brick investment and count on rent checks every month.

Where was Wiz? They had been talking about a Christmas in Paris, and the season was approaching. Despite the bad market, Fifth Avenue stores were putting up their wreaths and holly and mistletoe. The big stores had their elves and their Santas and the weather got colder and more blustery. A beautiful early dusting of white snow intensified the scent of the roasting chestnuts the street vendors sold. Wiz's secretary kept saying he was swamped with orders and sales and that he would get back to her. After another week, there was no more secretary. No one answered the phone.

Emily decided something was wrong and took the subway down to Wall Street. As she emerged onto Broadway this gray November afternoon, an even grayer pall was over the street. More men were taking off their hats and going into Trinity Church than seemed usual at two in the afternoon. Faces were grim, worried. There was none of the buoyancy that always so impressed Emily when she came downtown. And there were no cigars, no celebratory cigars. Instead, Wall Street was a Rue Morgue of tight, drawn men whose dreams had been obliterated by the harsh realities of a lean market. People were not speaking. The atmosphere was that of a city after a bombing, except all the skyscrapers, the monuments, the Exchange, the Customs House, were still there. Only the expectations had been destroyed.

Emily took the elevator at 48 Wall to the forty-fifth floor and got out into the marble corridor. At the end of the hall she tried to open the fancy oak door with the shining brass plate, "Radlow Securities International, Limited," but the door was locked. She rang the buzzer. She knocked. Nothing. An elderly black janitor in a brown work outfit with "48 Wall" sewn proudly on his epaulets came around the corner, hearing the noise.

"I'm trying to get in to see Mr. Radlow," Emily said.

"They'se gone," the janitor said.

"For the day? It's only two-thirty."

"I mean gone. Up and gone. Not for the day."

"Gone?"

"For good. They'se done closed up shop. Ain't nothin' in there but some desks. Not even no ticker tape."

"Where'd they go?"

The janitor shrugged. "Tha's what landlord like to know, too. One night they'se here, doing all their big business. Next day, they'se done gone. Whole lot of 'em's like that these days, ma'am. They take your money, too?"

Emily shook her head in despair. Wiz had taken more than money. She trudged to the elevator and rang the bell. An eternity seemed to pass. The old janitor stayed with her, his baleful eyes trying to comfort her. "It's a shame, these big shots losin' everybody's money. There ought to be a law, yes sir."

"Thank you," Emily said, and got onto the elevator.

On Fifth Avenue in the Nineties, a large Allied moving van was parked in front of Wiz's apartment. The highboys, the black velvet Queen Anne chairs, the Regency tables, all Wiz's English antiques, were being loaded into the truck by burly men in shirts that were sweat-soaked despite the near-freezing weather. Emily pushed past the doorman in the confusion of the movers and rode to the fifth floor.

The nude branches of Central Park could be seen through the big windows, past the open door. The Aubusson rugs were gone. The plush sofas were gone. Only a few stray boxes and some vagrant balls of dust were left of the once lavish flat. Then Emily heard Wiz's voice from a back bedroom. She ran to the bedroom door. Radlow, his back to Emily, was on the phone. He heard her and turned around as he talked. He was dapper in his ascot and hacking jacket. He was going to the country.

"We can go up to Darien and . . . and maybe . . ." His voice trailed off. "Let me call you back. The movers . . . yes. 'Bye." He hung up. "Emily, I . . ."

"You never called. What happened? What?"

"Ruined." Wiz threw up his hands, pointing to the empty apartment. "Finished. It's all gone. All of it. Everything."

"Don't worry." She took his hand. "We have each other."

He wasn't listening to her. He seemed vastly uncomfortable that she was there. He began talking like a runaway train. "The bond issue. Obliterated. Worthless. Shanghai General. Nothing. Luzon. Worthless. Phillips, Diamond Sugar, gone." He spat out the bad news like a ticker tape of doom. "Radlow International, bankrupt, Emily. Finished." It was a paper empire. He was a cardboard emperor.

"And all my other stocks? The New York Exchange stocks?" Emily asked.

"Forget it. They're not worth anything. I used them to speculate with."

"You don't have them?"

"I had your power of attorney. I thought I was doing you a favor. I was going to make you richer. I had no idea . . ."

"So there's nothing left?"

Wiz shook his head. He was almost grinning with the most profound embarrassment. "I want to . . . make it up to you somehow. I couldn't call. I kept thinking it would turn around. You're not just another investor. I'll do something," he mumbled.

"We'll make it back." Emily hugged him. "I have some savings. There's still the property."

He drew away again, ashamed to have her near him. "I'm sorry. I don't know what to do."

"I do. I know. You need to live. You were working way too hard. You need a holiday. You'll come back. We'll go to Europe. You need it."

"Don't be foolish."

"I'll pay for it."

"I can't do it, under any circumstances," Wiz said, kicking through the dust, staring at the park through the window. The howling winter wind shook the panes of glass, or perhaps it was a Fifth Avenue bus rumbling downtown.

"What do you mean?"

"I can't marry you," Wiz said.

"Who said anything about marriage?" Emily responded defensively. She knew he was reading her mind. "I just want us to be together. Don't you? Isn't that what the past few months were all about? The trip, the Paris trip, that's all you talked about. Wiz, look at me. Please. You didn't return my calls. You disappeared. I'm not a creditor. Wiz, I love you. Please . . ."

He turned around, his face a mask of avoidance and real pain. "This is the worst part. How do I say it? Damn!"

"Wiz, don't worry. I can work for both of us until—"

"Emily, I'm still married."

"You're . . . what?"

"I'm still married," Wiz said, looking at her with all the guilt on earth. Then he looked down at the floor. "I lied about my divorce. Constance . . . She lives in Connecticut. She's rich. Land. She won't feel a thing. She never believed in the market. You know how old money is . . ."

"But the ring . . . the nights we had . . ."

"It was a gift . . . not a commitment. I never promised."

"But why did you say you were divorced?"

"I lied . . . Wishful thinking. It was all wishful thinking."

"And you were married all this time. How could you do it?"

"Easy. Modern marriage is easy. Constance wanted a husband. She *had* to be married. She didn't care if I wasn't there. She had her clubs. I had the stocks. It worked."

He opened his alligator wallet and pulled out a photo of Constance. She was plain, very Connecticut. "I was selling cars. I sold her a Stutz. That's how we met. I came with the car." He tried to be light. "See, she doesn't hold a candle to you . . ."

"So? Then what were we all about? How could you?"

LULLABY AND GOODNIGHT

Emily felt cheaper and more used than with any man she had met through Polly. At least there was no deception with them.

"Emily, you won't believe this, but I loved you. I was going to divorce Constance. I was planning it. I swear. But Constance's family staked me to my business. If it wasn't for them . . . I'd still be nothing. They gave me class. They made me somebody. I was a poor schlepper from the Bronx and they put me on Wall Street. You don't spit at that. I thought I had enough to pay her back and say good-bye. Until the market killed it."

"And now you're going back to her? You're going back to someone you don't love?"

Wiz cut his eyes out the window. "I have to, Emily. I can't afford not to."

"All that talk. All our plans." Emily wasn't sure whether she wanted to plead with him or to strangle him. A romantic, she wanted to believe love was more important than money. Then she remembered how she had hurt Alex Foster. Was this how he had felt?

"The twenties are over. The party's over." Wiz shrugged. "We had our times. Now I have to go back home. Don't hate me, Emily."

"I don't hate you, Wiz. I hate myself. I hate myself for trusting you. I hate myself for ever believing a word you said."

"I meant it when I said it. I got carried away. I was crazy about you. You made me nuts. You're something, baby. You're the greatest. It's my loss—"

"Enough, Wiz. It's like the stocks. You'd say anything just to make that sale . . ."

"I'm sorry. I shouldn't have let it get so serious . . . I just fell for you."

Emily slipped the ring off her finger and laid it on the mantelpiece, above the fireplace where they had cuddled together and made love and talked about Christmas in Paris.

"Good-bye, Wiz," Emily said, and left him staring out the window at the dead branches.

55

Warren Matthews was relieved that he hadn't taken his tile company public. The investment bankers from Brown Brothers had been after him to turn Matthews Tile into a publicly held corporation. They said they could quadruple the value of the company by selling its stock. He would have millions of dollars in working capital to expand his operations—new plants, new sales force. Matthews Tile could have been a national entity. Maybe even international. But the crash saved him from his own ambitions. He had lost about a hundred thousand in the market, but he still had his company. He was still affluent. He thought about the speculators he knew who were wiped out. Poor fools. Half the homes in Bernardsville were up for sale at distressed prices. He thought about some real-estate investments as he scanned the pages of the *Wall Street Journal* in his snug den. Sitting by the fire, Warren Matthews lit a cigar and sipped his Scotch in his sterling-silver tankard that had been an heirloom of Isabelle's English cousins. McCarey had been right. Despite her outburst at the courthouse, Emily had not since bothered him. The visitation rights must have pacified her. He had his business, his society, his mistresses. All was right with his world.

Then Jessica passed through the hallway. "Jessica. Where are you going?" Warren called to her.

She breezed into the den. She was twelve. She had gotten taller. Her breasts were budding. She had on a yellow silk party dress—straight, clingy, short, to the knee. She was wearing heels. Pearls. Bright lipstick. Rouge. Bobbed hair. She looked older than twelve. She looked very feminine, almost provocative with those delicate ankles and the beginnings of a willowy figure. Warren was disturbed, but not by Jessica's growing up. What disturbed him was that she looked so much like Emily.

"To a tea dance, Daddy. With Julia." She puckered her lips, unused to the lipstick, but excited to dress up.

"In that?" Warren gazed at her askance.

"In what, Daddy?"

"That. That dress," Warren said as he reached out and fingered the fabric at her knee. "Or some part of a dress. It's too short."

"Daddy, it's the latest style."

"Who bought you that dress?"

"Mommy bought it."

"Your mother wouldn't buy something like that. That's not for us."

"Not Mummy, Mommy," Jessica said, backing away from Warren's fingers.

"Stop that mommy-mummy nonsense."

"Okay, my *real* mother bought it." Jessica was agitated. She was so proud to dress up. Emily spoiled her, let her have fun. Isabelle was so restrictive, so prissy. She was upstairs napping. She was always napping or playing bridge. Buying antiques. "Is that what I'm supposed to say?"

Warren dropped the *Wall Street Journal* and rose from the leather chair. "Don't be insolent to me, Jessica."

"I'm not . . . whatever that is. It's my dress." Warren grabbed her slender arm and squeezed it. "Ow. That hurts, Daddy."

"Take it off."

"What? . . . Why?"

"Because I said so. No child of mine is going to dress like a little tramp."

"I'm not a child," Jessica said, trying to get free of his viselike grip. "I'm not a tramp."

"Your 'real mother' "—Warren slurred the words—"is trying to remake you in her own image, and I'm not going to have it. Hear me?" He squeezed harder. The perfume was Emily's, too. For Warren, she *was* Emily. That drove him even crazier. The scent, the skin, the face . . . what had he created here?

"All the other girls have dresses like this," Jessica protested. "It's not fair."

"I don't care what they have. They don't have fathers like me."

"I know," Jessica lashed back.

Warren slapped her across the face. "You insolent little . . . I'm not going to let her ruin you."

Her face stinging, Jessica began to cry. Her makeup ran down her face as she began to walk away. "I hate you. I hate you more than she hates you!"

The mention of Emily by her image was a double shot that made Warren leap across the room and chase Jessica.

"No! No! Daddy!"

He hurled her down on the sofa. "Never! Never! Never as long as you live will you talk to me like this!"

Jessica remembered when Warren was naked on the floor with Emily, beating her, raping her.

"Do you apologize?" Warren demanded.

Jessica tried to get away. Warren grabbed her, ripping her dress. "You tore it! Daddy! You tore it!"

He didn't care. He ripped the sleeve completely off, revealing part of Jessica's little satin camisole. He tore down the other sleeve. He might have gone further, had he not heard Isabelle calling from upstairs, "Is anything the matter?"

Jessica covered herself. "Daddy. How can you?"

Warren's eyes gleamed sadistically, the same gleam Jessica remembered from the apartment in New York. "You are going to grow up to be a lady, even if I have to break your little neck!" he shouted.

"What's wrong?" Isabelle said, entering the den in her lounge coat.

"I hate you!" Jessica said to Warren. "I hate you!" she cried, and fled to her room.

"She's a problem," Warren groaned, sitting down and hoping Isabelle would not notice his erection.

"Just growing pains, I guess," Isabelle said rather non-chalantly. In a conditioned response, she poured some more of the expensive Scotch that his Tammany friends had given him for Christmas into her family's antique mug.

56
1930

One by one, the brokers stopped coming. By mid-January, Texas Guinan's was almost as "empty as Death Valley," Texas would say. There was some business. A group of Chinese diplomats from Peking played leapfrog on the dance floor. A Canadian bakery president who had come to New York to learn to make bagels spent five hundred dollars on champagne. The Broadway stars still stopped by. Nevertheless, Texas' bread and butter was businessmen, and when business was bad, they stopped playing, as did Polly Adler's patrons. "Sex is the first to go," Polly told Emily. Dates were infrequent. For the first time, Polly lowered her price. The men had begun to haggle. Texas let the band take a holiday, retaining only a black pianist whose favorite song, ironically, was "Makin' Whoopee."

The advent of the new decade brought with it every indication that the party that was the twenties was definitely over. Breadlines were forming. Unemployment rose. Stores closed. The local Communist party found its ranks swelling with hungry sympathizers. Thousands rioted at Union Square. Shoplifting arrests spiraled upward. The Municipal Lodging House was feeding four thousand people a night. The Salvation Army was serving over twenty thousand bowls of stew daily. The Emergency Employment Committee was paying men a paltry but welcome fifteen dollars for three days of work in the city parks.

Depression notwithstanding, Tammany Hall prospered. After the election, the first order of business of the Board of Estimates was to raise the salaries of most high public officials. Jimmy Walker's jumped from twenty-five to forty thousand dollars. When the press reported the raises, Walker typically defended things by laughing it off. "Twenty-five thousand. Forty thousand. What's the difference? In either case, I'll have nothing left at the end of the year," he told the reporters, and drove off in his Duesenberg to Broadway to pick up Betty Compton and take her to the Casino in the Park.

Betty was performing in the new Cole Porter musical, *Fifty Million Frenchmen*. Walker took Betty's mother to the opening. Despite the doldrums of Wall Street, despite the cost of six dollars and fifty cents for orchestra seats, *Fifty Million Frenchmen* was a massive hit. Its songs "You've Got That Thing" and "Find Me a Primitive Man" dominated the airwaves. When a visiting Oklahoma oilman at Guinan's asked Emily to go, she declined. The story line about a Midwestern girl in Paris hit too close to home. It reminded her of her trip with Wiz, the trip that never was. And then there was the photo she saw in the *Herald* of Michael McNaughton being decorated by Police Commissioner Grover Whalen for a record number of arrests in 1929. Emily stayed at home a lot, escaping into sleep.

The nation's depression only served to make Emily's depression that much more acute. What a futile, dead-end existence her life had become. "Loss" was *the* word in America shortly after the crash, and what the country had lost reemphasized to Emily what she had lost. When she had run away from the convent, she had been a sheltered little girl with big dreams and absolutely no sense of reality. Yet she had come close to Broadway success. She almost lived her fantasies. But that was at sixteen, and now she was thirty and had lost it all. She had been forced to grow up so fast that she never got to savor the pleasures of being young. Her twenties were a lost decade, gone like the American twenties, the gayest, wildest decade in the country's history, now a memory as evanescent as champagne bubbles.

Months passed. Emily, wearing her jade Chinese pajamas, was lying beside her electric fan in the stifling July heat. She had played "I'll Build a Stairway to Paradise" maybe twenty times today on the Victrola. Her phone was off the hook, and she was further escaping into the longest new book she could find, Thomas Wolfe's *Look Homeward, Angel*, when the doorman rang. "Mr. Alex Foster here to see you, Miss Stanton."

Emily was stunned. Why was he here? She looked terrible. "Tell him I'm not in." She didn't want him to see her. The last time he'd seen her, at the opening of his play, life had looked rosy for her. She'd been proud of herself. And now she was just as ashamed.

No sooner had Emily started to breathe easily, thinking that Alex had been turned away, than a commotion arose outside the door.

"I don't care what it is, I'm gonna call the cops," Emily heard the doorman say in the hallway.

"Please," Alex said. "It's urgent. I know she's there. Here's *ten* bucks."

"No, mister, I don't want to lose my job. You gotta go. Don't ring—"

Emily heard her bell ring. "Emily. Emily. It's Alex. Please open the door."

Emily stood by the door. Finally she flung it open.

"Miss Stanton," the doorman apologized. "Jesus. This man ran past me and said—"

"Alex!" Emily looked at him. "It's all right." She dismissed the doorman. "He can stay."

"Emily," Alex sighed. He was dressed in a blue cord suit. A newspaper was clutched in his hands. "Your line's been busy, so I got your address from Texas Guinan's. She remembered me. Said you've been off the last few weeks. Listen, I'm sorry to make such a scene, but I have to talk to you."

"Alex, I look so terrible. I've been under the weather. I just don't . . . I don't know what to say. Oh, hell, I don't want you to stand out there. Come on in."

"Why didn't you want to see me?"

"I don't want to see anyone, Alex. It's not you. Things are . . . you know . . . rotten."

"Well, you've got a terrific place," Alex said, admiring the art-deco apartment. "The last time I was in your place, it was the room on Essex Street. This is beautiful."

Emily had a surge of guilt, for Alex knew how she had acquired these surroundings. How she wished she could be back in her flat on Essex Street, starting over. "How are you, Alex?"

"I'm all right."

"And the show?"

"Closed after three weeks."

"Oh, Alex. I wanted to tell you how good it was. Really. It should have run for years."

"At least it ran. I'm working on another one."

"Sit down, Alex," she said, still uneasy.

Alex went to the sofa. "I never would have barged in on you you except . . ." He fingered the paper nervously in his hands.

"It's scorching in here. Want a drink? Iced tea?"

"Nothing, thanks." Alex fidgeted. "Emily, I have to show you this." He opened the July 15 issue of the *New York Times* to a small item on the second page. "Look."

Emily squinted at the headline: "SEABURY APPOINTED TO INVESTIGATE MAGISTRATE'S COURTS."

"Magistrate's Court? That's where I was sent . . ."

"Exactly." Alex took the paper back. "Listen," he began to read, " 'Albany. The Appellate Division of the First Judicial Department has appointed former State Supreme Court Justice Samuel Seabury as referee to head an inquiry into the city's Magistrate's Court system, which has been under recent criticism for illegal bribes, kickbacks, and sale of judicial office.' I'll skip this part about U.S. Attorney Charles Tuttle, Socialist Norman Thomas, Governor Roosevelt, blah, blah, blah. Here it is. 'Among the alleged abuses Governor Roosevelt has directed Judge Seabury to explore are the sale of municipal judgeships and'—get this— 'the framing of innocent women on prostitution charges.' "

"You're kidding," Emily said, suddenly as excited as Alex was. She had forgotten what a friend he was to her.

"It's right here. Read it." Alex handed Emily the paper. "At last they're going to get them."

Emily scanned the article, and there it was. Bribes, payoffs in the women's courts. "Judge Renaud. They mention Judge Renaud as one of the women's court judges to be investigated. That was the one. Judge Renaud."

"It's about time."

"Alex, how did all this happen?"

"Politics. Politics, for once, worked in the people's

favor. As you probably know, Roosevelt got elected governor because Tammany Hall backed him. But Albany's too small a town for Roosevelt. He wants to go to Washington. Remember how the U.S. attorney a few months ago tried to get those Tammany guys on tax evasion for all the kickbacks in the condemnation proceedings and the variances?"

"Yes, and they got nowhere."

"Well, Tuttle's a tough guy. And ambitious, and a Republican. He wants to run for governor. So he began putting the heat on Roosevelt, too. The Republicans are making a lot of noise, national noise, that Roosevelt's a Tammany puppet, that New York is a cesspool. You see, Roosevelt would rather be President than governor, so that's why he's going with this Seabury thing, to prove that he's his own man. Tammany can screw him in New York, but not for the White House. He's taking a calculated risk, biting the hand that feeds him, but he's taking it. Not to mention how he must feel about what's going on in this city."

"I never thought they'd investigate Tammany. I've heard of Judge Seabury. I thought he was dead," Emily said.

"He is," Alex laughed, further breaking the tension. "That's the only reason they can't corrupt him. No, seriously. He's been retired for fourteen years, after he ran for governor and lost. He has this big law firm downtown. He's rich and old, old money. *Mayflower* descendant. Above reproach. His father was an Episcopal bishop or something. His whole family were Episcopal bishops. We've got God on our side here, Emily. God and Roosevelt. We can't do much better."

"This is fantastic, Alex," Emily said. "It's the kind of thing I've been praying for, fighting for, all these years. It doesn't even seem real." Yet while Emily was speaking these words of happiness, her enthusiasm seemed to drain away. "It's great. I should be so happy. But . . . but . . ."

"What's wrong, Emily?" Alex asked.

"I've gotten so pessimistic . . . about everything. Tomorrow they may cancel the whole thing. You know politics. I know Tammany."

"No. Roosevelt's serious," Alex insisted. "If they nail

your judge, then you could go to them and they can overturn your conviction. And then . . ."

"That's the problem, Alex, going to them. That's the problem."

"Why?"

"I can't go to them," Emily said.

"Why not?"

"Because . . . because . . . you know what I am." When Emily had first started keeping her Tammany diaries, she'd thought they would yield her the kind of power that could be exercised through a lawyer, quickly, decisively, and above all, quietly and discreetly, to get back both Jessica and her name. But the Seabury inquiry was probably going to be a heavily publicized event. "Alex, with what I still am, how can I . . . ?"

"Still? No." Alex was more than surprised. "What about the guy I saw you with? I thought you were going to marry him."

"It didn't work out," was all Emily could say.

"I'm sorry," Alex said. "It looked so great for you."

"I know," Emily said ruefully. "Alex, you're so kind to think of me. You're too kind. But it's hopeless. Even if they expose what happened then, look at me now."

"Look at you. You're young and beautiful."

"Don't look too close, Alex."

"Stop it. You're still as beautiful as ever. I mean it. You could even start all over again on Broadway. You didn't deserve to have your life messed up. This is going to turn everything around for you, Emily. You've gotta believe that."

"Alex, if only I could. But I can't . . . can't let Jessica know about me, about what I do. At least I get to see her now. I don't want to lose that."

"Stop thinking about losing. Try to think about winning. I know you, Emily. You want to win."

"Yes, I do, Alex. We'll see. Whatever, there's one wonderful thing about all this." She put her hands on Alex's.

"It got you to come by."

At first, Emily had seemed hardened, by her life and by her losses, but now her softness and radiance were returning. Alex remembered exactly why he had fallen for her.

He wanted to kiss her, make love to her, but he didn't allow these desires to take over. He knew he was playing with fire by coming to see her.

"That night at the Biltmore, I never thought I'd see you again. I thought you hated me. I would've hated me too, if I were you," Emily said.

"I didn't hate you. How could I? I was just shocked."

"So was I. It wasn't me . . . isn't me." Emily glanced around the expensive apartment that her "career" had bought her. "It was the only way I had. I didn't think I'd get stuck in it."

"I understand," Alex said, gripping her hand. "And hell, who am *I* to judge? There but for the grace of God go I. We're two ex-cons, Emily. That's why I was crazy about you. Except you really didn't do anything wrong, and I did. So I would never judge you. It was just that I wanted you. I loved you. I couldn't stand the idea of other men having you. It killed me. I couldn't face it."

"Believe me, I did it to survive. I did it for Jessica. I was at a dead end. I wanted to get her back. I wanted to get my life back, some kind of life. I thought money could do it."

"Maybe Judge Seabury can do it. You've got to keep up hope."

"Alex?"

"Yes?"

"Will you be my friend again?"

"I never stopped being your friend."

Emily wanted to make love; she thought he wanted that. That would have been easy for her now, but she stopped short. She didn't want to go too far this time. She kissed him on the lips, not an erotic kiss, but a most grateful kiss.

"I think I'll have that drink," Alex said. He was glad he had come.

57

Emily took the subway down to Canal Street and wandered through the fringes of Chinatown to Foley Square, which was the center of government in New York. She had no idea, however, which of the grand, gray, and grim institutional buildings ringing the triangular green was where Judge Seabury was presiding. Her first try was at the grandest edifice, the Supreme Court Building, with its noble Corinthian columns and its almost-block-long ascension of steps.

"Could you tell me where Judge Seabury is?" she asked the first woman she saw.

"Never heard of him," the woman said and strode briskly by.

"Excuse me. I'm looking for the Seabury hearings," Emily tried again, with a man carrying a large briefcase.

"I'm in from Rochester, lady. Can't help you."

"I'm looking for Judge Seabury," she importuned an efficient-looking woman with files of papers under both arms.

"You mean Judge Stansbury."

"No. No. Judge Seabury. The Seabury Commission."

The woman gave her a blank stare.

Emily was concerned. What was about to happen was supposed to be very important, wasn't it? Only the blind man who ran the newsstand had heard of the hearings. "Seabury. Yeah. Across the street at the Criminal Courts Building, miss."

"Thank you so much," Emily said. The Criminal Courts Building. That was where Judge Crater's chambers had been. Emily crossed the square into the building she had seen only in the dark. It was exceptionally gray, even by daylight, and was connected to an even gloomier structure, a jail known as the Tombs, by the infamous Bridge of Sighs, over which prisoners were taken to face the judges.

When Emily finally found her judge, she was mightily impressed. Judge Samuel Seabury was the sternest man she had ever seen. In his dark judicial robes, the white-haired jurist resembled a biblical prophet. Here was the city's Avenging Angel, its pillar of rectitude breathing down on Magistrate Stanley Renaud, who, sitting in the witness dock, was as below reproach as Seabury was above it.

This was the match Emily had come to view. Yet she saw instantly that Seabury's imposing persona was not enough to carry the day for the forces of justice. He needed a bigger stage, a grander forum, and much more support. The little hearing room he had been assigned was hardly the setting for a showdown that would bring down the great Hall of Tammany. In fact, the room was two-thirds empty—a few ancient pensioners who Emily figured would attend anything that was free, two bums in the back who were looking for a warm shelter, a half dozen newspaper reporters. And that was it. Emily was terribly disappointed that there wasn't more interest. After all, the future of the city was at stake. Or was it?

Seabury sat on the bench as Stanley Renaud was being questioned by Seabury's chief attorney, Isidor Kresel. The bespectacled Kresel looked like an accountant who had been locked in a bank vault with ledgers all his life. He was hitting as hard as he could at the fact that, despite Renaud's magistrate's salary of twelve thousand dollars a year, despite the law that city judges could not engage in personal business while on the bench, he had managed to put almost two hundred thousand dollars in the bank in the last seven years. How could he get out of that? Despite the unimpressive turnout of the hearings, Emily was as thrilled as a fisherman with a big one on the hook.

"Judge Renaud," Kresel repeated, "during the last seven years, your wages have totaled eighty-four thousand dollars. Is that correct?"

"You can add as well as I can, sir," Renaud replied. Emily could see his waxed mustache twitch. With his slick hair and his ferret face, he didn't have a judicial demeanor at all. He seemed more like one of the sharpies who would guess your age and weight at a carnival sideshow.

"Could you answer my question, please, Judge Renaud?"

"Yes. I would say so."

"Thank you," Kresel said. The court stenographer tapped away for the record. Emily hoped this would be the scandal that would break things open. "And during the same period, your bank deposits totaled one hundred eighty-six thousand, twenty-eight dollars, and thirteen cents. Is that correct?"

"If you say so," Renaud responded.

"No. Do you say so?"

"Please answer the question, Magistrate Renaud." Judge Seabury raised an impatient white brow. He used the word "magistrate" with the ultimate contempt.

"If that's what it adds up to, your honor, that's what it is," Renaud finally answered, giving a false smile of accommodation.

"Then where did the extra one hundred and two thousand come from, Magistrate Renaud?" Seabury asked. This was a hearing, not a trial, but the distinction was blurred. "It didn't come from what you've earned."

"It's easy to explain, your honor," Renaud said unctuously.

"It is?"

"I've had a lot of luck at the track."

Emily couldn't believe the audacity. Neither could Seabury or Kresel. "A hundred and two thousand is a great deal of luck," Seabury said.

"I'm a compulsive gambler. Off the bench, of course," Renaud allowed, putting this outrageous icing on the upside-down cake of his finances.

"How can he get away with this?" Emily whispered to the old man sitting beside her. "Can you believe it!"

"Seeing is believing, lady," the man mumbled. "It's no big surprise. They all got answers like that."

Kresel tried one blind avenue after another. Finally he gave up. "You may step down," he said despairingly, and Emily left the hearing room in disgust.

Her revulsion would only mount in the weeks ahead,

as virtually every one of the Tammany magistrates, bail bondsmen, lawyers, and vice officers the Seabury staff called to the stand gave them as audacious a runaround as Stanley Renaud. They all had explanations for their property, all of which were untraceable. Having been stirred by Alex's exhortations about Judge Seabury and the hope that his investigation might weaken Tammany to the point where Emily's conviction might indeed be reviewed and overturned, even perhaps without major fanfare, Emily had followed the hearings in the papers with the same rapt interest most other New Yorkers reserved for the Yankees in their homestretch toward the pennant. But her initial hopes that Tammany would be exposed became dimmer as the already abbreviated coverage receded further and further into the back pages.

Judge Seabury's approach was simple, to compare salary and savings. The two rarely matched. The excuses were what made the show a circus. One vice officer accounted for eighty thousand dollars by card winnings he claimed to have stashed away in a trunk in his attic. Others had fortunate benefactors who had since died or couldn't be traced. Whenever a hard question came up, it was answered with a blank look that became known as the "Tammany trance."

The most celebrated of all the Seabury deponents and the one who astonished Emily the most was New York County Sheriff Thomas M. Farley, who had a three-hundred-thousand-dollar discrepancy. The Seabury Committee had reports that the fortune was made in Farley's district Democratic club, which was much more of a gambling casino than a forum for political debate. The bullish Farley, like all the Tammanyites, was indignant on the stand that he would even be questioned.

"Where did you keep these monies you had saved?" Seabury asked Farley.

"In a big tin box in a big safe."

"What is the most money you ever had in that tin box?"

"I had as much as one hundred thousand dollars in the box," Farley said proudly.

"When would you deposit the money?"

"Oh, from time to time."

Every time Seabury compared a year's salary and a year's deposits, Farley would always explain that the difference "came from the good box I had."

"Kind of a magic box?" Seabury almost groaned.

"Aye, it was a wonderful box," Farley said with the straightest of faces.

But rather than being outraged at Tammany's impudence, the public laughed. "Tin Box" Farley got the headlines that Judge Seabury did not. He became a minor folk hero, a fun-loving, rollicking Irishman who wouldn't hurt a soul. And what about the money? Anybody who had money, especially in the Depression, seemed to be admired, regardless of the means.

Meanwhile, at City Hall, Mayor Walker was proclaiming the entire Seabury investigation a witch hunt, a waste of taxpayers' money, a game of politics. The ringmaster of Tammany indignation, he cast the worst aspersions on Governor Roosevelt and his ambitions, saying that Roosevelt was using New York City as a pawn to be sacrificed so that he could become ruler in Washington. When asked about the frame-up allegations, Walker laughed. "They frame pictures. Nobody's framing innocent women." Then in his best thespian turn, he became dead serious. "But, by God"—he liked to invoke the Almighty—"you show me one of our officers doing something like that, and I'll single-handedly throw him off the force."

Emily saw that Roosevelt's public-relations skills were no match for Walker's. The framing of women was one area Governor Roosevelt assumed would galvanize the public against Tammany abuses. Illicit incomes were one matter; ruined lives were another. But the victims who testified, unfortunately, were unconvincing. The problem with these women who claimed to have been framed was that they lacked the brazen charisma of the Tammany men. As Emily looked at the pictures of these women, she realized that as terrifying as their stories were, the women themselves lacked drama, the drama that would sell papers. The Tammany men told their lies so much more effectively than these women told their truths.

One woman who came forward testified she was framed by a vice cop who had broken into her apartment, shielded by the noise of the Third Avenue elevated. He claimed she was a prostitute on the side, despite the fact that she was married. Her husband was away at work. Two of her brothers were priests, her sister a nun. She was scrubbing the kitchen floor when the undercover policemen barged in and arrested her. She paid five hundred dollars to a bail bondsman and was discharged by the magistrate.

Among the other women who came forward were a model who said she had been entrapped by a vice officer who picked her up at a Gramercy Park speakeasy; a masseuse who alleged she was "shaken down" by two vice cops who threatened to close down her "physical-therapy" studio as a front for prostitution; and a dance teacher who said a vice officer extorted seven hundred dollars to drop prostitution charges that the lessons she gave were of a far more intimate nature than tangos and rumbas.

One deficiency in these cases was that none of these women had actually gone to prison. Even if their stories were believed, they paid money, but they had their lives. More important, many of these lives, like those centering on modeling, massage, dancing, and the like, were lived in gray areas where the public could be persuaded that these women might have crossed the line into prostitution. Furthermore, the police who were called to face their accusers were convincing indeed. Each of the bad cops in question had a good story, a good excuse, a denial of any extortion.

The real harm was done to the women who went to prison unjustly, but most of them were so broken by the experience that they didn't have the heart, or the energy, to come forward. The damage was irreparable. The few witnesses who had gone to prison and did speak out before Judge Seabury had already been prostitutes when they were framed. Shaken down by the vice squad, they didn't have the money to pay. Once they got out of prison, they became prostitutes again. No one wanted to take the word of a hooker, not against New York's finest.

Emily thus realized that her story was unique. There was no one who had appeared before Judge Seabury who had *not* been a prostitute and ended up in prison. After all, the reason the innocent women were framed was extortion, and the vice squad knew their marks. Emily was the one "normal" woman who could speak out on the nightmares of being framed, of Bedford, of being stigmatized. But now she wasn't "normal" anymore. She was a call girl. How could she say anything and not ruin the new life she had struggled so to create? How could she ever let Jessica know? She wanted desperately to help Seabury. He needed help. But she couldn't destroy herself in the process. The dilemma was driving her crazy. The only one she could talk to about it was Alex. He had invited her to the new Museum of Modern Art on Fifty-third Street to see the Picassos, Mirós, and other avant-garde paintings and sculptures. Yet as they walked up Fifth Avenue to the museum, Emily's mind was not on art.

"I just can't go to Seabury," she said as Alex slowed down to see the book display at Scribner's.

"You're the only person they'd believe," Alex replied, not wanting to push her, but hoping that she would testify.

"There's got to be someone else," Emily said, walking on, not really thinking about anything except her own conflict.

"There hasn't been so far," Alex said as he ran to catch up with her.

"If I took the stand, they'd ask me what I do now. They'd find out."

"It's not what you do. It's what you know."

"They'd find out what I . . . do. They'd crucify me for it. And it's not me I care about. It's Jessica. For her to find out about Bedford, that would be bad enough. But if she found out about Polly . . . No! That would kill me. I can't do it."

"How can you be sure she'd find out?" Alex raised his voice to be heard above the rat-tat-tat of the construction of still another skyscraper on Forty-eighth Street.

"I can't take the risk. Any risk," Emily shouted back. "I'd rather leave things the way they are." But the status quo didn't appeal to Emily either. She didn't have a career. She didn't have a family. Most of the money she had saved came from an illegal profession that she hated but had become inured to. What did she have to look forward to?

Perhaps in the years to come when Jessica grew up, went away to college, had her own life, then they could be mother and daughter again. Until then, Emily would have to suffer the hell of her ignominy, of her loneliness. If she despised what she had come to do, how would her daughter feel about it? She wasn't ready to have that question resolved.

Inside the museum they were strolling through the Picasso exhibition when a small woman with a very animated yet tired face stood on her tiptoes behind Alex and put her hands over his eyes.

"See no evil," the woman said, surprising him.

Alex turned around. "Hi, Dorothy."

"Are you here for the art or just the dirty pictures?"

"Dirty pictures. Dorothy Parker. Meet my friend Emily Stanton."

"Hi," Emily said as she shook the tiny woman's hand. She wanted to tell her how much she liked her witty poems and stories in *The New Yorker*, but she couldn't get it out.

"I'm enchanted," Dorothy Parker said as she looked Emily up and down twice. "Who needs pictures, Alex? She's so pretty."

"Oh, thanks." Emily hated the compliment. She was *paid* for being pretty. She wanted to be something else. She consoled herself by thinking Mrs. Parker would love to be told she was pretty.

"Now I know why you never notice me," Dorothy said to Alex in a voice so clipped and fast Emily could barely keep up. "I know when I'm licked." She ran her tongue on the outside of her red lips. "And I know when I'm not." She winked and turned to go. "See you in my dreams," she said over her shoulder, and returned to her friend looking at a Modigliani.

"She's drunk," Alex said. "She's always drunk."

"Very fast company, Alex."

"I just met her."

"Do you have a seat at the Algonquin Round Table yet?" Emily asked.

"Not yet. I'm still at the square table at the Automat."

"Alex, I'm so proud of you. You're a produced playwright. You have Dorothy Parker chasing after you."

311

"There's no exclusivity to that."

"Seriously. You're doing swell. What more could you want?"

"You."

"That's the last thing you need."

"I'll always have a crush on you, Emily."

"You could have this famous writer. Or I'm sure you could have a beautiful deb from a fine family. What do you want with me? I'm scarred."

"I like scars. They add character. If the next play's a hit, I could write something with a part for you."

Emily sighed. "Write your play, Alex, but don't worry about me."

"Okay, okay. My mistake. Can I worry about New York? You might save the city."

"Doubtful. Alex, I'm depressed. I thought Judge Seabury was going to turn things around. It's the same old story."

"It wouldn't be . . ."

"If I risked my life. My daughter. No, I can't."

"These are the Blue Period, when Picasso lived in Paris," Alex said, changing the subject. "And this one, *Les Demoiselles d'Avignon*, had nothing to do with Avignon, where the popes went in France."

Emily looked at the museumgoers. All carefree, rich women in silk and fur and jewels. What was she doing here among them?

"This Avignon was a bordello in Barcelona where Picasso got his inspiration."

"Thanks, Alex."

"What?"

"I didn't appreciate that."

"You mean you're offended because I mentioned the word 'bordello'? Emily, please."

"Oh, God, I'm sorry, Alex. If I wasn't"—she pointed to Picasso's nude prostitutes—"I could go to Seabury and tell what I know. They've got my hands tied. They've got the city's hands tied."

"What are you doing for dinner?"

Emily hated to say it. "I've got a date. . . ."

58

The orchestra was playing Strauss's "Tales from the Vienna Woods." The ladies in their stoles, holding bags from Saks Fifth Avenue and Bergdorf Goodman, were eating little cucumber sandwiches and drinking sherry and tea in the Palm Court amidst fronds and marble, a classical rain forest. And Emily was there at the Plaza to have sex for a hundred dollars with a traveling dress salesman from Washington State in town to see his company's new line. "Wear extra nice lingerie, dollink," Polly had told her in giving her the assignment. "He likes fashion shows." Emily was surprised to run into Bridgit Lund lounging in the lobby, eating a napoleon and reading *Vogue*. She could have passed for a young society matron, except for her violet dress, which indiscreetly plunged too far.

"Bridgit."

"Hi, Emily. Taste this." She held out her pastry on a fork.

"No, thanks. What are you doing here?" Emily sat down on the brocade chair across the table from Bridgit.

"Same thing you are."

"Oh."

"I've got an appointment with"—Bridgit put on a mock Southern drawl—"a fine gentleman from Tennessee, or is it Mississippi? Oh, hell, it's all the same down there. 'Way down upon the Swanee River,' " she sang dizzily.

"You're happy."

"I'm going to do this really fast and go shopping. Do you like this one?" She held up the *Vogue* to a dress inside.

"Bridgit," Emily said, not answering her.

"Yes, ma'am?" Bridgit giggled.

"If you could be serious for one minute."

"Okay. But only one minute."

"Bridgit, what would you say if I asked you to see Judge Seabury?"

"You bet. How much?"

"Judge Seabury."

"I love judges. They're so stuffy, and I make them go so crazy . . . They're kinda tight, though."

"Bridgit, haven't you been reading the papers?"

"I only read them for sales."

"The Seabury hearings," Emily said impatiently.

"Oh, that."

"They're not getting anywhere."

"So?"

"I bet they're going to shut down. You could help. Not one of the other women who's come forward went to prison. *You* did. You could go and testify about McNaughton." Emily was proselytizing Bridgit the same way Alex was goading her.

"Me? Go?" Bridgit laughed. "Hey, Emily, are you nuts? I don't want to get killed."

"Who said you'd be killed?"

"I'm living like a little princess. I'm sitting here in the Plaza, dressed up from Bonwit's, sipping tea. I'm a little lady, baby. For the first time in my life I have money, and I love it. You want me to go up there with those poor hookers?"

Emily almost laughed at the word. "You could help New York."

"I ain't no patriot."

"You could help me. Help expose these people. Help me get my daughter back."

"I only make good impressions I'm *paid* to make. Hey, Em. I like you very much. I do. But I don't like you that much. Those guys kill for a lot less. I ain't no Jane of Arc."

"Joan."

"Whatever. The only stake I want's the one my date's taking me for."

"God, Bridgit, don't be so selfish. Think about somebody else for a change. Think of the other girls who've been ruined."

"I'm thinkin' about me, 'cause if I don't, nobody else will. I ain't a hero. You be the hero, all by yourself. You get all the spotlight. When you goin'?"

"I'm . . . not . . . I don't know."

"Are you serious? You send me and you stay . . ."

"I can't," Emily said. "I mean, if I testify, it'll be in the news. My daughter would find out. Bridgit, you don't have a kid. You could go. Your testimony would mean—"

"It's a bunch of hot air. You think this Judge Seabiscuit—"

"Seabury."

"Whatever, you think he can change anything?" Bridgit said, looking up at the big grandfather clock. "Emily, let me ask you something."

"What?" Emily hoped she would help her.

"Am I wearing too much rouge?"

Emily didn't answer.

"Well, don't be mad," Bridgit said as she combed her hair, collected her magazine and purse, and sashayed to the elevator to the strains of the Strauss waltz.

59

Isabelle had gone to Philadelphia for the weekend to an antique show. Eliza, the maid, had gotten sick Saturday morning and had gone home. Thus it was one of the rare occasions when Warren Matthews was all alone with his daughter. It was late Saturday night. Jessica had just returned from a dance Miss Draper's School was having with the Lawrenceville School in Princeton. She had danced with at least five of the best-looking young boarding-school boys and had a wonderful time. One boy with the grandiose name of Oakleigh Ridgemont IV had even given her a rose with his engraved calling card pinned to it, but she preferred another boy named Rink Pelham who had lost one of his front teeth as captain of the junior ice-hockey team. He wore a frayed tie, his father's old tweed jacket and hunting boots, and was generally rambunctious. He had a flask of whiskey and gave Jessica a sip. She thought he was the cutest one there and hoped to see him again.

Jessica had just gotten out of a long, hot bath sorting out the memories of the evening. She was drying herself off when she saw her father's reflection in the bathroom mirror.

"Daddy!" she squealed, and threw her towel around her. "I'm not dressed." She was so embarrassed.

She didn't know that he had been standing there for several minutes. "I want to talk to you, Jessica," Warren said.

Did I do something wrong? was the first thought that leapt into Jessica's mind. His coolness to her since their altercation over her party dress months before had heightened her fear of him. Was he going to punish her? Beat her? "Y-yes, Daddy." She held the towel around her. He kept staring. "I'll put on my nightshirt." She closed the door and dressed for bed, trembling.

When Jessica emerged from the bathroom, Warren was sitting on her bed. "Come here, Jessica." He beckoned to her and said in his deep authoritative voice, "Sit down. Here. We haven't talked much recently, have we, Jessica?"

"No, Daddy. I guess not."

"I wanted to tell you how sorry I was we had that fight about your dress, sweetheart. I didn't mean to get angry with you."

How vastly relieved Jessica was. Her face broke into a smile. "Oh, that's okay, Daddy. I didn't mean to make you mad."

"I can't stay mad with you," Warren said, and put his arm around his daughter. "You're too pretty to get mad with." Warren kissed Jessica's forehead. He saw that she was nervous. "Don't be scared of me, honey. I'm your daddy."

"I thought you were still angry," Jessica said.

"I'm not. And I want to spend more time with you. I'm proud of what a beautiful young lady you're becoming."

"Thank you, Daddy."

Warren held her tighter in his arms. Jessica liked being held by him. She had experienced so little warmth from her father. He was gone so often and he was so busy. Their life was formal, distanced. She had wanted him to love her, but it was a love she had never thought she could earn. She thought she had to be like *Mummy* to make her father notice her, but that hadn't done anything except make *Mommy* cross with her. And when she dressed up like *Mommy*, her father hurt her and scared her. As Jessica had gotten older, she had developed increasing pangs of desire for her father's attention. She was noticing boys, but none of them seemed as strong and handsome as her father was. She wished she could meet a boy who looked like him. And now, here he was holding her in his arms. He was wearing a dark green silk dressing gown over gray flannel pajamas and smelled of lime cologne and Scotch and cigar smoke. He reminded

Jessica of some of the stars she saw in the movies, something of Douglas Fairbanks, something of Ramon Novarro.

"Did you have a good time tonight?" Warren asked her.

"It was fun."

"I bet all the Lawrenceville boys were crazy about you."

"Not all of them."

"But a few, I bet."

"A few."

"Did you find one you liked?"

"Sort of."

"Did you let him kiss you?" Warren asked.

"No . . ."

"Did he try?"

"No." Jessica began to blush.

"Did you want him to try?"

"Maybe." Jessica began to giggle and buried her red face in her father's robe.

"You're going to break a lot of hearts, my girl," Warren said, pulling Jessica back and looking at her in a way that went beyond mere admiration. "You are really beautiful."

"No, I'm not."

"Yes, you are," Warren insisted.

Jessica found her father's warmth and praise so unusual, so exciting. "Daddy, I'm so glad you like me. I was never ever sure."

"I love you, sweetheart. You're my most special lady." He paused. "And none of the boys has kissed you yet."

Jessica shook her head.

"I'm surprised. They don't know what they're missing." Then Warren got a strange glimmer in his eye, drew Jessica to him, and kissed her lips. The feeling was burning and urgent, and though he had kissed her before, it was never like this. "You kiss beautifully, darling," Warren said in a low voice, and then he kissed her again.

Jessica was slightly scared, yet continued to be flattered that her father was noticing her. When he let her go the second time, however, her eyes caught something that made her wince in surprise. Warren's robe had pulled to one side exposing the opening in his pajamas. Jessica had seen such a thing only once before, years ago, the dreadful night she found Warren pinning Emily on the floor, forcing himself into her. The sight of her father's naked body was seared into Jessica's subconscious. Here it was again. Warren gazed at Jessica as her widening eyes traveled to his now exposed groin.

"That means that a man likes you," Warren said. "Go ahead. Touch it. Don't be afraid."

Jessica shrank back.

"Go ahead, sweetheart. I want you to."

Jessica gingerly started to place her hand on Warren but quickly yanked it away.

"Hold it. Hold it in your hand. It's all right," Warren said as he began unbuttoning Jessica's nightshirt.

"Daddy! Stop. What are you doing?"

"You're a perfect woman now," Warren said, as he refused to stop. He lifted Jessica's nightshirt over her head and gazed at her nudity. "You're beautiful all over. I'm proud of you. You're perfect," he repeated. He stroked her ripening breasts softly, sending warm lush feelings through her which commingled with the cold fear of the strangeness of the moment.

"But Daddy," Jessica pleaded anxiously. How could she be with her father like this, on her bed, among her dolls and her teddy bears. "Why? Why are you doing this?"

"It's all right, my love," he said in his reassuring voice. "I'm doing this because I love you. I don't want some strange teenage boy trying to teach you these things. This is my responsibility. You're grown up now and I want you to trust me. You must trust me."

No one had discussed the facts of life with Jessica, not Isabelle, not Emily, not her teachers. These were matters which were left unspoken. Jessica had no idea her father was lying to her. She had no idea what was going through his head, that he was in a trance, reliving his first sexual encounters with Emily, becoming more aroused and inflamed and convulsed with passion than he had been since that time. That was the erotic zenith of Warren's lifetime with women, and now he was surpassing even that with his thirteen-year-old daughter, his own *doppel-*

ganger of the wife he had destroyed, a wife whose memory, and the memory of the pleasure she had brought, was corroding him. Tonight he had the cure for his sexual malaise. Tonight was the ultimate.

"Daddy, I'm scared," Jessica was quivering.

"Do you love me, darling?"

"Yes. Yes, Daddy."

"Would I do anything bad to you?"

"No. No."

"Do you know how much I love you?" Warren kept caressing her breasts, his question producing a mesmerizing effect on Jessica.

But despite the authority, despite the flattery, something inside of Jessica told her this was wrong, terribly wrong. She pushed her father's hand away and stood up. "No, Daddy. I don't want to. Don't make me."

Warren stood up, too. "This is all for you, Jessica. All for you, my darling. I'm going to teach you about life and love." He tried to touch her again.

Jessica covered her breasts with her hands. She turned her body away from Warren so he couldn't see the front of her. Then she started to sob. "No, Daddy. Don't make me. I don't want to do this. Leave me alone."

Somehow, Jessica's tears stopped Warren. He couldn't seduce his daughter. He didn't want to force her. That wasn't what he desired. He wanted her to *want* him. She didn't. He backed off. But in being thwarted so close to realizing this fantasy, Warren became angry, both at the frustration and at the potential for his own humiliation if anyone found out. He glared straight into Jessica's eyes. His tone of voice changed from tenderness to menace. "You mustn't tell anyone, *anyone, ever* that this happened, Jessica. As long as you live. this was something very special just between us. Understand?"

"Yes, Daddy. Jessica replied. "I won't tell anyone."

"*Anyone!*" Warren repeated. "*Anyone!* As long as you live!"

"As long as I live," Jessica promised, knowing full well that however much she would like to break her word and share this trauma with her mother, this was one promise she dared never to break.

60

The sight of Michael McNaughton in his blue uniform with the brass buttons, the crisp blue flannel, the badge, dismayed Emily. He had all the symbols of authority. He was the institutionalization of evil. She was wearing a hat and dark glasses at the Seabury hearing. She had seen on the back page that he was scheduled to testify. After four months, Judge Seabury had been relegated to the end of the sports section. Emily followed the dwindling news each day, hoping for a breakthrough, which never came. Still, her curiosity, her anxiety, propelled her downtown. When Emily arrived, the same bums and pensioners were in the gloomy hearing room with its scratched benches, peeling plaster, and stale cigarette air. Most of the reporters were gone. McNaughton was explaining his hundred thousand dollars in the bank.

"Frugality, your honor. Wise investments. I work hard for my money. I make my money work hard for me."

"Did you ever accept a bribe for dropping a prostitution charge against a woman, Officer McNaughton?" Seabury asked. The judge looked older, wearier. He had a face that was always old, born old, owlish, wise, but now, if it was possible, he had aged. Tammany could do that, Emily thought. Here was St. George, but the Dragon was unslayable. Yet this was the question she had to hear the answer to.

"Your honor," McNaughton said in a modulated voice worthy of the stage, "I've been on the force ten years. I have not only the highest number of arrests, but the highest percentage of convictions to arrests of any man on the vice squad. I'm proud of that record. No amount of money could make me do anything to detract from that." He looked straight at the judge while he spoke, doing his best to try to shame this august jurist for daring to ask these questions. Polite, annoyed, indignant. Tammany style. He was the best of all the Tammany witnesses. He could have given classes.

"What about your ninety-nine-percent conviction rate? None of these women were framed?" Seabury pressed on.

"They were convicted, weren't they, your honor?" McNaughton said, and the judge somehow looked foolish for even asking. "I'm only a policeman, sir, not a judge and jury. It would take more than me to send them to jail."

Judge Seabury was more on the defensive than his witness. Several women had testified that McNaughton had framed them, but here he was, the exemplar of righteousness and high morality, denying everything and making these women appear to be not only liars but also fools for accusing him. "Officer McNaughton, for the record, do you testify here, under oath, that you never framed or extorted money from a woman?"

"Judge Seabury," McNaughton said as he propped his arm on the dock and assumed a colloquial let-me-tell-it-to-you-straight air, "I go to Mass every Sunday. I believe in God. I earn my living and I'm proud of the way I earn it. I'm proud to be a member of the New York Police Department, and I think they're proud of me."

Emily wanted to rush to the front of the room and tell them how proud he ought to be. She wanted to be Exhibit A. She wanted to tell the truth. She stirred in her seat, but a gravity held her back, the gravity of her life as a call girl, the gravity of the daughter she didn't want to risk losing. However tenuous her visiting privileges were, they still represented a tie, a bond. She didn't want to risk that bond. It was all she had.

A few weeks later at Guinan's, Emily was singing "Baby Face" to a half-filled house. Texas had lowered drink prices and, depression or not, New Yorkers and visitors to New York, at least some of them, had to go out.

"Hello, old stranger," Texas called out to Cassie Laverne, whom Emily hadn't seen for months. She had
gone to New Orleans to visit relatives, then had a date
for a Caribbean cruise with some Latin businessman, and
somehow Emily lost touch. Cassie looked like more than
a million dollars, swathed in an incredible ermine coat.
Behind her was a familiar-looking young man overdressed
in spats and pinstripes, a young boy trying to look
grown-up. Cassie introduced the boy to Texas. While
Texas was making a big fuss over him, Cassie approached
Emily, hand outstretched, to show her an enormous diamond ring.

"Well, honey, I told you miracles can happen."

"My God, a diamond bigger than the Ritz," Emily
said.

"Not just a big rock, love, an engagement."

"Oh, Cassie." Emily hugged her. "But . . . I know
him . . . I think."

"Of course you do. If it wasn't for you, you might be
married to him."

"Huh?"

"Remember the night at Polly's?" Cassie whispered.
"You passed him through to me."

"Tom Mix?" Emily remembered suddenly. The Chicago beef heir. Cassie? Engaged?

"It's the last roundup." Cassie smiled contentedly. "I
didn't want to say anything, for fear of jinxing it. He's
the one who took me on the cruise. We went to his cattle
ranch in Venezuela. God, if I see another prize bull, I
will die." Cassie gritted her teeth. "But hell, baby, we're
in a depression. Should I be fussy? Emily, I owe it all to
you. I promise to work something out. Can you believe
he proposed? At last, somebody proposed. To me."

"Is he nice?" was all Emily could ask. She was almost
breathless. The thought of losing Cassie set her adrift.

"Nice? I guess. If you can stand his cowboy routine.
But Nice"—she pronounced the *ee* of the French city—
"he's got a villa there on the Riviera and we're gonna
live our honeymoon year there. *Au revoir*, New York.
Bonjour, France." Cassie spun around, she was so happy.
"Maybe we'll find you some old duke and you can come
over."

"Honeymoon *year*?" Emily checked to make sure she was hearing correctly.

"The rich are different," Cassie said. "Even their time lasts longer. Come over and meet him, and never mention anything about Polly's. He's going to pass me off as a Creole heiress. Isn't that a kick? Emily, you look sad."

"No, no. I'm happy. Your getting married is such a shock. I'm just not ready for it. You're my best friend," Emily said as she wiped a tear from her eye. More began to fall. She couldn't stop. "Oh, Cassie, you did it. You got your wish."

"I owe it all to you. Stop it, crybaby. Stop." Cassie hugged her. "You're not losing a friend. You're gaining a stockyard. Come on and meet him."

Emily called eleven "A. Hunts" before she found the girl she had warned away at Guinan's the night two years ago when Michael McNaughton was attempting to frame her. Annie Hunt— Emily never forgot her name—had just moved out of the Three Arts Club to an apartment on Bleecker Street in the Village. She had gotten her telephone only a few days before Emily was going to give up on ever finding her. The timing was lucky. Despite the long passage of time, Annie remembered instantly who Emily was.

"That was the most miserable night of my life," she told Emily over the phone. "I almost quit trying to be an actress after that. I almost went back to Kansas." She told Emily she was still taking drama lessons and was working for a Methodist charitable foundation while waiting for her break. After an initial trepidation, Annie agreed to meet Emily for coffee at the Hotel Brevoort.

"It's still like a bad dream," Annie told Emily in the café overlooking lower Fifth Avenue, after hearing the story of Emily's frame-up. Annie was as wholesome as Emily had remembered her, natural blonde, innocent, farm-fresh. She would make a splendid witness for Judge Seabury, Emily thought. "I almost can't believe that they were going to set me up. I really, really appreciate your saving me."

"Then maybe you can help save me," Emily said.

"How could I do that?"

"By going to the Seabury Commission and testifying about what happened to you."

"But nothing really happened. I got away."

"Tell them that. Just tell the truth."

"It wouldn't make any difference," Annie demurred timidly. "Just because I went out for drinks with them doesn't prove they were going to frame me."

"Annie, he's a policeman, *not* a producer. The fact he was coming on to you like that, the same way he came on to me, that proves a *lot*. Please, Annie, I know you understand."

"He'd deny everything."

"Maybe he would," Emily said. "But I think people would believe you. You're an honest person."

"Why wouldn't they believe you?"

"You work for the Methodist Church, Annie. I work for Texas Guinan," Emily said. She didn't want to add that she also worked for Polly Adler.

"So you want me to back you up—"

"No." Emily hesitated. "I can't . . . really testify. I'm trying to protect my daughter. I can't risk the publicity," Emily said.

"You mean you want me to go alone?" Annie asked incredulously, a bit annoyed. "I'm sorry. I don't have a score to settle. I don't have a name to clear. But I do have a very short-tempered father back in Kansas who thinks the only time you should get your name in the paper is when you're born, married, or dead. Emily, I'd like to help you, but to begin with, I don't think, without you, my little story would mean a thing, and, beyond that, I'm fighting my dad tooth and nail just to stay in this city. The publicity would ruin all that. I don't see why you can't go."

"I just can't," Emily said.

"You have to fight your own battles," Annie said.

"I've been fighting," Emily replied, resenting Annie's tone. "I can't win all by myself. If I went with you, would that make a difference?"

Annie paused a long time. "I have to tell you the truth. No, not really. I want to make it on Broadway. I need my dad's support until I do. I can't go home to

Topeka. You can understand that. I love it here. I want to stay."

"I understand, Annie. I had to ask you, that's all."

Annie put one hand over Emily's, stopping her from reaching for the check. Annie opened her purse and left three dollars on the table. "Please, it's the least I can do." Annie looked at Emily with apologetic eyes. "I hope everything works out for you. You're a brave woman. I can tell. I wish I were my own person, you know. Then maybe I . . ." Annie's voice trailed off as she stood up. She shook Emily's hand. "God bless you," she said, and turned away to leave.

61

The week before Christmas, Emily received a telegram
that her mother had died of a cerebral hemorrhage. She
took the *Twentieth Century Limited* to Chicago and a
connecting train to Joliet. She hadn't seen her mother for
three years. The last time was when the Stantons had
come to New York for a prison wardens' convention. Mr.
Stanton refused to see Emily, preferring to stay at the
Hotel Pennsylvania and compare notes with other prison
keepers and go see the bicycle races at Madison Square
Garden. That night Mrs. Stanton went alone to Guinan's.
As the *Twentieth Century* roared across the dark hills of
Pennsylvania into the flat farmland of Ohio, Emily thought
about that last visit. How shocked her mother was, in her
dowdy wool coat and convict-made shoes, by the low-cut
silks and dancing and general debauchery of Guinan's.
She had no idea her mother was coming; her mother had
no idea what she would see. Emily remembered the look
of sadness on her mother's face, sunken from years of
submission to Emily's father, when she saw her daughter
cavorting around the tables to "Easy Street." Is this what
my daughter has become? the look said. Emily hoped
that the shock had not, in some way, hastened her mother's death.

Emily remembered proudly showing off Jessica's room
in her apartment, full of clothes and games and travel
books and paintings of animals, the room that would be
Jessica's when and if she ever got her back. This was her
shrine to her daughter, the room that kept Emily going.
Mrs. Stanton was skeptical. "Even if you get her back,

327

dear," Emily's mother said, "what kind of life are you going to bring Jessica into?"

"Not the one you saw, Mother."

"I'm glad your father didn't come. If I don't understand, how could he?"

"It's a means to an end, Mother." Emily made a defense she knew was falling on deaf ears. Thank God her mother didn't ask how she was really paying for the apartment. If she knew about Polly, she'd know that all Emily's father's anxieties—and worse— had come true. "I won't do this forever. I'll act again. I'll start a business. I'll do something. This is just a first step, Mother. I'm working. It's not easy, but I'm working."

She could see the despair on her mother's face. She could see her mother thinking: if only Emily had left Warren when their troubles started and moved back to Joliet with Jessica and met a nice local boy . . . Her mother's love was still there, under layers of her father's interdictions and her mother's own small-town prejudices about what a woman shouldn't do. Emily knew it was a lost cause. The price of her ambitions was the closeness of her family. Now, as the deluxe train sped on toward Chicago, as she lay motionless in her walnut compartment, the reality of that loss was setting in.

They buried Mrs. Stanton in a graveyard on the prison grounds under a giant bare oak. The weather was bitter cold. The prison walls and barbed wire stood unsympathetic vigil in the background. The only reminder of the season was a string of colored lights on one of the gates. The holiday was lost on the prison. A crowd of about thirty prison officials and townspeople gathered in the light snow to lay Mrs. Stanton to rest. Emily had arrived the morning of the funeral. Her father hadn't even kissed her. He treated her almost like a stranger. She went to the funeral home and kissed her mother's sad, beaten face good-bye. Here was a woman who had sacrificed her life to her husband, to all the conventional notions of rectitude and propriety, and what had it gotten her? An empty, forlorn life. She could have been a pianist, she could have had an identity, but she gave it up for love. But no, it wasn't love, Emily knew. It was security.

"Good-bye, Mom," Emily said with tears in her eyes. How she wished things had been different for them.

At the grave, dressed in her black veil and stylish suit, Emily was the object of small-town xenophobia. The townswomen cut quick, disapproving glances at her. They whispered to each other, not sharing their grief with her. The best she would get would be a "Sorry about your mother." She was the prodigal daughter. Joliet would not welcome her return. Emily retreated to stand alone by another old tree and cry to herself, behind her veil, as her mother was laid into the earth.

That night, after most of the mourners left, Emily found her father alone in his study. Mr. Stanton was staring at the dying fire. His face combined sadness and hardness. He would not let himself cry over the loss of his wife, no matter how much he mourned her death. He was simply staring, his thoughts unfathomable.

"Father," Emily said as she closed the door behind her.

"Yes, Emily," he said brusquely.

"I'd like to talk to you."

"Emily, I want to be alone."

"Father. Don't be that way, please. I thought if anything would have brought us together, this would have been it. I guess not, huh? Oh, Father. Daddy. Talk to me." She went over to him in the chair and touched his shoulder, hoping that he would respond, but he was as cold as her mother in her casket. "Mom wouldn't have wanted it to be like this. Oh, why . . . You're my family, my only family."

"Emily, I said I wanted to be alone."

"No, Daddy. I'm not going to leave you alone. You may not have anything to say to me, but I have things to say to you. I know you think I'm a fallen woman. You thought I was a fallen woman when I was still a little girl. You never gave me a chance, and I guess you think I lived up to everything bad you said I was going to become when I left the convent. Maybe I did, you know. But I didn't mean to. I know you don't believe I was framed. I know you think I got what I deserved. Don't you?"

Mr. Stanton did not answer.

"Well, I didn't deserve what I got," Emily went on. "Not from Warren Matthews and not from you either. You could have gotten me out of that prison. Was that asking too much? You could have at least written to me. You could have cared. You're my father. You're not my warden. My goddamn father. Why are you so goddamn hard?" Emily was crying now.

"Don't you curse here," Mr. Stanton said as he stood up and glared at his daughter.

"At least I got you to listen." Emily smiled through her tears. For once in her life, she suddenly knew she wasn't afraid of him anymore, and in that shedding of fear, she wasn't afraid of anything—not Tammany Hall, not Warren Matthews, not Michael McNaughton, not the press. "I don't know what's wrong with me, but no matter how cold, how cruel, how cut-off you are, some-how I'm still your little girl. I want you to be proud of me. I wanted Mom to be proud of me. I'm sorry she never got the chance."

"You should be sorry. You brought your mother nothing but misery."

"And what kind of joy did you bring her, Daddy?"

"Get out, Emily. Just get out."

"All right. But it's not over yet, Daddy. In a crazy way, I want to love you, and I want you to love me. I can't help it. Just wait. You're going to be proud of me," Emily said defiantly, her tears drying up. "Just wait. Good-bye, Daddy." She left the den, with her father gazing at the last dying embers of the fire, as the room went completely dark. She got her coat and called a cab for the hotel. She would be going back to New York tomorrow. Her mother's death had made a decision for her. She knew now exactly what she had to do.

LULLABY AND GOODNIGHT

answer. Curious, she knocked. No answer. And for some
reason, she tried the door, which Mr. Matthews always

62
1931

Emily couldn't figure out what was wrong with Jessica.
Sometimes she was bright and happy, and then, moments
later, would plunge into gloomy despair. When questioned, Jessica refused to explain, and Emily attributed
the mood swings to adolescence. What she didn't know
was how disturbed Jessica was over her father's sexual
advance. Jessica had thought she was in a hurry to grow
up, but now the process had seemed to go out of control.
Things were going too fast for her emotions to catch up,
and without anyone to discuss them with, Jessica felt
isolated and beyond confusion.

Emily was planning to go to the Seabury Commission.
Because Jessica didn't need any more shocks in her life,
Emily knew that she had to provide some cushioning for
the upcoming revelations. Accordingly, she decided that
the best way to tell Jessica what she was going to do was
to let her come to Texas Guinan's. Jessica got all dressed
up and sat with the hostesses, proudly watching her mother
sing "Easy Street." Jessica seemed to get rather upset
when one customer tried to flirt with her. When Jessica
snapped at him, "Leave me alone," and the man, embarrassed, retreated to the bar, no one had any idea what
she was actually reacting to. In fact, the hostesses
applauded her feistiness. They wished they could say no
as easily.

Back at Emily's apartment Jessica was draped in a pair
of her mother's satin pajamas, with the arms and legs
rolled up to fit her, lying in Emily's bed with her, talking.
For Emily, it was paradise being that close with her
daughter. Isabelle and Warren were on a cruise to Ber-

muda. They had grudgingly allowed Emily to have Jessica for the weekend, the first time they had ever so relented. How Emily wished that she and her daughter could have been doing this for the last seven years. "Texas is funny, Mom. And you're great. I can't believe how great. I'll never forget tonight." Jessica hugged her mother. "I love being with you."

Emily ran her fingers through Jessica's lustrous auburn hair. "You were a big hit with the men."

Jessica shrugged, uncomfortable at the thought of men. Before her father had come to her bedroom, she was beginning to be very interested in boys. Now she was guarded and distrustful. How she wished she could talk about it all with her mother, but she feared Warren's reprisal too much to even mention it. Instead, she looked for a way out of the stately home that had become a house of horror for her. "Do you think I could come and live with you someday, Mom? Sometimes I can't take it out there," Jessica blurted out.

"Why?" Emily asked.

"They don't understand me," was all Jessica could say.

"I'd like that more than anything, sweetheart."

"So? When can I come? I'd love to stay now and not go back there for awhile."

"We can't do that. But I'm working on it." Here was the entrance into the hard conversation Emily had to have with her daughter. She appreciated how completely alone in the world both she and Jessica were. She was sure that Isabelle didn't love this girl, certainly not the way she did. Terrified of her father (though Emily had no intimation of just how much), ignored by her stepmother, restricted from her mother, Jessica was as isolated as Emily was. In New Jersey she lived a life of false positivism, of good cheer and high spirits, just like the life Emily lived at Guinan's and with Polly's men. No one knew the dark turmoil seething beneath the gay facades of both mother and daughter. Aware of how brittle Jessica was, Emily agonized that the action she was going to take might somehow destroy her daughter. Jessica had forgiven her for "leaving" seven years ago. But could she ever forgive her if she found out her mother was a prostitute? Jessica might see that as the ultimate lie, the final betrayal by the only person she could trust. Then Jessica might feel she had no one, no one at all.

Emily was grateful that Jessica hadn't already been told about Bedford by Warren and Isabelle. They had to have some feeling for the girl to shield her from that. Nevertheless, as Jessica got older and Emily tried to get closer, Warren and Isabelle might retaliate by telling Jessica about Bedford. Emily had to set the record straight. And do it first. "Jessica, are you sleepy?"

"Not a bit, Mom. Sleepy? Here with you?"

"I want to talk to you about something." This was it, Emily realized. There would never be a better time. "Remember the night I never came home? When you were little?"

"The night you disappeared? Sort of." Jessica seemed to shiver.

Emily held her tight. She didn't want to scare her, but she had to prepare her for what was to come. "We've never really talked about what happened then."

"It doesn't matter." Jessica cringed.

"It does. You're old enough to know about this. And you're my best friend, do you know that? If I can't talk to my best friend, whom can I talk to?" Emily kissed her daughter. "Now, listen. Do you remember that night?"

"Sure I do," Jessica said. "Did you get in some kind of trouble?"

"Daddy, your daddy, my husband then, *got* me into trouble."

"He did?"

"So he could take you from me. And have you all to himself. You know how you told me he tore your dress and didn't want you to dress up and go out?"

"Uh-huh."

"Well, he felt the same way about me. He didn't want me to be in the plays I was in. He didn't want me to act. He didn't want me to do anything except wait on him and sit around and say nothing while he talked business with his friends."

"That's what Isabelle does."

"That's what he wanted. But it wasn't what I wanted."

"So what did he do?"

"Honey, have you ever heard of a prostitute?"

"I'm not sure," Jessica said. "What is it, Mom?"

"A prostitute," Emily explained, "is a woman who takes money to go on a date with a man."

"Money? Just to go on a date? Is that supposed to be bad?"

"Yes," Emily said. "Because the woman doesn't know the man first. The money lets him do whatever he wants with her."

"Whatever he wants, Mom? Like what?"

"Like . . . Oh, darling, we're getting off track. But like making love . . . having, you know, sexual intercourse with her. Do you know what that means?"

"Yes, Mom. I think I do."

"Anyway, Jessica, it's against the law for a man to pay a woman to . . . make love with her."

"Is it against the law, Mom, for a man and a woman to make love if the man doesn't pay her?"

"No, dear, of course not."

"Then why is it against the law if the woman lets the man do the very same thing with her, but he gives her money for it?"

"That's the law. I don't know why. I guess it's the money part that makes it bad."

"So it's against the law to pay the money, not against the law to do what they do."

The simple, syllogistic reasoning of Jessica, her child of only thirteen, was too much for Emily to handle. "Honey, I see your point, but it's . . . it's just against the law because it's against the law. That's all I can say."

"Okay, Mom, but it doesn't make too much sense to me."

"The point is that it's a crime to be a prostitute, and a woman can go to jail for it."

"Is being a prostitute the same as being a hooker, Mom?"

"Ah, yes, honey. That's it."

"We saw hookers on the street when they took us on our field trip to the planetarium. They looked so nasty," Jessica told her mother.

"Well, this is what I wanted to tell you. Your father paid the police to arrest me for being one of those nasty hookers."

"No! Him?"

"Your father," Emily said. "He wanted to punish me for being an actress. He wanted to take you away from me."

"No." Jessica couldn't believe what she was hearing. "They arrested you? The police?"

"And they sent me to prison, darling. For two years."

"But Daddy said you were sick, and then he said you ran away to be an actress."

"Your daddy lied."

"He lied?" He lied! Oh, God, Jessica thought, her whole world crumbling. Her father! How could he have done this to her mother? How could he have done what he did to her? The revelation of her mother's having been framed underlined and clarified to Jessica the heinousness of her father's behavior toward her. What kind of monster was he? "I don't understand, Mom," Jessica said. "How could Daddy pay the police? The police are supposed to help us."

"That's part of the problem I want to tell you about. There are a lot of policemen in New York who are very evil, bad men."

"Did Daddy really do that to you, Mom? Do you swear?"

"On my life," Emily said, clutching her daughter's hand. "It was the worst thing that ever happened to me."

If her mother only knew what had happened to her, Jessica reflected. "Oh, Mom," she sighed with more compassion than Emily could possibly know she had. "A prostitute. I thought maybe you might have done something wrong, like steal money. But to say you were a hooker and send you to prison. Daddy did that? How could he? Oh, he's just horrible. Horrible."

Emily told her about prison, about being blacklisted on Broadway and every other job because of it, about Cassie getting her the job at Guinan's. She didn't tell her about Polly Adler. Polly was one secret she hoped to be able to keep, at least until she went to Judge Seabury, and, if humanly possible, afterward. As they talked, neither mother nor daughter comprehended how much the other was suffering. Jessica's entire life with her father in New Jersey was now permanently tainted, poisoned. She wasn't sure how long she could endure there, but she was sure it wasn't for long. Maybe one day, one day soon, Jessica prayed she could go and live with her mother for good and, safe from Warren's reprisals, tell her what her father tried to do with her.

"A lot of women in this city are being framed like I was," Emily told Jessica. "We have to come forward and speak out, or else the crooked police and the crooked politicians will keep on doing it."

"But what if they try to stop you . . . hurt you?" Dawn was breaking. They had talked all night. Jessica was cradled in Emily's arms. They had not been closer, warmer, since Jessica was a baby and Emily held her then.

"I'm not worried," Emily assured her. "It's something I have to do. I had to tell you, because I want you to understand."

"I do understand."

"I'm going to go in front of Judge Seabury and tell the truth. But there are going to be a lot of newspaper reporters and they may say a lot of terrible things about me. I want you to be prepared for the worst."

"But, Mom, I'm more worried what they might do . . . what *Daddy* might do. I don't want anything bad to happen to you again." Jessica was trembling.

Emily didn't want to even consider that possibility. "No. Don't worry. They won't hurt me. They'll just say bad things. That's all. Now, stop fretting about that. I'm doing this to tell the truth and clear my name, and then I can take you to live with me. That's what you want, isn't it?"

"Yes, Mom. That's exactly what I want. I *have* to live with you. I *have* to," Jessic asserted in a panicky tone. "But are you sure Daddy can't do anything?"

"Not this time. Never. All he can do is call me names, and names will never hurt me. And if God is good to us, and I know He will be, you and I can always be together like this." Emily kissed her cheek. "Now, we better get some sleep, or we're never going to get to the museum tomorrow. So close your eyes," Emily said.

Jessica kissed Emily good night. "Mom, I love you so much. You just don't know."

"And I love you the same, my darling. Sweet dreams."

LULLABY AND GOODNIGHT

"Mom . . ." Jessica made one last request. "Will you sing me to sleep like you did when I was little?"

"I'd love to." Emily began humming Brahms's "Cradle Song" to her daughter, making up lyrics the way she used to.

Lullaby and good night
My darling sleep tight
And dream of tomorrow
When our lives will be bright
Lullaby and good night . . .

Emily's voice trailed off. Her angel, her reason for living, had dozed off in her arms. She blew out the candle on her nightstand, watched the sun rise over the East River in the distance, and dreamed of the tomorrow that she had sung about.

63

The Bronx's Grand Concourse was known as the Jewish Champs Elysées. The majestic eight-lane thoroughfare was lined with maple trees and gleaming new art-deco apartment houses in which lived newly prosperous, mostly Russian Jewish immigrants whose residence in this borough symbolized their success in the sweatshop jungle of the Lower East Side. At the top of the Concourse was Van Cortlandt Park, a former hunting ground of the Mohicans, with its herons and game birds, arched bridges and lovers' lanes, tennis and golf. Across from the park was the Woodlawn Cemetery, where Warren Matthews liked to go for walks with his clients amidst the mausoleums of American captains of industry interred there—Belmont, Gould, Huntington, Whitney, Woolworth—and dream about his own financial glories. He never noticed the small grave of Herman Melville. Books had never interested him.

Close by this sylvan area of nature and eternity at the northern end of the Grand Concourse was the Matthews Tile Corporation, a temple of the temporal, with its smokestacks and fiery kilns, and its columns upon columns of white tiles waiting to be shipped around the city and country. Warren Matthews' office in the plant was as serene and elegant as the tomb of a pharaoh. Oriental carpets covered the floor. Walnut display cases housed a museum array of ancient tiles—Ravenna mosaics, Pompeii red bricks, Persian terra-cottas. In his white shirt and gray suit, Warren held court like the J. P. Morgan he fancied himself to be, far removed from the grit-covered employees of the factory that roared and surged outside his thick oak door.

"You look very good, Emily," he said to his ex-wife, whose visit to the plant was completely unexpected. Before allowing her into his office, Warren had insisted she submit to a search of her person by one of the guards. He hadn't forgotten their last confrontation in the courtroom. "What can I do for you?" he asked.

Emily had agonized over this trip to the Bronx, which she had decided to take after her weekend with Jessica. When she had first made up her mind to go to the Seabury Committee, she had done so to clear her name, and to strike a blow for the women of New York at the same time. Then, as she held Jessica in her arms, she thought about the possible obloquy, the humiliation, the probability that her testimony would cause no more than a sensation that would do her far more harm than Tammany. She therefore decided to try one more time to settle things privately with Warren. She knew it probably wouldn't work, but for Jessica's sake, and her own, she had to try.

Warren sent his secretary, Carla Schwartz, out to lunch. He would receive Emily himself, play the magnanimous grand seigneur, and offer her some minor assistance. She could have had it all, Warren mused. What he had done to Emily often haunted him. He had his nightmares. He also had his rationalizations, in which he blamed everyone else. Emily, for being selfish, ungrateful. McCarey, for providing the opportunity, for baiting him. McNaughton, for actually carrying it out.

How good Emily still looked, how sexy, in spite of her troubles, Warren thought as he admired her, smelled her perfume, imagined making love to her again. She could always do this to him. He had never wanted any woman more, then or now. She was there in Jessica, but Jessica was a surrogate, and one with limitations. Emily was Warren's true obsession. One of the reasons he had had her framed, he reflected, was that he had snapped when he knew he couldn't have her anymore. He would have her sent away so no one could have her. The thought of other men with Emily made him insanely jealous. It still did. He wanted to have her again, right there in the office. "You're still beautiful. Look at that skin. How do you do it?" He tried to flirt.

"No help from you, Warren. In spite of you."

"Come on, Emily. I have my life. You have yours now. You've done all right, I see. All the rest is water under the bridge. Ancient history. Everything works out for the best."

"Best for you, Warren. Not for me."

"I missed you," he said. "Let's have a drink for old times, darling. Come on," he said as he stood up and went to his crystal decanter and poured himself a drink. "I've got this fabulous sherry from Bristol. You liked sherry, remember?"

"This isn't a social call, Warren."

"Have a drink. Loosen up. Tell me what you've been up to."

"I want Jessica back."

"So what else is new?" Warren laughed. "Of course you want her back, but we're sharing her, and it's not working out so terribly. You have your freedom. You live it up. I know you do. Why would you want a teenage girl? She can be a real pain. I love your dress. Have a drink."

"You know what else is new? Judge Seabury is new, that's what, Warren."

"So?" Warren was calm, patient.

"You've been reading the papers. You know that they're investigating."

"They're not getting very far."

"I could blow the lid off, Warren."

"What lid?" He didn't act worried.

"I could talk about Michael McNaughton and you, Warren, and what you did to me."

"Michael McNaughton? You mean the vice cop? Other than that we both belong to Tammany Hall, what in the world does he have to do with me?"

"Other than that he framed me for you, nothing at all, Warren."

"Emily, I think you've lost your mind."

"I almost did, Warren. I almost did."

"Emily, I have no idea what you're babbling about."

"I'll get down to specifics, then. You don't want your name dragged through the papers, Warren. You're much too much a pillar of the community. The papers would love it. You and Isabelle wouldn't. You and McNaughton. The Tammany connection."

"You always did have a fertile imagination, Emily." Warren forced a supercilious laugh. His tone had changed. Although his words were cool, Emily wasn't a sex object anymore. She was a danger.

"Wipe that grin off your face, Warren. It proves what a liar you are."

"Emily, you know nothing. There's nothing to know. Don't bait me."

"I know enough. I've met a lot of Tammany men."

"I'm sure you have," Warren mocked her.

"I knew Arnold Rothstein. I knew Judge Crater."

"They're dead," he said, with the implication that she might be as well if she didn't stop talking. He stubbed out his cigar menacingly on his brick ashtray.

"I know enough about Tammany to cause you a lot of embarrassment. It would ruin you, Warren."

"Extortion, huh? Is this your newest racket, Emily? You can spin tall tales till you're blue in the face, but who's going to believe you?" He sneered. "Who are you?"

"I'm your ex-wife, Warren. I am Jessica's mother and I want her back. It's your daughter or your brilliant future. You know what's more important to you, Warren. You know it."

"Jessica has the perfect life," Warren said.

"So perfect she hates it. You can't take that, can you?"

"What is it, money? Is it money you want? Here, take some of my money and get out." He opened a drawer and took out a big leather portfolio where he kept cash. "My time is money. What do you want? How much? I've got work to do, Emily."

"I want my daughter."

"You're not a mother. Stop deluding yourself."

"I was a mother until you tried to destroy me. You can't stop me from loving her, Warren. I want her back."

"How much, Emily? Come on. I'm in a hurry."

"So am I, Warren. I know a lot about Tammany. If they know you could have shut me up simply by giving me Jessica, and you refused, they won't be happy with you, Warren. You're a Tammany man. They made you, Warren, with all the kickbacks and fixed contracts and inside deals. I know, Warren. I lived with you. I was there. You don't want Judge Seabury going through your ledgers. They've got good accountants. Remember all those evenings with McCarey. You're a clay pigeon, Warren. You're a perfect target. This empire of yours"—she waved around the office—"it isn't founded on American ingenuity. It's founded on fraud. On cheating. On kickbacks. Governor Roosevelt will love to make an example of you."

"How much money do you want?"

"I want Jessica. Or I'll ruin you. If you give her to me, I'll let it go. If you don't . . ."

Warren stood up. But his fury didn't frighten Emily anymore. "Don't try to blackmail me."

"Why not?" Emily stood up, ready to defend against his mounting rage. "Turnabout is fair play."

Warren was torn between fear and rage. She could ruin him. Damn her. How dare she! He was so provoked he forgot what he had done to her. The past became the present. He still thought of her as his wife, a woman who owed him blind loyalty. She was turning against him, defying him, the same way she had done in choosing the theater over him and taking his daughter away from him. He felt a violent need to rape her, to control her. He couldn't control himself. "You dirty whore," he cried, and started toward her. "No one will believe you. No one."

"We'll see," Emily said, realizing that her gambit had not worked. But the very fact she had made the effort eliminated the last nagging doubt in her mind. The task ahead of her was completely clear. There were no alternatives now. The absence of choice gave her strength.

Warren picked up the mosaic brick ashtray and hurled it at Emily's head. She ducked. The brick crashed into a display case, shattering the glass. "Keep your temper to yourself, Warren. Did J. P. Morgan throw bricks at women?" she said, and proceeded, unruffled, toward the door.

Before she could get there, Warren stormed in front of the door, blocking her path. "What do you want from me?"

"I want Jessica."

"No. You won't get her."

"Then there's nothing else to talk about."

"Take your blood money, you filthy whore. What is it, ten thousand? Twenty? Thirty? What's your price, whore?"

"You can't buy me, Warren. No deal. I'm not Michael McNaughton. I'm not Judge Renaud." She knew she had him on the ropes. It was thrilling, gave her courage. If she only wanted money, she could be rich now. But no money was enough for her.

"How dare you come into my factory and threaten me? How dare you?" Warren breathed on her.

"I just want what's mine. I want back what you stole from me."

"I'll give you what's yours, you stinking bitch," Warren roared, and grabbed Emily by the arm and tried to strike her. But she was ready. She had been wearing a gray hat with a gardenia in the brim. Pulling out the hatpin holding the flower, she jammed it deep into his thigh. "Aargh!" he screamed, and doubled up in pain. She wanted to stab him again and again, but she restrained herself, as she had restrained herself all through the meeting. Her satisfaction was the terror in his face, his shriek, his squirming. "Aargh!" He clutched his leg, the blood seeping out onto his English suit.

"Thanks for your time, Warren," Emily said, carefully picking up the gardenia and wiping the blood off the pin with the handkerchief that had fallen out of Warren's coat pocket in the struggle. She adjusted her hat on her head, looking at herself in the reflecting glass of one of the display cases.

"Somebody! Get in here!" the immobilized Warren, not being able to reach the intercom, yelled. But the noise of the kilns drowned out his cries.

Emily put on her coat and softly closed the door behind her. She calmly walked past the hellish flames and dust and the flashing kilns toward the gate. She was deeply satisfied that, at least on this afternoon, she had beaten the devil.

64

Terence McCarey normally had all the answers for Warren Matthews. But today in Dinty Moore's, McCarey had no answer at all.

"What are you so worried about, Warren?" McCarey asked. "She's not going to do anything."

"She might. She just might. She's worked up enough."

"She's had enough embarrassment for one lifetime. Since when did you get so scared of her?"

"I'm not scared," Warren said. "I just didn't like the look in her eye."

"Or that needle in her hand. We could put her away on assault-and-battery charges."

"I want to avoid any publicity," Warren said. "She's dangerous."

"You should have thought of that a long time ago, Warren boy. You knew she was going to get out of Bedford one day. You knew she wasn't going to send you a valentine."

"She knows about our deal. She knows you have stock in Matthews Tile."

"How did she get all this information?"

"She heard us talk. She asked a lot of questions. They could subpoena the books. You could look bad. We could all look bad."

"Are you sure she knows about the stock?"

"Yes. She seems to know everything. She was talking, raving about Arnold Rothstein, Judge Crater, kickbacks, zoning payoffs. She probably knows enough to write a book."

"How does she know about anything?"

344

"She works at Texas Guinan's. She meets men. She's good-looking."

"Aye, she is that, Warren. Hell hath no fury like a woman scorned, and you sure as hell scorned her."

"But you're in it too, Commissioner. It's all of us. You know Seabury and his people. They're hungry bloodhounds. They haven't been fed for months. They could go for this."

"If she'll go," McCarey said. "If she'll go. I'm not so sure. She was a nice, quiet girl. Shy, almost. Lovely little lass. I don't think she wants to start a big fuss."

"I think she does. I don't trust her."

"Well? What shall we do? You don't want to give her the little girl."

"Never. That would be an admission. She could still turn on us. Uh-uh. She's *my* daughter. She's Isabelle's daughter now, too. I refuse to be blackmailed into destroying our family. I will never, *ever* give up Jessica!" Warren vowed.

"Then what?"

"I wish you'd talk to Charlie."

"Are you serious, Warren?"

"She's serious."

The main thing bothering Charles Sullivan was that his building was too short. He had moved his firm's offices to the new seventy-one-story Bank of Manhattan skyscraper at 40 Wall Street on the understanding that it would be the tallest building in the world. Sullivan loved views; he loved being number one. Now all he had were the views.

"Goddamn architect," Sullivan told McCarey, "he had a goddamn conflict of interest. His firm built the Chrysler Building. That was supposed to be nine hundred and twenty-five feet. Ours is nine-twenty-seven. That was supposed to be it. And you know, they had that spire all along to take Chrysler to a thousand-forty-six. We ought to get our money back."

"What the hell's the difference?" McCarey laughed. "What's another hundred feet up here in the stratosphere?"

"Because when I tell my clients they're in the tallest building in the world, it makes them feel special."

"I guess so. You can raise your fees."

"Why not? But this Chrysler thing . . ."

"Hell, Charles, when that new one, the one where the Waldorf was, the Empire State, is finished, that'll be even bigger. You can't stop progress, so forget about it."

"But this one was never the tallest. Not even for a day. That burns me up." Charles Sullivan looked out. The city was a magic kingdom of towering skyscrapers—all, save Chrysler, below him. The dislocations of the depression were as distant as traffic jams were when he was flying in a plane. The troubles of the world were below him, far below. Thus Charles Sullivan expressed annoyance when Terence McCarey brought up the subject of Warren Matthews. "Can't he take care of his own problems?" Sullivan said, puffing on his pipe, watching a silver bullet of a plane take off in the distance at Floyd Bennett Field and disappear into the billowing clouds.

"His wife, his ex-wife, seems to know a lot about the wigwam."

"I think I'm going to demand a rent reduction," Sullivan said, his mind drifting back to the skyscraper wars.

"Charlie," McCarey demanded his attention. "She knows about a lot of the deals. She was married to him, for Christ's sake. He says she's going to Seabury."

"Has she gone yet?" Sullivan asked in a bored voice.

"No, but that's the point."

"Don't trouble trouble till trouble troubles you."

"What does that mean?"

"Let it be."

"He wants to stop her before she goes."

"Stop her?"

"Stop her. You know."

"Seabury is Roosevelt's window dressing, but nobody's looking in the windows. The public's not buying it. Let it be."

"Matthews thinks she'll change all that. She really does know a lot. He's sweating it. Sweating heavy."

"That much? She knows that much?" Sullivan considered.

"She does. I'm afraid she does," McCarey repeated gravely. "Matthews has been a good man. He's been generous, Charlie."

"What does he want to do?" Sullivan asked.

"He wants to avoid embarrassment to the Hall. Is that all right, Charlie? All we need's an ounce of prevention."

"It could take a pound of cure," Sullivan said. "Whatever," he ended the conversation, rolling the little New York Central train model across a pile of contracts and swiveling his chair to the west to make sure New Jersey hadn't changed in the last half-hour.

65

The bald man with the suntan, the riding breeches, the boots, and the ascot had come to Guinan's three nights in a row, drunk martinis until Emily sang whatever number she was going to do, and left. On the fourth night, Texas joined him at the table, and after Emily finished "Easy Street," Texas returned to the bar to confer with her.

"You know who that is?" Texas asked.

"I thought he was someone from the horse show at the Garden."

"Different show, honey," Texas drawled. "That's Simon de Ville."

"The movie producer?"

"Yup," Texas said.

"Is that what he looks like? I loved *Just Desserts*. And *Allenby Bridge*."

"Tell him that. And take the rest of the night off. Go out with him."

"Why?"

"He's doing some big musical next. Said he was crazy about you. Thought you were better than the girls he saw on Broadway. He's handing out picture contracts like apples on the welfare line."

"Texas, are you trying to get rid of me or something?"

"I'm trying to do you a good turn. I'd go out to Hollywood, if I could do anything but pour booze. It's gotten too cold in New York for me."

"What's the catch?" Emily asked. She had learned to be suspicious of any generosity shown to her.

"*He's* the catch, honey. Go out and git 'im. You go become a picture star. I'd rather be able to say I gave

348

somebody famous her start than have her sit here and be nobody. That star stuff is good publicity. Look at us." Texas waved around the half-empty speakeasy. There were maybe thirty patrons. The fun of the past was gone. "We need some publicity. Now, git."

Emily remembered reading about Simon de Ville in *Photoplay*. Circus booking agent turned impresario. Despite his outdoor horse-and-hounds look, all he could talk about with Emily were deals and money. The stars and directors he knew were all fungible, basic budget items.

De Ville took Emily to the observation deck of the Panhellenic Hotel, a tall building off Beekman Place that was a residence for girls from Greek-letter sororities fresh out of college and hoping to make it big in the big city. It was a favorite place for de Ville to scout for starlets.

"I used to like that college-girl look," he said, looking more at the well-scrubbed graduates from Ohio State and Michigan State in the candlelit room than at the glitter of the skyline outside. "But with the depression, the college look is out. They're going to go for something new."

"Breadline? Peasant?" Emily joked.

"Too weak," de Ville said, taking any suggestion that related to his business with the utmost gravity. "Something more assured. A little worldly, let us say."

"Someone who's been around?"

"So to speak. A woman of substance, experience. A woman of the world. God, I love coming to New York. This city never stops going," de Ville said, turning his eyes to the skyline, then back hard to Emily. "And I think you'd love coming to Hollywood."

"Think so?" she said, not sure what he was getting at.

"We're making musicals faster than we can cast them. You've got something special."

"What is it?" Emily had heard every variation on the theme of flattery. But here was a person who could implement his hyperbole. That was his business. And he didn't seem to be looking for sex. That gave him a leg up where credibility was concerned.

"I can't define it," de Ville said. "But I can pay you for it. And pay you well."

"Mr. de Ville, a few years ago I would have died to get

an offer like this, but . . ." Emily was telling the truth, whether she believed him or not.

"I don't want you to die, Miss Stanton," he said, all business. "I want you to live. You'll be under contract. We'll get you a bungalow in the Garden of Allah."

She had read about that, too. The palm trees, the Pacific breezes, the mountains, the orange groves, the silver screen of her teenage fantasies raced across her mind. "I just can't do it." She wasn't a teenager anymore. She had a rendezvous with the Seabury lawyers in three days. After that, she didn't know what would occur.

"Your reluctance only enhances your market value. Five hundred a week and an open pass on the *Super Chief* to come back here whenever you're homesick."

"What about a rain check, Mr. de Ville? I have some very important unfinished business here. But maybe in a few months . . ."

"You should be in my contracts department, Miss Stanton. You're a shrewd negotiator. But as we dawdle here, the sun is shining, and the cameras are rolling. . . . Six hundred?"

She had always treasured her career, given up her marriage and, in the end, her whole existence for it. And now it seemed almost petty. Emily shook her head. She had something much more important ahead of her.

66
1932

At Man Gar Chung on Pell Street, the little apothecary in the mandarin jacket scurried among his jars mixing up a powder, which he ground with his mortar and pestle. Dried seahorse. Sliced deer horn. Blanched reptile. Bear's testicles. Ginseng. At the end, the foul-smelling concoction in the neat glass vial with pretty Chinese letters was advertised as a sexual stimulant.

"Maybe I should get some of that and slip it into your chop suey to see if it makes you love me," Alex joked to Emily as they strolled through the crowded streets of Chinatown, killing time. Alex was trying to keep Emily relaxed. At four o'clock they were going to the Seabury Commission.

"Oh, Alex, should I really?"

"Don't back out now, because if you ever change your mind again, they'll probably be out of business, and you'll never get to go. Besides, this isn't the public part. It's just preliminary."

"You're right, Alex. Keep reminding me," Emily said. She had been wavering back and forth, back and forth. She couldn't sleep, eat, sing well at all. She was deeply troubled.

They walked past the toothbrush shops, tattoo parlors, cigar stores that smelled like humidors. Past Hop Wing Laundry, Sun Fat Trading Company. Past houses, pagodas, the On Yung Lee Burial Association.

"First they bury them in the Chinese cemetery here," Alex explained in almost tour-guide fashion. "Then ten years later they dig up the remains, which have decomposed, and put them in little boxes and send them to

China for reburial. Very patient, the Chinese, and very frugal. They save on freight. It's important to be buried there. It's just too expensive to do it right away. Same with you. You've been patient and frugal. Now it's time to dig it up. It's a quarter to four."

"Let's go."

The unlined face of Robert Kohn, the young Seabury aide, gave Emily extreme doubts whether this boy, whose appearance gave every evidence of innocence, would be able to relate in any way at all to the horror story she was about to tell him. In her mind, going to the Seabury Commission had once been blown up to the grandeur of the Final Reckoning, with angels blowing trumpets and the Almighty himself, white beard flowing and lightning bolts crackling around his celestial throne, preparing to restore the equilibrium of a secular world rent asunder by evil forces. Instead, she was in a drab windowless room in the Criminal Courts Building where she once had had her midnight trysts with Judge Crater. Now she was with a mere boy whose father or grandfather must have been a friend of Judge Seabury's and wanted him to have some experience before moving on to draft genteel wills and trust agreements in the family law firm.

Alex and Kohn started talking school, Alex his Yale, Kohn his Columbia and Harvard Law, and gradually Emily felt more at home. Her story might have been falling on tender ears, but they were by no means deaf. Alex's education, his incipient success in the theater, all intrigued Robert Kohn. Alex's presence thus served to validate Emily and give her the respectability she needed to be believed.

"Warren Matthews. The tile man. Big Tammany supporter. You were married to him?" Kohn was impressed. The name had his attention.

"Yes, I was," Emily said matter-of-factly. "We were separated. Warren Matthews wanted custody of our daughter. She was six at the time. I have a feeling he may also have wanted a divorce, because he remarried very soon afterward. So, you see, the way he could get custody, and a divorce, was to have me framed."

"Yes, I see. I see," Kohn said, taking notes. "That

makes sense. Yes, but how did he do it? How did he have you framed?"

"I'm pretty sure he made some kind of deal with Michael McNaughton."

"McNaughton! We subpoenaed him. Top man in the vice squad. He was the one who arrested you?"

Emily nodded.

"When he testified, he tried to come across as holier than the pope." Kohn let his legalese lapse. "How did he set you up?"

"By pretending he was a Broadway backer named Amory Longworth."

"That's fantastic. Who was the judge in the case? Let me guess. Stanley Renaud?"

"That's the one."

Kohn's face lit up. "Could you excuse me just a moment? I want a couple of my colleagues to join us. This could be very important."

Kohn returned with two other young attorneys, Jack Rivkin and Dave Lo Bianco, for whom Emily related the entire story, about prison, about Texas, about Polly, about Rothstein, about all the men she saw and what she knew. They were fascinated. Also, they seemed envious of Alex for keeping the company of such a beautiful woman. None of them appeared to have left the law library for some time.

"What a great story," Lo Bianco said, constantly straightening his tie and brushing the cowlick out of his face, wanting to primp for Emily.

"The flaw is that there's no corroborating evidence on the Matthews-McNaughton deal," Rivkin cautioned. "If we had that, then we'd really have something."

"Without it," Kohn finished the sentence, "it's your word against theirs."

"But I think we should bring her before the judge," Lo Bianco said.

"Despite the inherent problem, I agree," Kohn said. "Warren Matthews is a major city contractor. Michael McNaughton is the police force's exemplar of what a perfect cop should be. Stanley Renaud is an extremely visible judge. Linking the three is a very important step."

"Tammany's not going to like this, not one bit," Lo

Bianco said. "A completely innocent woman and what they did to her. It's the kind of outrage that could finally turn the public off Tammany."

"Let's don't jump the gun." Rivkin played the tentative lawyer. "This sort of thing sells tickets, but legally, I'm not so sure what it'll do for us."

"It'll put some life back into this investigation," Kohn agreed. "We need to sell some tickets. Fast. Miss Stanton, we're going to want you to come back and meet with Judge Seabury before you go to the formal hearings. He's in Albany until next week, but he'll be delighted to meet you."

Lo Bianco spoke. "We can't thank you enough for coming. You're going to make a wonderful witness."

"It's very courageous of you to take this step," Rivkin said. "If there's any justice in the world, you should get your daughter back when this thing is over."

67

Jessica had called Emily to tell her that her class at Miss Draper's was going on a field trip to the American Museum of Natural History. Would Emily meet her at the dinosaurs? Of course, Emily said. One day a month wasn't enough, especially since Emily was going to see Judge Seabury next week. Emily needed at least one more moment of communion with her daughter, both to gain strength for herself and to give strength to Jessica. The Seabury attorneys warned Emily about what she already knew: a potential firestorm of publicity that would surely change both her life and that of her daughter.

Emily stood outside in the piercing February wind waiting for the bus to arrive on Seventy-seventh Street in front of the pink Romanesque building. She was early, wanting to go in and browse at the fossils and the gorillas and tyrannosaurus rex, but she didn't want Jessica to feel any anxiety trying to find her. Emily wanted to be there to greet her daughter. She drank in the cold air and wrapped her scarf tightly around her neck. Several museum guards clustered near the entrance, holding their vigil from within.

"This isn't your day to be with Jessica," Warren Matthews said from behind. He was followed by the two bodyguards who had intercepted Emily several years ago, Mac and Yuri, dressed in heavy overcoats.

"What are you . . ." Emily's voice trailed off.

"This isn't your day," Warren said.

"You don't own this street. You don't own the museum. You don't own Jessica."

355

"Move along, Emily," Warren said, inching forward with the two henchmen, a relentless mass.

"I won't move! I want to see my daughter."

"It's not your day."

"What are you afraid of, Warren? That I'll tell her about you? I don't have to tell her anything. She knows. She has eyes. She knows what you are."

"Move on," Warren growled. Mac and Yuri surrounded Emily.

"Afraid to face me on your own, Warren? Do you need protection from an innocent woman? Maybe you should call Michael McNaughton, too." Emily's only weapon was her voice. Subconsciously, it was rising, loud enough that passersby were beginning to stop and watch. The guards from the museum stepped out into the cold.

"Go on."

"You're nothing but a gangster! It's too late for you, Warren. The wheels are in motion. I've gone to Seabury. I'm going again. You can kill me, but now they know. It's on the record, Warren. It's on the record. Kill me, go ahead. Kill me. I dare you."

"You're crazy, Emily," Warren said calmly, coming closer. Mac and Yuri were almost at touching distance from Emily. She could smell their heavy breath. "You're insane. Go home. Leave Jessica alone. You can't have her. She's not yours. Stay out of her life. Stay out."

"Make me, you bastard," Emily screamed, and swung her purse at Warren. She charged toward him, clawing, kicking, a blaze of nails and toes.

"You've assaulted me once already," Warren said, as Mac and Yuri held Emily back. "I may have to press charges."

"I'm seeing Jessica. You can't stop me." A large crowd had gathered around. "I'm seeing her." Emily realized she was making a scene, and she was embarrassed. "He's trying to keep me away from my own daughter," she blurted out to the group of people who had assembled. They all stared back unresponsively.

"You won't see Jessica," Warren said. He turned and started walking back to his warm waiting limousine, his bodyguards following.

"I'll see her in a few minutes." I won, Emily thought. I

356

won. He gave up. All the yelling scared him away. She didn't care about the uncaring faces.

"The trip was canceled," Warren said over his shoulder, a faint trace of an evil smile breaking through. "Ice on the roads." Now he grinned and got into the limousine, which drove away into the frozen trees of Central Park. Warren had talked to Michael McNaughton. "Get her to make a public scene with you," McNaughton said. It was part of their new plan.

The crowd stared at Emily one more time and dispersed. "You animal," she yelled out, humiliated by his little sick joke. He had done this to scare her, to torture her, to show his muscle. She couldn't wait to meet Judge Seabury. "I'll get you. I'll get you soon!"

68

Emily didn't want to take any more dates, but she felt she needed the money. Thus, when Polly Adler called her for a two-hundred-dollar evening, she said yes. The date was with one of "Al Capone's dearest personal friends, dollink, who's in from Chicago. A real big spender." His name was Tommy Catania. He was staying in an apartment on East Fifty-second and the river. "He's very private," Polly told her. "No nightclub. Just a little homey evening, understand?"

As Emily took a cab across town, she was torn between virtue and vice. Virtue about going to Seabury, vice as her mode of support. In the last six months, each time she had done this, she had vowed never again. Yet, there were always extenuating circumstances that made her suspend her vow, and each new transgression blurred into the previous one. Once she had fallen, it didn't matter how many pieces she had broken into. Broken was broken. After Seabury, maybe she would take Jessica to Hollywood and start again, in a new mold, a new life. This would be the last, she told herself once again.

458 East Fifty-second. Emily thought she would be going to River House, the grand cooperative apartment shooting up from the East River, with its floating dock moored with the boats of the members of its River Club. On second thought, people with names like Tommy Catania didn't live in River House, even if they owned half of Chicago with Al Capone. But 458 was beyond River House. The sign at the end of the street read "Dead End." It was symbolic of the incongruous coexistence of wealth and poverty in this Sutton-Beekman Place

area. Old brownstones packed with poor dockworkers, dead-end kids, laborers from the nearby slaughterhouses, stood mere steps away from the august apartment residences of bejeweled dowagers, apple-cheeked prepschoolers, and sporting gentlemen in their yachting caps. Down by the river was the abattoir center. Occasionally, some sheep would get loose and wander up to Beekman Place. Many of the poor immigrant tenants of the waterfront tenements below River House still went down to the slaughterhouses to buy sheep's blood for a quarter a glass. To them blood was strong medicine; nothing was better when they were sick.

458 was a fairly dilapidated brownstone with hallways that reeked of urine and stray cats, and a few bare light bulbs. Emily climbed to the fifth floor, feeling ill-at-ease in her cocktail dress, high heels, and diamond necklace. She had thought she was going to River House. With each flight up, she grew more and more uneasy, until the door opened.

"Please excuse the building, Emily," a stunning Tommy Catania said, his teeth gleaming white, his smile putting her at ease. "It's better inside. Come on in. You're beautiful," he declared. He was dressed in an expensive vested suit, the jacket off, his hair slicked back, his silk tie perfectly knotted. He smelled of Old Spice.

"Hello, Tommy," Emily said demurely, shaking his hand.

"I heard you were pretty, but I wasn't prepared for this." Tommy took her coat. Inside, the apartment was spare, but clean and modern. All white, with a black couch and a black lacquer bar. The main attraction was a view over the dark waters of the East River, the swooping gulls illuminated by the lights of the barges skimming the water. "You can't tell a book by its cover," Tommy apologized for the exterior. "I hate hotels. They're always watching you, all the dicks on every floor. All the snoopers. I come to New York to get away. This is my little hideaway. I got some champagne on ice," he said.

"I'd love some. I'm thirsty from that climb."

"I bet you are, baby. Again, my apologies." His accent was vaguely foreign, more Spanish somehow than Italian.

"Salud," he said, raising a toast. "To the most beautiful lady in New York."

"To the handsomest man in Chicago." Emily smiled. If this was to be her going-away party, why not enjoy it?

There were a few odd touches. No suitcase. No clothes in the closet. Not even a toothbrush in the bathroom. But the champagne dulled her acuteness.

Tommy didn't know as much about Chicago as she did.

"I grew up in Joliet," Emily said.

"Nice place."

"I used to love Chicago. I thought it was the capital of the world."

"It is."

"State Street, Rush Street, Lakeshore Drive. Where do you live?"

"Here and there."

"I used to go for tea as a little girl to the Sheridan Palace—"

"It's a great hotel." He didn't let her finish. Odd that he spoke in the present tense, for the hotel had been demolished ten years ago and she only mentioned it as a preamble to a conversational gambit on how much Chicago had changed. But Emily had learned one rule of Polly etiquette: the customer is always right. Never correct him.

"I've never been to Cicero," Emily said, alluding to the Capone fiefdom.

"Me neither," Tommy said, curiously. "Who goes there? Hell, I don't want to talk about Chicago, baby. I ain't homesick. I'm in New York. I want to talk about you. Come sit next to me. I got big deals tomorrow. I gotta relax. This is our love nest. Let's float away to dreamland." Tommy lit up a stick of acrid marijuana. He gave Emily a puff. She took another sip of champagne, another drag of grass, and surrendered to his kisses.

He was a passionate lover. Curiously, all his love expressions were Spanish, not Italian. *"Mi amor." "Cariña." "Querida."* Emily paid no attention. The dope eventually made her very giddy and giggly. Thus she wasn't particularly taken aback when, with both of them nude, Tommy began to play games with her. First, he wanted to make her up. He went through her cosmetics case for rouge, eye-liner, lipstick. He was particularly fascinated by her lipstick holder. It was solid gold, engraved "To E. Love, A.R."

"Who's A.R?"

"A.R.," Emily said, as if he should know.

"*The* A.R.?"

"The A.R. Yes."

"Great man," Tommy said, and proceeded to draw hearts on Emily's derriere. Valentine's Day was the end of the week. "I'm an artist," he said as he nuzzled her and gave her a fabulous intermittent back massage. "I want to leave my mark on you." They painted each other and played more games. Tommy blindfolded Emily and made her grope around the room for him. She was high and having fun. The pot and the alcohol had caused her anxieties to vanish. Judge Seabury was completely out of her mind.

"That A.R., he was a man," Tommy kept saying, intrigued by the lipstick holder. "A man! I miss him."

"I miss him, too," Emily said. Suddenly drowsy, she drifted off to a deep, deep sleep for several hours. When Tommy took her downstairs at two A.M. and put her into a cab at First Avenue, she didn't notice that he had taken her lipstick holder.

69

The next morning, Carla Schwartz, Warren Matthews' secretary, left her family's apartment on East Tremont Avenue, took a bus to the Concourse, grabbed a buttered bagel at a soda shop, changed for the IND subway north to 205th Street, and walked the four blocks to Matthews Tile Corporation. She hung up her coat and powdered her nose in the ladies' room. The kilns were heating up. The noise was mounting. She checked to see that the orders to Philadelphia and Boston were being sent out, typed a letter to a Texas school board conveying a price estimate, and went to the ladies' room to adjust her makeup before Mr. Matthews arrived at eight. He always wanted her to look pretty, always commented on her clothes, which made her feel self-conscious and forced her to ask her parents to supplement her income so she could buy more dresses. Without the appropriate wardrobe, she thought she might lose her job.

At eight o'clock Warren Matthews had not arrived. He had always told Carla never to come into his office until he was there. He had been staying in town, working in the office very late all that week. The season was that busy. Maybe, Carla thought, he was sleeping late at his hotel. But by eight-thirty she began to be worried, because Mr. Matthews had said he had a ten-o'clock meeting with some important buyers from a California restaurant chain and wanted her to complete some dictation before they arrived.

At eight-forty-five Carla considered that perhaps Mr. Matthews had stepped in early while she was primping for him in the ladies' room. She rang the intercom. No answer. Curious, she knocked. No answer. And for some reason, she tried the door, which Mr. Matthews always locked when he wasn't there, and it was open. Impulsively she turned the brass knob and looked inside.

The lights were on. The room was still, but there was a strange odor. Perhaps he had been eating something when he was working late last night. He had forgotten to turn off the lights. She would straighten up the room before he arrived.

She walked in. Then she screamed.

Warren Matthews was sprawled on the floor beside his desk. On his face was the most incredible look of surprise and terror, all in one, she had ever seen. Fear and surprise. And death. Mr. Matthews had never looked surprised, but there it was. He was dead, yet his eyes bulged open with the shock that the last thing he had seen in life was literally the last thing he had ever expected to see.

70

The same morning at Pennsylvania Station the commuter rush was slowly subsiding. As the late commuters trickled through the grand marble waiting room, the tourists with their trunks and suitcases sat waiting for the *Gulf Coast Limited*, the *Palmetto*, or the *Orange Blossom Special* that would take them south to sun and warmth.

Michael McNaughton, in plain clothes, sat at one end of the coffee bar of the Savarinette. At precisely nine o'clock he left a dollar on the counter and walked out. At the ticket window, Luis Quito was buying a one-way parlor-car ticket to Miami on the *Orange Blossom Special*, which was scheduled to depart at nine-thirty. He went to a small locker area to get his expensive leather suitcase. As he pulled it out, he bumped into Michael McNaughton, who slipped an envelope full of hundred-dollar bills into Luis' hand. Luis pocketed it quickly.

"Excuse me," McNaughton said, pretending the encounter was accidental.

They both glanced furtively to make sure no one was watching them. "Have a good time in Havana," McNaughton said.

"I'll bet some money for you, screw a few showgirls, get a tan. How long should I lie low?"

"About two months. She should be on ice by then."

"She was some piece, man. But I don't have to tell you. You know."

"No I don't. We never got that far."

"She was fine. Really fine."

"Yeah."

"That was smart, that lipstick. How'd you know it would be engraved?" Luis asked.

"I didn't. Lucky hunch. I thought maybe her compact or something else. The fancy ones all like their names on things. Gives them class."

"But her and Arnold Rothstein's initials—you couldn't get better than that. Shows she's really in there with the bad guys."

"Yeah, and you got it, Luis."

"I always get something. I get what you tell me."

"You're good, Luis."

"Yeah, but you're the brain, *jefe*. And this time you nailed it. We were lucky."

"You're lucky, Luis. You're going to Cuba. I'm going to the Bronx."

"*Adiós, amigo*. The train's leaving," Luis said as he picked up his bag. "See you in the springtime."

"Kiss them for me, Luis," McNaughton said, and walked up into the streaming dusty sunlight of the concourse as he watched Luis descend into the labyrinth of tracks.

"The *Orange Blossom Special*, parlor cars and Pullmans, leaving on track twelve for Trenton, Philadelphia, Wilmington, Baltimore, Washington, Richmond, and all points south," the speaker blared out. "All aboard."

71

At some time after ten that morning, Emily's phone began ringing and wouldn't stop. At first the rings seemed to be part of some hazy, jumbled dream induced by the marijuana, the champagne, and Tommy Catania. But eventually, and annoyingly, the telephone woke her up.

"Yes, hello," Emily gasped into the receiver.

"I need a pound of lox and a dozen onion bagels, a container of sour cream—"

"Who're you calling?" Emily slurred.

"Caplan's Delicatessen, isn't it?"

"Wrong number."

"Sorry." The line went dead.

"Me, too," Emily muttered to herself. As she lay back down, she realized that she was still dressed from the night before. She hadn't even taken off her necklace and her earrings, which bit into her earlobes. She took them off, but was still too spent to undress any further. Her first disjointed thought was that she didn't really remember how she had gotten home. However, she had fallen fast asleep on top of her bed without even pulling back the covers.

Emily sighed and closed her eyes, waiting to float back away, to recapture whatever the fleeting dream was that the phone had interrupted. Sleep, however, would not come. Instead, Emily's mind began racing about Judge Seabury, about Jessica, about what she was going to testify, about how it was all going to change her life. But none of the thoughts were focused. She was too hungover. Never again, she promised herself, never again. She wasn't clear about anything else, except for the fact that her date with Tommy Catania was definitely, unequivocally, her last.

Emily rolled over and pulled back the bedspread for another pillow to prop up her throbbing head. As she did, she felt something on the bed next to her that jarred her into the clammiest, most frightening state of consciousness. It was a gun, a black thirty-eight-caliber revolver, placed under the pillow. Emily had never felt or held a gun before. She had no idea what to make of it. She couldn't imagine who could have gotten into her apartment to begin with, or who would leave such a sinister offering. She shook the gun gingerly, careful not to let it go off. It was heavy, and it felt like it was loaded. She laid it down beside her and dialed Alex Foster. There was no answer. She tried again. Alex was the only person she could trust. But he didn't answer.

She thought about calling Robert Kohn or one of the other Seabury lawyers, then decided not to. She thought that the gun might somehow be bad for her, although she wasn't sure how. Then she thought about simply throwing the gun away. She ran to her window. All of her windows faced the street. The winter winds were howling, rattling the panes. Below, the street was crowded with pedestrians. A garbage truck was roaring, collecting its loads. No, she couldn't throw it out there. Nor into the trash. It might go off. Someone in the building might find it and trace it to her.

Emily concluded that her only course of action was to get dressed and get the gun out of her building, perhaps hide it somewhere, in some park or garden she could come back to after she had gotten hold of Alex. Regrettably, she could barely walk straight. In a cold sweat, she hid the gun away in a secret compartment of her livingroom desk, where she kept her bankbooks Then she went into the bathroom and turned on the water for the tub. Maybe a bath would sober her up quickly, so she could get out and dispose of this terribly disturbing weapon.

The steaming water cascaded into the tub. Emily stepped out of her rumpled cocktail dress. What a mess, she thought. She rolled down her stockings and slipped off her panties. As she looked at herself in the mirror, she noticed the smudged lipstick hearts that had been painted on her buttocks. She cringed. "Never again," she repeated to herself.

The noise of the water obscured from Emily the insistent knocking that had commenced at her front door. She heard it only as she twisted the faucets closed and the water stopped. "Damn," she cursed. Who could it be? She was in no condition to face anyone. She hoped that it was the superintendent, or a handyman, and that he would go away. But the knocking continued, louder and louder. Consumed with a tipsy anxiety, she put on her bathrobe to see who was there. As she entered the living room, the knocking ended. For a moment, Emily breathed easier. Whoever it was had left. Then, in a terrible splintering crash, the door pitched in off its hinges. Behind it were policemen.

There were two plainclothes detectives and two uniformed officers. The revolvers the men in uniform were wearing were magnified by Emily's terror. They had broken into her apartment. They were armed. She was naked, except for her robe.

"I'm Detective Malley. This is Detective Shea. Sergeant O'Reilly, Officer Green," said the first, taller plainclothesman, who had a badly pitted face and a snowfall of dandruff on the shoulders of his dark suit. "Sorry to bother you, Miss Stanton," he continued mechanically, "but there was no answer, and a crime has been committed. You are Emily Stanton?"

"Y-yes, I am," Emily stammered.

"We're going to have to search your apartment. We won't make a mess."

"A search?" Emily gasped. "What for? What's the matter?"

"You don't have to answer any questions, Miss Stanton," Shea, the portly second plainclothesman said, leering at Emily in her white terry-cloth robe. He had a huge snouty nose that reminded Emily of a hog's. "But you do know why we're here, don't you?"

"No. I don't know . . . anything." Emily's first instinct was one of avoidance. She *didn't* know anything. But she did have that gun. Her mind was so sluggish. What should she do?

"You sure? Where were you last night, Miss Stanton?" Shea pressed her.

A chill racked her. Had they found out about her working for Polly Adler? Her fear of this exposure made her forget about the gun altogether, at least for the moment. "I was out . . . out with a friend."

"A friend?" Malley asked archly.

"Well, a blind date."

"Not a friend. A blind date, huh?" Malley said, his voice pregnant with innuendo. "Where'd ya go?"

"We . . . I . . . we . . . went . . . I don't understand what difference it all makes. I was on a date." Emily wanted to tell them it was none of their business, but she knew that would make her look suspicious. While she was being interrogated, she hadn't noticed that the uniformed cops had gone into her bedroom. "I went to a man's house . . . for a drink."

"We can't find anything, sir," Sergeant O'Reilly said, coming out of the bedroom empty-handed. "Not a thing."

"Go through everything. One more time," Detective Shea ordered in an annoyed voice. "It's got to be here."

Emily knew instantly what "it" was. She didn't want to let on, not yet. "What are you looking for? Please tell me."

"Where were you last night, Miss Stanton? Where were you really?" Malley returned Emily's question with his own.

"I told you. On a date. I'm still . . . a little dizzy. It was a long night."

"You don't say, Miss Stanton."

The cops in uniform began turning the apartment inside out, opening drawers, closets, the refrigerator, overturning cushions on the couch, looking behind books, banging the walls for secret panels as if they were a demolition crew. They had already gone through the desk and missed the compartment, behind another drawer that had a false backing.

"Dammit!" Malley pounded his fist when the elaborate search yielded no results. "Check the trash. Check her coat pockets. Check all the drawers again. Have you been outside this morning, Miss Stanton?"

"No," Emily said, her temples aching. Knowing that they would not give up, she didn't want to be caught concealing the revolver. "Listen, please don't destroy my apartment. Please stop. . . . Actually, I'm glad you're here."

"You are?" Malley glanced over at Shea. The others halted their search.

"The way you broke in . . . it took me a bit to get myself together . . . thinking straight. I think I sort of know what this is all about." Emily walked over to her desk and opened the false compartment. The policemen exchanged disgusted stares, reflecting their annoyance over their own failure to find the gun. "Somebody planted this here overnight."

Sergeant O'Reilly strode over to the desk and picked up the gun with a handkerchief and opened it. "One bullet left."

"That's it," Shea exulted.

"They planted it here, eh?" Malley asked.

"Not right here," Emily replied.

"Where'd they put it then?"

"Under my pillow."

"Like the good fairy," Shea said. The two uniformed cops suppressed a chuckle.

Emily forced a grin. "Yes. Like the good fairy. It's absurd."

"Why didn't you call the police?" Malley asked.

"I just woke up. I was going to," Emily lied, trying to make as light of the matter as possible. "The good fairy must have gotten me mixed up with some gangster. You'd only leave a gun for a criminal," Emily said in a nervous attempt at good spirits.

Malley examined the gun. "There was no mix-up," he pronounced gravely. "Most likely the same gun."

"Same as what?" Emily was beyond confusion. "What gun? What's going on? What's this all about? Please tell me."

"You tell us, Miss Stanton." Shea turned to her. "Were you in the Bronx last night?"

"Definitely not. Why?"

"Where were you then?"

Emily had nothing to hide. "I was here . . . here in Manhattan . . . with this blind date . . ." She hesitated over the phrase. "I went to his place."

"Where was that?" Shea asked.

"On Fifty-second Street. Near the river. That's where I was."

"You didn't go up to the Bronx?" Malley said in a tone that was much more accusatory than interrogatory.

"Why would I? What is this? What is this all about?"

"It's all about murder, Miss Stanton," Malley answered. "It looks to me like the same gun that killed your ex-husband."

"Killed my ex . . . Warren Matthews? Killed?"

"Yes, ma'am."

"Oh, my God." Emily grabbed the back of the couch to steady herself. "Killed? Killed where?"

"In the Bronx. At his office. Sometime last night," Shea intoned the facts.

"Killed?" Emily was stunned. "I don't understand."

"Five shots were fired into his chest," Shea said. "There's one bullet left in this six-shot revolver. Your gun."

"It's not my gun," Emily cried. "I was here last night. Here and with my . . . friend . . . at his apartment."

"And you say that was on Fifty-second, huh?" Malley noted, as if for the record, but without any real interest.

"I swear to God. There and here. That's where I was." Emily's mouth was as dry as desert sand. "I don't know how this gun got here. Something awful's going on. I don't know. Warren . . . killed? Is this some dreadful joke? Tell me. I swear, I swear on my life, I swear on my child's life, I wasn't in the Bronx. I didn't kill Warren Matthews."

"Then how come," Malley snapped, glaring at Emily, "how come, Miss Stanton, we found this lipstick case? *Your* lipstick case," he said as he took the carefully wrapped container from his pocket and thrust it at her, "at the scene of the crime, next to your ex-husband's body? How come? Huh?"

"Oh, no," Emily wailed, lunging at the lipstick holder. Malley pulled it away. The two officers seized Emily to

371

hold her back. Her robe flew open. The policemen gaped at her body. She flailed away to get free. It was impossible. The cops' sweaty palms squeezed her more and more tightly until she could struggle no more. Only when the outburst subsided did Emily realize that her robe was open. The cops let her pull it together, to tie its belt. Her embarrassment almost overwhelmed her fear, but fear won out. "He stole it," Emily wept, motioning toward the lipstick case Malley guarded. "Oh, God. Please believe me. It wasn't me. *He* stole it. This man. I was with this man who—"

"Save it for the station, Miss Stanton," Malley cut her off. "Go put some clothes on. We're going to have to bring you in."

72

Emily's sense of *déjà vu* was so overpowering that, at the beginning, she was virtually paralyzed by the nightmare she was being condemned to relive. The police wagon, the precinct house, the fingerprinting and booking were all just as they were seven years before, except that this time, even though she had been exposed to it before, the horror was even greater than it had been. The difference was in the alleged crime. That was prostitution. This was murder.

Another enormous difference between the two frame-ups was the presence of the press. A crush of reporters had gathered outside the House of Detention on Tenth Street, where Emily was taken after her arrest. They all seemed to be wearing glasses. They all shared that predatory hawkish intensity. Someone in the police must have called the press and furnished them with information, Emily surmised, shielding her face from the newsmen. Otherwise, the press would never have gotten here so fast, in such force, and with so much knowledge.

"Why'd ya do it? Was it money?" one voice cried out.

"Was blackmail involved?" asked another.

"Did he really frame you?" a reporter yelled.

"Did you do time at Bedford?"

" 'VIGILANTE MURDERESS.' That's my headline," still another newsman boasted.

"Keep it. I like 'SCARLET KILLER.' "

"Where'd a classy dame like that learn to pump lead?"

The press corps, eager for new sensations that would distract readers from the varied woes of the depression, buzzed with vicious gossip. Hearing it threw Emily into a hellish despair.

Who had framed her this time? That was all Emily could contemplate through the clinical blur of legal process as she was being booked. She was certain the answer lay in Tammany Hall, but with Warren gone, who, she wondered, was the new architect of this reprisal? How high up was this vengeance decreed? That the consequences of going before the Seabury staff could be so harsh, so sudden, even before she got to meet the judge himself, had taken Emily completely by surprise. She realized now that she had underestimated Tammany. Even Warren Matthews had turned out to be a pawn to be sacrificed in the Hall's ruthless power play.

Unlike seven years ago, Emily had been permitted to bring a suitcase of belongings with her. And this time she knew all about frame-ups. But this knowledge, by itself, rendered her just as powerless as she had been before. She needed a good lawyer. And she needed Alex. The police let her call him, but he was still not home.

They let her call Hiram Hogan, who she didn't believe was big enough or brave enough for this situation, but he was the only lawyer she really knew. But Hiram Hogan was in semiretirement, in St. Petersburg for the winter. His office referred a colleague from his building, a young man named Darrell Sweet. He, like Hogan, specialized in domestic-relations actions. Having never handled a murder case, Sweet did not inspire Emily's confidence, and he knew it. He offered to sit in on Emily's arraignment and promised to help her find what he called a "real criminal guy" afterward.

Within hours Emily was arraigned on a criminal complaint. The presiding magistrate turned out to be a woman. With Darrell Sweet by her side, Emily believed that she would be able to post bail and go home, find Alex, and prepare for the legal battle ahead of her. At least she had the money this time. The magistrate, Jean Norris, had soft blue eyes and a kind, forgiving face. In fact, it was a famous face. Jean Norris was not only New York's first woman judge, she was also its first celebrity magistrate. Because of her position of trust and her confidence-inspiring mien, she had been selected by Fleischmann's

Yeast as its spokesperson. Emily had seen Judge Norris'
image on billboards and magazines advertising Fleischmann's in her judicial robes, giving testimony to the
yeast's digestive properties and tranquilizing effects. An
odd involvement for someone in the judicial arena, Emily had reflected, but nonetheless a coup for Fleischmann's whose sales had soared. Emily had a similar surge
of confidence when she saw Judge Norris on the bench,
the only woman in a courtroom filled with the male
press.

Judge Norris informed Emily that she was being charged
with the "first-degree murder" of Warren Matthews. Darrell Sweet was disappointed. He had told Emily he thought
that she would "get away" with a second-degree charge,
which carried a several-decades prison term, as opposed
to the life imprisonment or possible death penalty Emily
now faced.

"How do you plead, Miss Stanton?" the judge asked.

"Not guilty, but it's all a frame-up, Judge Norris,"
Emily blurted out, snapping out of her haze of inertia.
"They framed me before. To get my baby. Now they
want to frame me to stop me from talking."

The bailiff lumbered forward to quiet Emily, but Judge
Norris held up her delicate hand, her nails painted red.
"Let her speak," the judge said.

Emily believed she had, if not a friend, at least a
sympathetic ear. "I was supposed to go to Judge Seabury
next week. They knew. They had to stop me." She
poured the words out breathlessly. "They—"

"They?" the judge stopped her. "Who is they?"

"They . . . Tammany Hall," Emily replied. "I know a
lot about them. . . . Oh, where do I begin? You see, my
husband, my ex-husband, Warren Matthews, paid Michael McNaughton, Officer McNaughton, of the vice
squad, to frame me . . . as a . . . prostitute."

"And you know this for a fact?" Judge Norris listened
attentively.

"Well . . . yes. Certainly."

"How? Do you have proof?"

"No. Not really proof, but Warren, Warren Matthews,
did so much for Tammany, and McNaughton, the officer,
he was in the Hall with Warren . . . Oh, Judge Norris,"

Emily sighed, her circuits overloaded with so much to say and so little time to do so, "I know a lot about Tammany, Judge Norris, and I know they don't want me to talk . . . And for some reason I can't yet figure out, they must have felt they had to do something to my former husband."

"So what you're telling us, Miss Stanton, is that they, Tammany Hall, and not you, killed your ex-husband?" Judge Norris asked, trying to take in all that Emily was saying.

"Not me. No, not me. Yes, I guess . . . that's what I'm saying. Yes."

"But you're saying that your husband was involved with Tammany? That he was an important man there. Why would they kill him?"

"I don't know. I just don't know. But I do know *I* didn't do it. This is an awful frame-up. I have no idea who planted that gun in my apartment. You have to have an investigation."

"Well, I'm sure the police and the district attorney's office will investigate this matter fully and thoroughly, Miss Stanton, but this is only your arraignment, and not really the time and place to discuss the matter," Judge Norris said in a soft feminine voice that rang with understanding. "But I'll keep an eye on this case. I promise you."

"Oh, thank you." Emily was delighted at this first semblance of sympathy.

"Meanwhile, because of your prior conviction and the extreme gravity of the charges against you, you will be held without bail," Judge Norris said, her sympathy suddenly vanishing.

"But, Judge Norris," Emily pleaded, after being stunned silent for a moment by the judge's pronouncement. "You've got to understand. You've got to let me out so I can help my . . . lawyers . . . help them find out what really happened. I have the money. Please . . ."

"Bail request denied."

"But you're a woman," Emily wept. She had been betrayed by her own sex. "You're a woman," she cried out, incredulous.

Judge Norris ignored Emily's outburst. She gathered her black robes around her and disappeared through the back door of the hearing room. Two bailiffs led Emily off to the women's cellblock, just a few barred doors down from where she had been incarcerated, en route to Bedford, seven years before.

The next step in the proceedings would be the grand jury. Though the grand jury had the theoretical power to refuse to return an indictment against Emily, in practice it was almost automatic that the jury would give the D.A. exactly what he wanted, an indictment for first-degree murder. This they promptly did, the very next day. Emily was told this together with one piece of "good news." The D.A. had elected not to seek the death penalty. Instead he would seek to imprison her for the remainder of her natural life.

73

Alex Foster was ebullient. He had spent the entire morning, and half the afternoon, with a group of potential backers for his new play, and he was confident that the potential was about to be realized. The play was *Wedding Belles*, a romantic comedy about three brash but impecunious sisters, each of whom sets her marital sights on the same shy tycoon. The Broadway angels, themselves all minor tycoons Alex had met through his advertising successes, found his presentation quite amusing and, more important, possibly lucrative. Depression audiences loved stories of fiscal reconstruction. Love and money were as surefire a formula as existed. "I think we have a deal," one of the investors said, patting Alex on the back in his best show of Wall Street bonhomie.

On his way home to his new apartment on Riverside Drive, Alex stopped at Child's for a celebratory stack of pancakes and maple syrup. But all his feelings of satiety, confidence, and hope were knocked right out of him as he left the restaurant and passed a newsstand where the afternoon papers had arrived. Emily Stanton was on the front page of every one of them. The *Times* was discreet: "TILE MAGNATE SLAIN." The others were not. "BLOOD FEUD!" "ANGRY HOSTESS, DEAD HUBBY." "NIGHTBIRD'S SONG OF REVENGE." "EX-HOOKER HELD IN DEATH OF TILE KING." Alex feverishly bought all of the papers, saw where Emily was being held, and leapt into the first cab heading downtown.

Emily gushed out the whole story to Alex in the windowless visitor's room. "All they talk about is Texas

378

Guinan's and Bedford and my prostitution conviction," she raged as she scanned the newspaper accounts.

"That's what sells papers," Alex said.

"Nothing about Tammany. Nothing about Seabury."

"And nothing about Polly Adler," Alex added. "We should be grateful for something."

"Give them time," Emily said. "You've got to speak to Jessica somehow."

"I will," Alex assured her. "I'll see her. Don't worry. I'll take care of that. But what about Polly? You're going to be depending for your alibi on her and that gangster, what was his name again?"

"Tommy Catania," Emily said.

"Tommy Catania." Alex spit out the name, unable to conceal his jealousy.

"I know how you feel, but it's all I've got, and it's true," Emily said. "What a mess. And the call-girl thing isn't even out yet. They just think I'm a bar hostess and they're crucifying me for that."

"You don't need a lawyer. You need Ivy Lee," Alex said, referring to the Rockefellers' famous public-relations expert.

"Alex, I need you. You're the only person I can talk to. I'm so ashamed. I don't know how I can make it up to you."

"By cleaning up your life when you get out of here."

"I will. Believe me."

"I've heard that before," Alex said, still smarting over the Tommy Catania date. "You've said that fifty times," he reminded her.

"Believe me this time. If I ever get another chance . . ."

"You will." Alex couldn't stop himself from forgiving her. Besides, she had far bigger problems to address than her own morality or Alex's jealousy.

"I've got to get out of here," Emily said. She had been defeated the first time she was here. This time she was prepared to fight, even if she wasn't sure quite how. Her major source of strength was her certainty that she would have the Seabury Commission behind her. "Alex, would you get in touch with Robert Kohn—as soon as you can?"

"I already did," Alex said, "while I was waiting to see you."

"Oh, thank you, Alex. They'll get to the bottom of this."

Alex didn't say anything. In truth, he didn't know what to say.

Emily sensed a problem. "Tell it straight, Alex. What? Come on. I can take it."

"Kohn said, off the record . . . Emily, are you sure . . ."

"Alex. I can take it. I can take anything."

"I'm not sure *I* can." Alex took a deep breath, then spoke again. "Kohn said . . . he said that the Seabury staff felt be-trayed."

"Betrayed?"

"He said you should have waited."

"Waited for what?"

"That you shouldn't have taken the law into your own hands. That your anger—"

"Anger!" Emily shouted, her voice echoing around the dim room. "Jesus! If they don't know a frame-up . . . This is straight out of what they're supposed to be looking into. Can't they see? They think *I* did it!"

"I said everything I could. I tried every—"

"I was supposed to be their star witness," Emily said, infuriated by the Seabury staff's failure to support her. "You saw how excited they were."

"I know, I know," Alex said. "They said having been a prostitute was bad enough. Being a murderess, well, that just killed it for them. They said you wouldn't have any credibility."

"They're talking like I've already been proven guilty. They're supposed to be lawyers, Alex. What kind of lawyers are they?"

"They're spineless," Alex answered.

"You mean they don't even want me to testify now? They're going to let Tammany win? They're doing just what Tammany wants!"

"Kohn said that with the way the press is handling it, you'd hurt Seabury more than you'd help. Using you would make them seem desperate, grasping at straws."

"Listening to convicted whores and accused murderesses. That makes sense," Emily said bitterly.

"I begged them," Alex said.

"Don't beg. If they can't see this is all Tammany, that this could be their biggest break, forget them."

"I'll go down there."

"No," Emily said. "Save your energy. For me. I've got somewhere else for you to go. First, get in touch with Jessica. Get through to her somehow. Tell her I'll be fine. Tell her I didn't do it. Tell her I'll be out of here. And tell her to remember our last night together and hold on tight to that."

"I'll tell her," Alex promised.

"That's the easy assignment."

"What's the hard one?"

"I want you to get me Sam Leibowitz," Emily said.

"Are you kidding?" Alex hesitated. "He's impossible."

"Do it for me, Alex. Please. Just get him down here to see me. I need the impossible."

74

The streets in Brooklyn Heights were named after trees and fruits—Willow, Poplar, Orange, Pineapple, Cranberry—but the giant trees that lined the streets of Victorian brownstones were all barren and the branches frozen, encased in February ice. Cold notwithstanding, Alex reflected that the Heights would be a splendid place to live, and to write, particularly with a bay window overlooking the docks below and the towers of Wall Street across the East River. It conjured up for him what he imagined London to be. Brooklyn Heights had a unique gentility, a splendid isolation that enabled its residents to see the city in all its splendor yet afforded them the luxury of being disengaged and living in a softer, kinder, earlier age, with all the energy of the present no more than a subway token away.

Alex made his way down the Promenade, observing the freighters from China and Japan unload their cargoes of jade and ivory and unnamed treasures. Then he found the residence of Samuel Leibowitz, a charming yellow clapboard town house that might have once belonged to some sea captain, and waited for the celebrated captain of the bar to come home.

In his new cashmere topcoat and silk scarf from Brooks Brothers, Alex had the appropriate English air for the neighborhood. No one would suspect him of loitering. He sat on a bench rereading *Moby Dick* to pass the time. Melville had been a customs inspector at the nearby docks. Alex read about Captain Ahab until the dimming winter light failed him. Then he gave up and waited, pacing to keep warm, thinking feverish thoughts of Emily and Tommy Catania and wondering how a woman he could be so infatuated with could make love for money with a gangster. He also played out several scenarios of what he would say to Samuel Leibowitz if and when he finally arrived.

This impromptu approach was the only way Alex was going to get to Leibowitz. He had tried the formal method for several days, calling the office numerous times about Emily's case and meeting a brick wall of indifference and avoidance. "Mr. Leibowitz is aware of that case and is not interested." "Mr. Leibowitz is not in." Even "Mr. Leibowitz is with Al Capone" from one secretary who was trying to scare Alex off. But Alex refused to be scared.

He went to Leibowitz' office. There were four secretaries, all with the same story. "Mr. Leibowitz is not in."

"But it's urgent. It's a murder case. You've read about it," Alex pleaded.

"Mr. Leibowitz gets dozens of urgent murder cases from all over the country every day. He's not taking on any more cases now."

"But we can pay."

"They all say that."

Still undaunted, Alex called a recent blind date who was a secretary at the New York *Times*. Her boss was a senior reporter who knew everyone's home address. Alex got Leibowitz by promising the young lady a dinner at Longchamps.

After over an hour's wait in the cold, the man arrived. Getting out of the cab, he was a large, rabbinical figure dressed all in black, bearing a briefcase so heavy and bulging that it gave the man another dimension of physicality not normally associated with someone of such a scholarly mien. Alex walked over to greet Leibowitz as he settled his fare with the driver.

"Mr. Leibowitz," Alex addressed him.

Leibowitz looked up with a start. Alex saw it as the fear of retribution from some criminal escaped from Sing Sing to get even with this vaunted mouthpiece for a failure of performance in not winning a not-guilty verdict. Then again, Leibowitz rarely failed, so the moment of anxiety was all Alex's illusion.

LULLABY AND GOODNIGHT

"Mr. Leibowitz," Alex said, adjusting his scarf to ward off the cold, "I'm Alex Foster. I'm a playwright. My *Fly by Night* ran last year on Broadway." Alex offered his hand.

"Yes." Leibowitz took it, without giving any indication whether or not he was aware of the production.

"I feel like Stanley and Livingstone here. I always wanted to meet you."

"Yes," Leibowitz said politely. He looked Alex up and down, mostly down, as Leibowitz was the far larger of the two. "What can I do for you, Mr. Foster?" he asked.

"I've got a case for you."

"You do?" Leibowitz replied. "If I only had time."

"It's the greatest case I've ever seen." Alex wouldn't let him get away.

Leibowitz surveyed Alex for a long moment, trying to determine what this wholesome young man could have in store for him. Then he spoke. "Well, Mr. Foster, we shouldn't be standing in this cold street talking about the greatest case in history, should we? Livingstone showed Stanley more hospitality than that. And this is Brooklyn, not darkest Africa. Please come in."

A major first step, Alex thought. "Thank you so much."

They sat in Leibowitz' library, overlooking the sparkling deserted canyons across the river, sipping hot tea with lemon in glasses, Russian style. Without his hat, the balding Leibowitz looked less like a rabbi than a wrestler. Beneath his impeccable three-piece suit and pindotted tie was a big man with the soul of a fighter, everything held tightly in check for when the battle call sounded.

Leibowitz was very polite, as was his wife, who served them the tea and left. His twin boys, Robert and Lawrence, came in to meet the visitor, who, Leibowitz told them after having heard a bit of Alex's background, was "going to write you both references to Yale."

Leibowitz was a great believer in education as the key implement of success in America. He told Alex how his father had fled the pogroms of Romania, prospered in the dry-goods business in Brooklyn, and sent his son to Cornell. "From the shtetl to the Ivy League in one generation," Leibowitz marveled. They talked about baseball, which they both played in college. They talked about Leibowitz' first criminal case defending a pickpocket who convinced Leibowitz of his innocence by picking the hundred-dollar retainer he had given Leibowitz out of the lawyer's pocket.

"The victim claimed he felt the pickpocket's hand," Leibowitz said. "And the pickpocket was insulted. He wanted to show me he was too professional to ever be felt. I won the case."

Leibowitz and Alex talked for over an hour, about everything except Emily Stanton. Then, as Leibowitz finished his last sip of tea, he said, "So, my good Mr. Foster, tell me about your splendid case."

"It's the Emily Stanton case," Alex began.

Leibowitz' high spirits, his interest, evaporated. For the first time during their meeting, he actually frowned. "That's a terrible case, Mr. Foster. You must be the fellow that's been to my office trying to set up an appointment with me on the case."

"Yes, I am, sir."

"How are you involved in that?" The "that" was definitely a denigration, implying Leibowitz' view that any involvement was beneath the dignity of a Yale man.

"She's a friend of mine."

"That's a terrible case. I've been following it in the papers. It doesn't sound like she's got a chance."

"It's a Tammany frame-up," Alex said. "They must have killed her ex-husband. All I know is that she's innocent. I promise you that, Mr. Leibowitz. But she needs a great lawyer, somebody who can stand up to Tammany, because it's Tammany who's out to get her."

"Her ex-husband, the dead man, he was a major Tammany man. They don't generally kill their own."

"If she killed him, sir, wouldn't she have gotten the gun out of her apartment? She's being portrayed as a calculating murderess. That's a bad calculation."

Leibowitz didn't say a word.

"And what about the evidence? The cops broke her door down. They didn't have a warrant. They had nothing. Couldn't you get the case thrown out on that alone? The police just can't break into people's homes. What about the Constitution?"

"Mr. Foster, the law works in bizarre ways. You're absolutely right about the Constitution and illegal searches and seizures. But even if the search and seizure is illegal, the fruits of the raid can still be used."

"That's absurd," Alex said.

"That's the law. *People versus Defore*, 1926," Leibowitz shrugged. "When we're more civilized someday, maybe the law will realize that if the search is illegal, the police shouldn't be able to use the evidence seized against the person in the same way they could have if they had acted lawfully."

"Yes. . . . And did you know Emily Stanton was going to testify before Judge Seabury?" Alex pushed on, trying another tack.

"I read that somewhere. Was she really?"

"Absolutely. That's the whole thing. Her husband had her framed as a prostitute in 1924, to get their baby and to get a divorce. He and Michael McNaughton of the vice squad, another Tammany man. She was going to testify about that."

"What proof did she have?" Leibowitz remained impassive, unmoved by Alex's presentation.

"Nothing directly, but she worked at Texas Guinan's, dated Arnold Rothstein and Judge Crater and your client Mad Dog Coll, to name a few," Alex said, this time, ironically, almost with pride. "Emily Stanton knows a lot about corruption in this city."

"That's not going to sway a jury, I'm afraid," Leibowitz said, shaking his head.

"You'll sway the jury," Alex said, without a trace of doubt in his voice. "You'll do it."

"I've got a full docket. More cases than I can handle. And I won't take a murder case unless I believe the defendant is innocent."

"Good. Then you'll meet her and see for yourself."

"No." Leibowitz backed off. "I can't win that case."

"Was Mad Dog Coll really innocent? How innocent is Al Capone? Sir, you're a courtroom wizard. You were willing to represent organized crime, weren't you?" Alex was pushing his luck, perhaps his welcome, but this was going to be the only chance he had.

"Everyone's entitled to his day in court," Leibowitz said.

"So is Emily Stanton. She deserves her day. And so does New York," Alex asserted, flying high on his own rhetoric at this point. "You love New York, Mr. Leibowitz. Here's a chance to do something to repay the city for being good to you."

"I appreciate that, Mr. Foster, but I'm just not the right man."

"You're the only man. Unless you're afraid of Tammany Hall, too. But knowing your reputation, I just can't believe that."

"I'm *not* afraid of Tammany," Leibowitz retorted, a flush coming to his cheeks. "But all I see is a crime of passion. Emily Stanton strikes me as an angry woman. If Matthews really framed her, she has reason. But these kinds of reasons don't count when it comes to murder."

"Meet her, sir. Talk to her. See for yourself. If you believe she's telling the truth, you're defending more than her. You can succeed where Judge Seabury so far has failed. Please, Mr. Leibowitz. Please do it."

Leibowitz paused for a while. He buried his head in his hands as if the thought process was weighing it down. "All right, Mr. Foster. I'll come and meet her. But that's all I'll guarantee for now."

"That's great!" Alex jumped up and shook the bearish counsel's hand. "You'll see!"

75

"That's not Tommy Catania!" Samuel Leibowitz exclaimed in the visitors' room of the Women's House of Detention as Emily Stanton, in her gray prisoner's frock that underscored her pallor, described to him the man she was with on the night of Warren's murder. "Rudolph Valentino? I've *met* Tommy Catania. He's more like Fatty Arbuckle. Who told you he was Tommy Catania?"

"Polly Adler," Emily admitted with humiliation. She was so honored that Samuel Leibowitz had come to see her, to consider her case, and now she was equally ashamed to have to tell him the entire truth about herself. She knew she was risking losing him completely, but he had insisted she tell him the unvarnished truth as a precondition of any possible representation. She had told him the whole story. She couldn't stop now.

"God help us," Leibowitz moaned. "So this was not your ordinary blind date."

"No."

"How much did you ask him for?"

"One hundred dollars."

"Did you get it?"

"No. He was supposed to pay Polly," Emily explained uncomfortably. "We rarely handle money. It's not done."

"Wouldn't that be something? Putting Polly Adler on the stand," Leibowitz muttered to himself. "Young lady, you've led quite a life. How'd you get to Polly?"

"She saw me at Guinan's. Recruited me, sort of."

"Ex-convict, cabaret hostess, call girl, alleged murderess. The prosecution's going to have a field day," Leibowitz said.

Emily's hopes sank. "I'm sorry it's such a mess. I guess you won't take it, then."

"Not at all." Leibowitz smiled. "I'm starting to like it."

"You are? Oh, Mr. Leibowitz. Thank you." Tears of relief came to Emily's eyes.

"Your background says you're guilty as hell," Leibowitz said, "but your face says you're innocent. My instincts are always to go with the person, not the past, but I must admit you have a past that would make Lucifer blush."

"I know," Emily said through her tears. "I know."

"You see, you might have been angry enough to kill Warren Matthews *after* you went before Judge Seabury, if you had gotten nowhere. And I honestly don't think your going there would have done any good, not without a tangible link between Matthews and McNaughton. But you would want your chance to talk before you started pulling triggers. This Tommy Catania thing's what intrigues me. Let me sleep on it."

"But you will take the case?" Emily asked, desperate to be reassured.

"I think so," Leibowitz said. "Maybe the challenge will be good for me."

76

Samuel Leibowitz began to do his homework. His first stop was at 458 Fifty-second Street, where he found out from the building's superintendent, Adolph Klein, an old German wearing the brown leather apron he had worn in his more rigorous years slaughtering sheep down First Avenue in the abattoirs, that the apartment where Emily had her rendezvous with Tommy Catania, or at least the putative Tommy Catania, had last been occupied by one Lyman Lipsky, a small-time bootlegger two months behind on his rent. Lipsky had been on the NYPD missing-persons blotter for the last two weeks. "I think he skipped town," Klein told Leibowitz.

"Has anybody come here looking for him?"

"The cops, they came by once or twice."

"Anybody in particular?"

"Blue is blue to me."

"No plainclothesmen?"

"Naw," the super said. "But Lipsky doesn't pay his rent by March 1, he is *kaput*. I throw his furniture in the street. Bum!"

"What'd Lipsky look like?" Leibowitz asked.

"Little guy. Belly. Looks like he drinks a lot of his own beer."

"Did he look like Valentino?"

"Valentino?"

"Rudolph Valentino."

"The dead one? The sheik?" Klein laughed so hard he shook. "You a comedian or something?"

"And the cops. Any of them look like Valentino?"

"They looked like lousy cops."

Leibowitz left, not knowing who Tommy Catania's stand-in was. He then paid a call on Polly Adler, whom he had met once through Al Capone, but had never patronized.

"No, I didn't see him," Polly said. She was wearing her best black Chanel suit for Leibowitz' visit and looked as respectable as she ever could. "But he had impeccable references. Al. Johnny Torio. Dollink, I don't need this kind of *tsouris*," she said. "As you can imagine, I'm a very private person."

"But this girl's life is at stake."

"So is mine, dollink, if this goes public. Sam, please. Al, your client, is my friend. I take good care of him when he comes to the city. If one of his boys wants a good time, who am I to deny it to him?" Polly provided no information other than that she had never seen Tommy Catania. "Let me introduce you to someone, Sam. On the house. Take an hour."

"I don't have an hour, Polly," Leibowitz said. He went back down to the Women's House of Detention with a sheaf of photographs. One was a mug shot of the real Tommy Catania— jowly, scarred, missing teeth, decades older than his impostor. Emily, who had been passing time reading a copy of the latest best-seller, *The Good Earth* Alex had brought her, could not identify him. Nor did any of the pictures of the members of the vice squad Leibowitz laid before her, nor any of the other photos—of dozens of criminals who specialized in impersonations— ring a bell.

Samuel Leibowitz fully believed that somebody posing as Tommy Catania had fooled Emily Stanton, and perhaps Polly Adler as well. Based on that deception, he formally signed on as Emily's defense counsel. His acceptance of the task kept Emily on the front pages.

77

Warren Matthews was interred in a white, marble-columned mausoleum in Woodlawn Cemetery, just one plot away from Jay Gould, who had owned the Union Pacific railroad and Western Union and had almost cornered the nation's gold market in 1869. The mausoleum was according to Warren's wishes. The timing was not.

"Warren Matthews was a good businessman. He was a good husband. He was a good father. He had a dream," the reverend from St. Thomas Episcopal Church intoned, waving his hand toward the smokestack of Matthews Tile in the distance. "His life was snuffed out, but his dream lives on. He will not be forgotten."

Jessica, in her black velvet coat, stood next to Isabelle behind the casket. Though she had built up an enormous resentment against her father, his death was still a shock and a pain. Nevertheless, she was glad of the cold, pelting rain that had started with the ceremony. It created the impression that she was crying for her father more than she was. She was, however, worried about her mother. Alex had tried to call Jessica, pretending to the servants who answered that he was a friend from one of the tea dances calling with condolences. But he couldn't get through. To avoid the press, Isabelle had taken Jessica to stay at her parents' home on Henderson Place, off East End Avenue. Jessica wanted desperately to see her real mother. But she knew she dared not even ask.

Thus when Alex slipped Jessica a note in the crowd of mourners leaving the cemetery, she was greatly relieved. "Dear Jessica," Emily's note read. "You must know that your mommy is innocent. So please don't worry, honey. I have the best lawyer in New York and everything will work out all right. The food isn't very good in jail, but I'm fine. Don't read the newspapers, honey, except the funny pages. They like to write terrible untrue things about people in my position. When we're together, I'll explain everything to you. We'll be back together soon. I love you, Mommy." That was all Jessica needed, and it was infinitely more comforting than all the mechanical hugs she received from the Tammany sachems.

Tammany had turned out in force. Terence McCarey dried a tear. Charles Sullivan sniffled and looked downcast, holding on to his walking stick. Jimmy Walker wore a white carnation and made a big show of introducing his new police commissioner, Edward P. Mulrooney, whom Walker had recently appointed to replace Grover Whalen in order to silence mounting criticism that Whalen was a dilettante and a dandy, only fit to give parades and not keep the peace. Mulrooney was a cop's cop, having worked his way up through the force. He had a gold front tooth, pronounced girl "goil," was tough and a hero as well, having saved many lives in a 1904 Hudson Day Line fire where hundreds of others perished.

Leaving the gates of Woodlawn, Walker, with somber face, praised Mulrooney's rapid solution of Warren Matthews' murder, adding, "Warren Matthews was a loyal man, a loyal Tammany man, and a loyal New Yorker. I'll miss him."

"What about Sam Leibowitz?" a reporter shot out.

"Mr. Leibowitz has a long history of association with the criminal element of this city," Walker replied.

"He never loses."

"There's always a first time."

"Wasn't Emily Stanton about to go to the Seabury Commission?" another reporter asked.

"She can still go," Walker said. "It's her husband who's dead. Not she."

"What about the vice squad?" still another shouted through the crowd. "Didn't she claim she was framed?"

"Gentlemen"—Walker held up his hand as his chauffeur opened the door of his black limousine—"you seem to forget who the victim is here. Mr. Matthews has just been laid in the ground. Miss Stanton is very much alive.

LULLABY AND GOODNIGHT

But thank goodness we have our own Sherlock Holmes right here," Walker bellowed, patting Mulrooney on the back, "and I think it's going to take more than Mr. Leibowitz' famous loopholes to prevent justice from being done in this case. Thank you, gentlemen."

"Mayor Walker! Mayor Walker!" the reporters cried and scrambled, but the mayor was finished. In the back seat of the limousine was Betty Compton. She didn't go out to pay her final respects to Warren Matthews. She didn't want to get her hair wet. She and the mayor were going to the theater that evening.

78

"A case so obviously tailor-made will never hold water before a jury of twelve reasonable men," Samuel Leibowitz told the swarm of pressmen on the steps of the Bronx County Courthouse, a blockhouselike building standing up the hill on 161st Street above Yankee Stadium. The Bronx had rarely experienced such attention in the wintertime. On the other end of the steps, Leibowitz' opponent, Bronx Assistant District Attorney I. J. Adlerman, pronounced that he had "an airtight case." Certainly the grand jury had agreed with Adlerman, readily indicting Emily for first-degree murder. Leibowitz told Emily not to despair. "It's the trial that matters. There was sufficient evidence for an indictment," he explained. Because nobody would be around at the trial to vouch that they had actually seen Emily the night of the murder, she knew she would have to be her own witness, and began steeling herself for that eventuality.

I. J. Adlerman was one of the Young Turks of Tammany. A wiry redhead, he was only thirty-two but looked a decade older. He held a grudge against Samuel Leibowitz, who had declined to hire him for his firm when Adlerman finished New York Law School. "He seemed too soft," Leibowitz explained to Emily. "I didn't think he could go for the jugular. I wanted an attack dog. Now, unfortunately, he seems to have become one, after all." Adlerman was fierce in the courtroom, stalking up and down in front of the jury box, snarling at witnesses, carrying on his own foaming crusade against crime in the Bronx. At rest, with his thick glasses, pale, narrow face, and too-short trousers, he seemed the stereotypical back-room clerk. The courtroom, however, brought him to life. It made him seethe and burn.

Adlerman was one of Tammany's best advertisements for a clean New York. Some outsiders saw him as window dressing, but window dressing was precisely what Jimmy Walker needed now. "He's a fine boy," Walker said. "He's turning the Bronx around." Adlerman was the pet, the golden boy, and the Jewish token of Bronx's Tammany Boss Edward Flynn, who was ever mindful of the borough's influential Jewish population. Some people called Adlerman "Alderman" because of his Chamber of Commerce pride. Others simply called him "Hangman." Devoid of any sense of humor, Adlerman was the perfect stalwart to avenge the death of a Tammany brave. "The woman is a murderer," Adlerman told the press. "A cold-blooded murderer. I can't wait to prove it."

Waiting for the trial to begin, Emily, in her cell, overcame her initial despair. Although powerful forces were seeking to destroy her life, and despite the flood of terrible memories of Bedford that her new incarceration generated, her spirit could not be drowned. She did smoke cigarettes to calm her nerves, and developed a bad cough. As at Bedford, the jail diet and harsh laundry soap wreaked havoc on her complexion. She kept a polite distance from the other inmates, most of whom were in and out in a matter of days, so no dangerous cliques were able to form. She could once again see the whole syndrome of defeminization and dehumanization that came with incarceration, but this time it didn't threaten her. For now she had a real lawyer. Now she had a date with justice.

She wrote letters to Jessica and she read everything she could get her hands on—Dos Passos novels, Charlie Chan mysteries, the newspapers Alex brought to her daily. The National Socialists were rising in Germany. Thomas Edison had died. The depression was getting worse, the unemployment lines longer. Yet there were also long lines on Broadway to see Boris Karloff in *Frankenstein*, Charlie Chaplin in *City Lights*. The city needed escape, and very few stories of the day were any bigger than Emily's. There came a curious sense of power from this notoriety that more than counterbalanced her sense of impotence sitting in the House of Detention.

The trial commenced on March 1 with the selection of a jury. Presiding was Judge Albert Katz, an intellectual-looking man with thick glasses shielding weary eyes that perhaps had seen more than he wanted. Katz was a Tammany appointee, another protégé of Bronx Boss Flynn. Early that morning Emily rode up to the Bronx in the back of a police car with Samuel Leibowitz. Although she was on her way to a rendezvous with justice that could conceivably result in life imprisonment, the very fact that she was going made her feel vibrant and energized. Simply getting out of the monotonous House of Detention and breathing the crisp winter air of the streets of New York filled her with life. She had been in jail less than a month, but the city looked sparkling and new to her. Driving up West Street by the docks, she could see in the distance the new George Washington Bridge's silver arc across the Hudson finally reaching New Jersey. The Empire State Building, that gleaming monument to the boom years of the past decade, was also nearing completion.

They turned across town at Forty-second Street. Even at this hour, Times Square seemed electric. The cacophony of the rush-hour mob, the blaring horns of taxicabs, were music to her. This was her city, and she wanted to return to it. She had her mission. She realized she should have been terribly apprehensive in view of the stakes and the odds against her. After all, she was going to do battle against Tammany Hall. At long last. But she had her courage and her rabbinical knight beside her. So she felt good, like a woman again. Never in her life had she so savored a morning of getting dressed, getting ready, getting out.

Although Mrs. Hattie T. Carraway, an Arkansas Democrat, had become the first woman elected to the U.S. Senate the year before, in New York State women were not eligible for jury duty. A pity, Samuel Leibowitz thought, for women would have been sympathetic to Emily Stanton's plight of having had her child taken away from her. On the other hand, Leibowitz realized that women would not be sympathetic to Emily's having become a prostitute, and a prosperous one at that. Thus, in his mind, the disqualification of women was a wash.

During jury selection, the *voir dire*, Emily sat silently, observing the proceedings from the defense table and doing all she could to avoid the stares of a courtroom packed with press and curiosity seekers. In picking the jury, each side was allowed twenty peremptory challenges. A prospective juror could thus be excused arbitrarily by the prosecution or the defense without any reason being given to the court. Leibowitz wanted men as intelligent as possible, because of the complexity of the frame-up. He was searching for compassion as well, but many of the compassionate-looking men were challenged by Adlerman.

Leibowitz' chief question to jurors was this: "You and I know what's going on in this city, don't we?" He didn't wait for a response. "If the evidence at this trial shows that the murder was by Tammany Hall, not my client, are you going to have the *courage* to cast a verdict of not guilty?" Most of the prospective jurors said yes, though some were a bit indignant about the lawyer's casting aspersions on the government of their city.

Because Adlerman's official position was that Tammany had nothing to do with the murder, he did not automatically challenge every juror who seemed willing to put Tammany on trial along with Emily. That might have looked too suspicious. Instead, he waited for other, less political grounds for exclusion.

"Would your decision be influenced by the fact that Emily Stanton might be described as a 'loose woman'? " Leibowitz asked a biology teacher from Evander Childs High School.

"Not at all," the teacher replied firmly.

The teacher was challenged by Adlerman, and Leibowitz lost a man he wanted.

"Do you believe that a prostitute is a bad person?" Leibowitz queried a bus driver from Stebbins Avenue.

"No, sir. Not necessarily," the man answered.

The prosecution also challenged the bus driver.

"Have you read the newspaper accounts of this case? . . . Which paper?" was a question Leibowitz frequently asked. "How often do you go to the theater?" and "Have you ever been to a speakeasy?" were two others, after which, if they drew too positive a response, Adlerman would exercise one of his challenges.

"Have any of you ever been to a vaudeville show?" Leibowitz asked the jurors collectively.

"I never waste my money on that stuff," one well-dressed clerk from the Concourse responded. Leibowitz challenged him. He wanted no teetotalers or philistines. They would be prejudiced against a cabaret hostess. But he wanted to avoid the florid faces. Real drunks might be sexist Tammany men. He also stayed clear of any Irish names. The Irish tended to vote the Tammany ticket, whether in the electoral ballot box or in the jury box. "Are you automatically inclined to believe what a policeman says?" was another corollary question. When Leibowitz asked, "Have you been reading about the Seabury Commission?" nearly half of the prospective jurors said no, a percentage that surprised Leibowitz, given the newspaper consumption of New Yorkers.

Adlerman was keen on addresses. He wanted east of Third Avenue, where the poor immigrants lived. They would be less likely to sympathize with a fancy courtesan. "Do you attend church regularly?" was another of Adlerman's litmus tests. The fire-and-brimstone people might regard Emily's past as something to be punished, and this would perhaps carry over to the issue of whether or not she was guilty of murder. And, finally, "Do you support your local police?" The intensity of the inevitable yes determined whether Adlerman (and/or Leibowitz) wanted the man or not.

After two weeks of parrying, weighing one prejudice against another, one hundred and fifty prospective jurors had been heard, and twelve had been selected: Daniel Lister, travel agent; John Frascati, salesman; Louis C. Merz, piano maker; Martin E. Ward, merchant; Max Ashman, dry-goods dealer; Franco Pisciotto, piano tuner; Lucien Clark, meter reader; Jerome Mathias, electrician; Herman Haubenhaus, clothing buyer; Louis Levine, salesman; John P. Novak, Jr., clerk; Albert O'Dwyer, electrical engineer. Of the twelve men, the oldest was Lister, at forty-eight. The most junior member was Mathias at twenty-five. It was an uncommonly young jury, and because of the enormous newspaper attention being given to the case, Judge Katz ordered it sequestered across from the courthouse at the Concourse Plaza Hotel for the duration of the trial.

"Electricians and piano tuners," Emily said, surveying the final list of the men who would decide her fate.

"They're precision men. They'll get all the nuances," Leibowitz explained. "Only one Irishman and two Italians, also," he said, with some pride. "I think we've pretty well shut Tammany out. It should be fair."

79

Samuel Leibowitz had told Emily to "dress for sympathy, not for fashion," and she found herself wearing a
black "funeral dress" from Best and Company similar to
that which Isabelle Matthews was wearing in the gallery.
Isabelle was there to dramatize the point that Adlerman
made in his opening statement to the jury. "The evidence
will show that *this* woman," he boomed, pointing at
Emily, seated at the defense table, "murdered *that* woman's husband in cold blood and took him away from her
forever." Isabelle was a superb exhibit for Adlerman.
Her eyes telegraphed her hatred for Emily as well as the
helplessness of being without a man in a life that Isabelle
was capable of leading only with a husband.

"This woman," Adlerman said, pointing at Emily again,
"hated her own life, but she hated the life her ex-husband
had even more. She begrudged him his happy life. Hell
hath no fury like a woman scorned. This woman was
scorned for good reason, for she was a failure, a failure
at everything she ever tried. She failed as an actress.
More important, she failed as a mother, and she failed as
a wife."

Emily wanted to leap up and lash back at Adlerman as
he stalked and glared and pointed at her. "She failed at
life. She succeeded at death."

But she had learned better. She was all control.
Leibowitz occasionally fortified her with a reassuring
glance. "It's his job," he whispered. Emily knew that
both sides were simply playing a game, the game of law,
at which attorneys maximized their advantages and did
everything possible to minimize their disadvantages. The
problem was that losing this game meant a life sentence.

"The evidence will further show, however, that this woman, Emily Stanton, was also a success in other areas," Adlerman continued. "She was a success at sex," he railed like an Old Testament prophet denouncing blasphemy. "She was a hit as a prostitute. And she was a hit as a murderess. We have the murder weapon, a gun found in her apartment. We have her lipstick holder, found next to the victim. We have the motive. We, the people of the State of New York, will prove to you beyond all reasonable doubt the guilt of this woman. Men of the jury, what we have here is a case of rage, a case of fury, and we never want to let that fury be free in the Bronx, *our* Bronx, ever again." He glared hard at Emily, then turned back to the jury. "Thank you."

If Adlerman was playing the Puritan evangelist, Leibowitz took the part of the Wise Man, all calm, unruffled authority. He approached the jury box and coolly told the male jurors that the evidence would show his client was innocent. "I'm honored to be representing Emily Stanton here today," he said in the mellowest, least adversarial of voices. "I'm honored to be a part of giving this woman her day in court. She's been in court before, but she wasn't given her day then. The evidence will show that seven years ago she came into a court, a magistrate's court, part of the Tammany justice system you perhaps have heard about through the Seabury investigations, the courts where the magistrates earn twelve thousand dollars a year but are banking fifty thousand. They are remarkable courts.

"My client, Miss Stanton, will testify that her ex-husband wanted custody of their little six-year-old daughter. He wanted to get a divorce so he could marry another woman. Now, you can only get a divorce for adultery, but Emily Stanton wasn't an adulteress. So they went one better. They not only made her an adulteress. They made her a prostitute!"

The word sent terrible chills through Emily, but she knew this was part of Leibowitz' task.

"In one fell swoop, an innocent housewife is transformed into a prostitute. How's that for the magic of the magistrate's court!" Leibowitz was no longer the calm scholar. An edge was creeping into his voice. He looked into the eyes of the jury. Though he paced back and forth before the jury, he never lost that eye contact. He didn't lecture the jury. He tried to make them his partners, partners in a search for the truth. If Adlerman was the salesman of guilt, Leibowitz was the gadfly of innocence. Leibowitz would operate by the Socratic method, raising rhetorical questions and letting the answers flow. And questions were the key to his quest for a not-guilty verdict. Questions were about doubt. He believed he could ask enough questions to create the reasonable doubt that would set Emily free.

"This trial," he said, "is more than the trial of one woman accused of killing her ex-husband. You, gentlemen of the jury, are participating in history, because it's not Emily Stanton who should be on trial. The evidence will show that the real defendant here should be Tammany Hall. The machine that runs your city, my city."

The courtroom let out a collective gasp.

"The best defense I can give to my client is to prove that somebody else other than she—somebody at Tammany Hall, to protect Tammany Hall—killed Warren Matthews. But who? And why? I'd like to know. *We need* to know, or else the evidence here is incomplete. But I don't have those answers for you. However the defense has no burden to provide the answers. Under the law of *this* land, the prosecution has the burden of proof. I think Tammany Hall has the answers in this case. And this is why I would like to place a challenge to the prosecution, right here *and* right now, to give us these answers by calling one Tammany man, in particular, who could be most helpful to us here. I can't call him to the stand, because if I call him, the rules of evidence won't let me cross-examine him. And to get at the truth I want to get at, I need to cross-examine this man. The man is Officer Michael McNaughton of the police department's vice squad. He's one of the most decorated men on the force. He's also the man who arrested Emily Stanton for prostitution seven years ago, the man Emily Stanton is certain conspired with her late husband, Warren Matthews, to frame her.

"I want all of you to hear Officer McNaughton, but the prosecution may decide to not call McNaughton, saying, 'that was seven years ago, that was another trial, that is history.' But history has a way of repeating itself. And I'll go so far as to say that the only way we can give Emily Stanton a fair trial is to bring Officer McNaughton to the stand.

"Tammany Hall is full of very arrogant men. Powerful men can be that way. But they shouldn't be, or they could lose their power. The Greeks had a word for it. *Hubris*. Overweening self-confidence. How Tammany thinks they can get away with this," he said, motioning toward Emily, "is Greek to me. The defense will prove that while Emily Stanton may not have had any power, Emily Stanton had knowledge. That knowledge gave her her own kind of power. Maybe that power was putting pressure on Warren Matthews. The pressure of the truth. Maybe Tammany Hall was worried about what that pressure might have done to Warren Matthews. Maybe Tammany Hall wanted to kill two birds with one *revolver*. What Emily Stanton knew was a real threat not only to Warren Matthews but also to the Tammany machine itself. A big enough threat that Emily Stanton had to be silenced. But if Tammany 'silenced' her, that might raise even more questions. '*You*, the people, silence her,' they laugh. 'You send her away for life.' "

Leibowitz stopped. Then he went into his conclusion. "But I say you the people can't be hypnotized. You the people are smarter than the machine gives you credit for. Tammany may be pretty smart. But I think you're even smarter. Emily Stanton was onto something, something about Tammany Hall. Let's give her her day in court. I am convinced that after we do, and after you men fairly and impartially evaluate the evidence in this case, you will return with a verdict of not guilty. I thank you very much."

80

With both Tammany and the prosecution stonily refusing even the slightest response to Leibowitz' call for McNaughton, Adlerman began the state's case. The first witness for the prosecution was Edward Armstrong, the Bronx County coroner. Armstrong was the antithesis of death—ruddy, beefy, robust. Using a clinical diagram of the decedent's body, Adlerman grilled Armstrong on the details of the killing. Two shots had gone into Warren Matthews' chest at close range. Three more after he had fallen. There were numerous bruises and lacerations on the head.

"He'd been kicked in the face when he was down," Armstrong told Adlerman.

"Are you sure he was down?"

"You don't get kicks like that standing up, not unless the person doing the kicking was a high jumper."

"What kind of person would attack someone after he's been shot five times?"

"I object," Samuel Leibowitz said, rising. It was obvious to him that whoever killed Warren Matthews had wanted it to look like a crime of passion—Emily's passion. "This calls for a conclusion of the witness. Moreover, this line of inquiry can only serve to inflame the minds of the jurors."

"Sustained," Judge Katz said, drawing his black robe tightly around him. A pipe in the courtroom had broken. The heat was off. The temperature was only in the low thirties outside and not much higher inside.

Coroner Armstrong placed the time of death somewhere around midnight, just at the time Emily was with

405

the would-be Tommy Catania. On cross-examination, Leibowitz asked Armstrong, "These bruises on the decedent's head. What kind of shoes caused them? Men's or women's?"

"I don't understand."

"Were there punctures?"

"No."

"Wouldn't a woman's pointed shoe or high heel have caused a different kind of injury than a round man's shoe?"

"Ah . . . some men wear pointed shoes too. You never know," Armstrong answered tentatively.

Adlerman's next witness was the watchman on the first two night shifts at Matthews Tile, a thick-set black man named Washington Jones who looked too lethargic to be effective in dispelling intruders. Jones established for Adlerman that Warren Matthews was working late the night of his death. "Missuh M. say he was gwine be workin' late, so I could go home."

"So he gave you the night off?"

"Yessuh. He do so right often. He was easy."

"How hard would it be, Mr. Jones, for someone to get into the plant after it closed?" Adlerman said.

"Well, ya see, Missuh M. he didn't like locks much, 'cause he was always forgittin' his keys. Not really forgittin', but, you see, Missuh M., he liked to dress real nice, and if you have to carry all those keys, they make some big bulge in your trousers, and Missuh M. like his trousers to hang straight."

"So he didn't carry a key?"

"No, sir. There was one door I always leave open for him."

"How many people knew about this door?"

"Oh, Missuh M. and Missus M. It was over to the side. No one else knew. You wouldn't think about it 'less someone told you."

"Did the first Mrs. Matthews know about it?"

"Yassuh. She used to come up sometime, help decorate the office, you know. She was different then, real nice."

"But she changed?"

"Objection." Leibowitz stood up, fuming. "This is irrelevant. It also calls for a conclusion."

"Overruled. You may answer," Katz intoned.

"Yessuh," Jones said. "All the actin' stuff done went to her haid. She stopped wantin' to be a wife."

"Do you see the first Mrs. Matthews in the courtroom?" Adlerman went on, obviously pleased with his witness.

"Yessuh, I sure do. She's the lady right there." He pointed to Emily. She remembered him, too. He used to be so courteous. Now he glared at her with a malice she'd never believed was in him.

"And that woman, Emily Stanton, knew about the unlocked door?" Adlerman pressed.

"Yassuh. She do indeed."

"Your witness," Adlerman said to Leibowitz, the same way a tennis player who has hit an unreturnable serve might gloat at his opponent.

"I have no questions," said Leibowitz, seasoned enough to realize that sometimes the best cross-examination was none at all.

Next up was Warren Matthews' secretary, Carla Schwartz, primly dressed in a brown suit that she would have dismissed as too drab to wear for her boss were he still alive. She testified about Emily's altercation with Warren, blushing that she had eavesdropped on the end of the conversation over her intercom, when she had returned from lunch.

"She really did threaten him," Miss Schwartz told Adlerman. "And it sounded like she was being violent."

"Did Mr. Matthews ever indicate how he felt about Emily Stanton?"

"Objection. That calls for hearsay," Leibowitz cut in, but Miss Schwartz answered over the objection as it was being sustained.

"He thought she was crazy and dangerous."

"I move that the last answer be stricken and the jury admonished to disregard it," Leibowitz said.

"The words 'He thought she was crazy and dangerous' shall be stricken and the jury is instructed to disregard them," Judge Katz ruled, knowing full well he was instructing the jury to do something as impossible as unringing a bell.

"Let me put it this way," Adlerman retreated. "How long have you been employed by Matthews Tile?"

"One year."

"Had you ever seen Miss Stanton before the day she came to see Mr. Matthews back in January?"

"No."

"What happened that day?"

"Well, she stabbed Mr. Matthews with her hatpin. I saw his leg when I came in. He couldn't walk. There was a lot of blood."

"Did you try to stop her from leaving?"

"It happened so fast. I had to help Mr. Matthews. She seemed so quiet, but . . . there was something about her . . ."

"What? What about her?"

"This . . . anger. She seemed so mad. I could hear her in the office threatening."

"What did she want?"

"All I heard her talk about was money."

On cross, Leibowitz tried to dilute some of Miss Schwartz's testimony. "You admit that the intercom was scratchy, that you didn't hear everything that was said."

"That's right. Not everything."

"And you didn't hear her say anything about her daughter, Jessica Matthews?"

"All I heard was about money. That's all."

During the first week of the trial, Adlerman called an NYPD fingerprint expert who testified that Emily's right-index fingerprint and right-palm print were on the gun found in her apartment and her left thumbprint on the lipstick holder at the murder scene. He called an NYPD firearms expert who testified that markings on bullets test-fired from the gun found in Emily's apartment matched up with those removed from the body of the decedent, and therefore he was able to conclude with "absolute certainty" that the murder bullets were fired from the gun in Emily's apartment "to the exclusion of all other weapons." Then Adlerman called Detective Malley, the chief investigating officer in the case, who testified over Leibowitz' strenuous objection that he was unable to discover any enemies of Warren Matthews or any other person with a motive to murder Matthews. A guard from the Museum of Natural History then testified that Emily had attacked Warren Matthews on the sidewalk in front of the museum.

"Yes, sir, she went right at him," the guard stated enthusiastically to Adlerman, as if he were reporting the blow-by-blow of a heavyweight-title prizefight. "She looked like she wanted to kill him right then and there."

"Did he make any move to strike her?" Adlerman asked.

"No, sir. He just tried to talk to her."

"And what did she do?"

"She yelled and screamed and went at him."

"Maybe you should try to get me declared not guilty by reason of insanity." Emily made this gallows joke to Leibowitz during a recess. "Half of New York thinks I'm a screaming banshee."

"Then we'll have to get the other half on your side," Leibowitz said. "Chin up."

In cross-examining the museum guard, Leibowitz tried to find out about the two thugs, Yuri and Mac, Emily had told him about.

"Did Mr. Matthews have any people with him?"

"There were some fellows who tried to pull the lady off of him. I figured they were good samarians."

"Do you mean samaritans?"

"Whatever you call 'em."

"Would you recognize these men if you saw them?"

"I doubt it. The lady, she drew all the attention. It was her and him."

"The two men were very large, burly, what might you call them . . . bodyguard types, is that correct?"

"Well . . . yes, they were."

As a final sop to Leibowitz' opening statement demand that the prosecution call Michael McNaughton to the stand, Adlerman did call Terence McCarey. He was Tammany's symbol of rectitude, of authority, of old New York at its heartiest Irish best. After he had established his long relationship with Warren Matthews, and that he had known Emily, Adlerman asked, "Commissioner McCarey, was it your impression that Warren Matthews was afraid of his ex-wife?"

"Objection!" Leibowitz interrupted. "Calls for a conclusion and also hearsay."

"Overruled," Judge Katz said, allowing McCarey to express his own opinion, rather than quote anything the decedent might have told him. It was a bad call, and Leibowitz seethed with disappointment, one of the few times during the trial his emotions got slightly out of his tight control.

"I believe so," the subway commissioner said. "Emily used to be so sweet, but when she went back onstage, in my mind she changed, got disagreeable, more demanding." At the defense table Emily seethed as well, deeply resenting the familiar, avuncular tone McCarey was using to denounce her.

"And when she got out of prison—I hate to think our prisons can do this to you—she seemed harder, tougher. I believe he seemed very worried about her seeing Jessica, worried about himself, which was odd, since Warren Matthews was a brave man."

When Leibowitz took McCarey on cross, he immediately went for the jugular. "Commissioner, did Warren Matthews ever give you stock in Matthews Tile?"

Adlerman had leapt out of his seat before Leibowitz even finished his question. "Objection, your honor. Objection. That is completely, absolutely irrelevant."

When Judge Katz sustained Adlerman's objection, Leibowitz demanded that both counsels approach the bench. "My question goes to motive, your honor," he pleaded with the judge. "Commissioner McCarey may have something to hide. Something big. Something worth killing for."

"Commissioner McCarey is not on trial, Mr. Leibowitz," the judge said peremptorily.

"I'm quite aware of this fact, Judge Katz, but I'm also aware that the best defense my client has that she did not commit this murder is to prove that someone else did," Leibowitz responded, echoing his opening statement.

"I know that type of defense in a criminal trial, Sam, but you need something much more substantial connecting McCarey with the murder. You're just on a fishing expedition, and I'm going to sustain the objection to this line of questioning." With this line of inquiry having been closed off, Leibowitz knew McCarey could do him no good at all.

Even further salt was rubbed into the defense's already festering wounds by the parade of Tammany sachems who would drop in at the end of the trial each day and then hold forth for the press, offering out-of-court testimony to the goodness of Warren Matthews and, by their grandfatherly presence alone, to the goodness of Tammany itself. The courthouse took on the ambience of a banquet hall, or an Irish wake, so many encomiums were being presented in the halls and on the steps. Boss Flynn came by; the new police commissioner, Edward Mulrooney, stopped over; Warren F. Curry, head of Tammany, made several appearances.

As the day of her testimony loomed closer, Emily Stanton was increasingly unnerved at the sachems' display of dignified solidarity. How could she impugn these stellar characters? How could she contend they were the architects of deceit and murder? This accretion of apparently heartfelt eulogies for Warren Matthews made Leibowitz' opening-statement gambit that Tammany Hall might have killed Warren Matthews seem increasingly preposterous.

"You know Sam, he always has to say something outrageous like that," Charles Sullivan told the reporters from the *Mirror*. "What else can he do? It's open-and-shut. Every lawyer, even Sam, can take the wrong case."

"But what about Michael McNaughton?" the reporter asked. "Why don't you call him to the stand? Don't you want to set the record straight?"

"Young man," Sullivan said, "the record *is* straight. And I'm not the prosecutor. Mr. Adlerman is. If he thought Officer McNaughton had the slightest relevant thing to contribute, I'm sure he'd call him. Mr. Adlerman is here to prosecute Emily Stanton, not persecute her."

"And there's not even a remote possibility that Tammany had anything to do with Warren Matthews' death? That Matthews might have been under pressure from his wife's impending testimony? That he might have talked in exchange for immunity?"

"I wish Warren Matthews was here to talk right now, son," Sullivan snarled.

LULLABY AND GOODNIGHT

Samuel Leibowitz, at least in public, mocked the Tammany parade of sachems. "The *lady*"—he referred to the Hall, quoting Shakespeare to the reporters—"doth protest too much." To Emily, however, he admitted that the tide was definitely against them, but that this was inevitable during the prosecution's case in chief.

Adlerman's final witness before he rested the prosecution's case, and perhaps his most effective, was Isabelle Matthews, who testified about how Warren was attacked by Emily outside the courtroom a few years earlier, during the custody hearing. "She would have killed him right then if she had had a weapon. It took three people to pull her off. I still have his tie. The one she tore when she tried to strangle him. It was his Tammany tie. He loved that tie," she said, fighting tears. "I always warned Warren she was dangerous," she went on. "He was so brave. If he had only listened to me. Oh, I miss him so. Oh, Warren," she cried out as she broke down and sobbed uncontrollably. Leibowitz did not cross-examine Isabelle. He wanted her out of the spotlight as soon as possible.

"I could see the disappointment in your face," Leibowitz said to Alex Foster after court was recessed. "I know you came to me expecting Houdini, and what you've gotten is a man who can't get out of the trunk."

"Mr. Leibowitz, you've been great." Alex tried to be polite, but couldn't conceal his dismay at how badly the trial was going. He was in the blackest mood. He thought he was going to be losing Emily forever, not that he had ever really had her in the way he wanted her. He felt that his glimmer of hope that she would be a free woman and have a normal life was going to be eradicated by I. J. Adlerman. "You've done everything a lawyer could do."

"Ah yes, I have, Mr. Foster. But you didn't want a lawyer, did you? You wanted a magician. Well, sometimes these trials work in strange and mysterious ways, and I think this is one of them. You see, I believe your friend Miss Stanton is going to be the magician in this one, not me."

81

When Samuel Leibowitz had tried to get in touch with Polly Adler again to see if she would be a witness to Emily's whereabouts on the night of the murder, he found out she had gone to the south of France to spend the rest of the winter. Texas Guinan was bedridden with a high fever that somehow would not seem to break.

"You're on your own," Leibowitz told Emily, who was hurt, but not surprised that Polly and Texas were deserting her.

Leibowitz decided, in light of the defections of both Polly and Texas, the absence of Tommy Catania, and the need to emphasize Emily's isolation, independence, and courage, that she should be, not just the defense's star witness, but its sole witness.

"I used to want to be a star," Emily said to Alex before taking the stand. She remembered the fantasies of her childhood, of her adolescent prisons of Joliet and the convent, of the "almosts" on Broadway. Now she was a star, at least in terms of attention, terms she had never imagined. The courtroom was going to be her stage, and that jury of twelve men was the toughest audience she, or anyone else, would ever play to. The Wednesday in March she was to be called to the stand, she wore a discreet beige suit and a peaked hat.

"The defense calls Emily Stanton," Leibowitz boomed, and the courtroom buzzed with whispers as the jammed gallery strained and craned for the best view of this main event of the trial.

Emily pushed her chair back, its metal legs screeching on the hardwood floor. She rose to her feet. For the first second, she was shaky. But the anxiety faded with her first step toward the witness stand. Striding forward, determined to be proud and strong, Emily regained her composure. This was her day. She was going to battle, with every molecule of strength in her body, to defend herself. She looked at Judge Katz with unblinking eyes. She looked at the stenographer, the clerk holding the Bible, the jury that would be determining her fate. She mounted the two steps into the burnished mahogany stand and turned around to place her hand on the black leather Bible.

"Do you solemnly swear to tell the truth, the whole truth, and nothing but the truth?" the stout clerk said in a rapid burst that sounded as if it were one long word.

"So help me God." Emily took the oath in the slowest, clearest manner. She summoned forth all the dignity she could muster for the indignities that lay before her.

I. J. Adlerman and his two assistant district attorneys sat at their table, hunters waiting for the season to open, this being their prize prey.

Samuel Leibowitz led off with his first question. "Miss Stanton, did you kill Warren Matthews?"

"No. I did not kill Warren Matthews," Emily said. Her tone bespoke with contempt the absurdity, in her mind, of the charge against her. "I didn't do it," she reiterated, turning to the jury and seeing a wall of faces that gave her no clues as to whether belief or disbelief existed behind those emotionless masks.

Leibowitz went through the day of the murder with her, outlining in tiny detail what she had done.

"I woke up at noon."

"Noon?" Leibowitz did his best to take the part of everyman, as well as that of advocate, so that the jury would sense they were getting an unbiased, unwhitewashed picture of Emily and her life.

"I had worked until five at Texas Guinan's the night before," Emily explained. "Those were my hours."

"What do you do at Texas Guinan's?" Leibowitz preferred that he, rather than the prosecution, bring out the negative elements of Emily's career.

"I sing. I dance. I'm a hostess."

"How long have you worked there?"

"Since 1927."

"How much do you make on a given night?"

"When I work, maybe twenty dollars. Maybe more, depending on the tips."

"Were you going to work for Texas Guinan on February 10?"

"No. I was taking the day off."

"Why?"

"Because I had a date that night."

"Tell me about this date, Miss Stanton."

Emily composed herself. This was the hardest moment of all, for she knew all hell would break loose in its aftermath. "I woke up when I got a call from Polly Adler."

"Can you tell us who Polly Adler is?"

"She is a madam whom I work for." The courtroom spectators stirred with a collective shock. This wasn't known at all. Whether Adlerman knew or not, he hadn't let on. In any event, Emily didn't have to incriminate herself. That was her constitutional right. But prostitution was also her alibi. She had no choice. There was a palpable rush of air into the courtroom as the reporters rushed out to phone in this latest scoop.

"How long have you worked for Polly Adler?" Leibowitz asked.

"Since 1928."

"How often do you work for her?"

"Two or three nights a week."

"Could you tell me what you do for her?"

"I go on dates. Sometimes I go to the theater. Sometimes dinner. Dancing. And usually . . . usually I'll go to bed with the man," Emily said, head high, concealing the shame she felt at this admission.

"How much do you get paid for this work?"

"Sometimes fifty dollars. Sometimes a hundred. Sometimes more. It depends on the man."

Judge Katz hammered down his gavel to quell the mounting rumble of whispers. "Order! Order in the courtroom! Please!"

"Why do you do this work, Miss Stanton?" Leibowitz asked, unfazed.

"Because it was the only way I could earn a living, at least a decent living, in New York City!"

"Could you explain?"

"Objection! Objection! Objection!" Adlerman shouted, furious that he had been preempted in his plan to demolish Emily's character. "This line of questioning is irrelevant. May we approach the bench, your honor?"

Katz nodded assent. Leibowitz walked over patiently. "If this isn't relevant, nothing is," he said to the judge.

"You're impeaching your own witness," Adlerman said.

"No, I'm not. I'm establishing the background for the frame-up in this case and also the basis for my client's whereabouts on the night in question. Other than that, this line of questioning isn't achieving anything at all," Leibowitz responded tartly as he looked to Katz for a ruling.

"Objection overruled," Katz said to Adlerman, who slammed his fist into his palm.

Emily first explained how she had been framed by Michael McNaughton and gone to prison in 1924. "When I got out," she said, "I couldn't get a job as an actress. I tried and tried, but no one wanted anyone with a prison record, at least not someone who wasn't a star to begin with. I gave up on the stage and got a job with Wanamaker's. But I lost that, too, because of the prison record. The only place I could get a job was at a cabaret, but I couldn't live on tips." She described how she needed money to hire a lawyer to get visitation rights to see her daughter. "Then I met Polly Adler. She showed me how I could make a lot of money by going out with men. I was very much against it at first. I thought it was awful. I really did. But I thought it was more awful not seeing my daughter. A lot of people don't like their jobs at first, and I didn't either, but they do them, like I did, because they have to. It becomes their life. It became mine. I wish I had had the chance to do something, anything, that was better. I'm sorry," she said, her head down in this public *mea culpa*.

"Were you ever arrested working for Miss Adler?" Leibowitz asked Emily.

"No."

"Did you ever solicit clients on the street?"

"No."

"At a speakeasy?"

"No. It was all arranged by Polly Adler."

"Did the men pay you?"

"They paid Polly. She gave me half. She took care of the business."

"I see," Leibowitz said, walking slowly back and forth before the witness stand, careful not to display any shock, matter-of-factly proceeding with this business of pleasure as if it were any other business. "Like a doctor and his patient. His nurse makes the appointments. She takes the payments for the doctor."

"Your honor," Adlerman lashed out. "He's dignifying something that's illegal!"

"Yes. Would counsel refrain from editorializing," Judge Katz snapped at Leibowitz. "You know better than that."

Normally Leibowitz would have displayed disapproval over any judge talking down to him. But he knew that because of his fame and stature in the bar, he was getting as fair a trial as he could possibly expect to receive from a Tammany jurist. He pressed ahead. "And this man, your date on the night of the tenth, who was he?"

"Polly told me his name was Tommy Catania. He was from Chicago. A friend of Al Capone's." There were suppressed gasps in the courtroom.

"Where did you meet this man?"

"In an apartment, 5B, at 458 East Fifty-second Street. He was staying there."

"He didn't take you to dinner?"

"No. He said he wanted to stay in, lie low."

"Did anyone see you with him?"

"No one. That was the idea."

"And what did you do with him? How did you spend the evening?"

"We drank champagne. We smoked marijuana. We made love."

More gasps. Many of the women in the courtroom turned red. Alex, sitting in the gallery, felt jealous again. Two reporters nudged each other with lascivious leers.

"Was there anything peculiar about the way . . . the way you made love that night?" Leibowitz asked as gingerly as possible.

"Yes," Emily said, after hesitating. "Tommy Catania wanted to make me up."

"What?"

"Put makeup on me. Lipstick. He wanted to paint my lips, do my hair, put mascara on my eyes. He wanted to draw valentines on my . . . back."

"I object to this, your honor," Adlerman said. He approached the bench, followed by Leibowitz. "This is unnecessary. And it's salacious."

"I do apologize for assaulting the lily-white earlobes of my colleague, Judge Katz, but this is what my client was doing when she was supposed to be in the Bronx doing away with her ex-husband," Leibowitz countered. "It may be salacious, but it's not murder."

"Overruled," Judge Katz said. Leibowitz smiled. Adlerman gave the judge a whose-side-are-you-on glance, which Katz did not return.

A titter went up with every disclosure Emily made. Titters, snickers, whispers. She blocked her mind from thoughts of Jessica and prayed the papers wouldn't print the testimony. More realistically, she prayed Jessica wouldn't read the papers, and, if she did, Emily prayed her daughter would forgive her.

"Wasn't this . . . making up . . . unusual?"

"Yes . . . and no," Emily said. "A lot of men have strange fantasies."

"And you let him?"

"Yes. It didn't hurt, so I let him do it."

"Are you sure, Miss Stanton? You say you drank champagne. You say you smoked marijuana. Are you sure you weren't imagining all this?"

"Yes. I'm sure."

"After this man used your lipstick, what did you do with it?"

"I don't know. I wasn't thinking. I didn't ask for it."

"Did he give it back to you?"

"Obviously not," Emily said.

"When did you know it was missing?"

"When the police broke into my house the next morning and said they had found it next to Warren Matthews."

"Miss Stanton," Leibowitz said, retreating from beside the jury box and standing in the center of the courtroom, "could you describe what this man looked like?"

"Yes. Tall, very handsome, elegantly dressed. He looked very much like Rudolph Valentino. With the slick hair. The teeth."

"The teeth?"

"He had perfect teeth. White and straight. Perfect."

"Miss Stanton, do you see this man who was introduced to you as Tommy Catania, do you see him in the courtroom?"

Emily looked around, scanning the seats front to back. She caught a glimpse of Alex, and was glad he was there.

"If it pleases the court," Samuel Leibowitz addressed Judge Katz, "I would like the defendant to step down for a moment— I'll call her back to the stand—and I would like to call Mr. Tommy Catania."

As a favor to Leibowitz, Al Capone had dispatched his "friend" Tommy Catania to New York. He was totally bald, pockmarked, broad as a house, with killer's eyes and two gold teeth. In his bulging sharkskin suit and polka-dot tie, he lumbered over to the stand.

"What do you do for a living, Mr. Catania?" Leibowitz asked.

"I refuse to answer on the grounds that it may incinerate me," Catania growled with an Italian accent. The courtroom giggled.

"You mean 'incriminate'?" Leibowitz helped him.

"Yeah. That's it."

"Were you in New York on February 10?"

"No."

"Where were you, Mr. Catania?"

"In Mexico. I was there."

"Were you in New York anytime in February?"

"No. See my passport."

Leibowitz introduced Catania's passport into evidence.

The Mexican stamps indicated that Catania had arrived in Veracruz on January 29 and had only returned to the United States the previous week.

"What were you doing in Mexico?"

"Sun," Catania grunted. In truth, he was involved in a tequila-smuggling operation for the Chicago franchise and would have remained south of the border had not Leibowitz called in a favor from Capone.

"Do you know Polly Adler?"

"No, sir."

"Have you ever used her services?"

Catania took an indignant posture. "I am a married man, sir. I am a religious man."

"Do you know this woman, Emily Stanton?" Leibowitz strode to the defense table and stood behind Emily.

"Never saw her in my life," Catania said.

Emily realized how tenuous her alibi was. On one hand, the presence of the real Tommy Catania could be construed to make her look like a liar. On the other, her countenance telegraphed nothing but candor and honesty, and Leibowitz' surprise move, he hoped, brought them one step closer to the truth, whatever that was.

"If the real Tommy Catania wasn't the man you were with, who was playing him?" Leibowitz resumed with Emily.

"I wish I knew," Emily said.

Leibowitz concluded with Emily's testimony about finding the planted gun in her apartment. "And you say that no one, not even your superintendent, had a key to your apartment."

"That's right. No one except me," Emily insisted.

"Why not?" Leibowitz queried.

"Because that apartment is the only place on earth that's mine," Emily said. "It's very special to me."

"So no one could have gotten in without your knowledge."

"No one."

"And you saw no evidence of anyone's having broken into your apartment before the police came that morning and broke the door down."

"None."

"Yet the gun was under your pillow. So someone had to have gotten in, is that correct?"

"Yes. Whoever it was had to have picked my lock. That was the only way."

"Thank you, Miss Stanton. Your witness, Mr. Adlerman."

I. J. Adlerman was at his most vicious when he cross-examined Emily. He was wearing a fiery-colored tie that almost precisely matched his hair color and certainly reflected his inner sentiments. He was out for blood. "Miss Stanton, did you hate Warren Matthews?" he bore down on her.

"Yes, I did," Emily replied.

"Did you want to see him dead?"

"Sometimes. But I didn't kill him."

"I see," Adlerman said snidely, as if talking to a child. "But you hated him enough to want to see him dead?"

"Sometimes."

"Why did you hate Warren Matthews so much, Miss Stanton, hate him enough to want to see him dead?"

Emily had fought with Leibowitz about telling the whole truth about hating Matthews. "Don't say you hated him," Leibowitz had counseled her.

"But I'm under oath," Emily had said.

"Use another word."

"There is no other word. I *want* to tell the whole truth. Please let me," Emily had insisted with a resolve that allowed no other course.

"When you say that, you're giving them a motive."

"But not a confession."

"Words like 'felt betrayed,' 'hurt,' even 'contempt for,' something a little less strong would help," Leibowitz had tried to sway her.

"I want 'hate,' " Emily continued to insist. "It's the truth. It's the only word that lets my life make any sense. If I didn't hate him, I wouldn't be human."

Leibowitz had relented, and now Emily was paying for her frankness. Adlerman had fixated on the word. It engendered an almost gleeful expression on his usually angry face. "Why did you hate this man, Miss Stanton?" he repeated.

"Because he ruined my life. He took my daughter. He turned me into . . . a . . . prostitute," she answered.

"He *turned* you into a prostitute?" Adlerman sneered.

"How? With a magic wand? Men can't *turn* you into a prostitute, Miss Stanton."

"He had me framed." Adlerman's barrage had made Emily so tense that she bit her lip and tasted the salty blood. Her head ached from the constant pressure of being alert, on the defensive, ready to parry the inevitable next blow.

"Yes, yes. We've heard that, Miss Stanton," Adlerman said impatiently. "Miss Stanton, you were duly tried, sentenced, and convicted. Your case was reviewed. The procedure was perfectly correct. I have your record in front of me," he said, brandishing a thick file.

"Yes, but," Emily said, "it was all rigged. The court took Michael McNaughton's word."

"So what does that have to do with Warren Matthews?"

"He paid Michael McNaughton."

"Do you have the receipt?"

"I know he did it. Look at all the money McNaughton has. Look at what Judge Seabury tried to prove."

"What Judge Seabury *tried* to prove," Adlerman said, "is of no consequence. What a court of law *did* prove is that you were a prostitute. What you yourself admitted on this witness stand is that you still *are* a prostitute. Do you want to recant your testimony, Miss Stanton?"

"No."

"Then you are a prostitute, or aren't you?"

Emily squeezed her fingers together nervously, out of sight of the jurors. She struggled to maintain her composure, but the strain was showing on her face. "I'm not . . . I am, I have been, but I wasn't then."

"You *are* a prostitute!" Adlerman said, wiping the sweat off his brow at the difficulty of extracting Emily's last statement.

"I worked as a call girl, but I'm through."

"Yes, Miss Stanton," Adlerman said.

"I'm not going to do it anymore," Emily said. Leibowitz subtly shook his head at her, indicating that she should elaborate no further, but Emily felt her honor, or what was left of it, was at stake. She had to repeat herself, for Jessica, for Alex, for everyone who was looking down on her. "I had no choice."

"You always have a choice, Miss Stanton," Adlerman

railed at her, pacing back and forth in a crescent between the witness stand and the jury box. He moved so furiously that his red tie had flown over his left shoulder and one of his collar points was protruding outside his vest. "Perhaps you just wanted to be rich. This was an easy way, wasn't it?"

"I couldn't get a job."

"You mean you couldn't get a job that paid what you wanted, Miss Stanton. But couldn't you have gotten some job, cleaning, waitressing, something perhaps not so glamorous . . ."

"Maybe, but . . ."

"So you admit that you could have gotten another job, a *legal* job."

"I needed more money."

"We *all* need more money. We all have fantasies of being rich. But does that justify you in breaking the law?" Adlerman asked.

"It's not a fantasy. I wanted to see my daughter. Warren Matthews wouldn't let me. I had to hire a lawyer to fight for visitation rights. Lawyers don't work for free. Would you have, Mr. Adlerman?" He didn't answer, and Emily went on. "Justice costs a lot. I couldn't afford it as a charwoman. I love my daughter, more than myself. A lot more. So I sold myself, yes, I degraded myself, to see my daughter. And you know what? It was worth it. It was worth all the pain, all the humiliation, all the torment, to see her. Yes, it was."

"Was it worth killing Warren Matthews?"

"I told you I didn't kill him. I love my daughter too much. If I had killed him, I'd go to prison or to the electric chair and then I wouldn't see my daughter and that's what I'm living for. Not rich men, not my apartment, not my clothes. These are props. That's my work. My daughter's my *life*. I don't want to be separated from her again. Ever! I may be angry, Mr. Adlerman, but I'm not crazy. I'm not crazy." Emily let go. She was crying for the first time in the trial. She couldn't stop herself. She didn't care.

"But you wished he was dead," Adlerman repeated again, as he had so many times.

"Wishing and killing aren't the same. He destroyed my

career. He destroyed my being a mother. He framed me—"

"Where is your proof, Miss Stanton? Just tell me that."

"I'm the proof," Emily screamed at him and stood up in the witness box. "Look at me! *I'm* the proof!"

"You have quite an imagination, Miss Stanton. And as everyone in the courtroom can see, quite a temper." Adlerman refused to look at her. Instead, he looked at the jury, with a self-satisfied look of pity for this insane woman he was certain he was going to throw away the keys on. "No further questions."

82

Samuel Leibowitz was very pleased with Emily's testimony. "You were sensational," he told her. "Very believable on both direct *and* cross. Adlerman made no yardage with you."

Despite her lawyer's praise and the catharsis her testimony provided, Emily wasn't optimistic. And she was bristling over I. J. Adlerman's announcement to the press after she testified that he was going to call Michael McNaughton to the stand "to show that this city," he said, "will bend over backward to give this woman a fair trial. And," Adlerman added, making one of his rare attempts at humor, "to save Mr. Leibowitz a trip to the Finger Lakes. He can have his own fishing expedition right here in the Bronx. But I'm afraid our lake is bone dry."

Leibowitz was delighted, both publicly and privately, at the chance to cross-examine McNaughton. He said Adlerman's move in calling the star vice officer to the stand showed that the prosecution realized they were in trouble. Emily's credible testimony, he believed, had put them on the ropes. But Emily wondered. Here, once again, it was her word against Tammany's, and Tammany was the law. Emily saw the upcoming McNaughton testimony as the final Tammany public-relations ploy, to show the city once and for all that Tammany was right. And that Emily Stanton was wrong, and Judge Seabury was wrong, and all the critics were wrong.

Emily was reading a tabloid piece about her alibi under the headline "WHERE'S TOMMY?" at the House of Detention when she was told she had a visitor. It was Bridgit

Lund, all dressed in a dreadful shade of reddish-orange, with too much lipstick and very high heels to match her overly tight chemise dress. Emily grimaced. Bridgit's presence reflected badly on her, if only to the guards at the jail.

"Emily, I feel so awful," Bridgit said, embracing her amid a cloud of perfume.

"Thanks for coming by," Emily said, trying to be gracious. "How are you?"

"Terrible," Bridgit wailed.

"Why?"

"I feel so guilty. I coulda helped you. I was selfish."

"It's okay, Bridgit. It wouldn't have mattered."

"Naw, it ain't okay. Polly was rotten to leave. And Texas Guinan playing sick. Nobody's helping you."

"It's all right," Emily said. "Please. Tell me about yourself."

"I shoulda gone with you to that Judge Seabis . . . Seabury."

"No, Bridgit. Stop worrying about it," Emily said. "One more word against theirs wouldn't have made any difference. But you're really nice to think of me." She was touched by Bridgit's outpouring of support. She hadn't thought the young woman was capable of such compassion.

"Us girls gotta stick together. I want to go to court now and testify for you."

"Thanks," Emily said as she leaned across the table and kissed Bridgit's brightly rouged cheek. "Bridgit, I wish you could, but it just wouldn't matter. You didn't see me that night."

"But I'd testify about McNaughton. How he framed me."

Emily had almost forgotten. "Bridgit, in the state I'm in, I didn't remember that *he* was the one . . . That *would* help. Of course it would."

"But that's not even the *good* part."

"What do you mean?"

"Remember back in Bedford when I told you how I got framed?"

"Sure."

"Well, the guy who picked me up, who introduced me to McNaughton, I had forgotten about him."

"So?"

"He was real handsome. Real charming."

"They all are," Emily said, not understanding what Bridgit was babbling about.

"Emily, I know you think I'm really dumb, don't you?"

"No, Bridgit, I'm just upset about all this, and—"

"Emily, I've been reading about your trial every day in the papers. I can help you. You see, this guy who introduced me to Michael McNaughton, the guy who set it all up, he looked a lot like Rudolph Valentino. I'm sure it's the same guy as Tommy Catania. It was him, the Sheik. I swear it was."

83

In his blue uniform, with his chiseled features and his military bearing, Michael McNaughton was the ideal authority figure, the kind of policeman who made New Yorkers feel safe to walk the streets at night. I. J. Adlerman had just finished with McNaughton on direct testimony, in which McNaughton denied, with indignation, the charge by Emily that he had framed her for prostitution and Leibowitz' implication that he was involved in Warren Matthews' death.

Leibowitz asked him on cross, "Do you like children, Officer McNaughton?"

"Of course I do," McNaughton said.

"Of course you do," Leibowitz echoed. "And I'm sure you remember the fire at the Allwyn Apartments in 1922."

"Yes. Certainly."

"Could you tell the jury how you were involved?"

"Yes. A young boy, Jimmy Frank, I believe he was five, was locked in his room during the fire. I was nearby, saw the flames, and came to assist the fire department."

"You were decorated for rescuing him, weren't you?"

"Yes, sir. I was."

"How did you get in to save the boy, Officer McNaughton? They had very big oak doors at the Allwyn, if I remember. Did you break the door down?"

"Not at all," McNaughton said. "I just jimmied the lock. It wasn't hard."

Adlerman, seeing the direction Leibowitz was going, as did everyone else in the courtroom, didn't dare object to the line of questioning. The relevance couldn't have

428

been more obvious, and any objection could only be construed by the jury as an effort on his part to suppress the truth. So he judiciously held back. What he could not hold back was the spontaneous cold perspiration that dampened his shirt.

"You have quite a heroic record, Officer," Leibowitz said. "Two years later you were decorated for saving the life of one Louise Minichelli. Is that right?"

"Yes, sir. It was a suicide attempt."

"Yes. It was in all the papers. She lived in that tall building on West Fifty-seventh Street. In one of the maids' rooms at the top. She was despondent that her employers were planning to move, to lay her off, wasn't she?"

"I believe that was the story, sir. Yes."

"And she was standing on the ledge outside her window, threatening to jump."

"She was halfway in and halfway out."

"Did you come to her on the ledge? That's a very tall building."

"No, sir. I came through her room."

"How did you do that without frightening her? She might have jumped before you got to her."

"I was very quiet. I surprised her from behind."

"But how did you get in? Was the door open?"

"No, sir. I opened the lock."

"Did you have a key?"

"No, sir."

"You're quite good with locks, aren't you, Officer McNaughton?" Leibowitz said.

"I wouldn't say that."

"But you can open a lock."

"Sometimes. Yes."

"When you were growing up in Boston as a teenager, didn't you work for two summers at the Heidelberg Lock and Key Store in Mattapan?"

McNaughton hesitated. He was as surprised by the question as was Emily, who looked back into the spectator section of the courtroom to exchange a wide-eyed glance with Alex. They were amazed at how well Samuel Leibowitz had done his homework.

"Yes, sir. I did," McNaughton answered.

"Officer McNaughton, did you enter the apartment of Emily Stanton early on the morning of February 11?"

"No, sir." McNaughton bristled. "I did not."

"I object, your honor," Adlerman yelled. "Who is on trial here? The defendant or the witness?" Adlerman was florid. His jaw was clenched. He stamped up to the bench, waiting for a ruling.

"Sustained," Judge Katz said. The court's ruling was irrelevant. Leibowitz' point had been made, in spades.

"Officer McNaughton, did you ever work with a man who looked like Rudolph Valentino?"

"That's such a subjective thing. It's hard to say. A lot of men on the force have sideburns and slick hair, but to me they don't look like Valentino did."

Leibowitz was all patience. "Very well. Officer McNaughton, did you ever work with a man who fits the description the defendant gave of the man she thought was one Tommy Catania?"

"What do you mean by 'work with'? I really don't understand."

"Someone who located or set up prostitutes for you."

"Of course not."

"Did you ever work with any man, on the force or off, who looked in any way like Rudolph Valentino? Please answer the question, Officer."

"No," McNaughton said at last.

"And you never framed Emily Stanton in 1924?" Leibowitz asked with sarcasm in his voice.

"Of course not."

"And you of course didn't frame any other women?"

"Of course not."

"And you of course didn't kill or have anything at all to do with the murder of Warren Matthews," Leibowitz went on.

"That's absurd."

"Let me ask you this, Officer McNaughton. If—perish the thought—you had murdered Warren Matthews, would you be honest with this jury and tell the truth?"

"Yes . . . I would. I'd never lie under oath."

"I see, Officer McNaughton. Even if you had the ultimate immorality to murder a fellow human being, you would never possess the terrible, terrible immorality to deny it under oath. That makes immense sense, Officer. No further questions," Leibowitz announced.

Adlerman stood up. "Judge, those weren't questions. Defense counsel is already making his summation to the jury. I would ask this court to reprimand counsel."

"You should have objected earlier, Mr. Adlerman, instead of listening so raptly to Mr. Leibowitz', quote, summation," Judge Katz said.

It couldn't have been more obvious to everyone in the courtroom: Samuel Leibowitz had not lost his touch.

Adlerman, now more worried than ever, proceeded to present evidence that Michael McNaughton could not have been the person who killed Warren Matthews. McNaughton's alibi was provided by his aunt, Billie Fitzpatrick, with whom he lived on Sixty-eighth Street and Third Avenue. Mrs. Fitzpatrick was a winsome but frail elderly woman with an Irish brogue. When she was rolled to the witness stand in a wheelchair, Emily's heart sank.

"Michael is a wonderful boy," she testified in a girlish lilt a half-century younger than she was. "Every week he brings me flowers."

"And on the night of February 10?" Adlerman asked.

"That night he came home around ten o'clock. I was awake, couldn't sleep a wink. He made me some nice warm milk. Tucked me into bed. He's the sweetest boy."

"Is it possible he went back out again, Mrs. Fitzpatrick?"

"Oh, no. He went to sleep."

"Are you sure?"

"Oh, yes. He said good night and went to sleep. You see, for the last month or so, he'd been working on the day shift. By ten o'clock, he was usually bone-tired. And besides, I'm a needle-and-pins sleeper. If Michael had gone back out, I would have surely heard it. The boy works so hard. He loves this city. But he always tells me. He's a fine boy, like a grandson to me."

"Thank you, Mrs. Fitzpatrick. I have no further questions of this witness."

"Mrs. Fitzpatrick, I want to thank you for coming to court today, ma'am. I have just a few questions for you," Samuel Leibowitz said as he commenced his cross-examination. "I know that your nephew, Officer McNaughton, has been working on the day shift for the past couple of months, but he certainly is out now and then at night after ten o'clock, is he not?"

"Oh, yes. Not too often. But from time to time."

"How often would you estimate, Mrs. Fitzpatrick?"

"Oh, maybe once a week. Twice. Michael's been working so hard, and I've been begging him to come home early and get some rest. I think he's finally starting to listen to me."

"Yes. Let's see. He started the day shift at the beginning of February and we're now in the middle of March. At the rate of once or twice a week, that would mean your nephew was probably out at night after ten o'clock between six and twelve times during this period, is that correct?"

"Yes, it sounds about right."

"Do you know what nights they were that he was out past ten during this time?"

"Oh, my golly. I couldn't possibly remember something like that."

"What is it, then, Mrs. Fitzpatrick, about the tenth of February that makes you certain that he came home at ten o'clock?"

"Why, he told me just a few days ago that he did," she answered without blinking.

"I see, Mrs. Fitzpatrick. Well, again, I want to thank you for coming to court today."

"Why, thank you," she said. "I've enjoyed talking to you, Mr. Leibowitz. I know you from the papers."

"There are certain things that are impossible to beat," said one reporter to another in the back of the courtroom. "One of them is an Irish grandmother in a wheelchair. But I think Leibowitz just did the impossible. They must be sweating blood at Tammany."

The courtroom wags wondered what Leibowitz was going to do next. After Adlerman was through on rebuttal, Leibowitz called Bridgit Lund to the stand on surrebuttal. Bridgit had been instructed to "dress down" for the occasion. Her idea of dressing down was to wear slightly less lipstick. Her black dress was more appropriate to a cabaret or dance hall than to the courtroom. Nevertheless, her testimony would have quickly dispelled any attempt to conceal her occupation.

"Miss Lund, could you state your occupation?" Leibowitz asked.

"You could say I'm a party girl."

"What is that? Could you explain, please?"

"Well, I go out and have a good time with people," she trilled, and the spectators smiled.

"And you do this for a living?"

"Well, I don't do it for my health."

The courtroom roared. Judge Katz demanded decorum. After a few moments, he got it.

"So you go out and have a good time for money, is that correct?" Leibowitz continued.

"Yes."

"In other words, you are a call girl?"

"Well, you could use those words. I don't like it, but you could put it that way." Bridgit pouted.

"Do you know the defendant, Emily Stanton?" Leibowitz said, glancing at his client.

"I do."

"For how long?"

"We go way back. Nineteen twenty-five it was. That makes me seem old."

"Would you please confine your answers to the questions asked, Miss Lund," Judge Katz interjected.

"Sorry, sir." Bridgit blushed.

"Where did you meet the defendant?" was Leibowitz's next question.

"At Bedford Prison."

"And why were you there?"

"I was convicted of prostitution."

"When were you arrested?"

"Nineteen twenty-four."

"By whom?"

"Officer Michael McNaughton."

"Where?"

"In the Cherokee Hotel."

"Miss Lund, could you tell us the circumstances of your arrest?"

"Well, I was at the Astor Bar, and I got picked up by this very charming guy who wanted to introduce me to his bigwig friend."

"Who was the man who picked you up?"

"His name was Oscar Salomon. Sounded to me like a fish. He said he was in the fur business. A fish in the fur business, imagine."

"And then what happened?"

"He said his friend was in from out of town, from Hollywood, that he was a big picture producer. I thought he might give me a break. I mean, it happens to girls sometimes. I've read about things like that. Why not me?"

"Miss Lund, could you please go on," Judge Katz said.

"Sorry, Judge. So Mr. Salomon introduces me to his friend and says maybe I could show him a good time."

"Did you?"

"I never got the chance. I woulda loved to. I mean, these were the two most gorgeous guys I've ever seen. But Mr. Salomon took off. And Mr. Producer, well, he talked a beautiful game, you know, all the big promises, my name in lights, but the minute we got up to his room, zoom, he threw the cuffs on me and tried to shake me down. Boy, one minute I'm in lights, the next I'm in the clink. Some luck!"

"And you did not ask for money or otherwise attempt to commit prostitution?"

"Like I said, I didn't get the chance. The big producer turned out to be a big cop." Bridgit described how the frame-up worked and how she didn't have the money to pay the bribe, and how she was sentenced to Bedford, just as Emily had outlined on the stand earlier in the week.

Then Leibowitz asked her, "Do you see this man who pretended to be a producer here in the courtroom?"

"I sure do," Bridgit said. "I couldn't forget a handsome mug like that. There he is. Officer McNaughton." She pointed at him in the spectator section. He didn't flinch.

"Thank you, Miss Lund," Leibowitz said. "And his friend, Oscar Salomon. Do you see him here today?"

Bridgit scanned the galleries and shook her head. "No, sir. He's not here."

"Could you describe what he looked like?"

"Easy," Bridgit said. "He looked just like Rudolph Valentino."

84

Bridgit Lund completed her testimony on a late Friday afternoon. On Saturday, the *Daily News* screamed in its morning edition, "VALENTINO LOOK-ALIKE SHAKES PROSECUTION IN STANTON CASE." On Saturday afternoon, Samuel Leibowitz had gone to his office to catch up on his other cases and read his mail. A major bootlegger in New Orleans named Lafayette Beauregard had been arrested for the murder of his chief rival, out in Plaquemines Parish. Beauregard's family had sent Leibowitz a first-class ticket on the *Southern Crescent* and a check for two thousand dollars to come south and discuss the case. He had just drafted a letter respectfully returning the ticket and the check to the Beauregards when he was surprised by a man and woman who knocked at his door. The couple apologized for the intrusion and introduced themselves as Mr. and Mrs. Ralph Fischer. The man, around fifty, with a weather-beaten complexion and heavily calloused hands, had a lumber business in Yonkers. His wife, Helena, was half his age, delicate and white, all indoors to her husband's outdoors. She was so distraught at first that Leibowitz thought he might have had another murder case to deal with.

"Mr. Leibowitz, I want to confess something," Helena Fischer wept.

"What is it?" Leibowitz inquired.

Her husband put his arm around her.

"I used to be a stenographer down on Wall Street," she stammered. "Mr. Leibowitz"—she took a deep breath

435

to stop her tears—"about five years ago, before I ever met Ralph, I got caught up in the whole crazy money thing. I never had enough, never thought I was ever going to get married, not unless I had better clothes and . . . you know, sir. Well, then I met this girl in a coffee shop, a beautiful girl, very beautiful, and she said there's an easy way to make some quick dough."

"Who was this girl?" Leibowitz asked.

"Her name was Candace Mitchell. Very tall red-head, very classy girl. Perfect creamy skin, I'll never forget."

"You met her in a coffee shop?"

"Yes. We used to sit at the counter and chat."

"Do you know where she is now?"

"Oh, no. She disappeared after it happened."

"Tell me."

"Yes. So this beautiful woman—and the reason I trusted her was that she was so pretty, I couldn't imagine anyone that pretty ever telling a lie—well, she told me she knew this very attractive, very rich guy coming in from out of town, from Santiago, Chile, big shipping guy, who wanted companionship. And he would pay me seventy-five dollars. I'm so ashamed," Mrs. Fischer broke down again. "I'm so ashamed."

"Go ahead. It's all right," Mr. Fischer encouraged her.

"I agreed to try it. It seemed like so much money. So much money for just a few hours. I was earning thirty dollars a week. So I said yes. The man, he was everything she said he was. His name was Ramon de la Cruz, I'll never forget it. But then he took me to this hotel, the Longacre, the same one I read in the papers Emily Stanton said she went to. And I thought, why was this big man taking me to this crummy hotel? And then this cop broke the door down and arrested me. Ramon de la Cruz looked just like Rudolph Valentino. And the vice-squad guy was Michael McNaughton."

"What did you do?" Leibowitz asked. "Did you go to court?"

"Never. I paid this bail bondsman my life savings, a thousand dollars, and he got the case dropped. He told me he knew someone. And the next year, thank God, I met Ralph. I never mentioned this to anyone. But when I heard about Miss Stanton pouring her heart out up there, and then her friend, I thought: I just have to help that woman."

The next morning, Leibowitz returned to his office on a hunch that some more unexpected callers might arrive on the Sabbath. He was so confident and so elated from the previous day's surprise by-product of Emily's testimony that he invited Alex Foster to come up and join him.

The lawyer's hunch paid off. They weren't in the office an hour when the telephone rang and a woman with a Southern drawl asked to make an appointment. Leibowitz had her come right over.

Amy Cross was a fine-boned girl in her early twenties from Wilson, North Carolina. Her father was a prosperous tobacco grower. She had lovely skin and graceful hands, slightly wayward hazel eyes, and an alluring throaty voice. She reminded Alex of the cotillion dances back in Charleston when the girls from the old families had too many mint juleps and thus, under the influence, abandoned their old-family constraints for tantalizing encounters on the verandas and in the rose gardens, only to regain their prim countenances for services at the Anglican Church the Sunday morning after. Leibowitz introduced Alex as "my colleague" to put Amy Cross at ease, and they talked about their Southern ties. In fact, under other circumstances Alex might have been quite taken by Amy. Under the present ones, he was only taken by what she was going to add to the case at hand.

"Two years ago I came up north to have a good time. As you know," she said, keeping a flirtatious eye contact with Alex, "there are a limited number of these good times back where I'm from. And Daddy said, 'You go on up there and have all the good times you want, long as you don't come back here with no Yankee husband.' So what I want to talk about is one of those good times. I blush when I say this, but I have a fatal weakness for a certain type of tall-dark-and-handsome man, and when that same man tells me he's not only rich but that he's a horse breeder from *Kentucky*—now, technically that's a border state, but he's certainly no Yankee—and that he's getting into the theater and producing this Cole Porter musical . . ."

Alex and Leibowitz turned to each other and both lit up in huge smiles that baffled Amy Cross. She went on to explain that this Kentucky gentleman, whose name was Ashley Lasell, invited her to his room at the Savoy, where he arrested her for prostitution. Ashley Lasell was Michael McNaughton, and Amy Cross was able to pay the twelve-hundred-dollar bribe to have the false charge dropped only by telling her father, who might not have understood or bought the prostitution frame-up, that she needed an abortion.

"He asked me if I loved the man. 'Cause if I did, he thought I should go ahead and get married. After all, I was twenty-one years old, and down South, as you well know, that's getting a little long in the tooth," Amy said, batting her long lashes at Alex. "So I was on the spot and I said, 'Daddy, although I like him, I'm not sure I love him, and I must confess to you that his last name is Levine and he is from Trenton, New Jersey.' Well, that was all it took. He sent me the money right away, really fast."

"We need your help, you know." Leibowitz said the obvious.

"I know. And I want to help. That woman. You know, I forgot about the whole thing. I figured New York, these are the kinds of things that happen in the big city. That this was *normal* up here. But then I saw how Emily Stanton was suffering, and I saw that Ashley Lasell lying through his teeth on the witness stand. I just thought: That man has *got* to go. Think of all the other women he's done this to. I want to speak my piece. I didn't do anything wrong. Besides, I'm moving to Atlanta in April. I've got nothing to lose."

Because of the emerging pattern, Leibowitz requested and was granted a four-day recess of the trial. Rosalie Gottlieb, a mother from Queens, had also been recruited by a stunning redhead for a paid one-night stand with a Venezuelan oil millionaire who looked like Valentino.

Dottie Bridges, a waitress from Washington Heights, moonlighted as a good-time girl until she met a Valentino look-alike at Billy La Hiff's Tavern. The man said he was an architect from Madrid. Michael McNaughton arrested her just as she was undressing and clinking champagne glasses with the Spaniard at the Piccadilly Hotel. She paid seven hundred dollars to the bondsman, who had the case disposed of. Elise Langley, of Santa Rosa, California, was, like Amy Cross, a well-to-do girl who had come to the big city for fun and romance. Instead, she found Michael McNaughton, again posing as a Broadway impresario, and after two dates and what promised to be the love of her life, ended up paying him fifteen hundred dollars to avoid a prostitution frame-up and the ensuing humiliation.

In all, twenty-three women called Samuel Leibowitz and offered to testify for Emily Stanton. Some had been prostitutes. Others had not. All had been framed by Michael McNaughton and his accomplices. Every one of them had paid the required bribe and gone on with her life, yet each cared enough about this woman whose life was on the line to do something to help her. Emily's own testimony had thus accomplished what Judge Seabury and all his hearings had failed to do: it got the women of New York to talk, to go public, to air the atrocities that, without Emily's pioneering confession, they were ashamed to let anyone know about. When the trial resumed, Leibowitz chose seven of these women to take the stand and tell their tales. Judge Katz refused to allow more than that, saying the evidence was cumulative.

"And all I ask you is, *so what?*" I. J. Adlerman said in his opening argument to the jury. "Have we found this dashing Latin lover? Have we found this stunning dragon lady? After all these years, don't you think someone would come forward and tell us who they are? Gentlemen, we are not trying the New York Police Department. We are not trying the vice squad. There are other tribunals for that. Don't you think Judge Seabury, with all his resources, can find that out?

"Michael McNaughton appeared before Judge Seabury.

He was not indicted for anything. Michael McNaughton opens locks, yes. To prevent suicides. To rescue children. Not to kill people. Not to frame people. And these so-called witnesses. These women you heard. Weren't most of these women engaging in prostitution? Weren't they committing a crime? And the others, they admitted they had come to New York for good times. Do we really know what kind of 'good times' they were having? Do we really believe them? But now they all come to court and cry for sisterhood. I think what we are hearing here is not about innocence. No, we are hearing about guilt.

"But let us get back to the crime at hand. We have a weapon, a motive, a victim, and a guilty woman. A very guilty woman. Gentlemen of the jury, what we have here is the unsubstantiated alibi of a convicted prostitute, a self-proclaimed prostitute, who serves illegal drinks and takes illegal drugs. You have her alibi. Against the thorough investigation of the finest police department in the world. Her prints were on the murder weapon. Her lipstick holder was by the body. Her hatred of her dead husband is emblazoned on her face.

"We came here to search for the truth. We have found it. Let us not turn this courtroom into Little Seabury. Leave that to the judge. We are here to do justice about a murder, a murder of a young, vigorous man with everything to live for and no reason to die, no reason except the hatred of a woman who wanted more than he, or any man, could give her. A man shouldn't die because he couldn't do enough for an insatiable woman. No, gentlemen. Let the truth be known. I know in your hearts you will do what is right, by the victim's family, by your city, by yourselves. I ask you to come back with the only verdict that is possible, the only verdict that is based on the evidence. And that is the verdict of guilty as charged." Adlerman sat down to a packed but silent courtroom.

Samuel Leibowitz paced up and down in front of the jury, looking at each man, one by one, almost like a shopper examining some fine goods, before beginning his summation. "Gentlemen, we have something remarkable going on here," he started, in his most sonorous, pleasant voice. "We have more than a trial. We have a new beginning. We have a city renewing its pride. We have people standing up for what is right and speaking out against what is wrong.

"People say New York is a cold city. A cruel city. An unforgiving city. Now, I don't believe that, but if I ever had my doubts, my doubts are over. We have seen woman after woman come forward, risking her marriage, her career, her reputation, to help another woman by telling the truth. These women not only wanted to help Emily Stanton. They wanted to help New York. Kindness to strangers is a beautiful thing. It makes me feel very good.

"Emily Stanton *is* guilty," Leibowitz said, setting off whispers. "Yes. She's guilty of bad luck, bad judgment, bad taste in men. But she's not guilty of murder. She's not guilty of killing Warren Matthews. Emily Stanton is no saint. She's made her share of mistakes, more than her share. She's done things you wouldn't want your wives or your daughters to do. But we're not here to pass judgment on Emily Stanton's morals. We're here to pass judgment on whether she is guilty of murder, and that's why I'm proud to defend her.

"At first I wasn't proud. I didn't even want the case. A prostitute who killed her millionaire ex-husband. Made sense to me. Sure, why not? She failed. He succeeded. The great equalizer was a gun. But a friend of Emily Stanton's sold me on giving her a hearing. And once I started listening, I decided the case wasn't so open-and-shut. But I was never prepared—and I'm usually prepared—for the outpouring of evidence from the women of New York City. We've heard not one, not two, but seven women. No, no one saw the smoking gun. No one knows who the Valentino look-alike actually is. But from the testimony of these other women, we know he is not a figment of Emily Stanton's imagination, and therefore we have every reason to believe her testimony that she was with him the night of the murder.

"No, I don't know who killed Warren Matthews. I do know Emily Stanton did not kill him. Surely, at the very minimum, you have a reasonable doubt as to her guilt, and, accordingly, under the law, she is entitled to a not-guilty verdict. This woman has bared her soul to you, admitted to being a call girl. If she were a calculating murderess, she'd have a more conventional alibi than that. No, what we have here is an elaborate frame-up by people who know all about evidence, all about Warren Matthews, and all about Emily Stanton.

"This is very sophisticated work. It's a perfect job. Too perfect. There's something nonhuman about this murder. It reeks of a machine, a machine you and I know the name of, a machine that has perverted the government of this city. That machine is Tammany Hall. It is a money machine, a graft machine, a murder machine. All it knows is money and power, and God help anyone who tries to shut it down. Emily Stanton was trying to shut it down. She wanted to talk. The machine didn't want her to. And this sophisticated machine decided to kill two birds with one gun. Warren Matthews was under pressure from Emily Stanton. He might have broken, so he had to go. And once he was gone, and Emily Stanton framed for it, the machine said, 'Let her talk now. No one will believe her.' Emily Stanton is the perfect setup. A hooker. She hated her husband. Who *would* believe her? That was the machine's scenario.

"I want to find out who really murdered Warren Matthews. So do you. So does Emily Stanton, because it will complete the mission she set out on. A not-guilty verdict will be a call to justice, a rallying cry, to restore good government to this city, to end corruption, to let New York flourish and live up to its destiny as the greatest city on earth. Remember, my friends, if the machine could do this to Emily Stanton, it can do it to you. Look at what is beginning in Germany, a fascist state where the citizens fear their elected officials. Let us not have a police state. Let the fear end. Let Emily Stanton go free. Let this city live in safety. Let your conscience speak to you. Come back with the only verdict there can be here, not guilty."

Although the courtroom remained silent, Emily smiled for the first time in months. Nor was her optimism shattered by I. J. Adlerman's final summation. After the salvo of his opening argument, the sting was missing from his words. He seemed to know that the Valentino issue smelled bad and could easily raise a reasonable doubt in the jury's mind. Nonetheless, he doggedly mouthed the words that "The evidence of Emily Stanton's guilt is overwhelming" and the cautionary "Don't be taken in by the eloquence of the counsel for the defense. Eloquence is not evidence." Adlerman closed with a plea for "justice in this city." It was, in effect, the same plea Leibowitz had made. At the end, Emily was no longer afraid of the result. Adlerman took his seat. She smiled once more.

85

On March 23, only one day after they had begun their deliberations, the jury announced that it had reached a verdict. All the optimism Emily had felt at the close of the final summations completely vanished. Leibowitz had told Emily that the jury might be out for several days, perhaps even a week. Why had the jury decided so quickly? she worried. As the moment of the verdict was now upon her, she dreaded the worst, that Tammany had so brainwashed the people of New York that they would instantly endorse whatever official position Tammany put before them, just as they would elect its slate of candidates. If Tammany said Emily Stanton was guilty, so be it.

Those were the anxieties that darted through Emily's fevered mind as she waited for the bailiff to lead the jury into the box. The courtroom was the most jammed it had been. Every seat, every place along the walls, in the aisles, was taken. Alex was sitting in the middle of the room, craning his neck, trying to catch Emily's eye if she turned around so that he could give her one last wave, one last wink of support. But she didn't move.

"All rise," the bailiff said, and brought the jury in. Emily stood, her heart racing, trying to tell from the men's blank faces what her future was going to be. The very blankness upset her. Why were they so dour? she fretted. Were they sending her away for life?

"Be seated," Judge Katz ordered. "*People versus Emily Stanton.* Gentlemen of the jury, have you reached a verdict?"

Daniel Lister, the travel agent who served as foreman,

rose from the first chair of the first row of the box. "We have, your honor."

"The defendant will please rise," Judge Katz said.

Emily again stood up.

"What is your verdict?" Judge Katz asked.

The wait was the longest five seconds of Emily's life.

"We find the defendant Emily Stanton . . . not guilty."

Emily stood petrified for an instant, as if unable to grasp the power and significance of these miraculous words. Then, bursting with joy, she threw her arms around Samuel Leibowitz and then ran to the jury box, kissing each and every member of the panel. Finally, the jurors smiled.

Dodging swarms of reporters with an ecstatic smile that said all that she had no words for, she and Alex escaped through the side door of the courthouse into a March on-and-off drizzle. They caught a cab to go downtown to her apartment. However, when they had crossed the bridge over the Harlem River at 135th Street and began driving down First Avenue, Emily decided to stop and get out of the taxi.

"I'm free," she cried. "I want to feel it with my feet."

"It's so nasty out." Alex hesitated.

"Not to me."

"You don't want to wait until Fifth Avenue?"

"Uh-uh," Emily said. "Let's do it now. Besides, they read different papers up here."

"It's your day." Alex smiled.

When they closed the taxi door behind them, the last gasp of winter in New York became spring in Naples. They were at 116th Street and First Avenue, Italian Harlem. The street market below the grimy four-story tenements was going full bore. Vendors in aprons hawked fresh *finocchio* and *calamari*, *scungilli* and *fagioli*, in operatic voices. There were gaudy *pasticcerias* flaunting statues of the Virgin Mary in the windows with the displays of sweets. There were fragrant pizzerias and neighborhood "social clubs" with names like the Palermo Benevolent Association, and ragtag clothing stores, and at least one barber shop on every block. Only the distant rumble from the Second Avenue el and an incongruous recording of "Minnie the Moocher" playing in a café gave any hint that not only were they in New York City, but that black Harlem was only blocks away to the north and west.

"I love this city," Emily said. "I never realized how much until right now. Do you realize it's been seven years since I've felt like a human being? Seven years since I was free. Even when I got out of Bedford, I was free but I really wasn't, because of the stigma. But now somehow I feel that the stigma is gone."

"I feel almost as good as you do," Alex said.

Watching the old Italian men playing *boccie* in the mist in Thomas Jefferson Park, Emily and Alex got so hungry from all the delicious aromas of baking bread and frying garlic that they decided to have a celebratory meal at the Amalfi Café, a crumbling storefront trattoria.

Inside there were wooden booths, the obligatory checkered tablecloths, and perennial Christmas decorations. Over a bottle of cheap but good Chianti, Emily talked to Alex about her first and highest priority, her daughter.

"Now I'm going to devote myself to getting her back," Emily said. "But can I?"

"You were vindicated today. Everyone in New York knows that you should have never lost her to begin with," Alex told her.

"Yes, but . . . everybody in New York knows what I do . . . *did*," Emily corrected herself.

"You said it all right there." Alex smiled.

"That's all over. Forever. It's a new life. But how do I go about trying to get her? I guess I have to go back to . . . ugh . . . court—I never want to see another courtroom—and . . . face Isabelle . . . and . . . Alex, it's another battle."

"You won today. You'll win again."

Emily kissed his cheek warmly.

While they waited for their food, Emily went to the ladies' room. Alex rushed outside to buy her a reduced-scale, primitive version of Michelangelo's *Last Judgment*. He had spotted it at a street vendor's stand and thought it would be an amusing way to commemorate this moment of Emily's triumph. It cost ten dollars. In the picture, God was depicted as a stern judge condemning the wicked. Demons were carrying off some victims. The boat of Charon was ferrying still others to hell. "Let's call the style Harlem Renaissance. May this always remind you of how you brought Tammany down," he told Emily as he presented the painting to her.

Emily hugged Alex. "Maybe. But this was just one day. One setback."

"I think this is the beginning of the end for them."

"I hope so, but I wonder," Emily said. "There's this poem, by Shakespeare, I think, that I read at Bedford. It ends, 'So out again I curve and flow to join the brimming river. For men may come—' "

" '—and men may go, but I go on forever,' " Alex joined her in completing the verse.

"Great minds think alike," Emily laughed. They toasted each other.

"The Brook," Alex said. "Tennyson. I love that."

"Tennyson, not Shakespeare. And here I was quoting poetry to the English major, the playwright. See how giddy I am."

"Quote away," Alex said. "I didn't realize we had poetry in common."

"We've got so much in common," Emily said. "Alex, you're the greatest pal a woman could ever have. I can't tell you how much I appreciate . . . No, I take that back."

"I don't understand."

"You always hated being a pal."

"I got over that a long time ago."

"Well, I've really been thinking a lot. At the House of Detention, I had nothing but time to think. And I thought a lot about you and how good you've been to me."

"That's what friends are for. I care."

"So do I. You know, when you don't love yourself, you can't really love anyone else. And ever since I've known you, I've never even liked myself very much. But I'm changing. Today I decided I'm all right. I'm not so bad after all. So I think, in the long run, you were right and I was wrong."

"About what?" Alex asked.

"About us," Emily replied.

Alex wasn't sure what to say.

"Alex, what do you think about Hollywood?" Emily

went on in an extremely animated way that had Alex completely off balance.

"The weather's supposed to be good," he said.

"Simon de Ville has kept writing to me. He's still pushing for me to come out for that screen test. Now that this is all over, if I can get custody of Jessica, I think maybe I'll do it."

"I think you should. It's a great chance, the pictures. Of course, I'll miss you terribly, but—"

"Why don't you come out with me? Write in the sun. You can take your pen and paper anywhere."

"Me?" Alex asked. "I mean, Hollywood is full of movie stars and millionaires. I'd be excess baggage. You could get lucky."

"I'm lucky right now," Emily said, and in front of the old people and young waiters leaned across the *linguine alle vongole* and met Alex in the longest, headiest, most intoxicating kiss either of them had ever known.

Back at Emily's apartment, Emily and Alex drank some champagne, played Duke Ellington's new record, "Dreamy Blues," and talked. For Alex, a great wall, a barrier of repression had toppled. He was finally able to love Emily, to speak the wild poetry he had been embarrassed to declare, to unleash the intense passion he had for so long strained to keep within him. As for Emily, she was able to look at Alex the way he had always wanted her to. She liked what she saw.

They were surprised by a knock at the door. The doormen had been given very strict instructions not to admit anyone, to say Emily had gone away indefinitely. But the knock continued, sending chills through Emily, recalling the insistent hammering of the police the morning they came to arrest her for the murder of Warren Matthews. Because she feared another break-in, Emily eventually flung open the door.

Standing in the hall was a beautiful teenage girl carrying a suitcase, better dressed but not that different from the beautiful teenage girl who had arrived in New York from Joliet with a suitcase in 1916. "Mom," Jessica cried, and fell into Emily's arms. "Mom. I'm here."

"Jessica!" Emily knew at last what happiness really was. "Darling, I love you, I love you. I love you!" They kissed and they cried and they looked and looked at each other as if they had never seen each other before. In a way, they hadn't. Not this way.

"How did you get here?" Emily asked.

"By cab from Penn Station. How else?"

"But . . . Isabelle . . . She *let* you?"

"I'm almost fourteen, Mom. She knows I'm going to see you whether she wants me to or not. But she didn't try to stop me. She's all right."

Jessica was glad to see Alex, too. They talked, and laughed, celebrated, like a family. When Alex went down to get some Chinese food for dinner, Emily took the chance to address the issue that was troubling her the most.

"Did you read the papers, darling?" she asked her daughter.

"I know you told me not to, but I did," Jessica said.

"Then I guess you know . . ."

"Know what, Mom?"

"What I did to earn a living," Emily said. "I didn't know how to tell you before. I hope you don't hate me for it."

"How could I hate you, Mom?" Jessica asked her.

"Because . . . because what I had to do . . . wasn't very nice. I hated it when I was framed for it, and then, this thing that I despised the most, that's what I ended up doing."

"Mom, don't worry." Jessica came across the living room from the chair where she was sitting and joined her mother on the couch. "I know women sometimes have to do things they don't want to do. I'm grown up now. I understand. These things just happen. The main thing is that it's over." Jessica thought about what her father had done to her. Now she had someone she could talk to about that. She wasn't afraid anymore. She was home.

449

Epilogue

Moored to the Hudson docks at the end of Fourteenth Street, the Italian liner *Conte Grande*, sailing that afternoon for Genoa, was the focus of hundreds of *bon voyage* parties. Glistening in the still waters in the hazy sunlight, the ship was pristine white, except for its two towering stacks, which were painted red, white, and green, the colors of the Italian flag. These were summer colors, and the *Conte Grande* was in spirit a summer ship, a party ship, transporting its revelers from the steamy September heat of the speakeasies and sidewalks of New York to the equally sweltering, albeit more romantic, *caffes* and *vias anticas* of the Italian peninsula.

A Dixieland band played "When the Saints Go Marching In," almost as if to speed the passengers aboard. White-jacketed stewards scurried about. Despite Prohibition, and despite the depression, champagne corks popped everywhere. In first class, cigar-chomping plutocrats clinked crystal with their wives amidst the cornucopia of steamer baskets brimming with fresh fruit, fine chocolates, and the maze of matching Louis Vuitton trunks, half-empty to allow for new acquisitions along the Via Condotti.

The real fun of the *Conte Grande* was not, however, in the stratosphere of the promenade decks that were once the exclusive preserve of captains and kings. Most celebrity voyagers seeking that sort of exclusivity wouldn't have chosen the *Conte Grande* anyway. The film stars, the sultans, the divas, the diplomats would usually sail on one of the "Big Three"—the *Berengaria*, the *Aquitania*, or the *Mauretania*. The *Conte Grande* was not quite in that league. In fact, its ambience was more that of a mad fraternity bash at sea.

The party was going on in the lower decks, where the many discount travelers were paying ninety dollars round trip to Europe and thereby keeping the luxury liners afloat. Today on the *Conte Grande* a group of Beta Theta Pi boys from the University of Colorado were clowning for a sailing-day photo. Their leader had a life preserver around his neck. A group of post debs and preppy boys from Cos Cob, Connecticut, were enjoying an *ad hoc* tea dance, fox-trotting around the squares on the shuffleboard court of the sports deck. A group of Underwood Typewriter salesmen from around the country were being rewarded with a European junket for their superior performance. They were receiving celebratory bottles of Chivas Regal from their national sales manager, with an accompanying admonition not to break the seal before they broke the three-mile limit.

Although there were no big "names" on the sailing list, the New York press corps was out in its fullest force, jamming the Italian Line terminal, waiting and craning their necks for the one passenger whose name was on none of the lists.

"The ship's sailing in five minutes. I bet this is all a false alarm," Emily Stanton said to Alex Foster on the veranda of the terminal. Worried about being recognized from her own tenure on the front pages the year before, Emily was wearing a big floppy straw hat and dark sunglasses. Today, however, the fourth estate's memory proved short, given the anxious distraction of the big story that was supposed to be breaking here on the docks.

"He's probably taking a train to Florida," Emily said. "This is a smokescreen."

"Nobody goes to Florida in September. He's going to Europe. I know it. Look at this, half the papers in the country are out here."

"When are we going to Europe? Look at the fun they're having."

"How much more traveling do you want? You're going back to Hollywood in December for that screen test."

"Don't look so forlorn, my sweet. You're coming too."

451

"Only if de Ville signs those damn contracts to film *Wedding Belles*. It's been six months."

"I won't leave without you."

"Promise?"

"Promise," Emily said, grazing Alex's cheek. "Let's go to Europe next summer when Jessica gets out of school. The three of us. It's supposed to be so cheap over there."

"Yeah," Alex agreed. "It would be great to go. It really would. But right now, I'd hate to leave New York even for a moment. Thanks to you, we've got a new town"

"You're giving me too much credit, Alex."

"I can't give you enough. Look at the record after you went to Seabury and all the other women followed you. The vice squad abolished. Stanley Renaud removed from the bench. Michael McNaughton in Sing Sing. And now this."

"Getting McNaughton was enormously lucky."

Alex agreed. "The real luck was that Luis Quito had the loyalty of a cockroach. Without him they could have never gotten McNaughton for the murder."

"Tommy Catania," Emily intoned sardonically. "Where is Quito now?"

"I think they deported him to South America. That was the deal. I'm not sure where—Colombia, I think— but I bet he'll end up a dictator someday."

"No. I bet he'll end up in London. That man was made for the stage," Emily rejoined. "Hey. Something's going on." A seismic rustle shook the pier as the reporters shifted their focus from the gangplanks to the terminal. A cordon of uniformed police was forming a flying wedge through the crowd.

"Mr. Mayor! Mr. Mayor! Your honor!" the reporters cried out. But for once in his life, Jimmy Walker, pale, gaunt, and dwarfed by his minions in blue, seemed to have nothing to say. He was dressed for a holiday in a double-breasted, brass-buttoned, blue-flannel blazer, blue-striped white trousers, blue shirt, black-and-white shoes, and a Panama hat.

This was Walker's very first public appearance since he had resigned as mayor of New York City nine days before, on September 1. The revitalization of the Seabury

Commission that had ensued from Emily's acquittal and subsequent testimony before Judge Seabury had caused the Commission to expand its search for municipal corruption until it eventually and inexorably extended to the pinnacle of city government. In May, Walker had been subpoenaed before Seabury, where for two days he gave evasive testimony regarding over a million dollars, most of it in cash, that had passed through Walker's banking and brokerage accounts since he took office in 1926. Walker hid behind the fact that the transactions had all been handled by his accountant, who had fled Seabury's long arm and was now reportedly somewhere in Mexico—just where, Walker insisted, he didn't know.

When ignorance was implausible, the mayor invoked charity. Another quarter of a million dollars was established as having come from a well-heeled friend whose ten-year-old son was distraught that the mayor could not live comfortably on his official salary. *The New Yorker* wrote, after Walker's testimony, that Walker was "the logical chief executive of this town. . . . He has come by large amounts of money with minimum effort. . . . He has spent it without stint. . . . He has traveled widely in foreign lands. . . . In other words, he's the man we all dream about being."

Although the people of New York City may have been amused by Jimmy Walker's fancy dancing before Judge Seabury, Governor Roosevelt was not. In August, the governor summoned the mayor to executive chambers in Albany, where he refused to tolerate Walker's attempts to sidestep his hard questions. Eventually, rather than talk, Walker elected to quit. In his letter of resignation, he denounced Governor Roosevelt as conducting "an extraordinary inquisition. . . . I feel that if I further submit I would demean myself as well as the citizens of New York who have twice honored me by electing me mayor by overwhelming majorities."

Walker slowly eased through the terminal. Emily stared at him. He seemed lost, his confidence drained. On one side of him was a dog, a gray wire-haired terrier. On the other side was a woman Emily recognized as his wife, Allie, dressed in dowdy brown silk and wearing an oversize orchid corsage. Following the Walkers in a small party of civilians were a grim man carrying a black leather doctor's bag, and an elfin man dressed in matching shades of yellow—hat, suit, tie, shoes.

"That's Blumey Blumenthal," Alex noted.

"The theater king," Emily acknowledged. Alfred Cleveland Blumenthal had made millions brokering the sale of chains of movie houses to the Hollywood studios. During the mayor's final crisis, Blumenthal had given him shelter on his Larchmont estate, where, according to nosy reporters, they swam with Ziegfeld girls, screened movies in Blumenthal's private theater, and were pampered by a staff of uniformed servants. Still, none of the alleged sybaritism had any ameliorating effect on Walker, who without his office seemed like a fish out of water, another man altogether. The swagger, the impudence, the charisma, were all gone.

Finally, the entourage stopped. Walker decided to speak. "I really am being shanghaied by a medical man," he told the press, and introduced the man with the black bag as Dr. Schroeder. "I'm leaving for my health," Walker reiterated in a low voice. "I need to get away from desks and telephones."

"Are you going to run again?"

"Will you try to block Governor Roosevelt's try for President?"

"How do you feel about Judge Seabury?"

"When are you coming back, Jimmy?"

The rat-tat-tat of questions from the various reporters had the effect of drowning each other out. The one question that no one asked was Walker's final destination. It was well known that his mistress, Betty Compton, was waiting for the ex-mayor on the French Riviera, but, in this instance, out of respect to his wife, Allie, the reporters held their tongues. One sympathetic pressman from the *Journal-American* did break through and grasped Walker's hand. "Everyone here is for you, Jim," he gushed. "All the world loves a lover."

"No they don't," Walker responded wearily. "All the world loves a winner."

The ship's horn pierced the din for several blasts. A loudspeaker cracked, "All ashore. All ashore. The ship is sailing."

LULLABY AND GOODNIGHT

The Walker entourage pressed on out of the terminal toward the gangway. The throng of reporters parted. Emily removed her dark glasses and stepped forward to get a final look at the man whose political machine had come close to ruining her life. Now, as Alex insisted, she had come full circle in ruining his. And while Emily resisted any temptation to gloat over such reversals— she had lost too much in her life ever to believe that she had truly won—she couldn't resist savoring a certain satisfaction that with Walker's resignation and McNaughton's conviction some justice, in the end, had been done.

As he passed her, Walker's bloodshot eyes somehow connected with Emily's. The old spark wasn't entirely extinguished. A pretty woman could always turn his head. He was about to smile at her. He was on the edge of flashing a bit of the old charm that had made him famous. But then something clicked. He hadn't seen Emily in person for years, the only time being in some speakeasy with Warren Matthews, but it was said he never forgot a face. And surely he had seen that same face, that delicate cameo face, in all the papers the year before. In any event, his smile vanished. He turned ashen. He stared at Emily for a second, at the face that had now destroyed him just as Tammany had nearly destroyed her. Then he cut his eyes away toward the ship. Haunted, he walked onward as if it were his last mile.

Alex joined Emily outside the terminal and watched as Walker kissed his wife good-bye and gave an even warmer embrace to his friend Blumenthal. The ship's horn blew once more. "All ashore. The ship is sailing."

Accompanied only by his dog and a man someone in the crowd said was his valet, Walker boarded the *Conte Grande* without looking back. In the lower decks, none of the collegians or secretaries or young marrieds seemed to notice what was going on onshore. They were looking east to Europe; New York didn't matter now.

As Jimmy Walker disappeared into the ship, Emily and Alex stayed on as the crew threw off the *Conte Grande*'s moorings and the flotilla of tugs shepherded the white vision, gulls flapping in its wake, into the great harbor. Night was beginning to fall. The woolly tufts of smoke from the ship's stacks disappeared into the dusk,

455

the ship's lights came on, and the endless rows of state-rooms twinkled in the deepening haze like diamond neck-laces. The liner had all the glamour of the city she was leaving and of the mayor she was taking away from it. Gathering steam, the *Conte Grande* sailed past the Statue of Liberty until Emily and Alex could see it no longer. Chilled by the hint of fall in the gathering September night, they embraced each other, out of warmth, out of triumph, out of the disequilibrium of change.

Jimmy Walker was gone. Tammany Hall, and New York City, would never be the same.

About the Authors

VINCENT T. BUGLIOSI received his law degree in 1964 from UCLA Law School, where he was president of his graduating class. In his eight-year career as a prosecutor for the Los Angeles District Attorney's office, he tried close to 1,000 felony and misdemeanor court and jury trials. Of 106 felony jury trials, he lost but one case. His most famous trial was, of course, the Charles Manson case, which became the basis of his bestselling book HELTER SKELTER. But even before the Manson case, in the television series The D.A., Actor Robert Conrad patterned his starring role after Bugliosi. His other two books, also bestsellers, were TILL DEATH US DO PART and SHADOW OF CAIN. He lives with his wife, Gail, and children, Wendy and Vincent Jr., in Los Angeles, where he is in private practice.

WILLIAM STADIEM was born in Kinston, North Carolina. He is a graduate of Columbia College, Harvard Law School, and Harvard Business School, and is a member of the New York Bar. He is the author of three previous books. Formerly a Wall Street lawyer, Stadiem currently lives in Los Angeles, where he also writes for the motion picture industry.